Help Wanted,
Desperately

Help Wanted, Desperately

Ariel Horn

AVON
TRADE

An Imprint of HarperCollinsPublishers

HarperCollins books may be purchased for education, business, or sales promotional use. For information please write: Special Markets Department, HarperCollins Publishers Inc., 10 East 53rd Street, New York, NY 10022.

FIRST EDITION

Designed by Elizabeth M. Glover

Library of Congress Cataloging-in-Publication Data

Horn, Ariel.
  Help wanted, desperately / Ariel Horn.—1st ed.
    p. cm.
ISBN 0-06-058958-2
1. Employment interviewing—Fiction. 2. New York (N.Y.)—Fiction. 3. Young women—Fiction. 4. Job hunting—Fiction. 5. Unemployed—Fiction. I. Title.

PS3608.O755H45 2004
813'.6—dc22   2004047742

04 05 06 07 08 JTC/RRD 10 9 8 7 6 5 4 3 2 1

For my parents,
Drs. Matthew and Susan Horn.
And for my husband,
Donny Levenson.
Nature or nurture, I'm your fault . . .

Acknowledgments

This book never could have turned into what it did without the wonderful assistance, support, and guidance of many, many people. Some might say it was a cast of thousands.

Tremendous thanks are owed to my editor at Avon Books, Lyssa Keusch, whose thoughtful comments and suggestions were consistently helpful and much appreciated. Her willingness to discuss all aspects of this book with me—regardless of how many times we'd talked about them—was unforgettably amazing. Tremendous thanks also go to May Chen, copyeditor Ellen Leach, managing editor Karen Davy, director of PR Debbie Stier, the PR team Pamela Spengler-Jaffee and Rachel Fershleiser, marketing director Lisa Gallagher, art director Tom Egner, associate art director Gail Dubov, cover designer Patrick Jones, and the publisher Michael Morrison. I am so thankful I had such a terrific team backing me up.

My agent, Jeff Kleinman of Graybill and English, has been truly stupendous throughout this entire process. King Among Men, he's helped me with every single aspect of this book, and has been nothing short of incredible in his patience, thoughtfulness, and guidance. I am unspeakably grateful that I've found him; only a restraining order could keep me away.

The list continues: appreciative thanks are also owed to Rachel Solar-Tuttle, Susan Schulz, Paula Marantz Cohen, Carolyn Hessel, Sessalee Hensley, Carol Fitzgerald, and Jennifer Wiener for encouragement and support.

This book could never have been possible without the unparalleled love and support from my family. Thanks (as well as a monument) go to my parents, who put up with endless conversations about how I was an unemployable, worthless wretch, and continue to put up with similarly bizarre and useless conversations. Thanks for not hanging up when normal people would have.

When my parents refused to answer call waiting (or perhaps blocked my number), my sister Jordana was always ready to talk, and it's because of her that this book even exists at all. Thank you for pushing me to write all my experiences down, for endless help editing, for standing in my corner always, and for forcing me to see how one person's misery can sometimes turn into another's beach read.

While Jordana gave me the idea to write this book, it was my other sister Dara whose own success writing made me believe that writing a book was possible at all. When Dara's incredible first novel, *In the Image,* was published (run, do not walk, to bookstores near you), writing a book stopped seeming like a pipe dream and more like a real possibility. Thank you for your success—which made me believe that my own was even possible. Somewhere out there.

To my brother, Zach, the best animator this side of the Mississippi, who endured his own job search as I dealt with mine: thanks for making me realize I wasn't alone. (Rest assured, he is now happily employed.)

Thanks and so much more go to my husband, Donny, who has always believed in me more than I've ever believed in myself. Thank you for going away to Paris during my senior year at Penn—which gave me newfound time to write this book. But more importantly, thank you for marrying me, loving me, and supporting me in spite of and because of who I am. You are truly, truly amazing.

Last, but certainly not least, thanks to all the companies I interviewed with; I didn't get a job—but I got something even better.

1
Panties and Pride

7 Months, 3 Weeks, 2 Days: The Countdown Begins

Call me naïve, but I hadn't expected fondling crotchless panties to be an important part of getting a job. A crotchless lifestyle had just never entered the picture.

In my unemployed, semi-delusional state, I had somehow anticipated that getting a job would be easy—that having someone pay me to do something I loved would be this simple five-minute endeavor that ended in my having a really swanky office, my parents boasting to their friends in the produce aisle about what a success I had become, and mountains of cash lining my bank account.

Under no circumstances had touching someone else's panties factored into my delusions of grandeur.

But last week, the second day of the first month of my senior year in college, that's exactly where I found myself: sitting in an electric blue armchair in the midtown Manhattan offices of *Trend* magazine, in a room decorated with leopard carpeting and magenta walls, surrounded by stick-thin thirty-something women brainstorming the top ten reasons why every woman should own a pair of sexy, satin, lacy, crotchless fuchsia panties.

Not being an owner of sexy, satin, lacy, crotchless fuchsia panties myself, I was at a loss for words. After all, having been raised in New Jersey, I come from the crotch-full cotton world, where "sexy" is a word we use to describe particularly clean strip malls.

As I sat wondering why thong-wearing fashionistas would even vaguely considered hiring un-sexy, cotton-crotched me, the lanky editors surrounding me erupted in a chorus of raunchy reasons why every self-respecting twenty-something sex kitten should own a pair of fuchsia crotchless panties. Apparently, I was trapped in some sort of alternate universe where women not only enjoyed but endorsed a perpetual wedgie.

Panting with the sort of unbridled excitement frat guys dream of and sorority girls fake, a platinum blonde jumped triumphantly from her chair and gasped, "I've got it! Put the 'ass' back in 'sassy'!"

A sullen redhead yawned and responded, "Too much like 'Put the Oh! Back in Orgasm.' "

The platinum blonde sat, devastated. "Ever since we did that depilatory cream article 'Hairless Wonders," I just can't come up with good cover titles anymore . . ."

Before I could even consider the painstaking hours of undoubtedly uncomfortable research that would go into such an article, Catalina, the long-legged, long-haired, and long-winded managing editor who would be interviewing me for the position of editorial assistant at *Trend* magazine, invited me to join her in her office.

Help Wanted, Desperately

As she catwalked down the hallway, Catalina's wildly curly black hair danced behind her and her dark purple dress hugged her amazingly (and surgically?) toned body—an ass that boldly and smugly screamed its proud ownership of crotchless panties. I wondered whether she was born with the ability to sway her hips like that or if she was taught to do it at the same place she bought her pointy, knee-high black leather boots. Catalina's ass continued to shake in a way that she probably knew made men want to hump her—in a way, I should add, that simply made me look—when I tried it—like I desperately needed to find a toilet.

Catalina turned the corner, ushered me into her office, and sat down in her plush pink leather armchair. Then, she simply, unabashedly, and confidently stuck her hands down the front of her dress and began to rearrange the position of her breasts.

Whoa.

"You really have to push them up and together if you want them to look perky all the time. And you need to position the nipples so they both face front at the same angle. Take it from me—I didn't get to the top of the fashion world with uneven nipples. Free advice."

Self-consciously, I tried to sneak a peek at my own chest before Catalina could.

"The left nipple is about three centimeters lower than the right, and it's not facing directly in front of you either. Didn't you think about that before you came on this interview?"

Apparently, I hadn't considered how crucial evenly spaced nipples would be to my professional success.

Catalina repositioned her nipples, rearranged her pink tulips and followed my eyes as they glanced around her glamorous office. It was just as stunning as I imagined my own postgraduation office would be, filled with awards, sleek metallic furniture and framed brilliantly colored magazine covers.

Witnessing my utter amazement and jealousy (over the room . . . not the nipples), Catalina snapped her makeup case closed and said, "Oh, it's nothing really. Don't gawk, it's unbecoming. I suppose this, and that, and everything else . . . Why, they're just the trappings of being a fabulous writer, doing fabulous things, and going to fabulous places. Would you like that sort of thing?"

I nodded mechanically, mesmerized by the fabulous fortune that had fallen on this thoroughly moisturized woman. She was right: There was no way any other job, even teaching kids on some tropical island in the South Pacific, could compare to this.

Catalina nodded back. "I bet you would." She sipped her fruit water and then tilted her head, her black curls falling like perfect little coils over her perfect blue eyes lined by her perfect black eyeliner. "Could you lean in? I want to look at something."

I leaned in toward Catalina, and she gently wrapped her warm, manicured, moisturized fingers around my chin. She turned my head to the left. And then to the right. Releasing my face, she said matter-of-factly, "Have you ever considered a nose job? You could be pretty with a nose job. Your face, as it is right now, just, well, just says 'I need a nose job' to me. Actually, a nose job or a chin tuck. You've got a little bit of an overbite."

With a dentist for a father and a middle-school career tortured by braces and then a watermelon-patterned retainer, I would have to say that hurt.

"Anyway. Rest assured that all this"—Catalina gestured to her office (and, I think, her nose)—"doesn't come without hard work. Oh, nonono, it doesn't! Before you get to be as successful as I am, you've got to pay your dues—and I assure you, my dear, paying your dues does not usually mean being invited to a staff meeting for *Trend*'s cover article on sexy lingerie. Believe me, not even our editorial assistants who have been here three years are privy to *that* sort of luxury."

Catalina shook her hair—in a way that I've only seen done in Pantene commercials—sat down, and crossed her legs (which combined were roughly the width of my left leg alone . . . when I was eight years old). "So let's get this straight. If you were to become my editorial assistant—a position, I'll tell you frankly, that people with far better noses than you have literally offered me money for—your responsibilities would range from the mundane—getting me my morning mocha, et cetera—to the more exciting—sorting through letters to the editor and that sort of thing. Oh, and little preferences for me too—for instance, I would hope that you would tell me if I was 'even' "—Catalina gestured to her chest—"before I went out on sales meetings and to fashion shoots. That would be part of the job."

Alexa Hoffman: Nipple Fixer Extraordinaire, at your service.

"Actually, what makes this job so enviable is," Catalina leaned toward me, and gestured for me to lean in as well, which I did, "between you and me, we're going to be giving the editorial assistant a *tremendous* amount of responsibility. Now, the editorial assistant will get to write the cute little headlines for the Uh-oh! column—like 'Gone Itchin','"for the girl who develops a yeast infection while on a romantic fishing getaway with her boyfriend, or—oh, this one's my favorite, 'Ringin' in the Rain,' for that one about the girl who lost her cell phone while having sex with some guy at some outdoor concert. Point being, my dear, that this position is for someone who will jump to do what I want and what I need. Don't come into this thinking you'll be writing for *Trend*, for God's sake. That won't come for another five, ten years, so don't even bother me with questions about *that*. Do you understand?"

I looked at Catalina and did my best to make my expression pleasantly say, "Of course I know what it's like to work hard in college and then be relegated to nipple-checker status for an eccentric has-been diva who Botoxes her worries away on a bi-weekly basis." Moving to Majuro to teach suddenly looked good again.

Catalina gazed around the room, her hands carelessly draped across her knees. Out of nowhere, a look of sheer and utter horror corrupted her moisturized face, and Catalina's eyes raced down to the spot on her leg that her hand had so carelessly brushed. A look of unbridled rage arched her eyebrows, and her eyes fixated on a particular spot right above the cuff of her left knee-high boot. Breaking her previously poised, glamorous façade, Catalina spat out, "Shit. I missed! I can't fucking believe this!"

"Missed?"

"There's this spot that's really hard to shave that I always miss—you know, the spot right above the bone on your knee? I missed that spot. Can you imagine me, one of the top fashion minds in America, *missing* a spot? I've got a cocktail party tonight too. Bare legs, Alexa, are only sexy when shaven. Write that down."

With this piece of advice, Catalina frantically opened all the drawers in her desk, and finally, finding the prize drawer, removed a rusty-looking razor and began to dry-shave her left knee. The office fell silent except for the scratchy, bristling, brushing sound of rusted blade against hairy knee.

When a woman starts to shave her knee in a job interview, you have to assume that the situation has skewed wildly out of control. One might even call the situation hairy.

Catalina seemed to be wrapping up, the wrinkle in her brow softened (thank you, Botox). She ran her finger carefully along the criminal kneecap.

In a desperate attempt to prove I was worthy of the job and to divert Catalina's attention from her newly shaven kneecap, I decided to ask Catalina whether she'd like to see any of the columns I wrote for my college paper. As I was about to open my mouth, Catalina shook her hair again and looked at her razor carefully.

"That's all we really need to know about you for this job—just that you're graduating in May, would be available the day after graduation, and that you attended a college. You *are* in college, right?" Catalina blew on her razor, and a small bushel of short black hairs separated and gently fell from the razor to her desk.

"And there's really nothing in particular required for this job in terms of skills . . . I don't suppose you have any questions, do you? Or skills, for that matter." Catalina took another tiny sip from her fruit water, her energy presumably spent from a rigorous afternoon rearranging her nipples and shaving her knee.

"You should really think about that nose job. I wasn't kidding before. You could actually be pretty if you got one."

For a moment, I was totally baffled. What do you ask a woman who has blatantly told you that if you work for her, your very best situation is writing headlines about women with yeast infections? A woman who has already told you that your nipples are unevenly arranged and that you're an impressive candidate for rhinoplasty? A woman who has dry-shaved her knee in the middle of your interview? A woman who, due to some inexplicably cruel twist of fate, essentially has your future sitting in the palm of her hand? Catalina stared at me expectantly, her eyes squinting as she scrutinized my face. Realizing that I needed to ask something, I stammered, "So, whose assistant would I be, exactly?"

Catalina paused before speaking, pursed her lips and looked at me. "Actually, I think it's more your chin. That's it. I really think your chin is a bigger problem for your face than your nose. I mean, the nose is bumpy, but the chin is just—out there. I think it's because you have a little bit of an overbite—or is it an underbite?—and *that's* what makes your nose look big.

"Have you ever thought about wiring your jaw shut? That might help—and you'd also lose a tremendous amount of weight. You could afford to lose a couple, if you don't mind my saying so. What are you, a size ten? We usually only have size twos work here." Catalina sippped her vitamin fruit water, and then let her hand carelessly glide over her newly shaven knee. "What were you saying again? Did you speak? I don't remember."

Catalina took out her moisturizer and began to reapply her aloe-vera-lanolin-honeysuckle-almond-rosemary-avocado-jojoba cream. "Oh, right. That assistant question. Don't look at this as an assistant position—you would be more like, well, more like my own second brain. Actually,"—she tilted her head, deep in "thought,"—"that's an overstatement, really." Catalina looked down at her chest, noticed that her nipples were still evenly lined up, and smiled. "I love when they learn to stay like that—don't they look perky?

"Anyway, I think we could more authentically say that you

would be more like my assistant *Lori's* second brain rather than my *own* second brain. So in a way, that would make you my third brain, I think. Can you imagine being the third brain to one of *the* most impressive and successful fashion editors in the country?"

No, I couldn't, but I was beginning to think it might be just as gratifying as being the unwashed pair of fuchsia crotchless panties gracing the ass of a self-obsessed, nipple-oppressed, unshaven, overly moisturized fashion editor.

Catalina picked up a picture frame on her desk. "This was the woman who started it all here at *Trend*. My God, if our original editor, Elyse, knew that I was even interviewing someone with your chin, I don't even know what she'd say! I can't even think about it. We don't usually have chins like yours working at *Trend*.

"But enough of *me* talking about me and your chin. Let's hear *you* talk about your chin. Kidding! Okay—only *half* kidding! Hey, would you be a dear and get me a mocha before you leave? And don't put any of those fake-y rat poison sugar packets in it either. The old girl used to do that. God, I hated her—oh, and her nose. God, it was even worse than yours."

And so began my unemployment woes.

Lessons Learned

1. Just because I wear underwear every day does not mean I am emotionally prepared or mature enough to fondle another woman's crotchless panties in an unironic way.

2. When your interviewer is more interested in dry-shaving her legs than talking to you, be sure to bring shaving gel to your next interview.

3. Do not, under any circumstances, challenge your interviewer's contention that you are a ripe candidate for jaw rewiring.

4. You may be the greatest candidate for a job, but what it all boils down to is this: you just can't get to the top of the fashion world with unevenly spaced nipples.

2

Dreaming of Dust Ruffles

7 Months, 2 Weeks

Let's not play games here: I've got way bigger problems than not owning crotchless panties and having chronically and unforgivably uneven nipples.

In exactly seven months and two weeks, I will be a college graduate. The Real World (a.k.a. "Life Outside of College") has been looming ominously overhead while I've studiously tried to avoid the fact that sooner-rather-than-later, the party will be over and it'll be time for me to get a job. To get a life.

I naturally assumed that this would be an easy thing—that getting a job in New York would be as simple as slipping on a pair of crotchless panties. After all, that was what had happened to my two sisters, and if we shared the same orthodontic problems, we might just be genetically linked in terms of our success rate too. Because I'm one of those people who everyone assumes "will be okay." Translation: I'll graduate college and find a decent-paying job, and then get married and have children who make dioramas of the Acropolis out of sugar cubes for their fifth-grade social-studies projects. And in the end, if all goes according to plan, *my* children will grow up in the same little New Jersey suburbs I came from, apply to colleges, and I, the neurotic mother, will eagerly await the mailman every day to receive their acceptances to the various reputable institutions I've forced my kids to apply to. Then my kids will accomplish great things (just as I did) and have children of their own, who will build papier-mâché volcanoes that spout lava for their sixth-grade science-fair projects, which will win not first but second prize, because the lava-spouting volcanoes always win second.

Whether this plan sounds fabulous or not, on paper I've been following it to a T without even knowing it: girl from New Jersey suburbs about to graduate from the University of Pennsylvania. The next step is to get the fantastic job easily and effortlessly.

Despite all my delusions of science-fair suburban grandeur, never once did I think that finding a job would somehow involve some overly moisturized Botox queen sketching out how rhinoplasty could change my life while simultaneously describing how inadequate I was for a "fabulous" job writing about yeast infections.

It was a sad, sad day in Alexa Hoffman history when I realized that getting the life I wanted was different from the life I was on track to get.

Don't get me wrong: I'm not that aimless girl who has no clue what she wants in life. Make no mistake, I know *exactly* what I want: I want my life to get *started* already. I'm sick of sitting in a holding pattern waiting for things to happen to me—I want to *make* them happen myself. This much I know about myself: I love to read, I love to write. The last math class I did well in was third grade. I love my family and I love Jared. I can easily spend over three hours sober at a karaoke bar and think I've found the meaning of life. I know I should exercise, but I hate paying to go to a gym, and I'd rather be eating popcorn and pretzels while watching an embarrassingly bad Olsen-twins movie on TV. And last but certainly not least: I desperately want a job in New York.

I just don't know what *kind* of job. I want a career that challenges me intellectually and rewards me financially. I want a life that doesn't involve me asking my parents for money and a job that makes me feel like I'm actually doing something worthwhile. And I want to know what life would be like if Jared and I actually lived in the same city. But more than anything else in the world: I want to be independent. I want something more than an Acropolis made of sugar cubes and a lava-spouting papier-mâché volcano. And I want it to happen now.

In fact, the real problem *is* I know exactly what I want, and that I just have no clue how I'm going to get it.

But wait—there's more. Here's the pièce de triomphe.

Last week, the combination of

1. my clueless lack of professional direction;
2. my inability to write in an unironic way about yeast infections; and
3. the fact that the economy is already drowning in what seems to be a permanent recession just in time for me to try and get a job

made me realize that desperate times call for even more desperate measures. So, two days after my *Trend* interview, with only seven months and three weeks until imminent joblessness, I signed up to leave the country. For Majuro. To teach.

When in doubt, flee the continent.

In an effort to avoid everyone else's Plan B (law school, med school, a masters degree, oh my!), I randomly decided I would sign up as a volunteer to teach elementary-school English on some random island in the middle of the Pacific. The program starts exactly one week after graduation.

In the big scheme of things, no matter how haphazardly I signed up, I know that volunteering as a teacher will probably be an amazing, incredible experience. I'll broaden my horizons. I'll live in a hut. I might actually make a difference in someone else's life. And hey, I might even snorkel.

But today, as I flipped through the Majuro brochure I had lying on my desk before submitting what felt like my ten-billionth resume online, I had a cathartic moment—the kind of life-defining moment of which college-application essays are born. It's actually more like the kind of cathartic moment I've bullshitted about in papers for the past four years. You know, the "aha!" moment, when a character in a book suddenly realizes, for example, that everything she's done up until that point in her life has been without purpose. The author's wasted hundreds of pages writing about some useless relationship where Elizabeths ignore Barnabys for Gregories, and then suddenly, like magic, Elizabeth realizes (except she realiSes instead of realiZes, because that's how British people do it), "I've been foolish! It's time for me to get my life in order by marrying the much less attractive but more wholesome man who has been obsessed with me while I've ignored him for four hundred pages! I'll marry him and then run away to Italy!"

Anyway, my catharsis wasn't nearly as drawn out as this Elizabeth-Barnaby-Gregory Bermuda Triangle of Boring, and I don't think it'll lead me to Italy, but it rocked my perspective of fleeing the country, the working world, and my place in it. As I sat at my desk, trying to avoid thinking about the fact that I was actually told that I could be someone's nipple-correcting third brain at a job interview, I came to a simple, but life-altering realization: I want a life in New York, and going to an island for a year isn't going to help me carve out a life for myself in New York any faster.

If all I want when I graduate is to be an employed, independent, full-fledged, push-and-shove New Yorker, will Majuro basically be a massive detour on the road to my life's beginning in New York? Would going to Majuro essentially be the same thing as waiting at the DMV for a year, and then leaving without getting the driver's license?

Enter catharsis, stage left: If what I really want is for my life to begin in New York, then I've got to get a job in New York in the seven months and two weeks before I get shipped out to the Pacific. Before it's time for me to enter a holding pattern. Before it's time for me to sign off on starting my life for yet *another* year. As if four years in college wasn't enough.

But here's the worst part: today as I submitted online cover letters professing why I'm destined to be a [fill in blank position] at [fill in blank company], which has a "unique commitment to developing its employees' expertise through teamwork and mentoring," I realized that in the big scheme of things, I'm not even really scared of being jobless.

What I'm scared of is becoming a disappointment. Of turning into one of those people my high-school friends' parents talk about as "having had so much potential" and then just missing the boat. I'm scared that I will graduate college, degree in hand,

and do nothing worthwhile with it. I'm scared that my life won't make a difference in anyone else's—that I'll be one of those people whose existence doesn't change or help anything. What keeps me from sleeping at night isn't the prospect that well, maybe I *do* need a nose job or my jaw rewired. It's the horrifying idea that I will never live up to the "potential" that everyone expects of me—and that I expect of myself.

Even nipples I can handle. "Potential" is a whole different story.

Enter the real revelation: maybe the problem with my trying to get a job isn't that we're in a "new economy." Maybe the real problem is that I'm still the same old me.

Well, as of now, it's the end of the old me. From this day forth, I'm going to fight with the big boys. Gone are the days of whining about not getting a job to my mother on the phone in the afternoon and whimpering like a wounded dog in my bed at night. From today on, I'm going to fight! I'm going to be the Scarlett O'Hara of the unemployed population. As God is my witness, I shall never go hungry again! I won't settle for withering away like some has-been loser who never was! I'm going to get a job in New York City—and I don't care what field, what position, what salary, or what it takes. I AM GOING TO GET A JOB. My ticket to Majuro is in precisely seven months, two weeks, twelve hours and eight minutes, which gives me that much time to get up, get into the world, get my foot in the door, and get me a job. I'm willing to do whatever it takes. Farewell, crotchless panties. Bonjour, potential.

Miraculously, after my submission of dozens more resumes (this time on "marble ivory" paper), someone in New York City is finally willing to interview me. Since my qualifications remain the same, I'm convinced it was the paper.

I had sent one of my classic cover letters to a large reputable company, Sweeney's Retail, for the position of a buyer: "My coursework as an English major, as well as my past internship experiences at *Style* magazine and *More Style* magazine make me an ideal candidate to work at your company and do whatever the hell it is you do."

Okay, I phrased it a little better than that.

Realistically speaking, you might ask why I would apply for a job when I have no real understanding of what the job actually entails, and know even less about the company itself. (Okay, maybe it's just my neurotic mother who would ask that.) And realistically speaking, I would answer, well, I know that I've got to start somewhere, and since I'm completely and utterly professionally directionless, I know that I have to put my time in at the bottom to eventually get to the top. I'm willing to do that, and in whatever industry that will have me, provided that I think I'll gain skills that will actually help me work my way up. So assuming that the company doesn't consider nipple-straightening an essential skill for top management, I figure at this point in the game—technically speaking—it's not unfathomably atrocious that I don't know anything about Sweeney's. Only mildly atrocious.

The irony is that most recruiters never really understand this essential point: many of the people applying for their jobs have *no* idea what their company is or what it is their company claims to do. Their catalogues and smarmy power-point "information sessions" teach us absolutely nothing, and just make us paranoid about the other hundreds of people surrounding us vying for the one position for which they will probably hire someone with an MBA. Someone ought to create a power-point presentation for all the recruiters on how to make an information session that includes substantive information. And yes, that means you can't include bulleted points that say "Geared towards innovation" or "Fast-paced corporate culture" or even (gasp!) "Create tailored solutions for client-based problems." (A phrase, I might add, I heard at a consulting presentation last May and frequently include in my own cover letters: "I am interested in creating tailored solutions for client-based problems.")

I frantically try to research the retail company on the Web so I don't make a total ass of myself at the interview ("Yes, I like shoes. In fact I buy a lot of them.") But, regardless of the fact that I know virtually nothing about Sweeney's Retail (except that I personally hate their crappy department store near my town which plays Christmas music year round), I'm actually excited, hopeful, and delighted in the fact that I have momentarily joined the Interview Elite at my college. At last, I have become one of those lucky few students who gets to strut to the Career Services building for on-campus recruiting interviews in their navy and gray suits and act as if they already have the job. I take advantage on my (one and only) walk over to Career Services and make my strut extra snobbish—before I know it, I'm doing the Investment Banker Mambo, the brattiest walk of them all! Strut, baby, strut. Livin' life large. I'm gonna bring home the bacon. Or at the very least a free pen from the interview. Which would be nice, because in my overstressed state, I have chewed all my plastic pens into unworkable drool-straws.

Naturally, I have carefully chosen my suit: Certainly the retail company will be interested in where I got my outfit, right? (Of course, I didn't get my suit at their store—they only sell clothing that my mom and I traditionally buy for my senile great-aunt at the nursing home, who refuses all clothing gifts except large floral-print housedresses, which, coincidentally, Sweeney's seems to specialize in.) Fortunately, in my attempts to get a job, I remember something my friend Ethan told me freshman year after I had "mistakenly" used my roommate's shampoo and spilled it all over the floor: "Remember, Alexa, sometimes honesty isn't the best policy. Lie, lie, LIE!" I am one hundred and ten percent ready to lie. Throw my morals out the window and get me a job! ("Where did you get your suit, Alexa?" "Wherever you want me to have gotten it.")

Mustering up all my moxie, I strut my way into the Career Services building. Instantly, my neurotic barometer skyrockets. Dozens of anonymous students wearing gray and navy suits fondle their embossed leather folders filled with "marble ivory" resumes just like mine. I suddenly feel grossly unqualified. I feel my heart suddenly start to pound as I spot a girl from one of my classes who has already started her own gourmet cheeses dot.com. It's already gone public, and everyone's eating up her Gouda like it's going out of style. My strut dissolves. I have no chance. I'm inferior, worthless, the dirt beneath these more-qualified applicants' shoes. It's over. I might as well take my free pen and go to Majuro. So much for New York City. And being with Jared.

Just as I consider walking out the door, a pleasant-looking Waspy woman wearing a pink cashmere sweater looks up from a clipboard, "Alexa Hoffman?"

"That's me." I walk over and give her a confident handshake. *I am professional. I am professional. I am professional. Wow, I'm kind of hungry. I could go for some Gouda right now . . . SHUT UP! I am professional!*

We sit down and tell each other something about ourselves, though naturally, I really don't care about "Mary Kate" and she doesn't really care about me. We just have to pretend to care for about a half hour, and then we can go on with our lives and forget about each other. It's kind of like a one-night stand.

Mary Kate looks at me and through her large, overenthusiastic grin begins talking: "Well, let me start off by telling you something about myself. First, I'm from Connecticut, and I have two children and a golden retriever named Muffy. I mean, the golden retriever's named Muffy—not my kids! As you might have guessed, I'm a buyer for Sweeney's and I positively, absolutely, love, love, *love* my job, with a capital L!"

As I start to wonder whether Mary Kate has spoken with her doctor about some sort of caffeine regulation in her diet, Mary Kate continues to gush, "In fact, it's so funny how I started out— I was originally a buyer of dust ruffles for Sweeney's, and then, well, you know how it is, one thing led to another and before I knew it I was on top of the world—a pillow buyer, can you believe it? It was just a dream come true! Isn't that funny?" Mary Kate is laughing so hysterically at her own good fortune that a small tear begins to form in the corner of her right eye.

I think Mary Kate and I have different definitions of "funny."

I guess it's supposed to be funny, so I laugh in that polite, "Oh, aren't you clever!" kind of way that I've mastered from being in seminars at college. Professors are always making jokes that under normal circumstances no one would ever find funny ("Sometimes my students *Kant* understand Kant!"), but since students worry that their final grades are directly proportional to how much they appear to enjoy the stand-up comic stylings of their professors, they always do the half-closed-mouth laugh, which seems to satisfy teachers who think they're on Comedy Central.

Technically speaking, it's really one of the more important skills I learned in college.

Mary Kate and I hit the interview questions back and forth, like a long, boring game of tennis.

"What are your best qualities?" Mary Kate poises her pen, eager to write down the gems that will undoubtedly pop from my lips.

"I'm outgoing, meticulous, and detail oriented."

"What are your worst qualities?"

I debate the tried-and-true "I'm a perfectionist" but decide to wing it with a Career Services counselor's suggestion: "I'm impatient for results."

Mary Kate raises an eyebrow, impressed. Unemployed Loser: 1. Mary Kate: 0.

"And what was your best class at college?"

"My marketing class, because it helped me hone my true passion for retail." (Best not to mention "Art History of Colonial America" here.)

"And how does your past work experience make you a good candidate for the position of a buyer?"

"Working at women's fashion magazines really helped me understand what influences fashion and what consumers want."

Take that, Mary Kate. Take that.

In reality, my past internships at women's magazines taught me how to use a color Xerox for personal entertainment, why "long-lasting lip color" can dry out your lips, and that many of the women who work at women's magazines, fascinatingly enough, are unattractive, unfashionable spinsters.

I pour it on thick for Mary Kate. And hope against all hope that Mary Kate sees something in me that she likes, something that can be trained to buy well, something that has potential. Especially since I haven't found that potential in myself yet.

By the end of the interview, I'm amazed to learn that I think I have utterly charmed Mary Kate. Perhaps the employment train *will* be stopping at Alexa Hoffman Central after all! Our interview goes ten minutes over schedule, since I'm so "fascinated" by Mary Kate's story of how a dust-ruffle buyer becomes a pillow buyer, and was so eager to hear Mary Kate regale me with more stories of how she "made it big." ("Your story really brings the advancement of a buyer to life! Thank you so much for sharing it with me!")

My second interviewer taps on the door, "Mary Kate, Alexa needs to move on—it's time for our interview."

"Sorry, Trish, it's just that Alexa and I are having so much fun!"

I bid Mary Kate a tearful farewell as Tricia enters the interview room and Mary Kate leaves.

Tricia seems a little less spunky than Mary Kate, perhaps because she has not been fortunate enough to have had the Horatio Alger rags-to-riches experience of going from dust-ruffle buyer to pillow buyer. Perhaps she still lives the tormented and conflicted life of a mere dust-ruffle buyer. Actually, Tricia seems downright jaded.

I think I might like her.

But at a closer look, Tricia bares a striking resemblance to one of my ex-boyfriends' mother, with her bright, fiesta-style makeup, overplucked eyebrows, and possible nose job. I try to ignore this fact, but as the interview begins, it gets harder and harder to avoid thinking about the resemblance, and suddenly I feel self-conscious and uncomfortable, as if this woman knows what I wore to the prom five years ago and thinks it was inappropriately revealing. (For the record: thanks to shopping with *my* mom, it was closer to a black potato sack than it was to sexy.) I try to shove visions of my ex's mother out of my head and focus on the issue at hand. For a split second, I frantically worry that my nipples are uneven.

Tricia wastes no time—there will be no pleasantries here. She glances at my resume and then smiles at me sourly. I'm a little scared, but I smile back.

"So this part of the interview is going to be situational. I'm going to posit certain situations, and you'll tell me how you'd react."

Tricia speaks slowly and deliberately, the way people speak English to foreigners who don't understand. I briefly wonder if she thinks I'm a foreigner. Do I look Slavic? I contemplate telling her that I'm not a natural blonde, that they're highlights, but I refrain. My interview mantra echoes loudly in my brain: *Do anything to make her like you, at any cost.*

Well, I might as well give the woman what she wants. I nod dumbly. I had learned in my (only) marketing class last semester that people have an innate desire to confirm their first reactions. So if it's an illiterate, mute foreigner Tricia wants, well, an illiterate, mute foreigner Tricia will get. And I'll give it to her.

"Where do you see fashion going next season?"

I have absolutely no fucking clue.

"I think the recession will affect buying patterns, and I think, um, that more people will be more reluctant to spend their money, and will be spending more time at home in order to avoid spending even *more* money. This means people will want reliable, comfortable clothing that's multi-purpose: something they can wear casually at home, at work, or dress up for the occasional night out." Wow. Where did *that* come from?

Tricia looks either impressed or nauseous—I can't tell through all the makeup. Apparently, the deaf-mute Slav can speak: pretty shocking. Too bad the question didn't really matter though. After all, Sweeney's stores only sell crappy floral house-dresses anyway. It's not like *those* will ever go out of fashion. As long as there are crazy old women in nursing homes who accuse their doctors of trying to kill them, Sweeney's retail will remain in high demand.

At the end of the interview, Tricia still seems impressed (or ill, depending on how you interpret the makeup). I ask when I'll hear from the company.

"Two weeks. And we will *definitely* be contacting you. But be sure to take your psychological testing. We can't evaluate you without it."

"Definitely be contacting me" to tell me I'm still an unemployed loser headed for Majuro in six months, two weeks and three hours? Or "definitely contacting me" to hire me? And what's this about psychological testing? *Does everyone have to do this, or just me?* I wonder in a brief second of paranoia. Perhaps the very type of paranoia they're testing for.

Uh-oh.

I slither home and go back to Career Services later in the day to take my test. A hundred questions. First, critical thinking ("Corn grows only when it is wet and cold. Cotton grows when it is warm and dry. Rice grows when it is wet and warm. Can any of these products grow together?"), and then, psychological testing.

I pick up pretty quickly that the point of the testing is to determine that I'm not a raving lunatic who's going to use freshly sharpened pencils as darts at the office. Like any well-educated lunatic, I answer all the questions accordingly. "I consider myself a trustworthy person. True or False?" "I would never willingly hurt another person. True or False?"

Cardinal rule number one of taking quizzes that claim to be able to determine your personality and demeanor: never, EVER admit to having faults, even if you do. Rule number two: lie, lie, LIE if you possess the bad qualities they're looking for.

Question forty-seven: "I respond well to criticism. True or False?" I briefly recall starting to cry when my boyfriend Jared told me that the brown suede skirt I owned (which I considered very haute couture) looked like something a caveman would wear while sinking his teeth into a large drumstick. Hmm. Yes, I respond well to criticism (after all, I didn't hit him, I just burst into tears). "True."

Forty-eight: "I rarely hold grudges. True or False?" Well, if we don't count that I'm still pissed at my second-grade teacher, Mrs. Ardman, for forcing me to use one of those handwriting correctors that you slip onto your pencil when your handwriting is terrible, then no. No, I don't hold grudges. "True."

After an hour, I'm exhausted. Lying to make myself seem like a well-adjusted, savvy candidate with no mental hang-ups has been quite an ordeal. They should give me the job for bullshit alone. I could be "Bullshit Coordinator." Or, since I would be entry level, a mere "Bullshit Assistant." Note to self: When I own my own company, create Bullshit Department.

Having finished the testing, I pick up my bag and leave Career Services again. I check the time and decide to call Jared on his cell phone. According to my calculations (read: unnaturally obsessive fixation with his schedule), he should be on his way to his statistics class, crossing Washington Square Park to get to Shimkin Hall at NYU, where he goes to school. I pick up my cell phone and dial his number.

"Jared, do you think it's morally wrong to bullshit your way through an interview?"

Jared sounds busy, like he's rushing somewhere. Perhaps late to statistics, if my watch is wrong. "Hey! Alex?"

"Who else?"

I can hear the smile in Jared's voice. "Hi. How'd it go?"

I switch the phone to my other ear as I wait for the crosswalk signal. "Well, I think it went okay. The women who interviewed me were pretty gung-ho about dust ruffles."

"What's a dust ruffle?"

"I think it's the little doily thing on the bottom of the bed . . . Whatever, not important. The weird thing was that they made me take this psychological test, you know, as part of the interview."

Jared's fading in and out of my phone. He sounds worried. "Did everyone have to take it?"

"I think so. It's no big deal. I'll pass, I mean, how can someone 'fail' a psychological test? You think I'm normal, right?"

A pause. "Yeah, I guess."

He "guesses" I'm normal? "What the hell is that supposed to mean?"

"Look, I'm just saying you're—it's not that you're *not* normal in the," Jared searches for words. "It's just that 'normal' can be defined in a lot of ways . . ."

Help Wanted, Desperately

Mouth agape, I make a dramatic "can-you-believe-this-guy" gesture to an imaginary audience. Someone passing by on the street glares at me and begins to walk faster. "You think I'm not normal. We've been dating two years, and you think I'm not normal. What does that say about *you*? Who's weirder, the circus bear in the tutu, or the bear who loves her?"

"I don't know where the hell that bear thing came from . . . and I won't point out the obvious by saying that that's pretty much the perfect example of abnormality, but would it help if I told you I love you because you're not normal?"

Giving up, I offer, smiling to myself, "Yeah, a little." I pause. "But seriously, what's not normal about me?"

"Do we have to do this now?"

"This is a once-in-a-lifetime opportunity, Jared. I'm asking you to tell me what's wrong with me. That's pretty much the equivalent of a girl asking you to tell her she's fat. You'll never have a chance like this again."

Jared takes a deep breath, and I hear a car honk in the background. "Okay, I think it's weird that you bite your nails and then chew them and swallow them when you think I'm not looking. That's not only weird—it's disgusting."

"They're just nails! It's easier than using the nail clipper! I'm a nervous person!"

"I don't care what it is—it's gross. Alex, you EAT your nails and it makes me want to vomit.

"Secondly, I think it's weird that you sing songs to yourself from The Man of La Mancha sometimes when you go to the bathroom—you know I can hear you through the wall, right?"

"It relaxes me! It's a tension reliever! *Normal* people do that!"

27

"While they're going to the bathroom? Alex, normal people *read* on the toilet. Thirdly, I think it's weird that you take on an all-purpose weird European accent zat soundz like zees whenever you're trying to decide between two entreés at a restaurant . . . Fourthly—"

"What, is this a power-point presentation?"

Jared, rushing off to his next class, responds, "Hey, you asked. And as far as 'weird' goes, don't get me started on Majuro. I could talk about that with you for hours." Jared pauses and then softly adds, "We *need* to talk about that for hours."

Changing the subject away from Majuro, which is always impossible to talk about with Jared, I ask, "So you still love me, even though I'm weird?"

"Maybe I love you because you're weird."

I smile. "What can I say, I'm weird and I'm proud. And for the record, I think it's weird that you won't let me share drinks with you."

"It's called hygiene. Or do they not have that in your little nail-eating world?"

"Jared, if I were 'unclean,' believe me when I say that there are a lot of ways you would be getting germs from me other than just sharing a glass of orange juice."

"Okay, that just put a lot of gross and uncomfortable scenarios in my head that I'd really rather not think about in the context of thinking about my girlfriend. Look, I have to go to class—call me tonight, okay? And I'm coming to Philadelphia this Friday, right?"

"You better. I expect a formal, in-person apology for false accusations of unhygienic weirdness."

"You asked for them!"

Help Wanted, Desperately

I smile and shrug. "I love you anyway."

"Always. Talk to you tonight."

Two weeks later: no word from Tricia or Mary Kate. I'm actually kind of shocked—for whatever delusional reason, I had thought that maybe, just maybe this would be my key to unlocking the happy door of employment. The interviews had gone well, I thought both Tricia and Mary Kate liked me. And on paper, I really *do* qualify for this job! I decide to take Tricia up on her instruction to "call if you have any questions." Oh, make no mistake. I'll call, Tricia. I'll call.

Voicemail message one (me, sounding perky and professional): "Hi, Tricia, this is Alexa Hoffman. We met three weeks ago when you interviewed me for the position of buyer. I was just looking to check up on the status of my application, since you mentioned that we'd hear either way two weeks after our interview and I haven't heard anything yet. Please call me back at your earliest convenience."

Voicemail message two: "Hi, Tricia, I called about a week ago, I'm not sure if you got my message, because you never returned my call, but this is Alexa Hoffman and I'm calling to get an update on the status of my application for the position of buyer. Please call me back when you get a chance. Thanks." (Muttering under my breath: "Heartless bitch.")

Voicemail message three: "Listen, Tricia. I'm fucking sick and tired of playing games like this. You want me or you don't want me? Pick one. But don't lie to me and tell me

29

that you'll 'definitely' call me when you're definitely not calling me. Was it my psychological testing? Do ya think I'm a psycho? Well listen up, Tricia honey, you better sleep with one eye open tonight, baby. You and your friend Mary Kate—and her little dog Muffy too."

Okay, so I didn't *really* leave that last message.

But I thought about it for a while, actually. In high school, when my best friend, Miranda, didn't get into Yale, she was pretty devastated. Granted, they had the courtesy to at least mail her the "good luck elsewhere" letter, but she was understandably irritated, especially since a couple of (not amazingly qualified) students from our high school had gotten in. So one day after school, she went home and sat down at her computer and began furiously writing her rejection letter for Yale along the lines of "I reject your rejection, you pompous bastards." After trashing Yale's admissions process, as well as the other applicants from our class who had applied and been admitted, Miranda closed it with the magnanimous salutation, "With hopes for your terminal cancer, Miranda Lewis."

She never sent the letter (we thought it might get around to the other colleges), but I've thought about the letter a lot since she wrote it. Why can't *I* have the honor of rejecting some loser company that makes floral housedresses? How is it that they don't even have the decency to send me a rejection letter after they "promised" they'd "definitely" be in touch? I'm not even asking that they type my name at the top of the letter if they don't want to. I'll happily accept a "Dear applicant: we've decided that you're really just a huge loser, thanks but no thanks" postcard, and then continue on my merry way.

Help Wanted, Desperately

As I change into my pajamas and crawl into bed, my house-mate Ethan knocks on my door and wanders into my room. He looks at me in bed, and then looks at himself in the mirror.

"Is it wrong that I honestly think I become better-looking every day?"

Rolling my eyes, I respond, "No. Narcissistic, yes. Wrong, no."

Ethan wanders to my desk and sits down in front of my computer, checking his e-mail. "So did you call those retail people back?"

"Ethan, why do you come in here to use my computer when yours is upstairs?"

"I like the change of scenery. And the lower altitude helps me breathe better."

"Yeah, I called. They're never going to call me back, basically, but, I guess retail just wasn't for me anyway."

Ethan turns to me, shaking his head, "Alex, you sleep in a ripped Mickey Mouse T-shirt with a pair of boxers you've had since you were twelve that say 'I just got my braces off!' in glow-in-the-dark puffy paint. Did you ever honestly think you would work in retail? I wouldn't let you dress my dog."

"You don't have a dog."

"That's not the point."

"This outfit is comfortable!"

Ethan stands up and pulls the covers off of me. "It's hideous. You're a beast."

Possessively grabbing my covers back and shrnking under-neath them, I shrug. "Anyway, I don't even care about dust ruf-fles or the 'new black.' The old black works for me. And I don't care about materials or fabrics unless it affects my dry-cleaning bill."

"Who even knew you went to a dry cleaner?"

"Seriously, Ethan, I'm not *that* bad. You make it seem like I'm some deformed, fashionless freak."

Ethan opens my closet and takes out a cream wool turtleneck sweater he truly believes makes me look like I'm wearing a neck brace. "All *I'm* saying is that given your daily wardrobe, it's both impressive and appalling you worked at *More Style* magazine."

"How could I think that retail was something I wanted to devote my life to?"

Ethan shakes his head and pulls a pair of green galoshes out of my closet. "Honestly, I really just don't know."

"If I don't want to go to Majuro to put off my life for a year, I'm going to have to try a hell of a lot harder than this to get a job."

"No kidding. I'm going upstairs . . . This is, amazingly, more boring than studying. Good night, fashion deviant." Ethan leaves.

As the door closes behind Ethan, I shift in bed, fully aware that the swine of Sweeney's are never going to call me, send me a letter, or let me know in any way that they don't want me. I'm going to have to infer from the silence that there's something so undesirable about me that I should never have even dreamt that they would call me. Am I, in fact, "weird"?

Or should I call again, one last time?

As I listen to the not-so-far-off sound of dogs barking at the veterinary hospital down the street and the too-close-for-comfort sounds of one of my housemates and her boyfriend having sex in the next room, I can't believe I'm going to have to go through this process all over again for every job I think I could possibly want.

This is not where I want to be.

Help Wanted, Desperately

*   *   *

It's now 11 P.M., four weeks after my interview, and six months, two weeks, two days, ten hours and thirty minutes until I'm either a) off to the island to pursue a year-long Waitlist for Life or b) galloping into the Real World with a Real Job, a Real Life, a Real Future. That means I have precisely six months, two weeks, ten hours and twenty-nine minutes to miraculously become happily employed in New York City.

I've not-so-reluctantly tossed my five-minute-long dream of being a dust-ruffle buyer out the window, and as I sit in my bedroom, again listening to constant frantic moans and barking of dogs awaiting kidney surgery in the veterinary school's emergency room across the street, I know what I have to do. In times of personal failure, disappointment, feelings of mediocrity, and general feelings of worthlessness, there's only one thing I *can* do: call my mom.

Nothing helps misery like spreading it.

The phone rings twice and my mother picks up. We go through the motions of our regular "Why are you calling me now? It's too late for you to call, I'm too tired to talk"—"Well, I'm bored and depressed and feeling worthless" exchange, and move on with the conversation.

"Mom, I'm *never* going to get a job! I'm going to be living in an alleyway eating free samples from the supermarket to keep myself alive. Doesn't that bother you?"

"Alex, you love those free samples."

"Mom! I'm a loser!"

"You're not a loser, Alex. And being a loser isn't about having a job or not. And besides, if you don't get a job, well, you know that we're here waiting for you with open arms to move back

33

home. Daddy and I just got such a cute new decal for the station wagon for you when you move home—it says 'How's my driving? Call my mom!' Isn't that adorable? We can even put our phone number on it so people can actually *call* us to tell us about your driving!"

I cannot move back home.

"Anyway, I'm sure this retail interview went better than you think it did. Honestly, you're getting all worked up over nothing. Have you talked to Jared about it? What does he say?" My mother pauses, and that's how I know what comes next. Ever since my sister Nina got engaged, my mother has developed this incredible ability to turn any conversation—with any person, including the guy at the gas station—into an animated discussion about when Jared and I are going to get married. And don't confuse me with a person who has ever actually *discussed* any M words besides Majuro with Jared in the first place. "Do you think he's going to propose soon—maybe before graduation, so we can set up the wedding for June, right after Nina's? Do you think you'd want a sushi bar at the wedding? Nina's wedding won't have one, but maybe yours should be a little different . . . Although if you got married a little later, maybe Nina would be pregnant or Julie would be married, God willing! And we'd have to go shopping maybe for at least one maternity bridesmaid dress, oh from my lips to God's ears! And—"

I *seriously* cannot move back home.

"Anyway, call the company tomorrow one last time, and if they don't call you back, who needs 'em anyway? So you wouldn't be a retail buyer. It wouldn't be the worst thing in the world."

Help Wanted, Desperately

Tuesday morning. Six months, two weeks, one day exactly. My hand shakes as I pick up the phone to call Sweeney's corporate office for the very last time.

The phone rings four times, and a voicemail message answers cheerfully, "Hi, this is Tricia. I can't take your call, so leave me a message and I'll be sure to call you back."

And then the long, bitter sound of the cursed beep. This is the part where I'm supposed to leave yet another stalkerlike message for Tricia, who probably won't call me back because a) she thinks that I'm an obsessive-compulsive, neurotic freak (which may or may not be true, according to the tests) or b) there was something so horribly wrong with my psychological testing that Sweeney's Retail was told to steer clear of me. (It's amazing what they can tell from that rice/corn question.)

But I refrain from leaving the obnoxious, pathetic message I desperately want to leave at the tone. Instead, I just wait, listening to the silence of the space where I'm supposed to leave my message. I'm amazed that there's nothing I can think of to say, so I say nothing. After two minutes of silence, the voice-mail operator voice picks up: "If you are satisfied with your message, press one. To record your message again, press two." I press one and hang up the phone. Take that, Tricia.

Disappointment Number 1: I have just casually been rejected from an unstylish retail company that specializes in floral pink and purple leisurewear for senile old women without even the pomp and circumstance of a letter, voice-mail message, or postcard. I'm not sure if this is a bad thing or a good thing. Regardless, it is a sad, sad day in Mudville.

But this time, no, Casey will not strike out. I refuse to be a disappointment this early in the game. I'm not going to fail my "potential." Yet.

This wasn't a strikeout. It was just a ball.

Lessons Learned

1. Never trust a dust-ruffle buyer for anything greater than selecting frilly pink flowered bed skirts.

2. When your senile, schizophrenic great-aunt claims the nursing home's secretary is trying to kill her, assume that thoughts of paranoia are induced by purple housedresses bought at Sweeney's Retail.

3. Being weird—in some ways—is sort of romantic.

4. Lying on psychological tests is useless. Unless of course, you are psychologically unsound.

3
Dwelling in Possibility

6 Months, 2 Days, 18 Hours

Two weeks since Sweeney's unarticulated rejection, and I've pretty much lost almost all incentive to look for a job, not because I don't believe I could at least find someone who would be willing to interview me, but because I wonder if that interview is even worth it. My days are spent eating Chinese food, spending ridiculous amounts of time on the phone with Jared, doing work that is relatively unimportant in terms of my "future" (whatever that is), and watching *Golden Girls* with my housemate Ethan. Not a bad alternative to employment, if you think about it.

Last night (another night of lo mein and eggrolls), I opened a fortune cookie that solemnly told me, "Nothing in life is achieved without passion." As soon as I got home from the Chinese restaurant, I taped the fortune up on my wall, next to the other fortunes I've taped up over the past four years: "A happy man is he who knows what he needs to do, but is happy with what he is doing instead," "Good things come soon," and "The best is yet to come." Today, as I sit staring at the fortunes hanging behind my laptop, I realize that I've reached a new low in Alexa Hoffman history. I'm seriously taking advice from a cookie. Which means it's only a matter of time until I begin searching for existential meaning on the backs of cereal boxes. I wonder how many days I have until I tape "You already know fiber is good for you, but did you know that fiber can play an important part in maintaining good health?" onto my wall.

It's a lazy Wednesday afternoon, I've just finished breakfast ("a healthy portion of fiber helps you start your day right") and know perfectly well that I should try to do something more meaningful than contemplating the cereal box's existential effects on my psyche. Fortunately for me, I don't have to wait very long to find a distraction, because with the mail comes a letter for me from "Volunteering for a Better Majuro." I open the letter and read:

Greetings, Alexa!

In Marshallese, the phrase Na ij rikaki eo ami kaal *means "I'm your new teacher." We are delighted you have chosen to volunteer your time, effort and energy to help educate the children of Majuro. As John Dewey once said, "Any genuine teaching will result, if successful, in someone's knowing how to bring about a better condition of things than existed earlier." We feel confident that your presence as an educator on Majuro will indeed bring out a better condition of life, education, and understanding for all those you teach. In taking the path less traveled by teaching on Majuro, we hope that the time you spend in the Marshall Islands will not only benefit your students, but will also broaden your understanding of humanity—*

*and your role in the world community—in new and profound
ways. Thank you so much for joining us on this exciting journey to a brighter, more promising future.*

As I read the letter, I wonder whether or not I should even
bother searching for a job in New York. Going to this island
would be so easy. I'd spend a year teaching children how to
read—I'd be bringing out "a better condition of things"! Do I
honestly believe that I would be doing that sitting in some office
in New York? Maybe there's no need for me to rush into life in the
hot-sticky-morally-vacuous-push-and-shove city. Maybe I *need*
to go to Majuro.

Maybe I need to stop dwelling on this.

Letter in hand, I decide to distract myself from all my mud-
dled, incoherent thoughts surrounding issues like, "Why should
I put my life on hold?" "Is it worth being on hold if you're doing
something valuable?" "Is finding a job that I want in New York
City so insurmountably impossible that I should flee the country
and give up on trying completely?" Fortunately, distraction lives
upstairs in the form of my housemate, Ethan.

I walk into his room and throw myself onto his bed. "I'm
going to die cold, alone, and unemployed. Possibly in the Marshall Islands."

Ethan ignores my comment and continues typing away at Instant Messenger on his laptop. "Okay, you'll never believe this,
but David got that job at that hedge fund!"

Moaning, on the brink of an entirely new level of self-loathing
at hearing the "great" (read: awful) news that yet another one of
our housemates has a job, I sigh. "What's a hedge fund?"

"I don't know, who cares what it is—it pays really well! He's

going to be making about fifty thousand dollars a year or something. You know how many egg rolls you could buy with fifty
thousand dollars a year? Let me get a piece of paper." Ethan, my
friend since freshman year who has watched me consume more
Chinese food than any other single person on the planet, knows
that in my life—pathetic as it is—egg rolls and currency can be
equated in a lot of ways. "Alex, that's roughly sixteen thousand
eggrolls. Before taxes."

"Yeah, but after taxes, you're screwed. About half the eggrolls then." I roll over on his bed as he types. "Anyway, so if you
could have a really great job but make like no money—or a really
bad job and make a ton of cash, what would you pick?"

"Can't we just watch *Golden Girls*? I have a good one on
tape . . ."

"I hate *Golden Girls*. If you want to watch geriatrics banter
with each other about sex they're not having, I'll take you to
South Mountain Home for the Aged where my great-aunt is and
show you what it's really like. She thinks her nurse is trying to
poison her."

Ethan rolls his eyes and puts a tape in his VCR.

Watching Blanche and Dorothy talk about something—it
looks like the Christmas gift episode—I shift onto my stomach
on his bed. "Seriously, what's the ideal job?" Staring blankly into
the TV screen, I ask Ethan, "Do you think it's wrong to do something because it's easy instead of doing something harder that
you really want? What if I want to take the path *more* traveled?
Does that make me a bad person?"

Ethan gestures to the screen, "Are you blind, woman? I'm
watching *Golden Girls*!"

After three pointed seconds staring at the TV, Ethan turns

away from the screen dramatically. Giving up, he offers, "Okay, well how much do I not like my job where I make a lot of money? Do I only sort of dislike it or do I really, *really* hate it? And what does 'really bad' mean?"

"I don't know—something where you're really, really unhappy. And you really, *really* hate it. Like say you have to shave middle-aged women's legs for twenty-two hours of a regular day. Or you have to tap your finger repeatedly to Gloria Estefan's "Conga" beat for hours on end. Or wait, this is a good one, you're the main cafeteria worker at a camp for fat kids and you have to tell the kids that they can't have a second serving—ever. And then they cry, and you can't do anything about it. Oh, and whatever you do—you do it alone."

Giving his full attention back to *Golden Girls,* Ethan turns to the screen. "Okay, that's just dumb. These things are so unrealistic."

"They're hypothetical situations. It's not supposed to be realistic."

"Alex, the whole point of a hypothetical situation is that it *could* be real!"

"Anyway, let's just say it's a job where you do a lot of busy work that's really time consuming but really doesn't matter for anything. And you have to stay until three A.M. every day doing it—and come in at five A.M. Oh, and you have no friends at work, no phone, and no e-mail. And you sit in an uncomfortable chair in a room without windows, and you're perpetually thirsty."

"I hate being thirsty."

Ethan tilts back in his desk chair, mulling over my hypothetical situation, "But I get paid a lot for it?"

"Oh *yeah.*"

"Well, I want the money, but that sounds miserable."

"Okay, then, so what's your *perfect* job? You tell me."

"I swear to God, if this conversation is somehow leading to me having to hear about fucking Majuro one more time . . . Look, you really have just got to relax. I mean, look at your life: You're graduating school, you're going to move to New York—"

"Or some random island."

Ethan rolls his eyes again. "Like I said, you're going to New York. You'll finally see Jared whenever you want. You should be as happy as a pig in shit."

"Lovely."

"Do you know how many people put this much effort into getting someone to date them? I feel like we've had this conversation a thousand times. You're in reruns again. It's a good thing at least that *I'm* normal."

"Oh, right, I forgot how 'normal' it is to make reservations under the name 'Mr. Marinara' when you go to Italian restaurants. Think on *that* for a bit. Anyway"—I begin browsing through Ethan's day planner—"in two seconds or less: best job. Go."

"God—fine. I'd say my ideal job would be making a ridiculous amount of money. Days are typically from ten A.M. to four P.M. Everyone I work with loves me. And I eat really fancy lunches all the time. Maybe I'm a theater critic. Or a Broadway producer. Okay, now I've *really* gotta go—I'm going to be late."

"Okay, later."

Ethan packs up his bag, puts on a Burberry scarf and a leather jacket and heads out of this tiny room that somehow he manages to live in. I shout after him, "See—you have goals! I don't have any goals. I'm professionally directionless. I'm a professional loser."

"Alex?" Ethan turns around—and looks like he's really concerned about me.

"Yeah?"

"Does this scarf match?"

Jesus. "Yes."

Content, Ethan smiles to himself. "Stop worrying. You'll get a job somewhere. You might get a hernia first, but you'll get a job too. And I shouldn't have told you about David—I wouldn't have said anything if I knew it would make you like this." Ethan fixes his scarf as he heads back to look at himself in the mirror, "You've got to get a grip on reality at some point. *Everyone* is in the same boat as you."

"Everyone except Jared," I mutter.

Ethan leaves, and I decide that maybe he's right after all. Maybe I should just suck it up, take a deep breath, and look for a job like everyone else rather than constantly contemplating my as-yet-nonexistent holding pattern. Maybe I'm exhausting too much energy worrying *how* I'll get a job rather than just doing it.

Maybe it's time for a little vacation to the land of normalcy.

Time to search for a job? Why not. Ah, the democracy of one.

I muster up some interest in employment and decide to surf the Internet for job listings, which is just about as dumb as surfing the Internet to find your future spouse—perhaps even dumber, because finding someone to love at least involves excitement and passion ("Nothing in life is achieved without passion"), whereas searching for jobs generally involves self-imposed feelings of depression, worthlessness, and boredom.

Not that I'm one to criticize how people meet and fall in love: My life is a fountain of embarrassing "how-we-met" stories.

Number one: I am literally a product of modern (now archaic) technology. While the rest of my parents' generation was wearing bell-bottoms, protesting war, and trying every drug imaginable, my parents were trying computer dating. ("Nerd" takes on a loving connotation in my house.) It was 1967, and my mother and father independently discovered the first computer dating system in the United States—actually, the first computer, which took up an entire building in Philadelphia. Each decided on a whim to check it out. Three children and four undergraduate and graduate tuitions later, they remain married. And their initial computer printout matching them up for an eternity of love and passion hangs triumphantly on the wall of our main bathroom, right next to the toilet. Ah, *l'amour*.

Thankfully, my parents' "romantic" meeting and its celebrated commemoration right next to the toilet brush diluted any delusions of grandeur I might have had about how I would meet the perfect guy. So when I met Jared for the first time at a Sheraton Hotel across the street from a prison in Newark, New Jersey, it just felt . . . right.

It was a typically smog-filled June day in New Jersey, and Jared and I met each other (and thirty-five other teenagers) in a conference room right outside Newark Airport (and an IKEA and a prison). It was the June before our senior year in high school, and we were going on a summer camping program to Israel. The conference-room time was our chance to mingle and get to know each other, and for me to avoid thinking about the fact that my parents were probably high-fiving each other in their car, so delighted were they to be free of me and my neuroses for one whole summer.

As I sat on the floor of the conference room holding back

homesick tears, which have plagued me since preschool, I noticed a good-looking guy—tall, sandy brown hair, blue eyes—walk into the room. And that was when I saw it: Around his neck, peeking out from his navy blue T-shirt, he was wearing a neck pouch to hold his passport and money. Arguably, it was the single most embarrassing thing a person could bring on a summer program, an instant ticket to teenage social alienation. A smile lit my face, and I triumphantly took my *own* neck pouch out of my T-shirt, marched up to Jared, and said, "You have a neck pouch too." After ten hours sitting next to each other on that flight, I had completely and totally forgotten about my boyfriend (whom I had cried about leaving the night before), and was completely and totally in love with just about everything about Jared, that sexy, neck-pouch-wearing seventeen-year-old.

Fast forward two years of sexually frustrated friendship and two years dating each other. The neck pouch is now framed in his dorm room. Right under the sink in a cabinet where he stores his unused garbage bags.

The point being, I'm not one to insult how people meet each other—or how people find jobs, for that matter. So I decide that it's better to take a chance, and that I at least owe myself the opportunity to try to find a job rather than torture myself about not finding one. Torturing myself can wait.

As I'm searching the Internet for employment, I arrive at one Web site where the search engine offers the usual categories: advertising/marketing/public relations, health/care, government, media, blah blah blah. But in addition to all these categories, there is another: the "other" category. Is a "hedge fund" something from the "other" world? As far as I know, I haven't yet searched "other" yet in my fruitless quest for employment, so, delightfully, I click "search." Maybe the reason I haven't found a job that's good for me or that wants me is because I'm a classic "other" worker.

A list of jobs pops up on the screen.

Janitor Needed.
Dancer Wanted.
Hair Model Wanted.
Dream Job! Be a Model Scout for Intrigue Models, Inc.!

A model scout? I click on the ad, which takes me to a Web site that asks for my personal information (but no resume), and then asks me to evaluate a series of twenty-one pictures: I must choose who is the most attractive out of each set of three. I fill out the "application," and hope against all hope that maybe, just maybe, "good things come soon."

It's two days later, I'm (unsurprisingly) still unemployed, and I'm beginning to take the cereal box's advice on my fiber intake rather seriously. My colon has never been happier.

As I'm about to head out to class, I check my e-mail:

Congratulations, Alexa Hoffman! Intrigue Models, Inc. would like to interview you for the position of Model Scout. Please come to our office this coming Wednesday for your group interview. Be prepared to stay at our office from 10 A.M. until 5 P.M.

The address is at the bottom of the e-mail. All I have to do is show up at the interview. It's almost too easy. And I'm dumb enough to buy it. Intrigue Models, Inc. must thrive on the stupidity of people like me. Hell, if I can't *be* talent myself, maybe I can find it in others. Look out, Intrigue Models, Inc: Alexa Hoffman is on her way.

My train leaves Philadelphia on time and pulls into New York City at 9 A.M. This is officially the first time in my senior year of college that I've come to New York for a reason other than visiting Jared at NYU. It's also the first time I've actually had to pay for my own ticket on Amtrak. To make a long (and bizarre) story short, during my sophomore year of college (right when Jared and I started "officially" dating), I was on a train going to Philadelphia from New Jersey. On the train, these two twenty-something hicks from Alabama began chatting with me about things to do in Philadelphia. Eager to avoid catching up on astronomy reading, I disobeyed the golden rule of not talking to strangers, and the guys and I talked for the whole train ride, about Philadelphia nightlife and restaurants. As the train pulled into the station, the guys turned to each other and whispered something, and then one of them said to me, "We've got a present for you." Assuming the worst (perhaps a "present" would involve one of them unzipping his pants?), I tried to get out of the car as quickly as possible—but one of the guys chased me and simply said, "You've been real nice to us. We used to work for Amtrak—we'd like to give you a couple of free tickets." I quickly said thanks and shoved the tickets into my bag. When I got home, I opened my bag to see that these guys hadn't given me "a couple" of free tickets: they had given me over five hundred dollars' worth, thus facilitating my entire long-distance relationship with Jared to and from Philadelphia and New York City. Some things, I suppose, are destiny.

But it hardly feels like destiny when I arrive four minutes early at the interview location—a shoddy, nondescript office building completely vacant of the sex and glitz I hoped would accompany my future career as a model scout. I take the elevator up to the thirteenth floor and sit down with the twenty other people who apparently were also invited to this "group interview." The crowd looks decent—a couple of people who seem about my age (one of whom has the largest nose I have ever seen in my life), and a couple of middle-aged "career changers" who seem tired, disillusioned, and wrinkly. This pair looks like a volunteer sample for Botox research. Fortunately for me, I have an edge on getting this job as a model scout. While most of the people here probably have to be trained to unfairly scrutinize the imperfections of other people's faces in order to find beauty, I've been doing this for years for personal enjoyment. For better or for worse (in most cases, for worse), I'm one of those people who never really learned that you're not supposed to stare at people's imperfections.

In fact, since I was fourteen I've used a classification system I invented myself in which I can divide every single person in the world into one of the following three categories in terms of his or her personal appearance: Duck, Rodent, or Elf. (To Jared's credit, this whole system may speak to the "abnormality" issue.) Duck people usually have big lips, a waddle to their walk, and large facial features. (I classify myself, Rosie O'Donnell, Regis Philbin and Elvis clearly as ducks.) In contrast, rodents tend to have sharp angular facial features (think snout of an aardvark or rat), dark hair, and either a sneaky way of moving around or eyes that dart around the room quickly. (John Cusack has darting eyes, dark hair, and a sharp nose. Therefore John Cusack = rodent.) Elves are the easiest to pick out: pointy ears and cute upturned noses, and they tend to be short and light and often have long eyelashes. (Winona Ryder is *classic* elf.)

I've often tried to explain this classification system to people. Some people take to it immediately and begin classifying people according to the system, whereas others simply look at me in baffled bewilderment, as if *I'm* some sort of freak, since I've just told them they resemble a rodent—something they should've realized years ago. Usually, their concerns are whether it is "better" to be a duck or a rodent, or "worse" to be a duck or elf, to which I reply, Is it "better" to have an uncomfortable rash that no one can see or a hideous-looking rash that gives you no pain? Is it "worse" to prefer the word *bongo* to the word *beef*?

This all coming from someone who, ironically, was insulted when Catalina told her she could benefit from a nose job or a chin tuck.

In any other situation, making unfair snap judgments is one of my worst personal faults. But in this room, on this day, at this hour, it is my greatest asset. As I sit back in my chair, dreaming up celebrity deformities, Patrick, Intrigue Models, Inc.'s office director, introduces himself. Patrick is lanky and tall, a bald thirty-something with a sharp nose that looks like it could poke someone's eye out. (Extra credit: See if you can classify Patrick.) His black suit hangs on his body, and the white T-shirt underneath his jacket looks wrinkled and yellowed—I think I see a spaghetti-sauce stain on his collar, and a tiny rip at the spot where his shirt meets his pants. Hardly the portrait of beauty I expected at a modeling agency.

"First of all, I'd like to thank you all for coming. I know this is the first time many of you have been to a modeling agency, and I'm glad you're here. I know this is kind of a strange job . . . As for me, well, I started a snowboard shop in Vermont when I got fed up with the modeling industry a couple months ago, but well, here I am again." Patrick looks up at the ceiling and sighs.

"It's actually a really hard industry to be in, you know, finding beautiful people all the time." Patrick pauses and then looks at the ground. "My girlfriend actually dumped me last week. You know, because she thought that I was spending too much time at work looking for good-looking people. And I tried to explain it to Kate." Patrick begins to pace the room. "But Kate said that when I went to Vermont to start the snowboarding shop she thought I was *sleeping* with this girl Liz that we both knew from when we used to go skiing together. But it wasn't like that at all. Liz was just a cool girl—and I was going to propose to Kate someday anyway. Really. She's just so goddamn sensitive sometimes . . . She forgets how much I love her, how much I need her . . ."

We all stare at Patrick, who looks like he's about to cry. In fact as I stare, I think I see a small tear well up in one eye, which he quickly wipes away before he turns to the window. Part of me wants to hug him, but the other part of me wants to run from the room. We continue to look expectantly at him, either for him to tell us more about Kate's emotional state or to tell us what we need to do to get this job.

Patrick turns away from the window and takes a deep breath. As he runs his hands over his bald head (perhaps searching for hair), he says, "Okay then. Sorry about that. Let's get back on track here . . . What I'd like you all to do now is break up into groups of four, with five people in each group. I'm going to give each group a series of a hundred model photos, or comp cards, as we call them here in the biz, and I want you to separate them into two piles: beautiful and ugly. Then I want you all to totally forget about the beautiful pile and go through the pictures in the ugly pile one by one, ultimately so you can tell me why the people you chose *are* ugly."

Everyone gets out of their seats and separates into groups. I wonder if I'm the only one who thinks this little exercise in eugenics is a strange way to test our model scout capacities. Everyone else obeys Patrick's command with relative ease. Sure, find the ugly people and trash them!, their faces seem to say. It's that easy! I'm shocked to find myself feeling somewhat uncomfortable as my group starts talking. Finding physical imperfections of other people in my head is one thing. Sharing them in a public forum is quite another. Despite my misgivings about our "project," I start listening to my group members' comments. One girl, about twenty-five or so (and no prize pig herself), begins sorting the stack into two piles.

"Ugly. Pretty. Pretty. Ugly, ugly. Ooh, REALLY ugly! Ugly. Pretty. Sort of pretty, sort of ugly, ugly, pretty, ugly, ugly. Where did he *find* all these *ugly* people?"

The rest of the group looks on, and some of my group members start sorting through the ugly pile to determine why they're ugly.

"This girl's fat. I hate fat people."

"This guy's ears are really uneven. And his nose is a little crooked."

"Look at this one! His eyes aren't even the same *color*! Let's put him in the ugly pile!"

"This guy must be British. Look at his teeth!"

"Ew—this guy's skin is *gross*."

I try to join in and point to a small detail on one face: "I don't like that birthmark." After all, finding people's imperfections happens to be one of my strengths. But as the group yabbers away about which person's lips are too thin, which person's nose is too long, which person's eyelashes are too fake, I suddenly feel like it's a Catalina flashback except instead of her telling me I should rearrange my nipples and get my jaw wired shut, we're now supposed to be doing this to other people.

Naturally neurotic, I begin thinking about the imperfections of my *own* face. The bump on my nose. The scar from stitches in my chin. My thinning eyelashes. The birthmark on my lip. And worse, my untoned abs of flab, and my thighs, which I haven't liked since I was twelve. The birthmark in my belly button that looks like it's just dirt. Then there's my horrible eyesight, my uneven eyebrows, my disgustingly bitten fingernails, the bags under my eyes that never go away, my unclipped toenails, the wrinkles starting to form on my forehead, and the scar on my back. The thickness of my upper arms. To say nothing of the shapelessness of my lips, the excessive curliness of my hair, the shortness of my torso, and the large and narrow size of my feet that makes it impossible to buy shoes. To my credit, I happen to have very lovely earlobes, and absolutely stunning kneecaps. But beyond those two things, I am hideously imperfect, borderline deformed. Look at me and mock me: I personally belong in the ugly pile. *Why* does Jared love me? I am a beast.

My group continues to argue about whether one girl is pretty or not. A dark-haired girl waves the comp card. "But she's got great eyes! Are you people blind?"

A chubby middle-aged man sighs and responds, "Look at that

mole on her face by her ear, though. It's practically a crater! She's a disaster."

It's then that I realize what a horrible person I am. Here, I've been doing this kind of thing in my head for years. And yet now that we've been told to openly find flaws in all these perfectly normal-looking people's pictures, it feels horrible, insensitive, cruel even. I can't help but remember how nervous I was throughout my childhood that I was never pretty enough—that my glasses' frames were too pink, my braces too small for my buck teeth, my clothes, coming from my grandfather's children's clothing store, never "cool" enough. Twenty-one years old, and I've still never owned "the right" jeans. Even my retainer color was all wrong. I remember how much it hurt when I was twelve at camp, my bunkmates trying to "sell" me as a girlfriend to Matt Marcus: "Look, if she didn't wear her glasses she'd be pretty!" and "Try to picture her without braces."

I can't believe people do this professionally.

Foolishly, I guess, I thought being a model scout would revolve around telling people how beautiful they are, not how ugly they are. Mistake number one: Jobs posted on the Internet are never what they say they are. Better to live life as a disappointment than to have this job, I think.

Patrick calls us all back together as a group, and then the group talks excitedly about people's physical imperfections. People start laughing as they realize that every group noticed the same moles, the same uneven ears, the same crooked noses. Patrick looks as if he has momentarily forgotten his break-up with Kate, and smiles in appreciation of the monster he has created: a room filled with people eager to criticize normal people's normal faces. Success.

Ariel Horn

Our group project ends, and Patrick begins to lecture us about the "basics" of finding "model material" on the streets of New York.

He hands us each a sheet of paper, with the heading "Model Scouting Guidelines," which lists the physical requirements necessary in a "good" model. Patrick explains, "There are all sorts of models out there, just waiting to be found. I'm sure you all think of models and you think Gisele, Cindy Crawford, Tyra Banks and all of them fashion models. But here at Intrigue, we also look for other types, you know, the 'everyman' model. Did you know that a fifty-five-year-old man that works for our agency makes at least a million five a year in print ads? I'm not kidding, folks. That's the kind of person you're looking for. Someone who can play a dad in an ad. A mom. A kid on the soccer team. You're looking for someone who's got that everyday edge. Someone people can relate to.

"We'll just run through some requirements real quick so you know. Fashion models, you know what they look like. Five eight to six foot, thirty-six-inch-or-less hip size, attractive, dress size is zero to six. Skinny—diets of cigarettes and coffee, nothing more. Men should be five eleven to six three in this category, jacket size forty regular to forty long, attractive. Basically, that's me, just taller and better-looking."

Patrick gets some obligatory laughs from the crowd.

"For commercial print models you're gonna want a girl who's about five three to five ten or a guy who's five seven to six two, with a wide face, good teeth, good skin, even features, high cheekbones. These people can be just about anyone. These are the everyman models we want. Then you got your promotional models, your petites, your plus sizes. Plus sizes should be five eight to six feet, dress size ten to twenty-four, attractive, shapely legs, proportional figure."

So ashamed am I of critiquing every normal-looking person in the world within a span of ten minutes that I tune out Patrick's little song-and-dance, until he mentions "plus-size" models. According to Patrick's standards, I, a size eight or ten, five foot seven, am too short to be a plus-size model, even though my dress size fits the bill. So not only is my body characterized by thousands of tiny imperfections . . . apparently, I'm also "fat." Fabulous.

Thank God for my earlobes: those bastions of beauty, a safe haven of purity on a body marred by numerous disgusting and horrid deformities.

Patrick wraps up his talk. "And that's what we're looking for. I'm gonna give you all about an hour for lunch, and I'd like you to spend that time doing some scouting of your own. Go outside, take a look. Practice your approach—how are you going to tell these people that they should be models? And if you really see one you think is terrific, you tell them to call Intrigue Models, Inc. Enjoy your lunch, and be productive!"

It is time for the Hideously Deformed like myself to find the Attractive, Shapely-Legged, Proportional-Figured Perfect Human Being. Let the search begin.

I go to lunch alone at a sit-down deli around the corner from Intrigue Models, Inc. and can't decide what to have for lunch. I desperately want a brie-and-tomato sandwich, but since I am apparently too dumpy and short to be a plus-size model, I skip the sandwich of choice and go for the more anorexic fruit cup. Despite my constant neurosis that I will develop brain cancer from excessive use of my cell phone, I take a seat by the window and decide to call my mother. I've got one thousand free minutes and I intend to use every single one of them—come tumor or neurological damage.

"Hi Mom. What's going on?" I cup the phone close to my ear so I can hear her above the noise of the crowded deli.

"Oh, hi, dear. How are you? I was just thinking of you. How's your interview? Are you still at your interview? You shouldn't be talking on the phone if you're at your interview."

"No—the guy gave us an hour for lunch, but then we go back. We had to decide whether people were pretty or ugly and put their pictures into piles. And this guy who's leading the whole thing is a total freak—he keeps talking about his ex-girlfriend. Apparently he owned a snowboarding shop or something in Vermont. The whole thing is pretty weird."

"I told you from the start, Alex, this is not the job for you. You're not going to be a model scout—who's ever even heard of that as a job anyway? You go to Penn so you can be a model scout? The whole thing's dumb. You should be going to law school, Alex. Or you could try to get an MBA. Anyway—are you seeing Jared today?"

"No, I've got to get back to school—I haven't done any of my reading and I have to write some stupid response paper too."

"I think you should go downtown and see Jared tonight. It's more important that you spend time with Jared than it is for you to do your reading. You can do your reading on the train."

This from the woman who pays my tuition.

"Mom, first of all, I didn't bring my reading, and second of all, Jared has a class tonight, so he couldn't even meet me for dinner if he wanted to. And I'm seeing him this weekend anyway."

"Don't you think he should skip his class? Alex, Jared is much more important than any job you're trying to get . . . jobs come and go." *Pause, Alex, wait for it.* "But Jared—he's going to propose to you this year, and I think you two should start thinking about where you want to live when you're married . . . or whether it would be best to get married after graduation in June or in August . . . I think you should get married in June and move to New Jersey, Nina might move to New Jersey—from my lips to God's ears!—it's much cheaper than New York, and you and Jared can commute. . . ."

Earth to Mom: there's no reason to commute to New York from New Jersey if you're living—unmarried—in Majuro.

"Mom, he's not going to propose."

"He has a wonderful job set up, Alex. There's no reason for him not to. *We* love him, *you* love him, what's the problem here?"

My mom constantly bringing this up makes me feel like she'll think I'm a failure if I don't get married soon—and not having a job while simultaneously not meeting my mother's standards for my life is enough to drive me into a dizzied spinster oblivion. And being constantly reminded by my mother that Jared already landed a fabulous job at Christie's auction house while I still have nothing doesn't help my self-confidence either.

"Mom, please. He's twenty-one, I'm twenty-one . . . I don't even have a *job,* I might be going to *Majuro* in six months! Should we plan the wedding to be in Majuro? Do they have rabbis in Majuro?"

"When I married Daddy he was just twenty years old. So Jared's already older than Dad was when we got engaged. Alex, you don't know what you're talking about. I just know this—

Jared is going to propose to you this year. Alex—trust me." She half jokes, "Make a life. Be a wife."

"Look, I'm going to go, okay?"

"Go see Jared tonight? For me?"

"Mom, I've gotta go."

"Good luck with the rest of your interview. Call me when you're back in Philadelphia. I think you should go to sleep early tonight—you're cranky. Love you."

And then it's just me and my fruit cup, my cell phone, and the newly imposed pressure to get married ASAP. You would think I was a teenage pregnancy case, the way she pushed this.

As I sit by the window, I start to wonder when or if Jared and I will ever actually get married. When or if I'll end up giving up and going to the middle of the Pacific. As I sit eating my paltry fruit cup as slowly as possible in order to trick my stomach into thinking it's getting more food than I'm willing to feed it, I notice a beautiful young woman sitting at the counter.

She's got long, wavy, sandy-brown hair, green eyes, and angular features. Something about her face is fascinating—strong features, an angular jaw. Gorgeous eyes. A face for the "beautiful" pile, no doubt. Looks about 5 feet 11 inches or so. Her eyebrows seem even. She has a well-proportioned figure. She chews her sandwich—nice teeth. Great skin. I look at her legs—shapely. She's wearing brown leather knee-high boots, a fitted, stylish denim skirt, and a white, breezy peasant blouse. A turquoise necklace. There's something about her—I can't take my eyes off of her. She just might have "the look"!

As I'm trying to muster up the courage to go up to her, to tell her that she's beautiful, I wonder if this is what it feels like to hit on a woman. Having no lesbian experiences myself to draw from,

Help Wanted, Desperately

I wonder how I should approach her. How to tell her she's beautiful and that she should be a model. How to seem sincere without appearing shallow.

What would I want a guy hitting on me to say? Noticing beauty is good, but not enough— too easy to write off. Too dumb and cliché of a line. I need something else. Something that will make her want to listen to me—to talk to me, to hear me out. I feel my palms getting very sweaty, and have to remind myself that this is not a person I want to date, just a person I want to scout.

I throw my garbage out and get closer to her. She's reading. That's good. I can use that as an entry point. It'll make me seem less shallow, smarter, worthy of listening to. I try to lean closer to see what she's reading: a collection of Emily Dickinson poems. She's smart! And pretty! I think I've found my dream woman! Calm, Alex. Not looking for a date. Looking for a model to scout. I squint my eyes to see what poem she's reading, and catch a glimpse:

I dwell in Possibility—
A fairer House than Prose—
More numerous of Windows—
Superior—for Doors—

A seat at the counter has opened up next to her.

I'm ready to make my move.

I try to look casual, brush nonexistent hair out of my eyes. Casual. "So, um, I noticed you're reading Emily Dickinson. I really love that poem, 'I Dwell in Possibility.' It's really, you know, a great poem. I read it in, in college." C'mon, Alex. Could I sound

any less confident? In one day I've become a hideous physical de-
formity, an unmarried, un-engaged wretch, and also a bitter, bitter failure at lesbian come-ons. What woman could ever love me?

She looks up from her book and turns to me. Emerald green
eyes that echo her turquoise necklace. And it looks as if the Goddess will speak to me! Oh happy day! "Oh, it's such a wonderful
poem," she says in a soft, low, sexy voice. "The idea of dwelling
in possibility . . . of dreaming of what can and can't be, and how
everything just *can* be if you want it that badly, well, it's really
something that I live by personally. My life motto." She flashes
me a smile. Not just good teeth. *Great* teeth.

Okay, time to tell her she's beautiful. I'm getting more nervous by the second; now it's not just my palms, it's my face
sweating profusely.

"I know this may sound really strange, but, well, I'm a model
scout for Intrigue Models, Inc."—*oh, good, Alex, when in doubt,
lie, lie, LIE!*—"and, well, I think you're really beautiful. You're
one of the most beautiful women I've ever seen in my life. You
could be a model for our agency."

The Goddess's eyes light up, and her brilliant smile gets even
wider. "You really think so?" The Goddess is gushing and I'm
blushing. I'm not a lesbian failure after all! "See, I just came to
the city about five years ago and you're just about the nicest
New Yorker I've ever met! What a wonderful thing to hear a
stranger say!"

I blush some more, and say, "Oh, well, I'm from New Jersey
and Philadelphia sort of, so you know, well, I'm not *really* a New
Yorker."

The Goddess smiles, lowers her voice and says in a deeper
tone, "Well, I'm not *really* a woman. I was born a man."

Help Wanted, Desperately

*   *   *

It's all really a blur after that moment. Words that I don't remember saying just spewed out of my mouth after she told me she was once a man. My venture into lesbianism failed: I was attracted to a wolf in sheep's clothing. I told her that "whatever she did to herself looked great" and that she should call the Intrigue Models, Inc. hotline to set up an interview date. She was thrilled. She asked me if I knew of many transsexual models. I told her I didn't know any really, but that that didn't mean that she couldn't carve out a niche for herself as the first transsexual supermodel. A trailblazer. As I was about to leave, she told me I had made her feel beautiful. She said that people normally don't treat transsexuals this way, and she was amazed at my sincerity. She said I had made her day—and her life as a woman. She told me she'll continue to "dwell in possibility."

I told her I would too. Then I left the deli, and didn't return to the Intrigue Models, Inc. office. And I didn't go to Jared. It was time for the Deformed to head home.

Lessons Learned

1. Avoid at any and all costs conversations with my mother that might in some inconceivable way lead to the discussion of my becoming engaged to my twenty-one-year-old boyfriend who has no idea about said conversations with my mother.

2. Do not engage in conversations over Emily Dickinson poetry with outrageously sexy women in delis while eating only fruit.

3. When your interviewer cries about his girlfriend during an in-

terview, assume that the job leads to unnatural psychological hang-ups.

4. Not having the right jeans . . . or the right thighs . . . or the right lip shape doesn't make me a bad person. But it sure as hell doesn't make me want to be a model scout.

5. Always, ALWAYS remember to apply prescription deodorant the night before an interview.

6. Do not—under any circumstances—interview for Internet jobs listed as "other" ever again.

4
The Perfect
Sit

5 Months, 3 Weeks, 2 Days

Clearly things haven't been working out for me in interviews. I decide that maybe it's time for me to readjust my warped perspective of the world: that is, just because I think I could maybe, possibly, perhaps be a suitable "rikaki" on Majuro doesn't necessarily mean that I'm well suited for any other job I might haphazardly apply for in order to avoid letting life pass me by. Maybe it's time for me to cut the bullshit entirely and try to focus on *real* reasons (if they do, in fact, exist) regarding why I could potentially work in any particular field. Or potentially live up to my, well, potential.

Both the interview with Sweeney's and the model scout "interview" taught me to hone in on a problem: I've come to rely on bullshitting as a way of life, even if there's no real reason to bullshit. Evidence A: During my freshman year of college, I decided that I really wanted to be a campus tourguide, to show prospective students and their parents around my school, but not in the traditional boring way tourguides normally do. Instead of taking them to the normal campus "don't miss" sites, I would give visitors the "behind-the-scenes" tour. I'd take them to the basement of the Fine Arts Library where I once spotted three rats engaged in what appeared to be a fairly run-of-the-mill sexual threesome (based on their blasé expressions, I'd be hard-pressed to say that the threesome was a) really doing it for any of the rats or b) particularly different from their usual sexual routine). Or even better, I wouldn't take them to the architecturally beautiful quad to show them the "college house community." Instead I'd take them inside the nasty highrises that resemble buildings in the Soviet Union circa 1974. And then, THEN, they could feel like they were making their decision on where to go to college with all the cards laid out on the table. I thought it was a noble endeavor of me to take on, truthfully. I would be doing these kids a service.

Naturally, I knew that my "idealized" tour wouldn't appeal to the student organization that selected tourguides. So at my interview on why I wanted to be a tourguide, I said all the right things. When they asked me if there was a safety problem on campus, I replied, "No, West Philadelphia is as safe by night as it is by day!" When they asked me what I didn't like about our school, I smiled sweetly and said, "That there's not enough time in the day to dabble in all the activities that our wonderful school has to offer." I was sure they had wanted me. I was going to get it.

I was rejected, since these interviewers clearly saw through what I thought was rather compelling bullshit. But just when I had given up all hope of being a campus tourguide and of telling the world the truth, a miraculous opportunity arrived in my e-mail inbox. I was "selected" by the admissions office to be one of the highlighted students on an admissions video to be sent through-

out the country to potential students. It was a dream come true—
fame, precious, precious fame! I mean, an opportunity to reveal
the truth.

But here's the strange thing: When I was finally offered my
golden opportunity to honestly "tell it like it is" about my school,
I couldn't do it. I was so steeped in the culture of bullshit my entire life that I found my lies growing exponentially with each film
spot. Truth was nowhere to be seen. Before I knew it, when I was
asked to talk on the video about my favorite place on campus I
was suddenly waxing poetic on how "wonderful the small pond
by the medical school is . . . like an idyllic slice of country in the
urban landscape."

But wait—it gets worse. They filmed me at the pond. Not just
sitting there, but feeding the ducks with little pieces of bread that
the cameraman had stolen from a cute three-year-old who then
proceeded to bawl (there's music over that bit in the video). I am
personally responsible for perpetuating that everything-is-
perfect-on-college-campuses myth. For shame.

The combined negative aftermath of my shallow, morally re-
pulsive model-scout interview and the run-in with my corrupt
psychological test at the Career Service's building has led me to
realize that in order to get a job, I'm going to have to learn how to
control my compulsion to bullshit. No easy task.

And where better to learn how to do that than at the Bullshit
Capital of the World: a bookstore offering an information session
entitled "A Guide to the Perfect Interview." Surely this will teach
me how to schmooze with the big boys. Convincingly. Just what
I need.

Rather than going it alone, I begged Jared—who's come to
visit for the weekend—to join me.

"Please, Jared, I just don't want to do this alone. It makes me feel like a failure. You don't want me to feel like a failure, do you?"

Jared, without glancing away from his book, rolls his eyes and says in a droning monotone, "You're not a failure." He shifts in his seat and puts his book down. "And I'll go if you make it worth my while."

"What's that supposed to mean?"

Jared's eyes focus on a piece of lint on my carpet, and it looks like he's deep in thought. "There is one thing you can do—and if you did it, I'd definitely go with you."

"Anything. Name it."

"Okay, you have to lick the information session leader's face."

"Jared, that's the dumbest thing I've ever heard. There's absolutely no way I'll do that." Putting on my jacket, fully prepared to leave without Jared and his bizarre expectations, I add, "You know, you really have no right to call singing 'Man of La Mancha' on the toilet weird after asking me to *lick* the information session leader's face."

Jared nods his head, still ruminating on what sort of condition I should agree to in order to have him come with me. "Okay, instead of actually licking their face, you can just ask, 'When is it appropriate to lick your interviewer's facer?' at the end of the session. But you have to ask it in front of everyone. When they say, 'Any questions?'"

Sighing, I hand Jared his jacket, "Done." We shake, and we head out of my apartment.

A small price to pay.

For all of Jared's strange, loving, and bizarre requests, the thing about him is this: He's employed. The E word. In many ways, it's more horrifying than the M-words (*Majuro* and *marriage*).

While losers like myself have spent the past month or so inventing ridiculous back-up Plan Bs to stave off feelings of professional and personal inadequacy, Jared has bypassed the entire mortifyingly pathetic job-search experience. Having sufficiently charmed his internship coordinator at Christie's, Jared was served the Holy Grail on a silver platter: a job offer that perfectly blends his academic fascination with economics and art history into a tasty little professional bundle. A job at an auction house.

Here's the "but." (There's always a "but," and anyone who tells you differently is lying. You can tell them I said that.) As much as I love him, as much as I care about him, as much as I really like the fact that he knows what he wants to do and how to achieve it, I can't help but feel this constant, unavoidable, sinking sense of self-mediocrity when I think about how he's got his life all put together already.

I'm still working on *getting* a life. The "put together" part will have to come later.

It's not that I'm not proud of him. He definitely deserves the job for working so hard (in contrast to my dedicated Instant Messaging all summer). It's just that in spite of everything, I find myself happy, jealous, and in love all at the same time.

When you have those emotions and it doesn't relate in any way to your boyfriend cheating on you, you know you've got deeper issues.

But in my ongoing two-year effort to avoid ever discussing anything with Jared that would in any way make him or me nervous or question our relationship, I make the healthy choice not to talk about anything pertaining to

a. my feelings of inadequacy born out of thinking about Jared's blossoming professional career in comparison to my own life

b. the fact that every day, with every ignored resume I send, with every failed interview I corrupt, and with every job offer landed by one of my friends, the idea of going to Majuro becomes a more likeable and realistic option.

Shoving anxieties about Jared out of my mind, I arrive at the information session only to find out, to my utter horror, that Margaret Kilmore, the universally-hated Career Services counselor would be leading the session. Jared looks at me, shaking his head, "I can't believe you're going to have to ask *her* about licking an interviewer." Jared knows my feelings for Margaret, and begins playfully massaging my shoulders as he smiles, "This is *totally* worth coming for."

Fifty-something and dressed (apparently) as a dust ruffle (I now consider myself a dust-ruffle aficionado), Margaret is decked to the nines in a floral Laura Ashley jumper, floral Laura Ashley stockings and a floral Laura Ashley headband. Pursing her lips, waiting for all the unemployed people to dutifully file into the room for their guide to the perfect interview, Margaret leans against a table at the front. Jared smiles angelically at her, no doubt anticipating what is sure to be another humiliating moment for me as I ask her whether and when it is ever appropriate to lick a potential employer.

At first glance, Margaret might appear to be a normal person. She drinks coffee like normal people, sends e-mail like normal people, and holds a steady job. But here's the catch: She absolutely, positively seems to hate her job. And, apparently, anyone who's unemployed. As a person who advises people on what professions they should seek, one would have thought that she would have the foresight to know beforehand that she herself would hate her job.

My first insight into Margaret's disdain for unemployed people came at a "Perfect Your Resume!" session, also offered by the bookstore. Essentially, perfecting my resume involved a "resume review," which is basically an excuse for career counselors to pick apart your resume and make sure that you appear to be much smarter on paper than you actually are in real life. My resume review went something like this:

Margaret looks at my resume quickly, purses her lips and then says in her prissy little way, "This won't do."

"What won't do?"

"You have here under 'Skills and Interests' that you're in a singing group. I wouldn't hire you."

Well, fortunately, I would never want to work for you.

"Why not?" I ask. Is there something seriously wrong with singers? Did career counselors get a memo that explained why employers hate singers? Part of me is baffled by this Taliban-esque ban against singing, but the other part of me, so desperate to get a job, to be told in no uncertain terms that I'm a worthwhile hire, listens to Margaret, scared of what she'll say.

"Because to me, this says, 'I have no marketable talents, I have nothing to say, and I'm unemployable, and therefore I'm going to put on my resume that I like karaoke.' "

I guess Margaret missed the "Professional Experience" part of the resume.

Naturally, I came home from that resume review more than a

little flustered, ready to call Jared, my sisters, my parents, anyone who would listen to me and tell me that it wasn't true—that just because I like to sing doesn't mean I'm an unemployable karaoke fiend.

As we wait for the session to start, I remind Jared of my resume review.

Jared hardly looks amazed as he remembers my story. "Alex, career counselors are *always* like that. When I went for a resume review at some job fair in New York last year, this guy told me, 'The problem is that an employer has no reason to want to hire you.' They're all just so bitter. I mean, granted, you'd be bitter if you worked with people like us too." To myself, I mutter, *You mean people like me. Unemployed people like ME.* Jared, oblivious, scans the room, turning to me as he smiles. "There are about fifty people here. And each and every one of them wants to know when you can lick your interviewer." Playfully, Jared takes my hand and licks it.

"You need to get out more."

"Maybe."

Scanning the room for fellow unemployed people I know, I casually ask Jared, "So, did your career counselor say anything else at your resume review?"

"Oh yeah, this guy told me, 'Quite simply, you may graduate without a job. Let me take that back. What I mean to say is that being unemployed is a *full*-time job.' That was a classic one . . . But hey, looks who's laughing now, right?"

Not me.

Regardless of my hang-ups about Margaret (and for that matter, Margaret's hang-ups about me), Jared and I decide to stick around for the "Guide to the Perfect Interview," if for no other reason than that I know they'll be giving out free mugs at the end. (After a month or two of career information sessions with more and more people coming back each time, the bookstore has finally realized that in the "new economy," they'll have to settle for giving us free mugs, pens, and stressballs, which are somehow supposed to compensate for the fact that four years of college education can't even get us the jobs that my mom once described as "below the poverty line.") As other people file into the room, Jared and I move to a particular pair of seats in the classroom—in the middle, but toward the back—where we can sink into our chairs, make snide remarks throughout the session, and pray that Margaret won't notice us or call on us for anything.

As we wait for the seminar to start, and Jared grows increasingly involved in a conversation about the quality of the bookstore chairs with a man sitting near us, I survey my surroundings, eager to see who else is unemployed. There's an annoying kid from my English class, who insists on calling everything he reads "incredibly Faustian," listening to something that's probably incredibly Faustian on his Discman. Next to him is an older-looking man with gray, thinning hair in a three-piece suit—he looks like he should be the CEO of a company by now. Across from me is a thirty-something woman rocking a baby in her arms while reading an informational pamphlet entitled, "How To Get a Job—Fast!" Margaret, at the front of the room, is pursing her lips and looking at her watch, taking deep, short, prissy breaths. A forty-something bald man near her seems to be editing his own resume. One of my friend's ex-boyfriends looks around vacantly, mistakenly makes eye contact with me, and then proceeds to pretend I don't exist. He fixates on a motivational poster showing a snowy mountain range and a placid lake with the one-word caption ACHIEVE. I wonder if he's really thinking about all he wants to accomplish in life. Then, noticing that I'm staring at him, he turns to me and says, "Dude, if I could just go to Vail and ski for a living, that'd be pretty sweet."

Sure would be.

But wait, there are even more posters, my first clue into just how crappy this seminar is really going to be. There's one poster that has a picture of an eagle flying over purple mountains, with a caption that says, BELIEVE! Another one has a crystalline blue lake with one tiny ripple in it; the caption reads, FOCUS. I wonder if there are people who actually find these posters even vaguely "inspirational." This collection could be more aptly called "Pathetic Attempt to Distract Me from Realizing That I Came to This Meeting Because I Still Don't Have a Job."

Margaret leading this seminar is one thing. But the posters are atrocious. I don't even know if this is worth the free mug anymore. I eye the door, but just as I think of making a stealthy escape, Margaret cuts me off. It's over. I'm a prisoner.

Just as Margaret is closing the door, a twenty-something guy with long hair and a pierced ear frantically tries to push it open, muttering, "Sorry I'm late."

Margaret turns to those of us unfortunate enough to be sitting in a room with her and says, "Remember this phrase, and write this down: 'Undeserving problem children of the elite.' "

To my horror, many of the jobless surrounding me furiously write down exactly what Margaret just said.

Margaret smiles her sickly "I'm pretending to be magnanimous and nice when really I'm an evil witch" smile, purses her lips, and addresses the latecomer, whose eyes dart around the room nervously.

Margaret smiles her icky-sweet smile again and says, "I'm sorry. You're three minutes late. But would you like some free advice? I don't tolerate lateness—and employers won't either. And cut your hair and remove that despicable earring. Then maybe you can try to get a job like an adult, not some silly little hippie teenager. You are no longer welcome here. Goodbye." Margaret quickly shuts the door in the anguished man's face. The rest of us prisoners remaining look at one another in repulsed awe.

I whisper to Jared, "She is *so* hard core."

Jared whispers out of the side of his mouth, "She's going to eat you when you ask about the licking."

Margaret walks to the front of the room and casually leans against the table again. She pauses for what seems like an eternity, apparently to make us think she's more interesting than she is, though I spend the free minutes thinking how I would give Margaret a makeover in my head, which is something I generally do with people when they take meaningful pauses. Dye-job for sure. Perhaps a diet with more fiber. And definitely some eyebrow-pluckage. Not "ugly pile" material . . . but not Intrigue Models, Inc. material either. As Margaret stares at all of us with her sickly, saccharine grin, Jared seems deeply involved in making faces at the baby sitting near us, who has started to cry.

Every time I feel jealous of Jared about the whole job thing, he does something that surprises me and makes me love him even more—like playing with a random baby just because it will stop the baby from crying, or talking to bewildered, lost tourists and giving them directions even when they're too nervous and flustered to ask for help themselves. And for that amazing fraction of a minute when I watch Jared do these things without his realizing I'm there, I forget that he has a job, I forget my pointless, repressed jealousy, and all I can think about is how lucky I am to be with that great guy who'll pay for the person behind him in line at Häagen-Dazs, just because. Changing the world, one ice-cream cone at a time.

Perhaps I should spend more time being jealous of who he is as a person, and less time worrying about who he is as an employee.

Margaret continues to stare at us until the baby—who now waves at Jared, her small, delicate hand opening and clenching to him like he's an old friend—has stopped crying. Finally, Margaret decides to bless us with her wisdom.

Margaret purses her lips and begins, "Many of you are not getting jobs because you are not good candidates. But others of you are not getting jobs simply because you have no sense of professionalism. Today, I'm going to try to rectify at least one of those problems.

"Some of you simply do not know how to behave like normal people, which is a problem."

I scribble a note to Jared on the informational pamphlet I picked up on the way in, "Takes one to know one, Marge."

"So today we're going to practice sitting. I'd like you all to sit now the way you would sit in an interview."

Everyone shifts around and glances at one another with the "Is she for real?" look that people usually have when they're near Margaret Kilmore. As the mother moves in her seat to sit properly, her baby begins crying again, and Majorie heaves out a sigh.

Jared, far too amused to be terrified by the Declaration of Sit, slides his butt to the back of his chair, straightens his posture, and winks at me. I smile at him, admittedly amused. The rest of us follow suit (minus the winking), assuming our very best sitting postures. I feel vaguely like a poodle at a dog show.

Margaret walks around the room for what seems like ten agonizing minutes and stares at each of us one by one. She squints in revulsion as she passes me. For a second I think she's going to spit on me, and I thankfully remember that I never took my raincoat off.

"Terrible. Were you raised in a barn? You sicken me."

Margaret walks toward Jared. "Oh God, surely you can do better than this!" Jared shifts in his seat and for the first time at this session, he actually looks nervous, and desperate for Margaret's approval. Margaret inspects him, and then tilts her head. "Mediocre at best."

Jared turns to me, as Margaret continues pacing the aisles, and whispers, "This is why people go to therapy. This is going to cost you *way* more than the licking comment."

Margaret then says to Faustian Boy: "Do they not have chiropractors in Cherry Hill? Certainly Mommy and Daddy would pay for a doctor for you. Your posture is atrocious."

She meanders over to the mother and child duo and offers, "Employers hate babies. I'd get rid of yours or hide it."

Margaret walks towards me and sneers. "*You* are a scoliosis-ridden troll. I can't even look at you."

Jared looks at me and sneers. "Who could ever love you, troll?" Seeing that I'm vaguely upset that I've just been told I'm basically a gnome, Jared offers me a tiny smile and says softly, "I could."

Then Margaret spots her prize pig and puts her hand to her heart. Jared and I look at each other frantically as an almost-human smile lights Margaret's face. She has found her Perfect Sit. Margaret crouches down to the floor to examine the woman's sitting technique from a different perspective. The prize pig shivers like a young piglet in the corner of a barn selected for slaughter. She looks around the room at the rest of us, her wide, frightened eyes begging that someone, anyone distract Margaret from her, to protect her. The rest of us look around the room, look down to the ground, ashamed and embarrassed that we're doing nothing to help her evade slaughter. Anything to avoid communication with the condemned.

Margaret pats her pig on the head. "You may release your sit. This, ladies and gentlemen, is a woman who is going to get a job! This is the sit the rest of you hunchbacks can only dream of! You, young lady, are getting a prize!" Margaret triumphantly walks to the front of the room, and pulls something out of her purse. The rest of us gnomes look on in mesmerized awe.

Jared—no longer holding his sit—turns to me and whispers, "That lady's gonna get a job AND a piece of candy? Alex, this is so not fair!" He nudges me. "Go tell Margie you deserve that prize, damn it!"

Margaret proudly walks back to the Perfect Sit and places magnets in the prized pig's hands. That's right, not candy, but refrigerator magnets. The rest of us heave a sigh of relief—at least we're not missing out on something good. Margaret smiles and says, "You, my dear, get magnets all about finding a job to put on your refrigerator! I'll read out some of the words for the rest of you. 'Success'. 'I can achieve!' 'Workaholic.' 'Job.' 'Astronaut.' 'Enjoy'." Absent are the more appropriate phrases, such as, "Still

Help Wanted, Desperately

an Unemployed Loser," "Person With No Sense of Sit," and "Applying to Law School Because I Can't Get a Job." Margaret must have given those magnets out at the "How to Live Within Your Means" seminar.

"Any questions?" Margaret scans the room for any fool willing to challenge her.

Jared looks at me pointedly, and I meekly raise my hand as I think, *I am a really, really good girlfriend.*

Margaret looks at Jared, looks at me, and then looks at my hand. She smiles sweetly. "I'm glad to see there are no questions." Then she just stares at the rest of us, the Deformed. (To consider yourself deformed twice in the span of one month is a very, very bad thing.)

Jared turns to me and shakes his head. "I can't believe I came for this and you didn't even get to do it. Now we'll *never* know when it's appropriate to lick your interviewer."

Margaret purses her lips, folds her arms across her chest, and looks unbelievably proud of herself. "You may pick up your complimentary mug at the door now. You are dismissed."

Jared and I get up to leave, the room still silenced by the aura of Margaret. I lean over to him and whisper, "Hey, maybe that job ringing the bell at Notre-Dame is available."

Jared lets a smile creep to his face, pursing his lips à la Margaret Kilmore and replies, "Well, you know, Quasimodo simply has *no* sense of sit."

Lessons Learned

1. A natural love of karaoke is a one-way ticket to unemployment.

2. I am a scoliosis-ridden troll.

3. If I knew how to sit, I'd be making over $100,000 a year, and could buy all the motivational refrigerator magnets I ever wanted.

4. I am no prize pig.

5
Maybe I'll
Be a Teacher?

5 Months, 2 Weeks, 2 Days

After a couple of days spent compulsively examining my posture in every mirror within a ten-mile radius, I'm ready to dive into the job search again. But which way to go? I check my e-mail and notice that I have my four thousandth e-mail from a job posting listserv I had signed up for at a time when I actually believed someone would hire me. Generally, these e-mails will have subject titles like "Interested in Naval Science?" or "How to Work for a Nonprofit." Sent out to about two thousand un-employees like myself, all desperate for jobs, the e-mails usually make their way rather quickly into our deleted files when we individually realize, "No, I'm not interested in pig breeding or saving all the tea-tree rain forests in the world," or whatever the flavor of the week is.

Well, that is, until last Valentine's Day, when one of the people responsible for sending out messages mistakenly sent a relatively harmless but entirely amusing love note to the listserv rather than to her boyfriend. It went something like this:

Ariel Horn

Dear Snugglekins,

Can't wait to snuggle tonight! Happy snuggiliciousvalentine-saversary!

—Snugglepoo

Ever since then, I usually read through all the listserv's e-mails, hoping to get some sort of snuggly-wuggly message. Regardless, I figure I'll open up the four thousandth e-mail, and that maybe, just maybe it would contain some inappropriate message which I can then forward to a bunch of people who might be entertained by it for about a minute and a half. I click on the "Do You Want to Be a Teacher?" subject line.

Do you want to have an effect on the future of America? Be a teacher! The following companies are teacher-talent search groups looking for young new teachers. The companies will interview you and place you in a pool of potential teachers for eastern-region schools. You can make a difference! Submit your resume by Friday.

Hmm. My mom's a teacher. Why, I've known teachers all my life! And if I go to Majuro, well, I'll be teaching. Why not teach in New York City?

I'm going to be a teacher! (Insert awe-inspiring music here.) I'm going to get off my duff and do something in this topsy-turvy world! Sure, I won't have a lot of money. But I'll have made a difference in the education of a child! And isn't that worth far more than the six-figure salaries my investment-banker friends will be pulling in? I have a vision! I have a dream! Most importantly, I have another resume to hand in. This one, I decide, will be printed on "taupe cream" paper.

I'm surprised that I'm actually called in for an interview for the teaching position. I played up on the fact that I had an internship at an educational children's TV show after my senior year in high school and did research there with three-year-olds and five-year-olds to determine the effectiveness of the show's programming. Truth be told, it was one of my only internships that I thought was actually worthwhile—really nice people, really valuable work, and they actually needed me. Maybe I *do* want to make a difference in the world, for real. What better way to live up to your potential than feeding into the potential of others?

I also played up the fact that in high school I worked as an "assistant teacher" (read: cookie distributor and juice pourer) at an extracurricular program geared toward teaching neurotic suburban parents' bratty, overachieving six-year-olds French so that they could someday get into the (Ivy League) school of their dreams.

Basically, I had decided when fixing my resume for this teaching job that no previous job was too small to mention. And they had taken my bait. Hook, line, sinker. This was going to be easier than I thought.

I walk into the room where my interview is to be held in the Career Services' building, but this time minus the strut. Teachers do not strut. They waddle, actually.

I wonder if this is what they talk about at teacher conventions.

I've mastered the waddle, but I immediately feel overdressed. My interviewer, a plump woman with gapped front teeth named

Charlotte, is decked out in typical teacher-wear: a sweater that has various multicolored bubble-font alphabet letters on it, a couple of kittens (wearing mittens, of course), and a gold pin that says A+! My "business formal" suit seems decidedly out of place. And so do I. Can I really become a teacher? Am I smart enough?

I don't even remember anything from geometry. In fact, I don't think I even *went* to geometry class.

I put my hand out to shake Charlotte's fleshy, fat, pink hand, and she's as bubbly as, well, a kindergarten teacher. It's nauseating, actually, and I wonder how I'm going to make it through the interview without feeling the irrepressible urge to imitate her mannerisms . . . or hit her, which, as we all know, is strictly forbidden in elementary school classrooms. It's gonna be a toughie. Good God, I'm already thinking like a teacher: What normal person uses the word *toughie*?

"Alexa! I'm so glad you're here! It's such a pleasure to meet you! I can't wait to hear all about your experiences!" Charlotte smiles warmly in a way that makes me hungry for sugar cookies and apple juice. "It's so wonderful to have someone who is as passionate as you about teaching at such a young age!"

Hmm. Maybe I shouldn't have put that bit in about how "passionate I am about teaching" in my cover letter.

"Okay! Why don't you first tell me why you're interested in teaching?"

Deep breaths, Alex. Try to be at least a little honest—just a little genuine. You do sort of want to be a teacher, you don't want to just go to Majuro to go to Majuro—you could help people and make a difference in their lives. And if it didn't feel like it was putting your life on hold, well, you might even go there just for the experience itself!

Help Wanted, Desperately

"I think America needs teachers who are dedicated to making a real difference in the future of American education. Teaching is one of the most valuable things a person can do with her life, it sets the building blocks for children's futures. I'm interested in teaching because I want to make that difference." Okay, good. Honest and safe.

But before I can control myself, more words pour out, "I want to know that when I leave work at three o'clock for the day, there's a child at home excitedly telling his parents how much he learned, how much fun his projects are, how excited he is to go to school the next day. I want to be a teacher because I want to inspire children as other teachers have inspired me. I want to make a difference. And only teachers can do that."

Jesus, that was laying it on thick. I mentally slap myself. That was too much. I try to keep my teacherly smile on, but it's hard. I have the sinking feeling that I've messed this one up—only five minutes into it. New record.

Charlotte takes a deep breath and puts her hand to her chest. For a second, I think she's choking on something, and I realize in a quick panic that I was absent the day they taught the Heimlich in seventh-grade health class. Instead of choking though, she takes her glasses off, wipes her misty eyes, and says, "Alexa. I have never heard such an inspiring reason for why a person wants to be a teacher. Honestly. Oh, just give me a moment. I want to get a Kleenex."

Wow. Even the kittens wearing mittens on Charlotte's sweater seem to sit back in silent awe. Strangely, I feel kind of guilty, which is very unlike me. (Though I lied about that on question ninety-four of Sweeney's psychological test.) After all, this is

Charlotte's profession. This is her life. She probably genuinely feels this way about teaching. I am a terrible, terrible person.

And right then, in the middle of the interview when I should be focusing on weaving more intricate webs about my passion for teaching, I suddenly feel somewhat depressed and sad all over again, over the fact that I really have no idea what I want to do with my life. I remember writing in a journal when I was seventeen that I really just wanted to have a job someday where I would enjoy what I did and look forward to going to work each day. Of course, I wrote that the summer I spent as an office clerk at my dad's dental practice alphabetizing hundreds of dental files, so it's hard to say if I meant that I wanted a job I really enjoyed in a serious, existential life-questioning way or a "I'm mad that there are a million *Rodriguez* patients and I have to file them all by their first name" kind of way.

Regardless, sitting right there in the interview, as I watch Charlotte tear up from hearing me so "genuinely" articulate a passion that was not mine but hers, I feel that little lump of despair, that comes when I'm trying very hard not to cry, well up in my throat. Who am I to bullshit about her profession? Who says I can even *make* a good teacher? Will I ever find a job where I'm truly happy? And is general happiness in the Real World contingent upon being in a job where you're happy?

Charlotte, having dabbed her eyes with Kleenex, jolts me back to reality fairly quickly when she asks me about my past experience with children. I harp for a while on the fact that I grew up in a family with two sisters with only a four-year age difference, and how there were always a ton of kids at my house, which in fact doesn't really say anything about *my* experience with children, but more about my mother's unbelievable ability to maintain her sanity. Talking about my family buys me time, and I eventually am able to give a coherent answer. I speak frankly about the research at the children's TV program, and how asking the children about what they remembered from the shows, or what they had learned, really made an impact on me. Then I throw in a bit from my French "after-school program" (more like an after-school pogrom—those kids were like wild miniature Cossacks), and before I know it I'm singing a little song for her that we used to teach the kids with the hand motions and everything.

"Qui est, c'est Alexa, bonjour Alexa, ca va? Non, ca va mal, ou comme ci comme ca?"

Charlotte is delighted and claps her hands loudly, as one would expect anyone used to sitting on the magic carpet in kindergarten to do. "So I take it you would want to teach younger elementary-age children?" Charlotte asks, pen poised to write down "elementary" on my resume.

And that's when it hits me that I actually *would* want to teach—bullshit aside and everything. Not whiny elementary students, but high-school students. People who are actually willing to learn (or at the very least work hard so they can get into college, but I'm fine for now with calling that "learning"). People who like to read—more important, people who know *how* to read by the time they reach me.

"Actually, not really. The teachers who had the most effect on me in my life were eighth grade and up. I'd really love to teach eleventh-grade British literature, or American literature." Wow. I'm not even making this stuff up! I really *would* love to teach eleventh-grade British literature! Have I finally found something realistic I can pursue? STOP THE PRESSES: I HAVE FOUND A LIFE!

Ariel Horn

Charlotte lifts an eyebrow at me. "With all due respect, you do realize it may be harder for us to find you a job then, since you have absolutely no experience with adolescents?"

In Interview-Speak, this means: "I don't respect you in the slightest. There's no way in hell you're going to get a job in high school, so stick with the babies."

I contemplate lying about tutoring high-school students. After all, I'm not moralist Jared, who doesn't believe in "embellishing" to increase your chances. It would be fairly easy to lie about tutoring, and I don't think I would have serious moral reservations about doing it either. Certainly I must have helped someone in high school with homework? Or I could just make up someone, let's call her Maria, who I tutored in high-school French? But I'm scared of falling into that "I'm lying about a passion I'm not sure I have" depression again, so I refrain from lying.

"Yes, I understand. I do think that I would make an excellent elementary school teacher, so I would hope that you might put me in that category as well." Goddamn it. I can just picture little brats whining at me now, "Miss Hoffman, can I go to the bathroom? Miss Hoffman, how do you spell *business*? Miss Hoffman, I'm having trouble with my cursive! Miss Hoffman, can we play silent desk ball?" Dear God. What have I done?

Charlotte nods enthusiastically and effuses, "Oh, I knew you'd be such a great K-five teacher! We need really passionate teachers like you!"

Here she goes again with the passion stuff. Okay, Charlotte. Party's over. I'm ready to go.

"Now, all we need you to do is write a personal statement on why you want to be a teacher, get three recommendations

86

from professors, write a cover letter, submit your resume again, and that's it! Great! Thanks so much for coming in, Alexa! It was a pleasure! You made me so proud to be a teacher!" Charlotte stands up to shake my hand, and then ends up hugging me instead.

That's it? Three recommendations from three separate professors? A personal statement? As I walk out the door, I swear to God I see one of the kittens wearing mittens on Charlotte's sweater sneer at me. This is going to be harder than anticipated.

I walk home from my interview feeling more than a little bit confused. Did that go well or go poorly? Will I ever hear from Charlotte and the Pussycats again? Maybe I *do* want to be a teacher . . . but can I really be in school forever? Won't I turn into one of those crotchety old tenured teachers—like my tenth-grade history teacher who told me I was "the poster girl for why parents should use birth control"? Or worse, what if I become so eccentric that I make my students sing my alma mater's song before we start class, like my high-school gym teacher? ("V . . . for Villanovaaaaa . . . V for victoryyyyyy . . .") If I become a teacher, am I doomed to wear sweaters with kittens and mittens on them? Will I suddenly have the irrepressible urge to call large groups of jaded teenagers "folks"?

What's it really like being a teacher? I remember helping my mother grade her seventh-grade students' tests and how one student had answered that Chinese citizens must take the "civil cervix exam" in order to be employed by the government. Or how several students answered a fill-in-the-blank question with the answer that "tempera paintings on walls" are called "crustoes" or "Cheetos." These kids need help. And someone like me to help them. Someone to teach them the ways of the world—to show them the metaphorical difference between a Cheeto and a fresco. (They can figure out the "civil cervix exam" versus the "civil service exam" on their own time.)

But most important: Can "real" people be teachers? And the converse: Are teachers "real" people? Once, when I was eighteen, I was in the mall, shopping for pantyhose. There, in the pantyhose department of Bloomingdale's, I spotted my British literature teacher. Buying stockings. And worse, underwear. A sexy black thong. Here was my fifty-something-year-old British literature teacher buying lingerie. In public, no less! Which served as proof that she probably functions just like a normal human—she doesn't sleep in the teachers' lounge every night as would be expected, and worse, she probably has sex—the kind of tawdry, wild sex that necessitates a thong! I remember feeling horrified at the realization.

As I unlock the door to our off-campus house, I actually start thinking that maybe this teacher thing isn't so bad. That maybe I really *could* be a teacher, and have a job that's meaningful and important—a job that really affects people's lives. I could leave my bullshit at the door once and for all and train *future* bullshitters!

I decide to send the appropriate materials in to Charlotte. As I sit down, preparing myself to type up a personal statement, one of the cookie fortunes taped on my wall falls ominously onto my desk.

"He who teaches one teaches the world."

Before I have a chance to think about divine intervention manifesting itself through crappy taping jobs and fortune cookies, the door to my room bursts open, nearly giving me a heart attack: Jared.

"Hey, sweets! I'm here!" He throws his backpack on the floor and takes off his coat. "The train was a nightmare today! I sat next to the most annoying woman—she kept talking and talking on her phone about some financial report. It was insane—the person she was talking to must have gone deaf."

Having satisfactorily messed up my room with his shoes kicked off in one corner, his coat on the floor, and his backpack's contents spread all over the place, Jared wraps his arms around me as I sit at my desk. "God, it's just so good to see you!" In between kisses he asks, "How are you? How was the interview? Did you lick the interviewer's face?"

"I don't know. Good, I guess, but who knows? And no, there was no licking." I tape the fallen fortune back up onto my wall as Jared hugs me, and the fortune falls down again. Great: God is playing Tetris with my life. Jared sits on the floor and pulls me down to join him as I ask, "Is it bad that I don't know what to do with my life?"

Jared pauses, rearranging himself on the floor so that I can rest my head on his chest. "Well, most people don't know what the hell they're doing with their lives. *I* don't know what I want to do with my life."

You have a job, though, I think as Jared continues.

"I mean, realistically speaking, I don't think there's one person in the world who is entirely happy in his or her job."

I think for a minute. "There must be *someone* . . . somewhere. Maybe someone in Germany loves his job. Someone named Rolf." I remove a notepad from under my back and throw it toward the bed. "I guess you're right. And it's not like a job is everything, right?" I might as well try to convince myself, since at this point it looks like I'm going to be permanently jobless, permanently volunteering, as I'm permanently waiting for my life to start.

Jared tucks my hair behind my ear. "Right. There's a lot more to life than a job . . . people work to live, not the other way around, you know."

Looking up at my wall of (mis)fortunes, I sigh. "I can't think about this anymore . . . too stressful. Anyway, how was *your* day? Anything exciting happen?" I nuzzle myself deeper into Jared's arms, enjoying the way he smells—like some old cologne I gave him years ago, Old Spice deodorant and sweat. His sandy brown hair falls over his left eye—which looks bluer than usual, almost matching his blue-gray T-shirt.

I brush the hair out of his eye. "Okay, I guess . . ." Jared pauses and I can see him focusing on his watch intently—like he always does when he's about to say something he's not sure he wants to talk about. "I felt sort of depressed today, actually."

"Why's that?" I glance at another fortune on the wall: "Your talents will be suitably rewarded." Does that mean I have no talent if I'm not getting rewarded for anything?

"I don't know—just depressed."

Shifting, I turn to face Jared as my fingers gently play with a birthmark on his neck. "Do you want to talk about it or no?"

Jared takes a long pause, and I can tell that there's something he's been holding in that he wasn't planning to talk about. "I really just don't want you to go to Majuro or wherever, and I was really nervous about this whole teaching interview of yours today and I was just, well, just really hoping it would work out . . . and that you would definitely be staying. In New York." Jared then says more softly, "With me."

For the first time today, a genuine smile spreads across my face.

Help Wanted, Desperately

I roll over and let my nose touch his. "I really want to be with you too, you know that. Look, I'm trying so hard to get a job in New York . . . Remember, Majuro is just the *back-up* plan. I want to be in New York. Hell, I *need* to be in New York." My fingers begin to tap-dance on Jared's chest as I start to sing, "I want to be a part of it, in old New York!" I gesture to the room surrounding me, "Seriously, though, I'm done with this, I want to go to New York and get my life going already."

Jared sighs. "Yeah, I know that's what you want—and I want it too, not for me, well, I mean, yes for me, but for you too." Jared sits up and offers, "But who knows, maybe Majuro *is* the right thing for you. Maybe it wouldn't be a holding pattern like you say it would—maybe you'd really love it. Maybe it'd change your life. Maybe not going would be this huge mistake . . ."

Now thoroughly confused, I sit up and face Jared. "What are you talking about? That's not the way it would be . . ."

"I don't know, Alex, I don't know. I'm just saying . . . I mean, look, I just want to be clear that you're coming to New York for New York's sake—not for me," Jared takes a deep breath. "What if you came to New York and you hated it and wished you were on some island . . . and then you hated me?"

A long, long pause now—kind of like the first time he told me he loved me, and I didn't hear him right, and asked him to repeat it . . . and then the pause . . . and then the repeat. I think about whether I should say what I want to say, about whether it will scare him or not, or whether he feels the same way or not. And then I close my eyes quickly, about to say it when Jared sighs and says, "Well, I just wanted to tell you what I was thinking about, I didn't mean to get into the whole Majuro thing." Jared gets up

91

from the floor and dusts invisible lint off his jeans, as if removing imaginary dirt from his pants will somehow erase this conversation. "I want to go take a shower, and then let's go out and do something, okay? Dinner?"

Jared takes a towel off the hook on my door and heads to the bathroom, and I hear through the wall the sound of the shower running.

Into the air, I then whisper something out loud that I haven't even thought about to myself really, "But what if I want my life to be with you?"

The sound of the rushing water in the bathroom continues, and I look around the room aimlessly as if there's something I'm supposed to be doing right now.

As I go to the desk to rearrange some pens, another fortune falls ominously onto my desk. Note to self: Buy tape that actually works.

There it sits in all its untaped and untapped glory: "A lost opportunity cannot be retrieved."

Terrific.

Lessons Learned

1. Never lie to a woman who is so perennially happy that even the kittens wearing mittens on her sweater seem to have achieved some sort of professional nirvana.

2. Learn the Heimlich maneuver so as to avoid future paranoia, in the event that an interviewer begins to choke during an interview.

3. When you find yourself singing French kiddie songs during an

interview, recognize that you are either drunk or unforgivably stupid.

4. Bullshitting a kindergarten teacher creates bad karma. Period.

5. I need either to a) stop missing opportunities, or b) stop letting fortune cookies run my life.

6
A Poet But
I Didn't Know It

5 Months, 21 Hours

After two weeks spent trying to fasten my fortunes to the wall again and one sleepless night trying to memorize the phrase *Na ij rikaki eo ami kaal* ("I am your teacher") at 3 A.M., I realized that my life should not be determined by whether or not I order moo shu vegetable. Period. (Such are the thoughts that plague the unemployed during bouts of perennial insomnia.) There is something seriously messed up about believing that destiny is dictated through fortune cookies that are mass-produced for fat Americans who are too lazy to look up their horoscopes and have to rely on esoteric one-liners in cookies for spiritual guidance instead.

I cannot be one of those people. I refuse. *Na ij rikaki eo ami kaal!* Teachers lead—they don't follow mandates from corporations on how we should live our lives.

So today, instead of letting my cookie-coated destiny control me, I'm going to control it myself. My fortune cookie last night read, "A knowledge of numbers will lead you far." Flying in the face of any dictated mathematical career, today I decided that I'm ignoring the fortune and will go with my strengths instead. After all, I'm an English major—what do I know about math? And what have I spent the past four years doing? Analyzing poetry, interpreting literature, and acting like I'm smarter than I am by pretending I've read things that I haven't even picked up. ("I think this work is really fascinating, and especially evocative of Goethe's romanticism in *The Sorrows of Young Werther*, don't you?")

I've got to try Plan F (which is somewhere before Plan Majuro). It's the obvious solution that any English major would come to: Throw me my black turtleneck, give me a beret, and call me esoteric and soul-searching. That's right. I'm going to join the ranks of Keats, Wordsworth, Dickinson, and Pound.

I'm going to be a poet. Desperate times, combined with a flyer I saw for an open mic poetry night, means desperate measures.

For now, I'm not going to worry about learning more Marshallese. The way I see it, if I can become a poet, and then sell a book of esoteric poetry that thousands of unsuspecting college students will have to buy for their classes, I'll be rolling in money, independence, and self-congratulatory pride before I can say "iambic pentameter."

There are two tiny little barriers to my becoming a poet though, the most serious of which is that I really and truly hate poetry, both because I find people who can't articulate their thoughts in simple, easy-to-read prose annoying and pretentious, and also because I can't write it myself, which is unambiguously the bigger reason why I hate it so much. And to top it off, my last experience with poetry had not been so great.

In my senior year of high school, I took a literature class that was devoted to "understanding the spoken word," which is really just a euphemism for "wasting forty-three minutes a day discussing whether the banana in the poem is actually a banana or a phallus." (Always a phallus.) Over the course of these agonizing classes, I frequently took bathroom breaks to stave off insanity. I later learned my teacher told the school nurse that she thought I had a bladder infection. Which, even now, sounds more appealing to me than this poetry class.

The class usually went something like this: Three or four students in the class would say things like, "I think, like, it's about, well, like, how people interact with one another?" or "Maybe the poet didn't want us to read into his work? Maybe we're just supposed to take it at face value?"

Then the teacher, Mrs. White (who my friends and I referred to merely as "the piece of chalk with eyes" since her skin was as milky as her name and she didn't talk much) would look at the student who "had the courage to share their thoughts with the class," pause for an endless minute, and say, "I see. Does anyone have anything to say in response to Elyssa's comment?"

And then the whole cycle would continue again while we waited as a class for someone, anyone, PLEASE, to raise their hand and try to say something pithy about the poet's intentions to end the horrible silence that teachers insist on "waiting out." (A hot metal prod might work better.) Then, after someone finally spoke ("Maybe the tree in the poem is supposed to be a symbol of life?"), Mrs. White, chalky as ever, would look at the "brave student" and slowly say, "I see. Does anyone have anything to say in response to Josh's comment?" And then we'd all have to wait until someone else came up with something, anything, to end the silence. I didn't learn much about poetry in that class, but I did get really good at drawing this really cute doodle which involved a piece of chalk with eyes using another piece of chalk (with eyes) to write on a chalkboard. It looked like this:

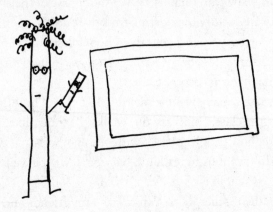

One time, after doing a particularly good doodle, I wondered what my doodle meant. That was when I realized that I had spent way too much time in our poetry class trying to "understand the spoken word."

The second part of Mrs. White's class was devoted to "our own creations."

On the first day, Josh eagerly volunteered to read his poem to the class. Mrs. White was delighted there was a "brave soul" who was willing to share his "creative genius" with us so readily.

Josh wandered up to the front of the room and said, "Um, this poem is about, like, my experiences with the college application process and stuff." Josh cleared his throat. I respectfully put down my pen, leaving my doodle with only one eye.

"There was no letter in my mailbox.
No, not today.

Help Wanted, Desperately

No letter in my mailbox today.
Nor tomorrow.
Nor tomorrow and tomorrow and tomorrow.
I hate the mailman.
I hate being judged by people.
Fuck the mailman.
Fuck being judged by people.
No letter in my mailbox.
Not today."

Josh ran his hand through his hair, looked up from his paper. "Thanks." He sat down. We all clapped politely. I resumed my doodling.

"I think that was a very good poem, don't you, class?" Mrs. White said. "Who'd like to help us unpack its meaning?"

Elyssa volunteered. "I think Josh is really fed up with, like, waiting for letters from colleges, and like, he's mad that people judge him."

Mrs. White looked at Elyssa. "I see. Does anyone else have anything to add to Elyssa's comment?" And so forth. This continued with more crappy poems, by myself and others, which were subsequently "unpacked" by Elyssa and Company.

But I've decided to give it a shot again, partly because I think people who say they're poets are half insane and half self-obsessed, and, I'm beginning to fit both of these criteria pretty well. So this is it. I'm journeying where I have never gone before: I am going to my very first "speakeasy." And I'm dragging Jared—who's visiting for the weekend—with me.

This "speakeasy," an open-mic "poetry, prose, anything goes" session (as advertised on the flyers) is being held at a coffeehouse called the Zodiac several blocks from where I live. I saw a poster for it the other day, and while the "normal" me would never think of going to a poetry reading, that very same "normal" me would never have thought that it would be this difficult to get a job.

As Jared channel surfs, lounging on my bed as I plan to head out to the Zodiac, I wonder out loud, "If I were a poet, what would I wear?"

Jared glances away from the TV and looks at me, "You'd dress as yourself . . . It'd be *so* postmodern."

"Postmodern, eh?" As I put on my black mock turtleneck, and ill-fitting stone-washed tapered jeans, I wonder to myself, *What the hell does* postmodern *mean?* And why does Jared know what it means, when he's studied economics and *I'm* the English major?

Jared, clearly amused by my latest attempt at employment, turns the TV off and watches me as I put on some dark eye makeup and heavy mascara. Feeling his eyes checking me out, I look at Jared.

"What?"

"Oh, nothing." Jared smiles to himself, and I can tell he is trying very hard not to laugh at me.

"Go ahead, laugh, I don't care! Poetry is important! What do *you* know about it? You're so . . . *not* literary." I go back to applying more mascara, and my eye starts twitching.

"Sure, sure. It's all very important. Very serious." Jared tries to look serious.

"You're a jerk, you know that?"

Jared reaches his arms out to me, and I put down my mascara wand and climb onto the bed where he's lounging.

Help Wanted, Desperately

Unable to open my left eye, I look at Jared with my good eye. "I think I'm blind."

Jared shifts on the bed and wraps his arms around me, and then chivalrously tries to pick away at my over-mascara'd eyelashes so that we can unglue my left eye. "So are we really gonna go to this thing?" He drops some black flecks on the bed. "Maybe we could find something a little more interesting to do around here . . ." Jared raises one eyebrow in a sexy, half-joking, half-serious way.

"Nothing turns me on more than ungluing black dirt from my eye."

He rolls his eyes. "So we're going, huh? As long as there's no Margaret Kilmore . . ." Jared starts to put on his shoes.

I contemplate putting in a fake nose ring, just to make myself a little more hip. I stick my head out of my room and scream out to David, my occasional-smoker housemate, "Got any cigarettes?"

Jared looks at me like I'm insane. And in a moment of self-contemplation, I wonder, *Am I?* Then David walks into my room, dressed in—as usual—nothing more than a pair of threadbare boxers. David states matter-of-factly, "Alex, you don't smoke."

Jared smiles and nods to David. "He's got a point."

"Oh Jesus, do you people understand *nothing*? I'm a poet! I am a POET. It's part of my look. Please. I need it." David, by now used to my bizarre requests (like the one that he not walk around the house solely in his unwashed, threadbare boxers), reluctantly throws me a pack.

My costume is complete: I have instantaneously transformed myself into "Brooding Young Poet."

As David leaves, I turn to Jared. "What am I forgetting? Poem. Right." Jared looks at his watch as I rummage through my desk drawer and come across one of the only poems I have ever written. During my freshman year, I was pretty disillusioned that I spent my first full weekend at college watching people in my dorm drink and then vomit for hours on the pink tiles of our hall's bathroom floor. ("Could you hold my hair back?" is a phrase that has molded itself to my memory forever.) So I did what any confused freshman would do: I put my emotions into a bad poem that no one would ever read.

But tonight that poem would meet the world. It was time for my transformation from unknown college student to renowned poetic genius.

Jared and I walk to the Zodiac and get there fashionably late (after all, how could I, brilliant poet, leave my house before finishing mon oeuvre?). I've dressed correctly—many people are wearing black mock turtlenecks and smoking cigarettes. Jared looks like he stepped out of a Gap ad by contrast in his dirty jeans and grey sweater. I look at him, raise an eyebrow, and say, "That's right. *I* fit in. This is my *life*. Poetry is my *life!*"

Jared, clearly uncomfortable with my new identity, asks, "How long is this thing gonna take?"

I casually whip out my cigarette pack to show the other poets, "Look! I'm one of you!" No one seems to care. There are little pieces of scrap paper at the door, and a sign that says, "Write your name and put it in the fishbowl." Strange, but I do it anyway. After all, a poet doesn't question reality. She *writes* about it.

Jared looks at me, "There's no way in hell I'm putting my name in there."

Wiping residual mascara gunk out of my eye, I respond, "Your loss. But at least you'll be able to witness my genius. Some people come for that alone."

Jared takes my hand as we search for seats. "You're one eccentric little diva."

Looking behind me, I whisper urgently, "Don't hold my hand, maybe I'm supposed to be a lesbian!"

Jared drops my hand and we finally take two seats in the back behind a girl named Melanie and her friend Patrick, both of whom I know from a class I took last semester called Literature of Social Change (except when I signed up for it, it was called Contemporary American Literature and by the time we got to the "social change" part, it was too late for me to change my schedule). Melanie pushes her dark brown dreadlocks behind her ears and tells Patrick, "I just really think it's unfair of people not to recycle. This is our world! This is the legacy we leave our children! How can they be so selfish?"

Patrick scratches his goatee and replies, "Mel, how can you even consider recycling a priority issue at a time when children all over the world are starving? We need to concentrate on getting these people food, homes, and ample health care. Otherwise we're living merely in a state of organized anarchy, don't you think?"

Melanie and Patrick are the type of people I have generally tried to avoid my entire life. Melanies and Patricks can be found all over—they're those annoying self-righteous social activists who think they can save the world by camping out in public places and coffee houses with signs that say CRUSADE FOR UGANDAN PET CARE, RECYCLE AND SMILE, and HOMELESS ARE PEOPLE LIKE YOU—BUT WITHOUT HOMES. Any time a social issue comes up, it's people like Melanie and Patrick who are the first to jump on it, verbally castrating anyone who disagrees with them. I am unspeakably terrified that if I do go to Majuro, even if I really love it, all the other volunteers will be just like Melanie and Patrick.

After Melanie and Patrick are done arguing about the problems with health care, they turn around and acknowledge me. Melanie adjusts her beaded necklace and checks Jared out. I protectively grab his hand, though he resists ("Stop, you're a lesbian!") and I see a glint of light on Melanie's tongue as she opens her mouth to speak. "I didn't know you were a poet."

"I didn't know you had a tongue pierce."

The lights dim, and a guy with long, stringy brown hair tied back in a ponytail named Gary jogs to the front of the room.

Jared looks at me, "You owe me. I must really love you."

I quickly respond, "I'd like you to show a little respect for my potential future profession. You don't see me making fun of auction houses."

"It's hardly the same thing."

I turn to Jared and snottily reply, "You're right. As a poet, I *create* art, and at an auction house you just sell it to the prestigious and wealthy, robbing from the disillusioned middle class, the people who need it most."

Jared, stunned, stares at me. "Who *are* you? *What* are you?"

I take Jared's hand and squeeze it, as if to say everything I want to but can't. Instead, I just think to myself, *I love you for coming with me to this. If I become a successful published poet, I won't have to leave. I'll have a job, I won't be jealous of you, I'll be making it on my own. I love you for loving me even though I don't have a clue who I am or why I'm worth loving at all.* I squeeze his hand harder, hoping that somehow mental telepathy will transfer my thoughts from my mind to my hand to his. Jared looks down at our hands, confused as to why I'm squeezing so hard. "What?" he whispers.

"Nothing. I'm sorry for what I said before. That was mean."

"Whatever."

At the front of the room, Gary rubs his hands together and starts, "Hi, I'd like to welcome you all to the Speakeasy!" (The crowd snaps their fingers. I don't get why, but I snap too. I look at Jared who smiles at me and enthusiastically joins in.) "Could someone hit the lights? We're gonna get some mood goin' on in here." Someone turns the lights out, and Gary walks around the room and lights a couple of candles. Immediately, I sense that this is going to get way too touchy-feely for me. *Just for one night, Alex, try to see if you can do this. One night. And then we'll see if we can make it a lucrative lifetime commitment.* I shift around in my chair, suddenly uncomfortable, feeling very, very alone in this room filled with more people and black turtlenecks than I would have imagined. I turn to Jared, who ignores me, looking thoroughly fascinated with Gary. Or thoroughly unwilling to deal with me.

Once the candles are lit, Gary goes on, "Before we start, I'd just like to remind everyone that this is a place that's open, a place for us to share our emotions through whatever form we want to— our readings, our writings, whatever. This is our special, safe place. No one judges you here, so feel free to be who you are, no mind games." Josh from my twelfth-grade poetry class would feel at home here. I remember that he didn't like people judging him.

"Okay. With all that out of the way, let's start! I'm going to pull a name from ye Fishbowl of Fate to start us off with a reading. Ummm"—Gary moves his hand around in the bowl and pulls a piece of scrap paper out—"Is Ray here?"

Ray stands up and heads to the front of the room with a pair of bongo drums he seems to have pulled out of thin air. He sits down on the stool at the front of the room, makes himself comfortable, and says, "This is called 'Taryn.' It's about my best friend." Ray closes his eyes, runs his hands over his shaved head, and licks his lips. Then he begins to pound the drum, with no particular rhythm. He plays the bongos slowly and sensitively, and then more angrily, loudly, and then he hits the drums only once every four seconds for about a minute.

I look around the room. Is this guy for real? Even Jared looks interested, and he starts tapping his foot to the nonexistent beat.

Ray's furrowed brow is now emitting large amounts of sweat. He furiously pounds the bongos, his arms shaking and his eyes bulging out of his head. At the end, Ray shouts: "TARYN!" Then he puts his head down. The room erupts in snaps.

Did I miss something here?

Gary pats Ray on the back, "Amazing, Ray, absolutely amazing." Melanie and Patrick look at each other, stunned. "That was un-fucking-believable."

It sure *was*.

Gary puts his hand in the fishbowl again: "Yelena?"

Yelena pushes her way to the front of the room. She's tall, with short choppy black hair, broad shoulders and fishnet stockings. She's wearing a chauffeur's cap and smoking a cigar.

Jared pokes me and says, "Man, she's sexy! Perhaps we'll find a date for my lesbian girlfriend here tonight, huh?"

Yelena begins to speak in a loud, assertive voice, "Hey, everyone. This poem is a post-lude to my poem from last week, 'Hurt

Me.' I've been working really hard on this, so I hope you, well, I hope you get it. It's called 'I Am Yelena.' "

Yelena drops her cigar on the floor and stomps it out.

Jared looks impressed, "That was *hot.*"

Right.

Then Yelena says:

"You stomp on me, you fucking bastard, hurt me,
    hit me, help me.
You are the ravager of my heart, destroyer of my mind,
    bargainer with Fate,
You've fucked me, ravaged me, destroyed me, attempted to
    bargain with me.
But I am not fate. And I am not your fate.
    I defy this destiny.
Because if this is what God has given me, then I DO
NOT
WANT IT!
because
I am Yelena,
Strong, young, above all, more
Than you can handle
in this ocean of forever which has tied me to you.
But I will not be beaten, no,
I am not Poseidon's bitch, to be touched, bitten,
    stabbed with that sharp
Trident you call your love.
I
am Yelena.
Strong, young, above all, more.

You can ravage me no longer: I am beyond your touch
Because
I
am
Yelena."

Apparently, Yelena has said something incredibly meaningful that I have missed entirely. This time, the audience pounds their feet on the ground, snaps their fingers so loudly I think their thumbs will bleed. One person barks: Where the hell am I?

This time I really need to hold Jared's hand. "You still love me, right?"

Jared, looking totally stunned, responds, "We'll see."

Gary winks at Yelena, who responds by sticking up her middle finger. "Fuck you," she whispers to Gary as she sits down. Perhaps Gary is the ravager of her heart? The destroyer of her mind? The bargainer with fate?

I look at the door and realize there is no possible way for me to leave, short of the window, which I'm seriously considering at this point. Let Jared worry about himself. For whatever bizarre reason, the room has filled up, and the path to the door is blocked. But that's not even my biggest problem. My name remains in Ye Fishbowl of Fate. And there's no way for me to take it out now. I am screwed. I am not strong and young like Yelena. I am weak and very, very scared.

Reading my thoughts, Jared, clearly amused, whispers in my ear, "You are so *very* screwed."

Gary dips his hand into the fishbowl. *PLEASE GOD do not let that name be mine.* I could have gone after Bongo Ray, but don't make me go after strong, young Yelena.

Help Wanted, Desperately

"Alexa?"

Fuck.

I look at Jared, who smiles and happily whispers, "This is going to be hysterical! I'm *so* glad I came."

Gary looks around the room. I try to sink down in my seat and at the same time search the room with a "Who is this Alexa?" look on my face. *Please God, I will eat my weight in the margarine substitute Benecol if no one notices it's me Gary's calling up. I will never classify another person as a rodent, duck or elf in my mind. I'll never make fun of a dust-ruffle buyer, I'll never lie in an interview, I'll never dwell in my own anxiety that I'll never find a profession that will make me happy. I won't stress about getting a job in New York. Hell, I'll actually willingly put my life on hold in Majuro. I'll stop complaining, I'll show Jared how much I love him, I'll never ask for anything else, ever again, just please do not let them find me.* My butt is slowly sliding off my seat as I try to sink lower and lower. If I'm very quiet, they'll think I left . . . Jared watches me with a look of sheer amusement, and with my eyes I beg him with all my heart not to tell them it's me.

But then Melanie turns around and points at me. "She's right here. She's just shy." Melanie smiles her little "save the world" smile and I know that she's doing this to get back at me for the tongue-pierce thing earlier.

"Yeah, I'm here. Sorry, I just couldn't find my poem." As I walk up to the front of the room I stumble over a candle, which momentarily sets everyone into a panic as it softly ignites a tiny corner of the rug. Bongo Ray furiously stamps it out with his feet as Jared runs out of the room searching for an extinguisher. Smooth, Alex. Very smooth. For the first time, I catch eyes with

Jared as he returns to the room, and he actually looks sort of sorry for me.

I take my time getting to the front of the room. "Well, um, I'm new, and I hope that you don't think this is, you know, not good enough or anything.

"My poem is about my freshman year, when, um, I wasn't feeling too at home at school." Could I sound any dumber? Why don't I just read them my second-grade essay, "What I Did This Summer"?

"Okay, here it goes."

"In this black-panted world
Where short skirts and tighter shirts tell us to drink more
*   and think less*
I go back in my mind to the days in time
When my sweet little naps and my sitting on laps
*   weren't a turn-on*
But a way to turn off
That bad girl inside of me who ate her crayons instead of
*   her carrots for dinner."*

I pause for dramatic effect, and to see if I have mortally embarrassed myself yet. Strangely, everyone seems interested. I knew I smelled pot when I came in here.

"The good news is that now I eat my carrots.
The bad news is that everyone wants me to be the bad girl
But she's still sitting in the thinking chair somewhere
*   in the second grade*
Where maybe I should've stayed.
The thinking chair awaits, Mother Teresa."

Help Wanted, Desperately

I look up again. The bong has clearly gone around another time. Jared winks at me encouragingly.

"I wish for the days in the seventh grade
When instead of seeing vomit I could read The Hobbit
   on a Saturday night
Without the sight
Of a black-panted girl in this black-panted culture
Where khaki-panted boys attack like khaki-panted vultures.
But I'm not here to save the world."

I look pointedly at Melanie and Patrick, who don't get my directed stare.

"I just don't want to see it end
Because in this black-panted world where short skirts and
   tighter shirts
Tell us to drink more and think less, I am ready
To think more instead."

I dare to glance at the crowd. Melanie doesn't look too repulsed. She snaps. Jared smiles at me and winks, and then joins in with Melanie's snapping. Others begin to snap. And with that, I am silently inducted into the poetry community of the Zodiac.

The night continues. Melanie reads a story about what it was like to protest against "the Man," and Patrick does some sort of weird word association that involves saying one word at a time very . . . slowly—"Home . . . You . . . Gone . . . Alone . . . Me . . . Dark . . ."—and Jared starts to nod off. Gary plays a song on his guitar called "Motion," and Yelena leers at him as he sings. While she's busy leering, I notice that Jared is snoring very quietly and contentedly.

The kick of poetic genius has lost its spark for me, and for an utterly boring moment when a girl named Kasey outlines her eating disorder through interpretive yoga to an Enya song, I briefly consider taking up smoking to stop the boredom, if only for a moment. I suddenly understand why poets always carry cigarettes.

As soon as everyone finishes their final snaps, I stand up, grab Jared's hand and rush toward the door. "Jared, let's get the hell out of here."

So eager to leave the whole poetry scene, I pull Jared's hand harder as he questions, "You weren't that bad—what's going on?" As we hit the exit, Melanie shouts, "Where's the fire?"

"I have to write something down!" I shout back. Surely a poet could understand that need.

The second we get home, I run up to my room, and open my notebook where I keep a list of all possible job opportunities, and write in very neat handwriting, "I am not a poet."

Lessons Learned

1. Ignore people who crusade for Ugandan pet care.

2. It's time to accept the fact that I will never in my life be able to interpret interpretive dances.

3. When a man plays bongos so furiously that you think his eyes will bleed, accept your initial suspicion that he's probably dealing with some sort of deep-rooted emotional or sexual healing—the likes of which you cannot even begin to imagine, let alone understand. That, or he wishes he were Tito Puente.

Help Wanted, Desperately

4. Militant feminists don't like "bargainers with fate." They do, however, like cigars.

5. When you ignite a carpet before you are about to recite your own poetry, accept the blaze as a sign from God that hearing your poetry read aloud is something just short of a natural disaster.

7
The Real Me

4 Months, 27 Days

Okay, I may not be a poet, but I will admit this: I *am* a snoop. There are few absolute certainties in this topsy-turvy world, but among those unalterable, inalienable truths is this: If your personal belongings are lying out unattended, I will, without any moral reservation whatsoever, rifle through them.

Yes, I'm that girl you hid your stuff from at camp.

Shortly after igniting the Zodiac's carpet, I decided I needed a break from the stress of the job search and my gloom-and-doom prediction that I'll be shipped off to the Pacific, leaving my "potential" to be picked up at the baggage claim upon my return a year later.

Since I've been home in New Jersey for a break (exactly four months and twenty-seven days until I'm off to Majuro, to be exact), I've taken to rummaging through other people's things—which isn't really a new hobby, just one that I've been enjoying more lately. I've been an "explorer" for quite some time now, with one of my most famous expeditions occurring when I was twelve. As I carelessly flipped through my mom's day planner as I waited for her to come home from the supermarket, I fell upon December 24, which was marked with big, red, relatively unclear cursive letters that said, "Depart for Zooch." Zooch, I thought to myself? Where the hell is Zooch? And why the hell didn't anyone tell me we were going there? Spy that I am, I quickly ran up the stairs to my sister Julie's room to tell her the news.

Gasping for breath, afraid that someone had followed me, I told her wide-eyed and excitedly, "We're going to Zooch for vacation!"

"Where's Zooch?"

For the rest of the week, we tirelessly scoured through maps, atlases, and all the geographic reference books we could find. Even Nina helped. But by the end of the week, we were still stumped. Where the *hell* was Zooch? Thankfully, there was an end to the madness. One night at dinner, my parents announced to us that we would be going to Zurich. As in Switzerland.

"No Zooch?" I asked my dad, somewhat upset. By this time, I had my heart set on December in Zooch. I imagined it was a lovely place to spend New Year's Eve.

"Where the hell is Zooch?"

Right now, that's sort of the way I feel about Majuro.

For the most part, I've spent the past three days spacing out, thinking about all the jobs I don't have and will never get. As Nina whines away, explaining why she simply can't have "déclassé" little baby hot dogs at her cocktail hour, I continue to think about my life and ultimately end up at this profoundly disturbing question: Is it morally repugnant and embarrassing that, essentially, I'm planning to go to Majuro just so I won't have to admit to myself, my family, Jared, and my friends that

Help Wanted, Desperately

I have absolutely no potential, when they seem to be drowning in it?

In efforts to tear myself away from depressing visions of me in Majuro, I decide to distract myself by embracing my old hobby: revisiting the world of Zooch, so to speak. It's time for some good old-fashioned "exploration." As my parents frantically argue with Nina in the kitchen that the wedding in fact *does not* need caviar busts of Nina's and Brad's heads to be "the beautiful wedding of their dreams," I decide to set out on a new expedition, a covert operation which I have cleverly titled, "Open All the Cabinets in the Living Room and See if There's Anything Good Inside."

As I open the first cabinet, my mom calls me to dinner. "We have Chinese tonight! Alex, you love Chinese!" I ignore her, and she hits the breaking point. "ALEX, get in here, NOW!" As she continues to shout for me to come to the kitchen, I open another cabinet and discover an archaeological trophy buried beneath the rubble of old and yellowed Tom Clancy novels, my dad's dental textbooks, my mom's college yearbook, and a really ugly clay ashtray I made for my parents at camp when I was eight years old. (Who could forget the ashtray's joyous reception by my parents? "We don't smoke, Alex." "Does that mean you don't like it?")

The third cabinet reveals piles upon piles of manila envelopes with dates on them ranging from 1973 to 1998. There are roughly three manila envelopes per year. Perhaps my parents had a covert operation of their own, and this was their big plan, sketched out day by day. And I, Super Sleuth, Queen of Zooch, have found it in no more than ten minutes. Great hiding place, Mom and Dad. Next time, why don't you just label your plan in big, black magic marker, PLAN TO TAKE OVER THE WORLD, and leave it on the kitchen table.

"Alex, come to dinner right now! Nina's eating your lo mein . . ."

"I'm not eating it! I was *tasting* it!"

I continue rummaging as Nina and my mother loudly and enthusiastically debate the nutritional value of lo mein ("Are the vegetables steamed or fried? And is it stir-fried in cooking spray or butter?"). Ignoring their deafening conversation, I look over each of my shoulders and take out a handful of envelopes. Let's start at 1979. I open the envelope, only to find four pages of capital and lower-case letter Bs. "Bb. Bb. Bb. Bb. Bb."

Then I open up another envelope. This one's from 1980: All it contains is a piece of colored construction paper with a big painted yellow blob on it. Beneath the blob, it says, "There are ducks in the park" in very neat, bubbly handwriting. On the bottom right corner there are words in my mother's neat handwriting, "Nina, age 4. Nursery." I look back at the "B" envelope: "Julie, age 6, first grade."

So this is the cabinet where my parents collected our childhood schoolwork! Where are *my* envelopes? I rummage through the manila mess to find my schoolwork, and I keep my eyes peeled for envelope labels like "Our Favorite Child," or "Precious Little Perfection." No such luck. I do, however, find one that says "Alex, age 4, nursery school." It must have been mislabeled.

Artifact number one: a shoddily painted noodle necklace. I smile to myself. I've had zero artistic talent for such a long time now.

Artifact number two, a picture on pink construction paper drawn in crayon: five stick figures, four of whom are wearing stylish triangle dresses. In bubbly teacher handwriting above the stick figures, it says, "My Family."

Help Wanted, Desperately

"If you don't get in here right now I'm throwing your dinner away! I mean it, Alex. *Come. Here. Now!*"

And then, the crown jewel. Artifact number three: a stapled packet that proclaims, in bright blue bubble letters, "When I Grow Up!"

For the past three years, and more specifically, the past three months, I have tortured myself over what I want to do with my life. I've spent nights lying in bed at three in the morning wondering if I'll ever make anything of myself, or if I'll just be another person on the street . . . or worse, another person on the streets of Majuro. And yet here, in the very same quivering hands that once made tiny blue handprints on yellow construction paper lies the Holy Grail, the Fountain of Youth, the pièce de triomphe of all my covert rummaging operations. All I had to do was open it up and see what I had wanted to do when I was in nursery school, and then go with my pure, unadulterated four-year-old wisdom. It was almost too easy.

"FINE, Alex, we're throwing out your dinner! This is unacceptable family behavior!"

"Mom, if she does this at my wedding, I'll kill her."

My hand trembles as I begin to flip the page; four-year-old Alex was about to tell twenty-one-year-old Alex what to do with her life. Minus the clay-pot throwing and the shirtless Patrick Swayze, why, this was just like that scene in *Ghost* where Swayze comes back to tell Demi Moore to move on with her life! I turn the page and find that this packet is not some soul-searching manuscript on my four-year-old professional yearnings, but rather a compilation of what *all* the kids in my nursery school class wanted to do with their careers.

Damn.

The first page, interestingly enough, is my lifelong friend Miranda's page. In teacher handwriting it says in bright blue letters, "When I grow up I want to be . . ." (and this is where the teacher recorded Miranda's worldly four-year-old wisdom) "a ballerina. When ballerinas grow up they can be Mommies and Daddies. I will go to work and a babysitter will have to stay with my children. Sometimes I will yell because they do things bad sometimes."

Already, as a preschooler, Miranda had a clear understanding of "good" and "bad." Logic. As a four-year-old, she was practically the nursery-school authority on John Locke's theories of rightful punishment. It's only fitting that now she wants to go to law school.

If Miranda's blurb was right, who knows what my blurb has in store for me!

Other classic responses include Leslie's, "I really want to be a teenager" (Leslie has probably followed through on that dream. Way to set reachable goals, Leslie!); Beth's desire to "buy Adidas clothes"; and Lauren, who "wants to be a Mommy. I will drive a car. I will wash dishes and clean the house. I will shop for food and cook sometimes. I will buy bananas." Ten bucks says Lauren is a women's studies major now at Smith whose favorite book is *The Feminine Mystique*. She no longer wants to be a mommy ("motherhood is a prison"), and eats nothing but freshly bought bananas.

And then there's Matthen. Poor, poor Matthen, who is probably "Matthew," though his self-printed name attests otherwise. Matthen says, "When I grow up I really want to be somewhere in the Army . . . on a different planet or Siberia."

Help Wanted, Desperately

I think Matthen didn't get a lot of hugs as a kid.

And now, it's the moment of truth. I can see through the paper that the next page is mine (the sophisticated, artistic style of the triangle dresses give it away). Though I know I shouldn't, I actually feel nervous, as if maybe, just maybe, this piece of paper might shed light on my "potential." I can't help but hope against all hope that with the turn of this page, I will miraculously know who I am, what my destiny is, and what my purpose is on this planet (or Siberia). Or at the very least I'll find what my ever-elusive "potential" is. And how it can get me out of Majuro, into New York, into a life I can be proud of.

"When I grow up I want to be a mother, because I like taking care of people. I like to dance and spin. So I'll be a ballerina. I like writing too."

That's it? Here, I come searching for the meaning of life according to my four-year-old self, and all I'm supposed to be is a ballerina? Jesus, Yoda could've done better determining my destiny. Hey, Four-Year-Old Alex—have you seen these hips? Made for birthin', not dancin'.

Defeated yet again in the Unending Quest for My Nonexistent Future, I flip through the rest of the pages and as I read about the ambitious dreams of entrepreneurial and fantastical four-year-olds, my thoughts keep wandering back to Jared and the fact that he probably had his life figured out *in utero* while I was busy doing the mundane: growing fingers, developing an intestinal tract, etc. I love that he knows what he wants, but knowing that Jared is a person who will always achieve his goals while I'm a person who seemingly has no goals to achieve other than moving to New York kills me. I try to remember a time when Jared didn't know he was interested in art, and can't. Ever since we met, Jared has always had this fire in him that would just ig-nite whenever someone started talking about an artist—it didn't even matter who the artist was, or if Jared had ever heard of him (though he usually had). The only time I "ignited" was when I accidentally lit the Zodiac's rug, and that hardly counts.

As I read about Kimmy's desire to "make pretty dresses that me and Mommy would wear," I start to wonder why it is that I'm the only one who seems to have missed out.

What happened to *my* dream? Contrary to Four-Year-Old Alex's prophecy, I can't dance and spin around for the rest of my life. I want to go to New York, yes, but what the hell would I do there? What kind of job is appropriate for the girl who has no idea what she wants or who she should be?

Unsurprisingly, my attempt to interpret my four-year-old will isn't the best way to go about unlocking my hidden potential. There has to be a better, more logical way to go about finding what my career should be. And, indeed, what would be a more rational way to determine my future than taking an online career test? Operation Find Alex a Future, Part Two commences.

Having missed dinner already, I decide to go downstairs to the computer to find some online tests. As God is my witness, I've de-cided I'm not leaving until I discover what career I'm cut out for.

I search the Web for "career testing" and come up with several sites, and decide to go to the one that looks the most professional, because, after all, I am trying to be a professional myself. I begin taking the test called Career Finder.

Forty-two jobs are listed below. Click the button next to each one of the jobs that interests you—jobs that attract you in some way. Do not click on jobs you are undecided about, or jobs that you think you would dislike.

The task is easy enough, even for an unskilled, unemployable wretch like myself who serves no purpose on this planet other than to suck up the valuable oxygen being used by skilled members of society who can pull their own weight by working. (" 'Bitter,' party of one?")

I look at the job offerings. Bus driver—no. Librarian— maybe. Insurance clerk—God, no. Truck mechanic—no. Fish and Game warden. Fish and Game warden? What the hell does a fish and game warden *do*? Stand with a whip outside a pond and smack the fish that try to escape? Or does he or she coordinate games for fish to play? No. Radio TV announcer—perhaps. On to Section Two.

I like to work with animals, tools, or machines.

Umm, about as much as I like picking the grime from underneath my toenails and then eating it. (I only bite, chew and sometimes swallow my *finger*nails, which is a *totally* different story, thank you.) No. False.

I like to study and solve math or science problems.

VERY false. In fact, when I switched schools in the fourth grade, I was put in a remedial math course in which I was the only native English speaker. And the worst part is that all the kids who couldn't speak English *still* did better than me. I think two of them are at MIT now (the other one had to settle for Harvard).

I like to do things that help people—like teaching, first aid, or giving information.

I guess so, compared to these other options. True.

I value success.

True. I just wish I could achieve it.

Time to hit the DONE button and see where it takes me. C'mon, Career Finder—find me my career! Baby needs a new pair of shoes! (And more importantly, a job that will give her a salary to buy those shoes.)

But just as I'm about to seal my professional fate, I remember the Fortune-Teller Incident, and that makes me wonder just how much value I should put on the results of this test. My family was at a Kiwanis carnival, and for whatever reason, my sisters and I wanted to have our fortunes told by one particular bald, toothless fortune-teller, whose sign claimed he was "always right." The fortune-teller furrowed his (excessively hairy: think five inch) brow and looked closely at Julie's hand: "Very smart, very smart. Great fortune in future." Nina's hand: "Good brain. Good heart." And finally, mine: "Will marry bald, fat foreigner." Thanks for giving me the rest of my life to look forward to.

I nervously click on the DONE button.

"Congratulations, Alexa Hoffman! There are several jobs you are especially well-suited for: mail carrier, correctional officer, drywall installer, and hazardous-materials-removal worker."

They all seem so glamorous, it's hard to choose. A bald, fat foreigner to pleasure me at night, spackle and chemical waste to keep me happy during the day.

Just as I am about to resign myself to a year-long purgatory in Majuro drywalling huts, my mother pokes her head into the room, "Are you coming up?"

"Coming up for what?"

My mother pushes her hair behind her ears and just says, "Alexa, you didn't join us for dinner, and that was bad enough. I'm going to pretend I don't care about that. But now, it's important. Come upstairs." My mother turns around abruptly and heads up the stairs herself.

I drag myself upstairs to the living room, where Mom, Julie, Nina, and my father are casually lounging on the couch. Julie is passed out from having clocked forty billable hours already on her three-day vacation. Nina happily and obliviously compares two swatches of fabric as my father calmly tries to explain to her that the silk costs almost ten times more than if the dress were created in the other fabric.

As Dad and Nina's argument grows louder, my mother waves a pink folder in the air and says, "This is our Death Folder."

"Your what?"

"Well, things are going really well right now. Julie has a great job at the law firm"—my mother strokes Julie's hair, and Julie allows herself to collapse into my mother's lap—"and Nina's getting married, and Alexa . . ." My mother looks at me, puzzled. "Well, Alex is going to . . ." my mother's eyes desperately search out my dad for help, and my dad jumps in. "Alex is going to figure out what she wants to do with herself."

A lightbulb seems to go on above my mom's head and she offers, "And Alex is going to move back home with us!"

Dear God. As if the news that I'm a drywalling ballerina isn't enough.

My mother continues as Julie begins to snore. "The point is, things are going well, so we need to plan for the worst."

"But we already have the potassium iodide pills you gave us for nuclear disaster, Mom," I offer. Normal parents send their children care packages of cookies. I got pills to protect my thyroid from nuclear radio waves.

Nina chimes in, "And we've got the EvacU8 hoods for leaving a smoky room, too." Ah, yes. Who could forget our Chanukah presents.

My mother shakes her head. "No, no, no. This folder is for when *we're* dead." My mother continues on, as if she's telling us how to cure a rash, or how to make sure we don't bleach our clothes in the laundry. "See, when Daddy and I die, this folder has all the information on where we want to be buried, where we bought our plots—"

"Well, we didn't actually buy them," my dad happily interjects. "Grandma and Grandpa bought them for us as a one-year-anniversary gift."

Nina looks up. "I'd rather have a silver tray or something, just FYI."

My mother, annoyed at the interruptions, glares at us as she continues, "So when we die, you look in this pink folder and it'll tell you all the important stuff. You'll know it's the right folder because I made a label at the top— 'If Mom and Dad Are Dead.'" I look at the folder, and sure enough, in purple magic marker bubble letters (with glitter) it says, IF MOM AND DAD ARE DEAD. All it's missing are scratch 'n' sniff stickers.

"Inside, there's all the information you need—and just so you know, one of you should move back in here. It'll be better for the taxes . . ."

Nina rolls her eyes, "Mom, I hardly think this is necessary. No one's dying."

"Believe me, girls, when I'm dead, you'll be happy."

Majuro or not, I *cannot* move back home.

My mother gets up and heads into the kitchen, shouting behind her, "So who wants a fortune cookie?"

Dad, unfazed by the whole death talk, happily shouts, "I do!"

I wonder if I'm trapped in some weird parallel universe where "death folders" and potassium iodide pills are normal.

My mother comes back into the living room with a plate of cookies and bowl of cherries. As she tosses a cookie into my hand, she says, "Oh, Alex, this letter came for you last month, I don't know why they don't have your Philadelphia address. Did you give this"—my mother scans the envelope for the return address—"this Majuro Volunteers person our address?" My mother drops the letter in my lap and then suddenly seems to remember something important. "Oh, and Alex, this is important. Maybe most important. When I'm dead, or God forbid, if Daddy and I die before the wedding, I want you to help Nina plan the whole thing. Julie's too busy with work."

Kill me first.

Nina cracks open a cookie. "Can't I just hire a professional wedding planner?" Nina reads her fortune, " 'Good things are being said about you!' Of course they are."

My dad opens his cookie. "Absolutely not. A wedding planner, that's ridiculous. Over my dead body!"

Nina and my dad laugh, and Nina offers, "That's exactly how I'll do it!"

Where the hell *am* I?

Dad continues, "Alex will help you plan the whole thing, you know how much she loves this stuff." My dad winks at me and reads his fortune. " 'Your spirit of adventure leads you down an exciting new path.' Whatever. The spirit of Nina's wedding is leading me into debt."

My mother happily crunches her cookie, and through a mouthful she reads, " 'If you lead, others will follow.' Well, that's *definitely* true for me. Alex, open yours."

Before I crack open my cookie, I open the letter my mother has placed in my lap from Majuro and read aloud:

Dear Alexa,

Benjamin Franklin once said, "Dost thou love life? Then do not squander time, for that's the stuff life's made of." As a lifelong educator, Benjamin Franklin knew the value of time, especially insofar as it affects the way we, as teachers, plan for our students and ourselves. We hope that in these five remaining months before your upcoming journey to Majuro, you'll thoughtfully reflect on the following questions regarding your teaching practice:

What is your philosophy of teaching?

Where is the crossroads between pedagogy and practice?

Before I can continue reading, Nina offers, "I'm pretty sure the crossroads are Boring Street and Waste-of-Time Boulevard."

My mother throws a cherry at Nina. "Nina! Teaching isn't a waste of time! It's one of the most valuable careers someone can have! Now, teaching in Majuro," my mother turns to me pointedly, "now, *that* is a waste of time. How can Jared propose to you if you're all the way in Majuro, huh? How can Jared *date* you if you're all the way in Majuro? Look, if Alex can't get a real job, she should just go to graduate school. From my lips to God's ears, you should just apply to law school already."

Ignoring Nina and my mother, I continue reading:

Other more practical, precautionary questions you should consider before your move to the Marshall Islands include:

If for any reason you perish while abroad, do you have your financial and personal matters settled?

Have you thought about consulting a lawyer and writing your will? In the case of your death, who will be responsible for collecting your remains?

Would you like your remains shipped to the United States, or to remain on Majuro as a tribute to your experience?

While you may not be thinking about issues such at these, as a volunteer on Majuro you will be your own responsibility, and we urge you to carefully consider important matters such as these before your arrival.

And remember, as Edward Hopper once said, "There are two kinds of people in the world: those who are alive, and those who are afraid!" We are glad you have chosen to enrich your life and the lives of others by joining us on Majuro."

I slowly put the letter down and look up at my family, wide-eyed with horror. Nina starts to laugh. "You're gonna die while you're volunteering!"

Ignoring Nina, my father thinks aloud, "I always *assumed* that as her parents we would be responsible, but maybe since she's over eighteen, she really is her *own* responsibility at this point . . .

Hey Julie, in-house counsel, could you help Alex write her will? Alex, what kind of assets do you have?"

Sweating profusely I sputter, "Oh, God, Dad, how could I have any assets if I don't have a job? I don't have any money! I don't want to die!" For the first time since I've thought about Majuro, I can feel my heart racing as I morbidly picture various ways I could die there: slipping on drywall material in my hut, drowning while snorkeling, murdered by one of my students unhappy with her grade . . .

Always sympathetic, my mother offers, "Then you shouldn't go to Majuro, end of story. You'll live at home with us, Jared will propose to you, and you can drive the Buick. What about that setup isn't great? And if that doesn't suit you, well, just go to law school."

For the first time, Julie sleepily interjects, "It's just another form of death."

My mother stretches her legs out and puts one foot up on the coffee table. "Anyway, I can't talk about Majuro anymore. Alex, did you get a cookie?" Overwhelmed by the fact that my Majuro holding-pattern plan has just turned into Majuro the Morgue, I absentmindedly take my cookie off the coffee table and crack it open, taking out the fortune just as Nina and my dad steal my cookie out of my hands and split it between them.

My mother asks me, "Well, what's it say?"

"Nothing." Disbelieving, I flip the slip of paper over to check. "It's blank."

Nina starts laughing hysterically. "Ha, that sucks! That letter said you're going to die and now you have no fortune!" She's convulsing in laughter, and I see that my dad can't help but grin too.

My mother, refusing to believe the Fortune Cookie Gods'

cruel judgment on my life, leans across Julie—"Let me see that!"—and snatches the slim strip of paper out of my hand, searching for the fortune I can't find.

"No, she's right! It's blank." Mom turns it over and over, looking for a fortune—a future—that's not there.

My dad sympathetically offers some pure Dad-humor as he spits out a cherry pit: "Hey, life's just a bowl of cherries, right? Who cares about fortune cookies? Hell, make your own fortune!"

"That's *so* Alex's life, isn't it? Ha!" Nina shakes her head. "God, that sucks."

Sure does.

Lessons Learned

1. Avoid conversations about the Death Folder at all costs.

2. Anticipating my nursery-school classmates' professional failures based on their four-year-old aspirations brings me a sick, unhealthy feeling of unbridled satisfaction. Hours of therapy might be in order here.

3. It's time for me to learn how to spackle and drywall.

4. My mom is prepared for death. I can't even prepare for life.

8

Help Wanted, Desperately

4 Months, 13 Days, 12 Hours, 13 Minutes, and 11 Seconds

Two days ago, ten days after I learned that the combination of fortune-cookie "wisdom" and death preparations are enough to drive me clinically insane, four months, thirteen days, twelve hours, thirteen minutes, and eleven seconds until I'm off to Majuro (to die), I have a serious career revelation: No matter how depressing it may be that I might not be able to get an "important" or impressive job in New York, certainly I can at least get *a* job, right? Any job? If I can't specify what I want out of a career anyway, why not pick the things no one wants?

So that's it. I want to be an earthworm breeder. Well, that, or a phone-sex operator.

Granted, most people don't wake up one day and think, "Today I'd like to breed worms in the comfort of my own home," or even, "Today I'd like to verbally pleasure thousands of perverted, lonely, and crotchety sixty-year-old men from my own telephone." And don't get me wrong, I didn't think those things either. I don't even like *gummy* worms, let alone living, squirmy, slimy, oozing worms—the human male type *or* the worm type. But as I'm reading the paper, I scan the Help Wanted ads, since I figure I'm a person who wants to be helped . . . desperately, and therefore maybe the classified section will miraculously rescue me from the dearth of employment opportunities.

I see page after page of ads searching for dental hygienists and executive assistants, but no other jobs. Which means, yet again, that the unemployed like myself have three critical choices:

1. To become hygienists and resign ourselves to wearing lab coats every day that have teeth with faces on them, with toothbrushes that they use to brush themselves (See picture).

2. To accept our futures as professional interns and reconcile ourselves to alphabetizing Rolodexes for the rest of our professional lives.

or

3. To come up with last-minute, relatively stupid, and desperate alternatives to becoming either dental hygienists or executive assistants.

I choose option three.

Help Wanted, Desperately

As I reach the very last dental hygienist ad, I come across an opportunity that speaks to (screams at) my desperation:

R U Ready to Make Lots of Money?
Breed earthworms in your own home. Big $$$.
If you want a real chance at real money, just call.
No previous qualifications necessary.
Earthworm breeding is an investment in your future.

All along, I thought the "real money" was in business, law, and medical careers—or more specifically, careers that I am grossly unqualified to have. But here I was wrong! The stock market may be going to pieces, but if there's one thing you can rely on in this topsy-turvy universe we live in, it's this: earthworms. The new plastics.

Alexa Hoffman: Professional Earthworm Breeder. Nice to meet you. It rolls off the tongue.

Despite my general distaste for worms, I decide to give worm breeding a chance. Beggars can't be choosers, and for people like me with only four months, eleven days, six hours, and thirteen minutes left until we must resign ourselves to a year-long wait at the metaphorical DMV, earthworm breeding offers a desperately needed potential refuge from unemployment. Fortunately, my lack of professional experience meets their qualifications perfectly. I call the number at the bottom of the ad and am greeted by a recording of a pleasant female voice.

"Welcome to the Earthworm Benevolent Society. If you're interested in becoming an earthworm breeder, please leave a message at the tone with your name and home phone number.

Please note that this is not, repeat, NOT Earthworm Safe House Inc."

Thankfully, I don't even know what Earthworm Safe House Inc. is, though I imagine it's a place where rescued or escaped earthworms go so they can get back on their feet—or whatever it is earthworms have—again. A sort of noble earthworm halfway house. I decide to leave a cheerful, professional message at the tone: "Hi, my name is Alexa Hoffman, and I'm really fascinated with earthworm breeding and am very interested in breeding worms in my own home."

At this point, I should end the message. But in my frenzied, unemployed delirium, I (typically) continue rambling: "Actually, there's nothing more interesting to me than helping young worms maximize their potential." Perhaps I *should* seek social-work opportunities at the earthworm halfway house.

It gets worse: "You know, it's really hard for worms to make it on their own these days—they really have to battle the odds. I'd like to help those frightened and nervous worms. To help them turn a worm profit. To help them . . . help themselves." *Alex: shut up.*

"After all, a worm is a *terrible* thing to waste. Please call me as soon as possible."

Unsurprisingly, the Earthworm Benevolent Society never calls me back. Apparently, there must be at least one qualification for becoming an earthworm breeder: You can't appear to be a psychopath on the Earthworm Benevolent Society answering machine. Perhaps they don't call me because they are just trying to protect the precious worms that might be in my care. To watch out for maniacal potential worm breeders like myself so that their worms wouldn't have to slither out my window, escaping in Underground Railroad–type organizations through the sidewalk cracks on the street to the safety of the earthworm halfway house.

Worm breeding apparently was not written in my stars. But that doesn't mean that I'm giving up on Help Wanted ads. Make no mistake. Help is wanted—desperately.

As I am about to throw away the newspaper that contains the worm-breeding ad, I decide to give it a final look. What if I've missed an opportunity that I'll never find again? My eyes scan the pages until I come to an ad that says it all:

> Employment Opportunity
> Phone Sex Operators wanted.
> Great pay & work from home.
> Must have proven ability to satisfy a
> Wide range of callers.
> Adults only.

My first thought: Can I really be a phone-sex operator?
My second thought: Why the hell not?
My third thought: Would Jared be mad at me?
My fourth thought: What would my mother think?
Rather than second-guess what I anticipate to be my mom's response ("Are you insane?" "We didn't send you to college for this." "Are you trying to kill me?" "How are you going to get engaged to Jared if you're a phone-sex operator?"), I decide to go straight to the source, and amuse myself if only for a couple of minutes with the sheer and utter horror my decision to become a

phone-sex operator will surely induce in my mother. I pick up the phone and call.

My mom, who has the uncanny ability to know who it is before she even picks up the phone (without Caller ID no less) answers: "Alex? Why are you calling me? Shouldn't you be in class?"

"Mom, can I ask you a serious question? What would you think if I said I wanted to be a phone-sex operator?" I draw out the words *phone-sex operator* extra slowly for her benefit. Let the words resonate. This will show her that going to Majuro is better than at least *some* careers. I pause for a moment, relishing that sinfully delicious and delightful moment of anticipation right before my mother freaks out.

"I don't think it's a bad idea. Go ahead. Listen, Alex, I'm heading out the door right this second—I can't really talk now. I'll call you later. I'll be home around four-ish. Love you."

My mother hangs up the phone nonchalantly.

The silence of the phone echoes in my ear—I'm dumbfounded, not really sure what to think. No pressure to get engaged? And explicit approval of my X-rated career choice? No discussion of why I should forget getting a job, go to law school, and live at home, driving the Buick in New Jersey? What the hell is this world coming to? First I can't get a job . . . and now my mother has gone completely crackers.

This could mean one of three things:

1. My mother has given up on my search for employment. Depressing, horrifying, terrifying. Even my own mom doesn't think I can get a job.
2. My mother has given up on her belief that Jared wants to

marry me someday, thus implicitly suggesting that I
have somehow become undesirable, unattractive, and
unmarriageable.
3. She wasn't really listening to me.

Considering the fact that my mother has never before mentioned any aspirations for any of her three daughters to become
phone-sex operators, I figure she just wasn't listening to me.
But having that casual seal of approval makes a difference—a
big difference.

I'm going to make the call.

But first, I call Jared. Might as well see what he thinks about
the whole thing, what with him being my boyfriend and all. I
wonder if phone-sex operators' boyfriends have jealousy or rage
issues.

"Hi there, handsome."

"Hi—what's up? How's your day going?"

"Okay, so far. I should be going to class right now, but I
sort of found something cool in the paper—it's this Help
Wanted ad . . ."

"Why do I already feel like this is going to be something
weird?"

"This ad—it's for phone-sex operators. Apparently you can
make a ton of cash doing this sort of thing."

"Alex. Are you kidding? This is as dumb as the model scout
thing."

"Why is it dumb? Look, I'm just trying to find something to
do here. Imminent departure to Majuro is right around the corner, and I've got nothing. N-o-t-h-i-n-g. I feel so depressed. Are
you upset about the phone sex thing?" I ask.

"Look, I know you're depressed about this. And no, I'm not mad at you, I just don't think you could ever do it, that's all. You're not a phone-sex-operator type of person."

"What's *that* supposed to mean?" My boyfriend doesn't think I'm sexy? What? Shoot me, please.

"Oh please, Alex. Don't take this the wrong way and blow this out of proportion. It's just . . . you're not that kind of person, that's all."

"That's so mean!"

"What do you mean? Alex, it's a good thing! Phone-sex operators are so depressing—they just talk to gross, masturbating old guys all day . . ."

"I know what this is about, Jared. You don't think I have a sexy voice, do you? Why don't you just say it? You don't think I have a sexy voice. We're dating two years, and I can't believe you've never told me that. Look, this is as sexy as they come in New Jersey. And I'll show you sexy, you big hunk of man, you . . . Would you like to know what I'm wearing?"

"Shouldn't you be going to class?"

"Don't you want to talk to me though, lover? Tell me, what's your wildest fantasy?"

"All right, I really can't handle this right now. Go do your little phone-sex thing and call me later. You are so weird."

"Jared?"

"Yeah?"

"But I'm lovable, right?"

"Sort of, yes. But right now you're just freaking me out."

"Sort of the way a phone-sex operator would freak you out, right?"

"Alex—GO TO CLASS."

Help Wanted, Desperately

"Okay, okay, but first I'm going to apply to the phone-sex thing."

"God, you're one messed-up kid."

"Talk to you later, you big sexy man, you. Call me when you're done with class, okay?"

"Okay—or you call me when you're done wanting to be a phone-sex operator."

"Whichever comes first."

"Love you."

"Always."

With my emotional and romantic qualms about applying to be a phone-sex operator somewhat sated, I head out the door, ready to be my big, bad, sexy self. But where should I make the call? If I call from my own apartment, won't these phone-sex people have my number on Caller ID, and therefore be able to harass me, sending me unwanted hairy, horny-old-men callers? What if I decide not to leave my own number? What if Ethan overhears me? Do I really want to be known around the house as Alexa, everyone's "special telephone friend?" I've got to go to a phone booth.

But which one? I rack my brain, trying to remember the most desolate phone booths in the city. The ones where people are least likely to walk by. I instantly think of a phone booth right near a movie theater several blocks from where I live, and I'm off.

As I walk, I speak to myself softly in a slow, sexy voice. "I'm wearing a Gap T-shirt and Steve Madden flip-flops. What are *you* wearing?" My attempt at "sexy" sounds more like a congested, sixty-year-old smoker waitress named Fran than a seductive, flexible, curvaceous sex machine named Candy. Also, my guess is that horny old men named Gus and Harvey aren't ex-

141

actly interested in Gap T-shirts and Steve Madden flip-flops. But so help me God, if I can try to be an earthworm breeder, certainly I can at least try to be a phone-sex operator. There's a certain sliminess to both careers that I know I have somewhere inside of me. This is, after all, a Mother-and-Boyfriend-Approved mission.

I walk several blocks, all the while testing out my phone-sex voice, which elicits more than a few strange looks from various passersby on the streets, all of whom must assume I'm a self-obsessed nymphomaniac passionately attracted to myself. (Alternatively, they assume I'm just another over caffeinated college student.)

Despite my very conscious understanding that being a phone-sex operator is probably not the career for me, I arrive at the phone booth, in an area with more people traffic than I had anticipated. But I have no choice. I call the number, which accesses, yet again, an answering machine.

A sexy female voice sounds in my ear. I imagine this is what size-double-D breasts would sound like if they could talk.

"Thank you for calling Erotic Pleasures hotline." The Breasts emphasize the t's. Mental note: emphasize the t's in my own message. "If you think you can drive a man *wiiiiild* with your creativity and sexy voice, we want *you* to join our talented team of erotica operators. At the tone, please leave a message with your name and phone number. Then, answer the following questions: What are you wearing right now? How would you describe yourself to your male customers? What's your most desirable fantasy?"

The tape pauses for a second, and then I hear a long beep. My cue. Panic. Sheer and utter panic.

Help Wanted, Desperately

I take a deep breath, mustering up all the sexiness I have in me—which, admittedly, is not that much at all. Use the throaty smoker voice, Alex. I open my mouth: "My name is Alex and I— "

But before I go any further, I start laughing and hang up the phone. A homeless man I recognize from the area points at me and screams "Beans!" which only makes me laugh harder. I can't believe this is what my job search has come down to— I don't know whether to laugh or cry, but laughing works, so I don't stop.

After a minute or so, I calm down, stop laughing, wipe the tears out of my eyes. I can't decide if the laughter is from genuine amusement or sadness that this is what it's come to. Regardless, I haven't had this much fun since fifth grade, when my friend Kristy and I called up 1-800-TAMPONS and told the operator our periods were navy blue. Good times.

As I finish collecting myself, poising myself to call again, I look over each of my shoulders. Six innocent passersby, one of whom looks like he could be an Erotic Pleasures hotline caller. I try to shrink my way into the phone and cup my hands casually around the receiver. Alexa Hoffman Tries To Be a Phone Sex Operator: Take Two.

The Double Ds pick up the phone again, and I wait until the beep comes.

"Hi," I say in my best "sexy" voice. "My name is Alexa and . . . my phone number is . . ." I look around the phone booth and spot an ad: "Free short female haircuts, call the following telephone number." Suddenly too scared to leave my real number, I figure this one will just be for practice, and I give the phone number from the ad. (How often is it that you meet a phone-sex operator who also gives free short female haircuts? What a bargain!) "I'm wearing, um," the sexiness starts to slip out of my voice. "I'm wearing uh, jeans," I look down at myself, "and um, a white T-shirt. And flip-flops." Erotic, Alex. Not NEUrotic.

"Oh, and underneath?" I whisper sexily, "I'm not wearing any panties at all." As the words slide out of my mouth for the first time in a vaguely sexy way, I turn around and see two ruggedly attractive twenty-something guys walking past me. Suddenly, they smile at me. Without slowing his pace, one of them looks me up and down, checking, I think, for underwear. I crouch further into the phone booth and look away mortified. Just so he knows, I dramatically pick at a nonexistent wedgie. Wouldn't want to keep him wondering.

"As far as, you know, my sexual fantasies go, well . . ." As I'm about to make up some ridiculous sexual fantasy that would appeal to dirty old men (Moisturizing liver spots?), I hear a beep on the other end of the line. "Thank you for calling." A click. The phone call ends.

That wasn't nearly enough time to finish what was sure to be a fantastically boring, unsexual (if not antisexual) message. If Erotic Pleasures hotline thinks they can get rid of me that fast, they've got another think coming! I decide to call again. I look over each shoulder. A preschooler and her mom. A businesswoman. Two third graders. So much for the desolate-phone-booth idea.

I pick up the phone.

As the sexy voice repeats the message, I think about why men actually call phone sex hotlines. Not enough sex at home? Maybe. They don't feel loved? Probably. Nothing good on TV? Definitely. All these things have one thing in common: loneli-

ness. These guys just want some girl to make them feel appreciated. They want attention. Some of them probably just want
someone to talk to them. Maybe they don't even *want* phone sex
at all—maybe they just want a friend.

And therein lies my answer.

The message beeps and instead of a sexy, guttural voice, I
speak like normal, nondescript regular old me: "Hi. My name is
Alexa Hoffman. I'm twenty-one years old, have curly hair, and
am about five foot seven. I have two sisters, and I go to school in
Philadelphia. I'm terrified that I won't ever be able to get a job,
that I'll never make anything of myself, and that I'll be a disappointment to all of my family and friends. I'm worried that I've
worked so hard up until this point in my life—and it won't make
a difference. If you feel the same way, and want to talk, call me."
An overwhelming sadness takes over me, and, without leaving
my number, I hang up the phone.

It's too early in my life to have a career this depressing.

And that may just have been the worst phone-sex-operator
audition known to mankind.

Surprise, surprise: Neither a career in breeding worms nor one
spent sexing it up on the phone with hormonal geriatrics is in my
future.

My cell phone rings: Jared.

"So did you call them?"

"Yeah, I did."

"And . . . ?"

"And nothing."

"Alex, are you okay? You don't sound like you. Is everything
all right?"

"Yeah, I just . . . it was sad, doing that. Really depressing."

"The phone-sex-operator thing? Alex, please. It was a job as a *phone-sex operator*. It's *good* that it wasn't right for you. I'm glad you thought it was depressing."

"I know, it's just that it feels like nothing is for me . . . like I'm destined to be some boring nobody who shouts 'Beans!' in the streets."

"I don't get the beans thing. But Alex, you're anything but boring. Why would I want to be with someone who was boring? One of the reasons I'm so in love with you is because you're so strange and interesting."

"Well, Jared, I hate to be the one to tell you, but you're really getting the bad end of the deal here. You're much more interesting than me—you have an actual goal in your life. A career at an auction house. An international lifestyle surrounded by art and people. You *have* a life. I'm just blah. I'll work wherever, whenever. And worse: No one wants me to do whatever, whenever. And because of that, I'm going to end up skipping out on my only real dream of moving to New York to move to crappy Majuro, where I'll teach kids while perpetually fearing death. Don't you think that's sad and depressing?"

"Look, Alex, part of what's so great about you is that while you're so worried about finding some job, you try *everything*. You're not afraid of doing things other people would run away from. I love that about you. Among other things. And as for Majuro, well"—Jared sighs into the phone—"that's your choice."

Rolling my eyes, I answer, "Jared, Majuro isn't a choice. It's a sentence. It's a year-long sentence that basically means I'm a nobody. It means I can't make anything of myself so I have to run away for a year so nobody will remember that I'm not good enough, I'm not smart enough, and no one would ever hire me."

Help Wanted, Desperately

I hear Jared try to interject, but I interrupt him, "But you couldn't understand that, I guess. You don't know what it's like to worry that everyone you know will think you're a loser because you just can't get a job, and therefore you can't get a life, and not for lack of trying."

Jared spits back, "When are you going to realize that life isn't about all these stupid jobs? Alex, there's a difference between having a job and having a life. You already *have* a life. I feel like my life is so great because of you. And I hope you feel as happy about your life because of me the same way. Does that make sense? I really love you. That's better than any job—and I hope that I make you happier than you think any job would."

"Of course you do, and I know, I know it's better than a job. And you do make me happy. It's just that I want to be able to make myself happy independent of you. I want to stand on my own two feet. I want to be proud of who I am, and what I do. But I do nothing . . . I can't explain it. Look, I love you so much— you're too nice to me. Why do you put up with me?"

"How could I not? You're the best person I know."

"You need to expand your circle."

"Alex . . ."

"Look, I'm sorry I'm such a pain in the ass. I just need . . . something. And for what it's worth, I think you're a much better conversationalist than a horny old man would be."

"Thanks, I think."

"No, that was definitely a compliment."

"Well, don't be sad about this phone-sex-operator thing. There's always something else. And I'll give you a hug on Friday— I'm coming in on the six-o'clock train."

Stage left, in walks the age-old dilemma: What next?

147

*   *   *

Instead of letting my recent defeats with Help-Wanted ads get in the way of what I desperately hope will be a prosperous future living in New York (as opposed now to dying in Majuro), my run-ins with worm breeding and overpopulated phone booths have made me realize that I probably have a lot of untapped talents that I haven't even thought about. Making cheese is a good example. Sure, I've had rotten, curdled milk in my refrigerator just begging to be transformed. And yet I've never gone that extra step to making it into cheese. I'm a negligent dairyman. But just because I've never tried it doesn't mean it's impossible.

With these thoughts in mind, I listen to the radio, contemplating my future. In between songs, I hear an ad: "Be the new voice of *Meow TV*—a TV show all about cats! Entrants will recite the famous Meow Mix jingle or create one of their own using our catchy tune." This is ridiculous. America really is getting dumber by the second.

I pick up the phone and call Jared.

"Jared, what are you doing tomorrow?"

"Hi there, beautiful! Um, class?"

"Do you want to do something really cool?"

"Alex, your 'really cool' and my 'really cool' are not the same thing . . . What is it?"

"Please, first just promise you'll go. I swear I'll do anything if right now, you promise to go with me."

"Will you taste herring?"

"Why are you so hung up on me tasting herring? There's no way I'm doing that."

"Alex, first of all, as far as hang-ups go, you're *hardly* one to talk. It's just herring. Taste it. What's the big deal?"

Help Wanted, Desperately

"It looks gross. And I'd hate it. And you want me to try it just because you know I'll hate it. That's cruel."

"Fine, then I'm not doing whatever you want me to do tomorrow. I'll just see you Friday. And you don't know that you hate it unless you try it."

"Jared, I really, really don't want to taste herring. Isn't there something else I could do? Like snorkeling or something?"

"Nope. Herring. If you do it, I'll do whatever you want me to do. Deal?"

"Well, that certainly sounds kinky! But fine, deal. Anyway, tomorrow, I'm going to come to New York to audition for *Meow TV*. It's this TV show for cats, I just heard about it on the radio. Will you come with me?"

"Are you serious?"

"Yes! I think it'll be cool—what if I win and become an American cat-spokesperson-feline thing?"

"Alex, not to dredge up bad memories, but let's not forget your role as Vietnamese Refugee Number Twenty-seven in *Miss Saigon* last year at school . . . Not exactly the crowning dramatic achievement you hoped it would be . . ."

"This is different! This is about *cats*!"

"Alex, you hate cats."

"That's not important! You said you would come! You promised—I eat the herring, you go to this thing with me."

"I can't believe I'm agreeing to this. Call me later and we'll work out all the details, okay?"

"Jared, you are the best, most wonderful, super-est person in the universe. You're my favorite person in the world. What does that *feel* like?"

"Ask me tomorrow when I'm escorting you to audition for

some cat TV show. Alex, cats don't even have opposable thumbs. How can they pick the station to watch the cat show? I'm telling you right now I am *not* auditioning—we're doing this for *you*. I'm there for moral support. Or moron support."

"Okay, I promise I won't make you audition. I'll take you out to dinner this weekend, as a reward. In addition to the herring. I love you so much, you know that, right?"

"Yeah, yeah. I love you too."

"I'll call you later. You're the best!"

"You're going to be eating a lot of herring."

Fame, fortune, lifetime supply of cat food, here I come.

Admittedly, it's strange that I've decided to audition for Meow TV for several reasons, the most important of which being that Jared is right: I truly, wholly, completely, unequivocally, and utterly despise cats. I hate the way they smell, I hate that they're secretive, I hate the way their eyes glow in a creepy way in certain lights. I hate that people always name them clichéd cat names, like "Buttons" and "Socks," and carry pictures of them in their wallets as if they were children or grandkids. I hate the way you never know if they're in the room . . . lurking. I hate the fact that all the cats I've ever known in my life have had elaborate health problems (diabetes, end-stage renal disease, etc.), which require their owners to give them injections every day at the crack of dawn. Cats strike me as lying, deceitful, manipulative creatures who own their owners more than their owners own them. (And having read Garfield comics my entire childhood, I was also appalled to learn at age eight that cats don't *actually* eat lasagna in real life, thus proving my suspicion that cats are liars.)

Despite my hatred for cats, I have the sinking feeling that this is something I can actually win—that I could actually be the voice of *Meow TV*, and while it may be unconventional, it would still be a job and a ticket off of the island of Majuro and onto the island of Manhattan, right? Jared and I arrive at the building where the auditions are being held. Before we enter, we notice a car parked in front shaped like a large orange-and-red cat. Instead of a license plate, the car has a mechanical tongue wagging back and forth. Its wheels are covered by feline haunches, and above the windshield blink scary secretive mechanical cat eyes that dart back and forth.

"Alex, I can't believe I agreed to this. Start thinking about the truckloads of herring you're going to have to eat."

"We agreed on tasting. There was no mention of 'truckloads.' "

We walk into the building and arrive at a promotional tent, where a woman (wearing a *Meow TV* baseball hat) introduces herself as Meghan, and enthusiastically asks us to fill out the Meow Mix *Meow TV* contest application. Though there are no living cats visibly present, Meghan's *Meow TV* clothing is covered in cat hair. As she tells us about the rules of the contest ("you have only fifteen seconds to sing your jingle, so make it good!"), I realize even she looks sort of like a cat. Neither rodent, duck, nor elf, she is the exception to the rule, defying all categorization.

Jared and I look at each other frantically with the first question: "How many cats do you own?" Do they mean living, breathing "real" cats, or stuffed-animal cats? I see no specification as to whether the cat is a real cat or a stuffed-animal cat. I write down "1" on my answer sheet. Jared smiles at me, and writes down "1" on his. After all, my parents *once* had a cat for two weeks—which, I still believe, they got to replace me when I left for college. That should count for something. Granted, they hated it and returned it to the shelter, but still.

Question 2: "What are your cats' names?" This could get messy. Just one second ago, I signed a waiver and release form that I didn't even bother reading. Can a person get sent to jail for impersonating a cat lover?

As I brood over the moral implications of re-creating a cat that only I myself knew for three days, Jared happily scribbles away on his questionnaire. I peek at his paper. For question two he has responded, "Kersplatt." Apparently, Jared has a cat named "Kersplatt" that I never knew about. I tap him and point to his answer expectantly. He shrugs, and I write down on my answer form, "Kersplatt." Jared whispers in my ear, "We call him 'Kermie' for short. We named him Kersplatt because when we first got him at a rescue center and brought him home he immediately sat on top of the TV, fell asleep, and then fell to the floor. Hence, Kersplatt!"

Jared goes back to writing, and I look at him for a long, long time.

When you've been dating someone for two years and known him for four, there are certain things you expect of him: to know you absolutely hate walking on the open grates on the sidewalk, to know you would willingly eat nachos with artificial cheese for the rest of your life and nothing else, and to know the name and address of the one restaurant in New York that consistently makes you have a peeling, disgusting rash under your left eye. You expect him to know that when you say you want the eggs you really want banana pancakes. And that even though you roll your eyes at him because he still laughs uncontrollably when he sees a gerbil slip and break its hip in a bathtub on *America's Fun-niest Home Videos,* you still secretly find his laughing at it really, really cute.

You do not, under any circumstances, expect your boyfriend to have a host of stock responses to questions about a cat that you know he does not actually own. And yet now, standing next to Jared, I'm actually starting to believe that we have a cat named Kersplatt. I tap Jared on the shoulder. He looks up at me from his questionnaire.

"Does Kersplatt like me?"

"Of course! He loves you. He sits on your lap all the time and you love petting him right underneath his left ear. He's really going to miss you when you head off to Majuro . . ." Jared goes back to writing.

And in this relationship, *I'm* considered the strange one.

Content that our fictional cat loves me, I look back at the questions. "How often do you purchase dry cat food?"

Just as I'm about to look up at Jared he says, without looking up from his own questionnaire, "Once a month, seven-pound packs, and we exclusively buy Meow Mix. We've had Kersplatt for how long, and you still don't know all of this? Honestly, Alex."

Am I insane? Or is he?

At question 7 Jared looks as baffled as I am. "Does your cat watch TV?" I look at Meghan, the "MeowMixer" who greeted us, and I ask her, "Why does it matter whether or not my cat watches TV?"

Meghan looks at me as if I've just told her that my cat doesn't have regular veterinary visits. "Why, because *Meow TV* is going to be a half-hour TV special geared toward entertaining cats!"

Jared and I turn to each other, amazed.

I look at Meghan incredulously. "What do you mean? I thought this was for entertaining cat *owners*. You know, people."

"Oh, no! *Meow TV* is the first television programming in the history of the medium targeted specifically at *cats*! The whole point of this contest is that we're looking for a voice to go along with the visuals that'll be on the show—you know, stuff that cats like, like birds, mice, bouncing balls and yarn. I can't believe you didn't know this! Isn't it a terrific idea? I mean, how many times have you *wished* that your cat had a good show to watch?" Meghan looks at us expectantly, with her eyes glowing like a cat's furtive glance in the darkness.

Without missing a beat, Jared smiles and says to Meghan, "Not a day goes by." Meghan smiles at Jared and offers him a *Meow TV* baseball hat, which Jared promptly puts on.

Where the hell *am* I?

Meghan shyly dusts off some of the cat hair on her shoulders, and then offers Jared a cat key chain. She smiles at him, batting her eyelashes, and says, "You should finish up your question-naires soon . . ."

Question 8: "What types of programs does your cat watch?" Jared and I circle *soap operas* and *animal shows*.

Question 9: "How does your cat respond to the television? Eye movement? Tail posture? Swatting? Vocal sounds? Kneading?" I have no idea what any of these things are, so for kicks I circle *kneading*. I look at Jared's paper, relieved. He circled *kneading* too. No one knows Kersplatt like Jared.

We hand in our applications, and Meghan hands us a sheet of paper that says "Write your own lyrics for the Meow Mix Song." Jared and I say goodbye to Meghan, and Meghan says goodbye to Jared, ignoring me as if I was leftover cat shit in Buttons's litter box. We walk down the hallway, sit on the floor, and start to write our lyrics to match the annoying tune of the Meow Mix jingle that goes "Meow-meow-meow-meow-meow-meow-meow-meow-meow-meow-meow-meow-meow-meow-meow." (Trust me, you've heard it.) I start to put my poetic genius to work; Jared looks deep in thought.

After several moments, I ask Jared, "What do you think of this one? 'I love Meow Mix, I'm a human, Meow Mix Meow Mix keeps me pooping!' I look at Jared expectantly.

Jared rolls his eyes. "Alex, *pooping* doesn't even vaguely rhyme with *human*."

"If you say 'poopin' ' instead of 'poop*ing*,' it rhymes a little . . . poopin' . . . human . . ."

"Do you really want to go in front of total strangers and sing about poop?"

I sigh and look down at my lyrics sheet. I thought the 'poopin' ' thing was good.

Jared writes something down frantically and says, "Listen to this: 'If your cat rejects his vittles, give him Meow Mix Seafood Middles!' "

I look at Jared, awestruck. Here, I come up with *pooping*, and Jared instantaneously creates what could very well be the next Meow Mix jingle.

Jared smiles proudly, and we continue working. Our finished jingle sings like this:

I love Meow Mix, it's delicious
To deprive your cat is vicious

Ariel Horn

Muffy likes it, it's so tasty
Socks won't eat it, he looks pasty

If your cat rejects his vittles
Give him Meow Mix Seafood Middles

Why'm I singing, this looks yummy,
I want Meow Mix in MY tummy!

(Obviously, Jared came up with the first and third verses, I came up with the "brilliant" second and fourth. "Yummy" and "tummy" = pure English-major genius.)

With hope in our hearts, Jared and I set forth into Meow-Mix wonderland. We walk down the hallway, turn the corner, and arrive in a ballroom filled with screaming children, all of whom are covered in face paint to make them look more feline: gray whiskers and pink noses. Some of them are wearing cat ears. One four-year-old angelically practices "Meow meow meow" in preparation. Her mother—not a soccer mom, but a cat mom, which I soon learn is ten times worse—sternly looks at her daughter.

"Lindsey, sweetie, you are NOT focusing right now! I need you to work really hard at this. Mommy really wants you to be the *Meow TV* voice. You don't want to make Mommy mad, do you?" Lindsey shakes her head and looks like she's about to cry. "Mommy will love you more if you win!" Lindsey nods her head. "Now try it again, Lindsey. And this time I want you to do it like you really mean it! Do it for Mommy!"

As Lindsey's mom continues to beg Lindsey to "do it with feeling," the hundreds of children (and handful of adults) wait-

156

ing on line to audition are called up one by one to the micro-
phone. Each kid is introduced by an overzealous MeowMixer (all
of whom seem to be covered in cat hair) and then told to sing
"their original lyrics" (which more often than not means that the
child whines atonally, "Meow meow meow meow," with adoring
parents looking on). A forty-year-old man auditions, singing in a
deep, booming and resonant voice, "Meow-meow-meow" to the
tune of "New York, New York." One child forgets to sing the
"ow" part of "meow," and bursts out into hysterical tears on
the stage.

Jared, turning into a cat mom himself, asks me to practice.
"Okay, Alex, you've got fifteen seconds to do this. I'm going to
time you. Go!"

Jared stares at the second hand of his watch as I tear through
our jingle. I notice a woman lurking over my shoulder, and
quickly snap my head around. The competition to be the voice of
Meow TV is fierce, and I wouldn't want some manipulative cat
lover to win because of our poetic genius.

A woman wearing a *Meow TV* T-shirt begs, "Oh, don't stop
singing! I absolutely LOVE your jingle! I work for Meow Mix—
and your jingle is terrific! C'mere, I want my boss to hear it."

Before we know it, Jared and I are escorted over to this
woman's boss, and I'm singing the jingle all over again. Her boss
is impressed and says something along the lines of "This kid's
really onto something!" I feel like I'm trapped in a world with
crazy people obsessed with cats, which is, perhaps, not so far
from the truth. Sure enough, the original woman's boss takes us
over to meet Harry, *his* boss.

"Harry, you gotta hear this. Her stuff's fantastic!"

Once again, I sing the jingle. Jared looks on, as proud as a person impersonating a cat lover can be when his girlfriend wows the team at Meow Mix.

Before I can say "Meow Mix Original Flavor" someone is introducing me to the CEO, for whom I immediately begin singing our jingle. The CEO looks at me as if I'm, as it were, the cat's meow.

The CEO grabs me by the shoulder, and leads me toward the front of the audition line. "You're purrr-fect! I want you to audition *now*—go to the front of the line." The CEO gestures to an overweight man in a *Meow TV* shirt, who looks very unhappy with his job. "Hank, take this girl to the front of the audition line. I want her videotaped, recorded, and pictures taken. Now!"

I look at Jared, my eyes shining, as I'm led to the front of the ballroom. Jared just shakes his head and smiles. Could it be that I will finally have a job in New York—and not just any job—but a position as the cat-lover icon of America?

Transformed from unemployed loser to queen of Meow Mix, I'm hurried to the front of the audition line, much to the chagrin of a pack of eight-year-olds dressed as cats who scream in unison, "No fair! Cutting!" I shrug my shoulders at the kids, resisting the urge to stick my tongue out at them and shout, "Ha ha, I'm better than you losers!" You know you have serious insecurities when you feel the need to taunt eight-year-olds dressed as cats in order to validate your own self-worth.

I get to the front of the line, and Hank introduces me to the crowd. He looks down at my application. "Everyone, this is Alexa. Can we say, 'Hello, Alexa?'" The crowd of disgruntled eight-year-olds looks unimpressed; some of them pick their noses and wipe their boogers on each other. For a second, I think I see a Meow Mix Seafood Middle fly at my head.

Help Wanted, Desperately

"Alexa's going to sing her own jingle for us! Isn't that exciting? Okay, Alexa, when you hear the beep, I want you to start singing." Video cameras come close to my face, and the flash of camera bulbs burns my eyes. So this is fame. I finally understand what Julia Roberts must feel like every day of her life.

I take a deep breath as the room goes silent. The CEO looks on excitedly. Jared smiles and gives me a tiny wink. The four-year-old who was supposed to go next angrily sticks his tongue out at me. And then, the beep cues me in. I sing the jingle with as much feline energy as I can muster, and when I finish, the crowd erupts into applause.

For a brief four seconds, I savor the moment: hundreds of adoring fans, applauding me. The CEO of Meow Mix clapping wildly. Meow Mix board members whispering to one another and taking notes. Fame. Sweet, delicious, precious fame! Let my body be your temple!

Jared runs up to me, hugs me, and kisses me—which repulses a four-year-old nearby who displays his displeasure with fairly loud vomiting noises. The CEO of Meow Mix smiles and says to me, "We'll let you know tonight if you're our New York City finalist. Good luck." The CEO winks at me.

And with that, Jared and I head back to Jared's dorm room, amazed, appalled, delighted, and dumbfounded.

For the first time in my entire job search, I feel filled with overwhelming hope.

This is what my life has come to.

For the rest of the evening, Jared and I sit in his dorm room, cuddling on the bed as we talk about the audition and watch *Animal Planet*. (It seems appropriate.)

As we watch, Jared begins to carelessly stroke my hair in the way one would pet a cat, and I look up at him. "Jared, do you think I'm going to win?"

"Do you want to win?"

"I don't know. It's weird—part of me really wants this. I mean, I'd have a job. In New York. No Majuro to deal with. No Death Folder to create. But then, part of me, I think, would be really, really embarrassed if I won. I don't know . . . I'm sure it won't work out. Story of my life."

Just when I think my moment in the sun has ended, the phone rings. Jared and I look at each other, and he gestures for me to pick up the phone. "Oh please. I'm sure it's your mom or something."

I pick up the phone. "Is this Alexa Hoffman?" an excited voice asks. "My name is Marissa, and I'm calling from *Meow TV* to inform you that *you* have been selected as the *Meow TV* New York City finalist! Congratulations!"

There is a moment of silence on the phone. I'm not sure whether I should laugh or cry.

I repeat Marissa's words slowly. "I'm the *Meow TV* New York City finalist?" Jared looks at me, his jaw drops, his eyes light up, and he starts jumping up and down on his bed doing some sort of triumphant victory dance I've never seen before.

"That's right! Now, here's how it's going to work. We're going to visit eight more cities to find the eight other *Meow TV* finalists, and then in the beginning of September, we'll call to let you know if you're our grand prize winner. If you *are* the grand prize winner—how exciting would *that* be!—you get to be the new voice of *Meow TV*'s original half-hour pilot program!" Marissa sounds like she's going to die of excitement. It's as if she herself were the New York City *Meow TV* finalist. "And, even better, we'll provide you and a guest with an all-expense paid trip to Los Angeles for the *Meow TV* premiere of your episode! If the program takes off and you're well received as the voice of *Meow TV*, this could turn into a full-time contract! Isn't this exciting?"

Almost speechless, I reply in a daze, "Yeah, yeah, it's great!"

"Oh, and before I forget, for tomorrow we've set up a radio interview for you on NPR. So be ready at twelve o'clockish to be on the radio, okay? And congratulations again! We'll be in touch!"

Marissa hangs up the phone, and I try to take it all in. Instead I collapse onto Jared's bed as Jared hugs me, laughing, kissing me everywhere. "And you thought it wouldn't work out! This is *worth* the herring, right?"

I actually have a fighting chance at being the new voice of *Meow TV*, a program geared toward entertaining cats. Is this really what I want to do with my life? My fifteen seconds of fame are going to happen because I've spent the past ten hours impersonating a cat lover. And I'm going to be on NPR as the New York City *Meow TV* finalist. Across the nation, people will hear that Alexa Hoffman is the *Meow TV* New York City finalist.

I don't even have a real live cat.

The Meow Mix radio interview with NPR is today, and I decide to skip my class in Philadelphia this morning to do the phone interview in New York. Last night, I dreamt of cats filling my apartment. Hundreds of them, pawing and licking me in my bed. I woke up in a cold sweat when one of them tapped me on my shoulder with its paw and politely asked me if I would please feed it Meow Mix Seafood Middles. Later I realized it was Jared trying to wake me up.

This cannot be my life.

As I lie in bed, contemplating my future as the icon of cat love in America, the phone rings: It's the woman from NPR.

"I'm just going to ask you some really easy questions, and I'd love it if you could answer them. When you hear the click, I'm recording the interview, which should air around four thirty today." I hear a click: We're rolling. Jared looks excited, and I feel nauseous. I put the phone on speaker.

"So, what did you sing in your audition?"

Still amazed that I'm being interviewed for NPR, I stutter out, "Oh, my boyfriend and I just made something up, this jingle, and it was great." Good answer, Alex. This should make for some *really* fascinating radio.

The interviewer seems unimpressed. "You know you're going to have to sing it for me, right? Can you sing it?"

Before I know it, I'm singing our newly famous jingle on national radio as Jared dances to the sound of our literary genius.

The interviewer laughs in the way that interviewers have to when they can't believe they're doing a story far dumber than any other story they've ever done before.

"That was great, really great!" The interviewer fake-laughs. Jared is nearly dying of laughter, and I briefly wonder if I should get him a glass of water so he doesn't choke. "Now, let me ask you, why did you decide to audition to be the Meow Mix girl?"

Starting to enjoy the interview, I feel myself turn into a charming cat lover. I roll over in bed and respond, "I think that sparks another question . . . Why *wouldn't* anyone audition to

be the next Meow Mix girl? It's the opportunity of a lifetime!"
The interviewer chuckles. "No, seriously, I just thought it
would be a lot of fun." Probably best to leave out the "desperately unemployed /terrified about my future/don't want to die
in Majuro" part.

"Great, great. Now, I understand you have a cat. What's his
name?"

Yikes. Lying on national radio. I shoot a look at Jared, who is
no longer laughing: he looks as nervous as I feel. Is this illegal?
Which is worse: drug possession or pretending you have a cat?
"His name's Kersplatt. We got him at a rescue center in New Jersey, and now he lives with my parents." Sort of.

"Terrific. Now, if you could give one piece of advice to all the
cat lovers out there with high aspirations, what would you say to
them?"

I pause for a second, reflecting. Not actually having a "real"
cat myself, it's hard to say what kind of advice I would give to cat
lovers. But I can't admit that to this woman—it would be scan-
dalous. The *Meow TV* finalist doesn't have a cat? It would be all
over the papers. Imagine the horror and riots that would rip the
nation apart. I can see the headlines now: ME-OUCH! KERSPLATT
A LIE!

I think quickly and blurt, "I would say that those people
shouldn't just look at their cats as soft, lovable, furry things"—
did I just call cats "things"?—"but as a source of inspiration. As
a muse." It's as if I've actually been eating Meow Mix Seafood
Middles . . . I've gone completely and totally insane.

The interviewer thanks me, and the interview ends. Jared and
I look at each other and laugh nervously, as if I've done something wrong that can't be fixed. Jared repeats the phrase that in

the past day has become a fixture of our conversations: "I can't believe this is happening." It is shortly followed by, "I can't believe you lied on national radio, Alex. This is really, really bad."

A few seconds later, the interviewer calls back, off the record, to ask me what Kersplatt looks like. I think fast: "Um, he's gray. And um, he's really cute." She asks what breed he is and I say he's "mixed" and that "I don't know, since we got him at a rescue shelter."

"You have no idea what breed he is?"

"He's just really, really cute."

She laughs and says, "Oh, that's rich! Now, does he have long hair or short hair?"

"Um, I . . . it's short. Very short." The interviewer hangs up the phone with me and before I know it, Kersplatt has become a living, breathing lie. And one that needs some substance.

If I win this thing, I'm going to need to get a cat. And fast. A gray one with short hair. And it's got to be really, really cute.

Jared and I start listening to NPR at 3:30 in the afternoon in eager, unbridled anticipation, though the interview isn't supposed to air until 4:30. At this point, I'm so involved in what is sure to be my newly acquired fame that I have almost completely forgotten about Philadelphia, class, and even the fact that if this doesn't work out I'm going to have to start writing my will for Majuro.

As 4:25 rolls around, I feel my heart rate speeding up: I've told my entire family, as well as everyone I even vaguely know (which includes the security guard for Jared's dorm at NYU), to listen to NPR at 4:30. The *Meow TV* people will be listening for sure. There is more than a lot riding on this. It's my reputation as a cat lover, my future as a cat voice, and basically, a real possibility at a job. My heart beats faster by the second, and I feel myself growing more nervous by the minute.

Four thirty passes. We hear a story about piranhas. Then four thirty five passes. At four forty, the voice on the radio program *All Things Considered* says that there's going to be a new TV show geared toward cats. Marissa, the woman from *Meow TV,* is interviewed. And then they move on to the next short news story.

Just like that, my interview and my brief shot at NPR fame are dashed. They nixed my interview. They didn't play it. "All Things Considered" indeed.

Jared looks at me. "There must be some mistake. They're not just going to forget about your whole interview. Let's keep listening."

Jared and I lie on the couch, wrapped in each other's arms, silently listening until 5:30. My fifteen seconds of fame, without any warning, have just turned into two hours of disappointment. No NPR. No fame for today, just dozens of disappointed relatives and friends, all of whom I've forced to listen to boring NPR in hopes of my interview being aired. I am outraged and appalled. It is another sad, sad day in Alexa Hoffman history.

This morning I wake up, back in Philadelphia, saddened at the memory of NPR's major dis. (I might add that a story about blow-darts aired, but my interview didn't, which is perhaps the greatest insult of all.) Still reeling from the pain of being an NPR reject, my head heavy as if riddled by a hangover, I hear the phone ring and pick it up, dazed and sleepy. It's Julie. I look at the clock: 8:15. These working people have *no* understanding that those of us who are unemployed sleep at least until nine, and more often than not, we sleep until twelve.

"Alex, have you looked at CNN online?"

"No, I just woke up. Actually, *you* just woke me up. What time is it? It feels like four in the morning. What happened?" I wipe the crust from my eyes and notice that despite the fact that a couple of days and several showers have passed since my *Meow TV* audition, I still smell like cat food.

"There's an article all about *Meow TV*! I'm not even kidding! The CEO says that they're looking for 'the Vanna White of cats' to host the new show! Alex, you *are* the Vanna White of cats! Aren't you excited? Who needs NPR when you're going to be the Vanna White of cats! Aren't you happy? This is so much better than Majuro or law school, right?"

Julie and I talk for a while, and I regain hope. The glimmer of a bright future has not yet faded. I may not have earthworms. I may not have dirty old men. But I've got a future of cats—and thousands of cat viewers, eager to hear my voice.

Come September, I just might be the voice of *Meow TV*.

Me-ouch?

Lessons Learned

1. Help Wanted ads are for *employers* who are desperate . . . Never, never should they be abused by desperate job seekers.

2. Never assume your mother believes in something you plan on doing simply because she didn't say otherwise.

3. When leaving voice-mail messages in response to job opportunities, refrain from acting like a deranged worm-molester.

Help Wanted, Desperately

4. When I try to sound sexy, I sound like a sixty-year-old smoker.

5. It's never worth eating herring—no matter how badly you want to con your boyfriend into doing something relatively stupid with you.

6. Fictionalizing ownership of pets can lead to potential employment. Translation: bullshit reigns supreme.

9
Blitzkrieg

4 Months

"On September 1, 1939, Hitler launched one of the most impressive military offensives ever known to European warfare: a military tactic known as 'blitzkrieg.' "

Professor Kidd pauses for dramatic effect and scans the audience. Some students are frantically taking notes. Some students are sleeping. Some students are poking sleeping students. And me, I'm just staring at the latest mailing from Majuro—a pamphlet describing where we'll live once we get there. The huts actually look pretty nice, and on the cover of the pamphlet, well-adjusted humanitarians smile, looking happy, cheerful, and *satisfied* with their lives. Inside, well-adjusted Marshallese children sit at rainbow-colored desks, looking happy, cheerful, and satisfied with *their* lives. As Professor Kidd drones on about the war, I wonder, if I go to Majuro, will I be satisfied? Maybe my inability to get a job—my inability to have a future—is some sort of divine intervention that means I'm destined for Majuro.

I look over at (already-employed) Amy, who is happily writing her signature over and over again and then glance down at my Majuro pamphlet at a photograph of an American teaching a group of Marshallese children. The kids look studious. The teacher looks involved and important. I doubt I would feel involved or important at a job in New York . . .

"Blitztkrieg," Professor Kidd continues, pacing the stage, "was calculated by the Nazis to create psychological shock, which would result in the disorganization of enemy forces through, as I've said, speed, agility, and an impressive combination of land and air action.

"It was war like Europe had never seen!"

I stop working on my grocery list and begin taking notes mindlessly, knowing full well that the fact that this was a "war like Europe had never seen" would probably not help me on the final exam. In between notes I let my mind wander to whether or not I should write my will and whether or not I should just give up on the job search and go to Majuro, and then, if I go to Majuro, what would happen between me and Jared?

"Yes," Professor Kidd clasps his hands together, "On September 1, 1939, with Hitler's blitzkrieg, lightning-war invasion of Poland, the Germans showed Europe that Germany was no longer some National Socialist joke."

Would going to Majuro make me feel like a professional joke or make me feel like an important member of society?

"Hitler had decimated Poland in a mere month. And no one in Europe knew what would come next. Blitzkrieg succeeded: it created psychological shock throughout Europe like never seen before. See you next class." Will Hitler take over Europe? Will the West bring Hitler to justice? Tune in next time on *Days of Hitler's Life.*

Help Wanted, Desperately

As I'm packing up my bag, I suddenly realize how World War II is relevant to my life and my job search. Here I've been sitting on my ass doing nothing like the rest of Europe. Waiting for something, anything, to happen to me in the job department to spur me on to make my next move. But sitting around and waiting doesn't get anything done—hell, Hitler could've told you that. What I need is a lightning war. A blitzkrieg of my own to show all these employers out there that I'm not some whiny unemployed kid to be shoved aside—I'm a force to be contended with!

And that's when I decide my next tactical move in the job search. To avoid the holding pattern in Majuro, I am going to have to take strategic advice from Hitler. Were I to utter that sentence out loud, I would know that it is a bad idea. Fortunately, stupidity, unlike its told-ya-so partner hindsight, isn't 20/20.

So on January 1, I will launch the greatest employment offensive that the working world had ever known. It is time for blitzkrieg, baby.

It's hard to say what made me think to apply Hitler's military strategies to my personal career search. Sleeplessness? Possibly. Anxiety? Perhaps. Unrelated Jared jealousy and anxiety about what would happen if I gave up on trying to get a job I wanted and went to Majuro? Maybe. Desperation and fear of overlooking "my potential"? Absolutely.

There are a couple of reasons why I suddenly decided on the resume blitzkrieg, the most important of which being that the weekend before Professor Kidd's lecture on blitzkrieg, I had been at Nina and Brad's engagement party. Julie and I labeled the party "Ninafest," as if it were some amazing rock festival

171

rather than our aunts, uncles and cousins crowding around the newly engaged couple, new baby cousins, the buffet and the bathroom.

Though people claim that family events and get-togethers are times for family to catch up, in reality they're simply socially acceptable bloodbaths where various relatives from your extended family have the right and opportunity to make you feel paranoid and terrible about your pathetic and uncharted future so that they themselves can feel more successful. (Okay, maybe that's just me.) Anyway, Ninafest was no different.

There I was, standing on the buffet line, innocently picking up some more grilled vegetables, when the bloodbath began.

My great-uncle Jerry started it. "So, nu, how's Philadelphia?"

Delicately transferring a grilled pepper from a platter to my plate, I respond carefully, "Really good. How has Boca been lately?"

"Oh, you know, Boca's always terrific! So are you excited to be Nina's bridesmaid?"

Shuffling along through the buffet I shrug my shoulders, "I guess."

"And if you don't mind my asking, that handsome kid over there—that's your boyfriend, right? What's his name—Jeremy? So when are you two kids gonna get married? Your great-aunt Sophie—her memory is a blessing—she and I got married at twenty, right after the war!"

"So is there a dessert table at this buffet, you think?"

Uncle Jerry shook his head at me, waving a finger accusingly. "I know what you're doing, Alex. You can't fool Uncle Jerry! Next year we'll be at *your* wedding!"

Thankfully, Uncle Jerry spotted a baby who he felt the irrepressible need to pinch, thus freeing me from questions he was no doubt sent by my mother to ask.

Just as I was recovering from Jerry's invasion, one of my thirty-something cousins hit me with the question he knew would bring me down, downtown to Chinatown.

"So, I heard Jared's got his act together! I don't remember, did I meet him? Your mom can't stop talking about how great he is and how he has that fabulous job set up at the auction house. Your mom was talking about your going to law school? What's the plan, kid?"

He smiled pleasantly and put some Greek salad on his plate. My heart stopped. Checkmate. I'd been caught, ensnared, tricked through pleasantries into thinking that this might be a normal conversation. I writhed in the trap like a mouse with its feet stuck on the sticky poison paper that I had in my room in Philadelphia. As if in slow motion, the grilled eggplant on my plate rolled over and dropped to the floor.

Here I was, without eggplant, without a job, without an answer.

I thought about answering with "I'm actually waiting to become the voice of a cat on a TV show for cats; you have no idea how prestigious it is," but decided to skip it since it might be even more embarrassing later if he passed it along through the family and then I didn't even get the job. I gave up and went with the tried-and-true "I'm not sure yet." I thought about adding "I might go to Majuro so I can hide there, thus preventing everyone I know from thinking I'm a disappointment," but opted out in favor of the jovial, I-don't-care-that-people-will-think-I'm-unemployable laugh, complemented by a carefree smile.

Someone, please kill me.

Ariel Horn

* * *

Slowly but surely, the answer to the "Do you have a life?" question has devolved into "Whatever job wants me can have me." It gets a laugh and allows me a quick getaway: I don't have to tell the relatives that I am completely desperate and have no idea what I want to do with my life and have resorted to searching my nursery-school files and fortune cookies to determine my career. I don't have to tell them that in order to avoid their head-shaking disappointment at my inability to find employment, I'm planning on fleeing the country.

With my ambiguous "whatever job wants me can have me" answer, I can pick up the proverbial dropped eggplant strip and move on my merry way. If, of course, you ignore the fact that for the rest of the day I feel like a complete and total disappointment to all the people who expected more from me. But I guess at this point it's really just the backdrop to my life.

But with friends, the answer to the "What are you going to do in the 'Real World'?" question takes on a whole new tenor, depending on whom I'm talking to. For instance, when I happen to bump into any ex-boyfriend, my response is always something grandiose to make him feel small and pathetic, such as "I'm applying for a Rhodes scholarship, and I'm also training for a decathlon," or "I'm writing a nineteenth-century historical novel that draws from both Dante and Shakespeare. Oh, and P.S., I'm smarter, funnier, and prettier than when we dated."

When my high-school alumni committee e-mailed me asking for an "update" on my life for our class newsletter, I e-mailed them back: "It's been quite an exciting year for me. I spent the summer modeling in Kristiansand, Norway, and have spent the past six months establishing a literacy program for children in Ghana, geared toward developing their cognitive processes and teaching them about AIDS." Somehow, "Looking for a job, and worried I will never be happy with who I am while everyone else from our class instantaneously becomes successful, happy and rich" didn't sound as good.

It's very rare that I'll actually tell someone that I have no plan for my life, or even about Majuro at this point. That is, except my childhood friend Eric Gillers, whom I met at play group when I was six years old. As a child, Eric was always obsessed with He-Man in the usual six-year-old way. He would bring Skeletor to play group, and show me how Skeletor was different from He-Man, why Skeletor would never succeed in ultimately defeating He-Man. ("Because He-Man is so much better! He is MASTER of the Universe!") As I talked with Eric about why Barbie would never like He-Man, he taught me the ins and outs of the world of action figures and how to easily pop He-Man's head back on (the trick worked for Barbie too).

As Eric and I grew up, I grew out of my Barbies and my dollhouse and into more teenage interests: going to the mall, passing notes, learning how to drive, crying over boyfriends, slamming my bedroom door and talking on the phone for hours. Eric, however, remained in stasis. While other teenagers worried about getting into college, Eric, apparently, had bigger fish to fry.

One rainy day my senior year, I drove Eric home after high school. It was raining hard, and my 1986 wood-paneled yellow station wagon could hardly move its windshield wipers fast enough to let me see the road. Eric, realizing this, invited me into his house, for the first time since play group, until the rain let up and Wild Thang could take the road.

And that was when I saw it: an eighteen-year-old guy's room like none I had ever seen before. Where other eighteen-year-old guys had pictures of naked women posted up inside their closets, a computer screen saver of Heidi Klum, some school textbooks, maybe video games lining the walls, and a couple thousand CDs, Eric had nothing of the sort. His walls were lined with nothing but He-Mans (He-Men), preserved lifelessly in their plastic boxes.

Every inch of the room was covered with He-Man, Skeletor, and She-Ra paraphernalia. I looked at Eric's bed: He-Man sheets. I glanced at his computer: He-Man screen saver. And I looked in his closet and saw the worst of it: boxes upon boxes of even more He-Man figures—too many to fit on the wall space.

I was stunned.

Eric saw the look on my face, and began spewing out words in his defense, as if I had just discovered four hundred decapitated heads in his closet and bloody gloves to match on his desk. His rapid-fire responses made an effort to be casual. "I haven't cleaned my room in forever." "It's just an old collection." "I'm just too busy to clear this away."

But as I started to pick one of the He-Man figures off the wall, Eric ran across the room and smacked my hand away. "Don't touch that! Do you have any *idea* what that's worth? It's a discontinued model of He-Man from 1988!" Haven't cleared it away, huh, Eric? Indeed.

Eric finally admitted to me that the collection was not only new, but also growing by the minute. He did not just like He-Man. He loved He-Man with the very core of his being. As he rambled on about why He-Man was so great (it was kind of like we were both six again, except I wasn't stroking Barbie's hair), he finally got to the best part:

"And I know this sounds crazy, but what I really want to do with my life—God, I can't believe I'm telling you this—well, what I really want to do is to create and become the curator of the very first He-Man museum in the United States. It's actually what I'm writing my essay about for my Michigan application."

And that was when I proudly blurted it out to Eric. "I have no idea what I want to do with my life!"

Eric was a unique situation. His career goal was just pathetic enough that my failure to have a career goal seemed impressive by comparison.

Between responding to the "What are you doing with your life?" question from relatives and telling or not telling various people my age what I plan or don't plan on doing with my life, I've reached all-out desperation. And the fact that I am slowly starting to think that maybe Majuro would be good for me, that maybe I don't need to go to New York, that maybe I would love Majuro more than I would love any entry-level job in New York, has made me realize that I've reached an entirely new, unprecedented level of desperation. I've genuinely started to lose hope in myself. Hence, the blitzkrieg. But there is one more reason to plan my blitzkrieg right now.

When I was twelve years old, I saw a bumper sticker that said, "Today is the best day of your life." I found it kind of hokey but inspiring at the same time, in the way that only a twelve-year old could. I went home and wrote on an index card in black magic marker, "Alexa Hoffman, today is going to be the best day of your life!" Then I pasted the card next to my bed, so when I woke up in the morning, it would be the first thing that I saw (provided Nina didn't hold my nose to wake me up, which had been a trend at the time). So each day, when I woke up, I'd say out loud, "Alexa Hoffman, today is going to be the best day of your life." And then maybe it would work. That was the plan.

Granted, it never worked—I can't remember any of those days being the best of my life (especially that day in the eighth grade when I danced with the chubby unpopular kid at some middle-school dance and then he claimed we were dating). But when I got to college, I put the sign up again during my freshman and sophomore years, for old time's sake. Maybe the more you believed the day would be the best one of your life, the more likely it would come true.

But sophomore year, I had a bout with insomnia. I had simply forgotten how to sleep. Night after night, I would try to will myself to sleep, but I just couldn't do it. I took sleeping pills. I took Tylenol PM, and I even bought really terrible CDs that promised they would "lull me to sleep." (What they really did was make me pissed off any time I heard Pachelbel's *Canon in D*.) There was nothing I wouldn't do to bore myself to sleep: I read roommates' economics textbooks; I blindfolded myself with black tights; I cried on the phone to Jared, begging him to keep his eyes open just a minute longer to keep me company. I used earplugs; I recited all the lyrics to *Joseph and the Amazing Technicolor Dreamcoat* in my head. But to no avail. I just couldn't sleep. I was exhausted and horribly lonely at 4 A.M., night after night.

So on a cold March morning at 5 A.M., as I sat crying in my bed, bewailing the misery known as sleeplessness, I wiped the tears from my eyes and got out of bed. But first, I ripped the index card next to my bed off the wall and violently tore it to pieces. "Alexa Hoffman, today is going to be the best day of your life." My ass, it is. And that day, I checked myself into my school's counseling services. Surely there was something wrong with me: not only couldn't I sleep, but I also was living life by the mores of fortune-cookie and bumper-sticker wisdom. Maybe I could've solved my problems through other stickers, but somehow "Don't worry, be happy!," "Jesus saves!," "Vote Republican!," and "My Kid's an Honor Student at Ridgewood Elementary" didn't seem to come in handy. It was time for a professional.

My therapist, Sheila (who wore galoshes on sunny days), tried to explain to me that I couldn't sleep because I was depressed. I was having trouble at home. ("No.") Mad at my boyfriend? ("No.") Maybe I had an anxiety disorder? ("Possibly.") We worked on some breathing exercises that would allegedly help me sleep. Inhale for three seconds. Exhale. Inhale for three seconds. Exhale. Picture the air slowly entering your body and then leaving it. Inhale for three seconds. Exhale.

Eventually, I got so pissed at Sheila (who liked to exhaust all her energies giving me eating disorders, agoraphobia, and paranoia) that I spent all my time bitching about her to friends, and soon I completely forgot that I couldn't sleep. And I slept. Since then, I've decided I'm going to put the index card up again, since bumper-sticker wisdom back in the seventh grade proved more motivational than some woman off the streets wearing galoshes who fancied herself the next Sigmund Freud.

This is partially why the blitzkrieg has begun: I want to believe that each day can be the best day of my life, that each day isn't one day closer to Majuro but rather one day closer to possibility, employment, eternal happiness with who I am, and knowledge of what I really want in life.

Slap that one into a fortune cookie.

Also, I never want to see Galoshes Lady again, which is, I think, what will happen, since I've started to have trouble sleeping again.

Between answering relatives' questions on what I want to do with my life, knowing people like Eric's future plans, and putting this damn index card up again, I have no choice. It is as clear to me as it was to Hitler. There will be blitzkrieg. The surprise and speed of my resume dropping will be calculated to create psychological shock, and result in the disorganization of the enemy forces (read: human resources departments). No matter how nice the huts are in Majuro, I'm not giving in just yet. And I'm definitely not memorizing the Marshallese words for "I am your new teacher." Forget about writing my will or making a Death Folder.

This morning, I dropped over thirty resumes for positions including a commercial real-estate finance analyst, a consultant, assistant account executive, a project manager for a consulting firm, an investment banker, an editorial assistant, and park ranger with the City of New York Parks and Recreations Department.

Four months until I'm off to New York, *not* Majuro. The blitzkrieg has begun.

Lessons Learned

1. There is nothing sadder than an eighteen-year-old guy gushing about his lifelong passion to open the first He-Man museum in the world. Sad because it's He-Man. Sadder yet because it means he has a passion—however bizarre—and I don't.

Help Wanted, Desperately

2. Family gatherings that occur under the pretext of sharing in each other's joys are, in reality, no-holds-barred celebratory bloodbaths during which it's every misguided, cruel cousin for herself.

3. Imagining far-fetched analogies between Hitler's strategic wartime endeavors and your own life is probably both a recipe for disaster and a serious cry for help.

4. Never take advice from a woman who wears galoshes on sunny days.

5. If "today is going to be the best day of my life," I'm not setting my alarm for tomorrow.

10
From Texas With Love

3 Months, 17 Days, 22 hours, 10 minutes, 14 seconds

I should've known better than to model my strategic plan after Hitler.

Suffice it to say that the strategy is not going as expected: It's almost two weeks since my resume blitzkrieg began and all that's come of my lightning war is that the park-ranger people have informed me that there's a "hiring freeze." Adieu, cute little park-ranger outfit. Farewell, "Smokey the Bear" presentations. "Only *you* can prevent forest fires," indeed.

Understandably, the investment bank didn't want me either, as my "business" experience is basically limited to my ability to spell "business" properly without Spell Check (which is more than I can say for "hors d'oeuvres").

As I sit in my room, drowning in feelings of inferiority, I call my mother to bemoan my futureless state.

"Mom, I'm a useless member of society."

"You're only useless if you let yourself be."

"Would you tell me if you thought I was stupid?"

"You're not stupid, Alex—you're stupid if you think going to Majuro is going to solve your problems. They don't have rabbis in Majuro, Alex. I looked it up—you couldn't get married there. I don't even think they have a kosher caterer."

Horror of horrors.

"I can't even deal with talking about that now. Mom, do you know if you have to be employed first to get unemployment pay?"

"It doesn't matter—Jared will take care of you."

"Mom, do you think I'm a failure?"

"No, but you should be applying to law school right now."

Miraculously, as I hang up the phone, an e-mail arrives in my inbox. It's from a small consulting firm. They are (gasp!) willing to meet with me!

I check the e-mail address to make sure that it hasn't somehow been misdirected—sent to me by mistake, when some other worthier, more talented and skilled person was waiting for it. But lo and behold, it *is* my name in the address! This isn't some freakish accident, like what happened freshman year when my friend Matt sent me a pornographic e-card that he had meant to send to his girlfriend—this is deliberate! This e-mail is like a beacon of light spreading warmth all over my war-ravaged terrain. (That might be my overheated halogen, though.) I have triumphed. Victory. Sweet, delicious pre-interview victory. Look out, world! Alexa Hoffman is back in the game and ready to play ball!

Having never studied business except for two marketing courses in which I mainly focused on what I was going to eat for lunch, I know this interview will require more honest thought

than my usual bullshit. I figure I will have to study for this interview. Off to the bookstore I go, to hide in the aisles and read *The
Guide to the Case Interview.*

Question One. Brainteaser: "Why are manholes round?"

Oy.

Question Two. Guesstimate: "How many babies are born in
Japan per day?"

Double oy.

Question Three. Typical Case Question: "A shrimp farm we
work for has rapidly dropping profits. Why?"

Triple oy.

I'm not sure if I have a hard time answering these questions
because I'm stupid or because I'm lazy or because—for some in-
explicable reason, probably relating to a fear of ending up in Majuro—my brain no longer processes questions that don't have
direct relevance to my day-to-day life. Could be all three. Regardless, I study. And memorize how many people live in Los
Angeles (3.5 million). How many households there are in the
United States (100 million). How many people are connected to
the Internet in the United States (90 million). For kicks, I try to
find out how many people live in Majuro, but can't find an exact
number. Instead, I learn that unemployment in the Marshall Islands runs as high as 30 percent.

As I consider why a shrimp farm would be losing money, I
can't help but feel for a brief second that at least if I was on Majuro, I wouldn't have to bother myself with contemplating the
boom and bust cycle of crustacean creation. And if the unemployment rate in the Marshall Islands is 30 percent, well, I'd feel
right at home there! Perhaps I'm not the first person to consider
fleeing the country so that no one knows I'm unemployed.

After a week of mulling over crustacean reproduction, I think I'm ready.

Somehow, God willing, an excessive understanding of the economics of shrimp farming will help me in my interview.

Alternatively, I could just become a shrimp farmer myself.

I arrive in New York and find my way to the consulting firm. It's a new firm—about four years old, and the building is small, homey, quiet, and nondescript. So far, not intimidating. I can handle this. I am a mature, working woman. Except for the mature and working part.

The elevator takes me up to the sixth floor, where I enter a beautifully Zen lobby. Huge pink flowers in the corner, sitting in a vase of pristine water surrounded by smooth rocks. Inviting brown leather couches. A mahogany coffee table with issues of the *Wall Street Journal* carefully laid out.

As I'm admiring the environment, an overwhelming, overpowering, beanlike, split-pea-soup smell enters my nose. But, no. No soup could possess a heart-stopping smell as foul as this odor, so pungent I can feel it burning my retinas in the way that rotten hot salsa does when I eat it two weeks after its expiration date. (Not that that's ever happened before. Or happened more than twice, at least.) The smell nearly blinds me, and I try to slowly, casually back out of the lobby toward the door before anyone sees me. There's still a chance for one sweet breath of delicious and pure odorless air.

Surely no job is worth suffering like this.

As I back up toward the door like a caged animal suspecting imminent danger, a girl (the receptionist?) comes over to me and says, "Welcome! Are you Alexa Hoffman? Let me take your coat."

Help Wanted, Desperately

No time to inhale one last breath of unadulterated air. I am doomed. I will have to live in the stench. And smile. And appear comfortable in my new surroundings. I think back to Margaret Kilmore's guide to interviewing. I know how to sit, but I don't know how to ask for a surgical mask.

"My name is Ellen, and I'll be giving you the first interview. Then Yale will interview you next."

Whoa. Hold the phone, honey. Ellen looks about a year younger than me. She looks like a girl I knew from nursery school. Same big, dark eyes, same gummy smile with tiny white flecks that look more like Tic Tacs than teeth. And now my future is in her hands. And what kind of name is 'Yale'?

As we walk toward the interview room, Ellen explains, "Most of the consultants here are young, many of them, like myself, having just graduated college. I graduated from Princeton two years ago, and Yale, ironically, graduated from Cornell."

I briefly wonder if I should ask Ellen the consulting question that truly has no answer: Why would a well-established Fortune 500 company that has been run by business-schooled senior management for years upon years hire a bunch of recently graduated college students, most of whom were liberal arts majors, to solve their biggest financial problems? I refrain. Bad karma to insult the interviewer's job during the interview.

That and I really desperately want this to work out. Not because I want to be a consultant, really, but just because I want to want *something*. Anything. I want to want a particular job, to want a field, to feel like I belong somewhere. More than anything, I want to belong in New York, and prove to everyone that I've made it, that I can do it, that I can support myself in this city, no matter what everyone else says about my having to go to law school.

I wonder if Ellen has ever felt like this—if, when she walked down this hallway for an interview two or three years ago, she too had no idea what she wanted to do with her life. I doubt Majuro was in the picture, but did Ellen have a back-up plan?

We sit down, and Ellen and I chitchat about my experience at college. My favorite class ("The Life and Times of Oscar Wilde" may not have been the right answer. . .). Why I'm interested in business. Why I want to work at this particular consulting firm over any other. (I suppress the urge to respond, "Um, because no other consulting firms wanted to interview *me*.")

Ellen seems mildly interested, but I can tell we're just not meshing. I bet she flashes that vacant gummy smile at every interviewee. I want to shake her so those little Chiclet teeth fall out from her smug little mouth onto the table. I want to shake some humanity into this lifeless Tic-Tac-toothed girl, barely two years ahead of me. But there's nothing I can do.

"So, Alexa, it says here you've been a columnist for your university paper for two and half years . . . what was your favorite column?" Ellen looks at me expectantly, flashing her gummy smile again.

A descriptive question. I can shine here. I can really shine. This is gonna be my big break. I pause, and think about what I want to say. Part of me thinks, *Tell her about the time you wrote an editorial about how the opinion page needs to be fact-checked to maintain its journalistic integrity! Tell her about how you stood up for what you believe in! Tell her how you've used your column to shape university life! Do it, Alex, do it!*

But then the other, dumber (and therefore louder) voice inside my head seduces me. *Don't lie, Alex. Tell her which column was really your favorite. Lighten the load. Befriend her. Make her laugh. Show your personality!*

The obvious choice is my gut inclination, so naturally I decide to share the second (and incorrect) response. The amazing thing is that as I make that choice, I have a distinct and concrete understanding that I am about to say something that will be very stupid—that if I tell this certain story suggested by Voice Number Two, I will irretrievably ruin all possible chances of working here. But despite my better judgment, my cognition of my own stupidity, I can't help myself. I know I'm going to do the wrong thing. And in that split second before I open my mouth, I wonder if I'm doing this on purpose to myself—if this is my mind's way of telling me I really don't want this job, I really don't *deserve* this job, I don't belong here, this place isn't fit for me, and that maybe I should go to Majuro.

"Well, a lot of my columns are geared toward reaching out to the 'everyman' at our campus—I don't represent a minority, and I don't write about politics. I like to think that I provide that writerly soapbox for students about everyday college issues. As for my favorite column, well, it's a strange one, and I can't believe I'm going to talk about it at an interview, but . . ."

Right here, if there were a director in my day-to-day life—please send resumes and cover letters to the attention of Alexa Hoffman—he would shout, "CUT!" At that moment, I should've stopped, brainstormed, and done some sort of pre-emptive damage control. Because anyone knows that once the phrase, "I can't believe I'm going to talk about it at an interview but . . ." seeps from your lips, you really should just shut the hell up, no questions asked.

Great, a new "skill" to add to my resume: "Will speak against better judgment."

"I wrote a column for the first day of school my junior year, and it was about how people need to change their expectations. What I mean is that people need to realize that what they expect to happen at college might not happen. My column was about how people need to ignore their expectations and roll with the punches. But the way I wrote it was that I used an anecdote from my freshman year as a metaphor."

As that last sentence leaves my mouth, I realize I'm babbling and that Ellen really couldn't possibly be interested in this. As I watch her gummy smile melt into gummy boredom, I squint my eyes and try to make out what she's writing down about me—it either says "choc. milk" or "cropkeflog." Helpful.

"Long story short: It's the first night of my freshman year at college, and everyone is going to other people's rooms, introducing themselves, chatting about what classes they're taking, where they're from, etc. So I'm in one of these rooms with a group of people, and on the dresser I see a shower caddy, shampoo, perfume, notebooks. Not surprising, right? But then I see a blue thing that's shaking. I point to it and ask the girl who lives in the room, 'What's this?' She looks at everyone both amazed and repulsed by my clear stupidity, and says, 'Why, it's only the Magic Wand 2000!' I still look confused. And then she says, 'It's my VIBRATOR!'"

Oh

my

God.

I have just said the word *vibrator* at an interview. What the *hell* is wrong with me?

Help Wanted, Desperately

But what's this? Ellen is smiling. She's laughing! I've made this uncaring, lifeless Gummy Bear laugh! But is it a "this girl's an idiot" laugh or a "this girl's got panache" laugh? I squint to see what Ellen is writing down now. "Rupliggst."

"So basically, the column is about how you shouldn't live by your expectations. I mean, I never expected to hold a throbbing blue . . . thing in my hand."

Ellen is thinking of me right now holding a *throbbing blue phallus* in my hands. I officially need my foot surgically removed from my mouth.

"And the general point of the column is that you need to keep your mind open, don't expect things, and roll with the punches . . . or quake with the vibrations, I guess."

Ellen is done laughing. She writes something down and then mutters, "Interesting."

Interesting. Great. It's time for me to leave the office, stand in the middle of an intersection and wait for a car to hit me. Everyone knows that "interesting" is unsubtle interview code for: "I'm bored/there is something tragically wrong with your qualifications/we're not hiring you."

Regardless of the fact that Ellen clearly can't care less about me, she continues with the interview and goes on and on about different consulting jobs she's done. The smell of B.O. wafts through the room. I suppress a gag. What does Majuro smell like? Surely the salty sea breeze would be a beautiful smell to wake up to. Another gag. This does not bode well.

As Ellen drones on and on, I heave a big sigh—which Ellen unfortunately takes note of and writes down (if that's what "lormgak" means)—and I realize that what it boils down to is that I just have the wrong mind for consulting. I really don't care about

191

these consulting situations. I don't care about Internet business. I don't care about global expansion. There are a million other places I'd rather be, and right now, Majuro is actually one of them. I could see myself in a classroom, teaching children meaningful things that have nothing to do with globalization, profit sharing, competitive research and IPOs. I don't care about ROIs. I just don't care at all.

As I nod and smile at Ellen, I realize I want to leave the B.O. smell. I want to be anywhere in the world but in this room, in this consulting firm, with Ellen talking away about God knows what. What am I *doing* here? If this is the life I'm searching for in New York, do I even really want it anymore? What about Majuro isn't better than sitting in a dark, smelly office contemplating shrimp farming? I do not belong here in this pungent office, with this Zen furniture, these pink flowers and with Chiclets-toothed Ellen, Queen of the Employed.

Ellen looks at her watch, sighs what she had clearly hoped would be an inaudible sigh of relief, and wraps up our interview. "It was a pleasure meeting with you. I'll get Yale to come in and interview you next."

It seems cruel to continue an interview that I've already blown. But on the upside, it really couldn't get worse than this, could it? Note to self: When meeting Yale, do not mention vibrators or anything that can be described as "throbbing."

After Ellen leaves the room and before Yale enters, I allow myself one small, quiet, exhausted, terrified moan.

Yale walks into the room, and looks about a year older than me. "Hey, I'm Yale. What's up?"

Yale—uncomfortably trapped between boyhood and manhood—still has that skinniness of a seventh-grader that some men, even after graduating college, never seem to lose, along with a couple of zits on his forehead and what looks like the beginning of a balding pattern. I can tell just by the look of his face that Yale probably still goes home after work to play hours of video games.

Despite his clear desire to be maneuvering a joystick rather than talking to me, Yale is charming in the way that most unattractive and un-intimidating guys are. After glancing at my resume, he asks me casually about the NoteGoats, an a capella group I'm in, and admits readily and happily that just last year, he was in the "Treblemakers" before he graduated college. "It was awesome." I am bonding over college a capella with a prepubescent twenty-two-year-old who now holds my future in his hands. "Pathetic" has a whole new meaning.

"But now I'm working here, and seriously, I love it. It's great." As an aside, Yale adds conspiratorially, "Trust me, it's just as good as being in the Treblemakers."

Great to know that life outside of college a capella can compare.

"So I guess I kind of have 'the weird question' for you." Yale shifts in his seat and smiles at me. "And look, I don't expect, like, a really definitive answer, I just want to see how you think and how you reason. Sooooo . . ." Yale pauses for dramatic effect.

"How many haircutters are there in the United States?"

I really thought it couldn't get worse than with Ellen. There was no way. And yet now, here I am, sweating like a pig in heat as Yale stares at me expectantly, his pencil poised to write down the numerical gems which are expected to pop gracefully out of my mouth. Did I mention that my college level math course was entitled "Math for Poets"?

"That's an interesting question." Remain calm, Alex. Do not panic. "I guess there are about three hundred million Americans . . ."

"That's a good start," Yale smiles and his face lights up like a neon scoreboard. Hooray! In the video game occurring in Yale's mind right now, I've just scored one hundred points!

"And, let's see . . . Let's split the population down the middle into male and female."

"I like where you're going with this." Two hundred points!

"And then, um, well, here's a question: Do we consider people who cut their own hair to be haircutters, because in the literal sense, they do in fact cut hair, and are therefore haircutters. You know, if not in the professional sense, then, well, I mean, technically speaking, they are haircutters." Smooth, Alex. Buy some time.

"No. We don't consider people who cut hair privately to be haircutters.'" Minus fifty points.

"Okay, um, maybe I should do this a different way . . . There are about one hundred million households in the United States."

"Okay . . ." Yale doesn't look too convinced.

"No, really, there are one hundred million households in the United States." I read it in the consulting book!

"Okay, go on." No, no, Yale is not too convinced at all.

"And, um, well." It's time to pull out the bullshit here since I *really* have no idea what the hell I'm talking about. "So, let's say that every household has a couple haircutters. My family, for instance, has . . ." I calculate the haircutters in my mind—there's Jon and Carlos and Renata and—"oh, about four or five haircutters."

"Mm-hmm." I can almost hear my score going down in Yale's

mind. One hundred fifty . . . one hundred forty . . . one hundred thirty . . .

"So let's say then that there are fifty million haircutters so far by this estimate, the idea of there being two per household and then there being a lot of overlap, since, well, I mean, for me personally, I've had my hair cut in my lifetime by—oh, I don't know, let's see—probably over twenty or thirty people." Where exactly am I going with this?

"Where exactly are you going with this, Alexa?"

I open my mouth, to explain something, anything, but nothing at all comes out.

Yale cocks his head and writes something down, only looking at me to say, "Actually, I think we'll end the case right about here."

Yale writes down in big clear letters, "50,000,000 haircutters." GAME OVER.

NO! Stop, Yale! I wasn't done! Let me finish! I obviously was not saying that there are fifty million haircutters in the United States! Granted, my town at home has about eight haircutters per town resident, but still, I don't think there are really fifty million haircutters in the United States! I mean, that would be roughly one sixth of the population! And if I can never make an appointment with my haircutter at a reasonable time, that must mean she's busy constantly, which means there are *millions* less than fifty million haircutters in the United States! Yale, no! Let me finish! For the love of God and all things non-Majuro, let me finish!

Yale turns over his piece of paper where he was taking notes on my "reasoning" and says, "Alexa, let's stop here and talk about other approaches you might have taken."

And that's the nail in the coffin. Yale thinks that I think there are 50 million haircutters in the United States. And he will tell people who would consider hiring me at this consulting firm that I think there are 50 million haircutters in the United States. And then I will become the office joke.

Yale explains "other approaches to the problem," and my eyes glaze over as I tune him out and take a deep breath to make sure I still seem poised and confident, though Yale must now think I'm the dumbest person he ever met. The B.O. smell chokes me, and I feel tears welling up in my eyes. It's time to go home.

Naturally, Penn Station is a mess and I barely make my train. After walking though six cars, I finally find a seat and plop myself down between the window and a middle-aged, red-headed man with a mustache. I take my heels off (bought exclusively for the interview), put my hair into a ponytail, and stare out the window mindlessly. I'm a complete and utter failure, destined for a lifetime spent humiliating myself in important situations and dwelling for the rest of the time in sub-mediocrity on Majuro.

Rather than crying on the train, I decide to pick up my cell phone and call Jared, who had already told me he'd be too busy with some new-job orientation thing at Christie's to meet me for late lunch. Not that I'm bitter.

He picks up. "Hello?"

"I'm a failure, I don't know what I want to do with my life, and I'm going to die cold, poor, unsuccessful, and unemployed. In Majuro."

"So tell me really, Alex, how was *your* day?" Jared sounds

happier than usual, and I wonder if it's because his orientation went well.

"Please don't be a jerk . . ." I shift the cell phone, which has begun to grow uncomfortably hot, to my other ear, "I think I'm having a mental breakdown. I just royally fucked up that interview. It's almost like I'm *trying* to make myself fail. Maybe this is a sign that I should go to Majuro . . ."

"Alex, who knows? Maybe this job wasn't for you anyway. It's not like you ever had some burning desire to be a consultant. I mean, do you even *know* what a consultant does?"

"Sometimes it has something to do with shrimp farming, I don't know. Anyway, that's not important right now, Jared—the point is that everyone has their life set up. God has handed out futures to everyone except me. I mean, seriously," I shift my phone so that I can massage my temples, "The only thing I can do 'professionally' is mess up interviews. Jesus Christ, I told my interviewer about the vibrator thing!"

I can hear Jared's pained look on the other side of the phone. "Yeah, that's not good." Jared takes a breath, "Look, it may take a while, but you *will* get a job, I promise."

"Why, Jared? How can you make that kind of promise? Just because you got a job? Anyway, do you know about some job that I don't?"

"Well, sweets, I don't want to get your hopes up, but if you want to come to my apartment and clean it, I'd pay you like, oh, I don't know, six bucks an hour? That's a job! You could wear a little French maid's uniform and I could call you Monique . . ."

"You're a jerk."

"Gimme a minute. I'm thinking about you in a French maid's uniform . . ."

"JARED."

"Okay, seriously, you need to relax about this . . . You're a mess. It's unhealthy. It's not normal to get this upset about an interview."

"*I'm* not normal. 'Normal' people do not intentionally talk about vibrators in interviews. And this isn't about an interview: This is my life. This is me resigning myself to the fact that in about three months, I'm going to Majuro. I surrender. HR wins, I lose. Here's me waving my white flag—whee!" I wave my imaginary white flag through the air.

"Oh, Alex. Listen, all joking aside, you're going to find something. I *know* you will. And who knows, maybe you *should* go to Majuro. What's not good about Majuro?"

Has Jared gone mad and completely missed my life for the past four months? I mean, even Diego, the security guard at the convenience store, knows about Majuro by now. "Jared, Majuro's the holding pattern, remember? It's not the goal . . . It's the detour on the *way* to goal."

"Right, whatever. Well, I'm just saying, you never know. Anyway, wanna know how *my* day was? Or are you not interested?"

Selfish, self-consumed girlfriend at your service. "Right! I'm completely interested! I totally forgot—how'd it go? How was orientation? How're the people? What's the office like?" Nothing like a little self-pity and self-loathing to make you realize what a terrible girlfriend you are.

I can hear how happy Jared is through the cell phone, and in that second I realize how horrible I've been to him—how impossibly selfish it is that I've been secretly jealous because he got the job he really wanted, he's moving on with his life when I'm just sitting here in eternal stasis. I love that he got what he wanted, and I love that it makes him so happy. For the first time all day, I feel a smile creep through my self-hatred. I love him. And I love that he's somehow been able to see past my neuroses well enough to love me back.

"It was amazing, actually," Jared's voice starts to rush, his words tripping over each other, and I can tell he's excited in a way he hasn't been in a while, which makes me smile even more, "We met all these specialists—there's a guy who focuses on Old Masters paintings, and he's just ridiculously smart, and he talked to us about acquisition and all that. Oh, and then there was this woman who works exclusively in trusts and estates, which was a little morbid, but she says she's been all over the world to these rich, dead people's apartments and appraises their art, and then the auction process begins. Once they found this Van Gogh sketch in some woman's apartment and it was just crinkled at the bottom of some closet under a pair of shoes, can you believe that? I mean, what kind of person—"

Hearing Jared so happy, I can't help but feel even more in love with him than usual, and more appreciative than ever of how passionate he is, how he remembers every tiny detail of everything. Interrupting him, I offer, "God, it's just so good to hear your voice and hear you so happy. I really love you, you know that?"

Jared, too involved in his story to have a romantic moment, continues, "Yeah, me too. Anyway, you'll never guess who else is working there!"

Jokingly, I say, "Oh, did you get me a position?" No, seriously, did Jared get me a position? Did Jared get me my Get-Out-Of-Majuro-Free-Without-Losing-Self-Respect card? Praise GOD, I knew I had the best boyfriend in the world.

"*Lyric* was there! How crazy is *that*? What are the odds, right?"

Slowly, Jared's words begin to register with me and my smile instantly dissolves. Quietly and calmly I ask, "Lyric as in 'Lyric, your ex-girlfriend'? Or Lyric as in 'new person named Lyric, whose name is as stupid as your ex-girlfriend's'?" Seriously, what *were* the odds that Lyric—whom Jared dated for a year—would be working there? If the nation is made up of 50 million haircutters, the odds are pretty slim. Lyric should be a barber.

"Oh, Alex, give me a break. Anyway, I think Lyric is a nice name. And you never met her—she's nice."

Slowly I respond, "Lyric is a dumb name. What's her middle name, 'Limerick'? 'Sonnet'?"

I can hear Jared roll his eyes, "Anyway, yeah, so she was there, and it was really good to see her. She looked pretty good, you know, a little thinner than the last time I saw her."

Kill me now. My boyfriend's ex-girlfriend has lost weight.

"Well, she was pretty skinny in those glossy pictures I've seen of her." *You know, Jared, those two wrinkled pictures of her at the bottom of your closet that I desperately want you to throw out?*

"Well, they always airbrush those comp cards anyway."

Lest we forget that Lyric was a model. Wouldn't want that to slip my mind.

As my neurotic barometer begins to skyrocket, I try to sound interested in the fact that this weight-losing, gorgeous girl Jared amicably broke up with three years ago is suddenly back in the picture, working conveniently one cubicle over. Breathing deeply to calm myself, I slowly ask, "Doesn't Lyric want to model anymore?" *Because I really care about her career.*

"Alex, it's not like she was making some huge career out of modeling or anything. She was a hand model for some nail polish company. That was it."

"Yeah, I agree, she totally looks like an alien. She has these buggy weird eyes and she sort of looks like a big potato too . . ." You know, if potatoes look like leggy, green-eyed redheads, then yeah, she looks like a big potato.

"Who said she looks like an alien? And a potato? I think she's pretty, and she looked good," *Yes, thank you, that's the second time you've told me your ex-girlfriend looks good.* "She really wanted to be a yoga instructor, you know, 'cause she was always really into yoga and organic stuff." *Glad to hear my boyfriend's ex-girlfriend was flexible.* "But then her dad knew someone at Christie's who got her this job. Amazing, right?"

"That's one word for it." I apply to every job within a twenty-mile radius of New York City for four months and get nothing. Twiggy the Hand Model asks her dad for a break from yoga and ends up at Christie's. Lovely.

A pause.

"Alex, what's wrong?"

"Nothing, I'm glad you had a fun day with your little alien ex-girlfriend. I'm so thrilled you'll be working with Lyric, though I mean, you'll have less of her to work with, what with her losing weight and all. And hey, I'm glad to hear she's into yoga. I'm sure you guys had a lot of good times together. Good ol' lotus position." No job, no life, and now a boyfriend working with his fantastic hand-model, yoga-fetishist ex-girlfriend. It's almost worth going to Majuro now. For permanent self-imposed exile.

"Alex, don't tell me you're jealous? Come on, I haven't seen her in two years!"

"How lovely that you two could meet up again."

"Oh Jesus Christ, Alex. You've got to be kidding me. You're a billion times more beautiful than her, a trillion times sexier, smarter, and funnier . . . Don't make me do this. Anyway, all she really cares about is yoga and her hands! And hey, she's a potato, remember? An alien? Perhaps even a troll?" I can hear Jared trying to cheer me up, but it's not taking, and I can't fight the sick feeling in my stomach that this is it, that this is how it's supposed to end, that I'm supposed to head off to Majuro so that Jared can live happily ever after in Organic Yoga World with Lyric, the Ever-Thinning Potato.

"Alex, gimme a break. When did having a conversation become a crime?"

"Great," I mutter, "have some great 'conversations' with her. For someone who didn't 'commit a crime,' you're pretty damn defensive."

"Can't you just be happy for me that I had a great day? That I'm doing something I'm proud of?"

" 'Doing something' you're proud of. As opposed to 'doing someone.' Save that one for next week's orientation with Lyric . . ."

"All right, Alex, this is fucking ridiculous! How can you *talk* to me like that?" Jared's voice gets louder, and I can tell the man next to me on the train can hear Jared yelling. "Alex, I can't do this, I can't *be* with you if you're going to be like this. All day I was waiting for you to be out of your interview, for you to call, so I could talk to you. All I wanted was to hear your voice, to tell you how happy I am, about the job, everything. And then you're so selfish you can't even be happy for me!"

My cell phone grows hotter against my ear, and I feel myself filling with fury as Jared continues, "And this obsession with Lyric, I don't know where the hell that's coming from, but I don't want to be a part of it, and Jesus Christ, if you can't realize yourself what I see in you that's so incredible, then fuck it. It's not worth it. Be miserable by yourself, dwelling on some loser ex-girlfriend of mine. And you know what? *Go* to Majuro, see if I care—"

"Jared, you don't mean that—"

"Because if you're going to be like this when you come to New York, shit, I don't think I can handle it. I love you, and you know that, but if you can't get a grip on reality and throw your fucking insecurities out the window—about Lyric, about your job, about your *life*—then there's just no way that it can work out between us. Period."

I can feel the tears welling up, and the lump in my throat getting bigger. My head feels hot against my phone, and suddenly I'm furious. Incapable of turning my anger into words, I lamely sputter out, "Have fun with Lyric, Jared. Rekindle your lost organic love. I'm sure you two will have great yoga-sex."

And that's when my cell phone battery goes dead.

Jared is gone and I'm left alone listening to the void, staring out the window blankly, listening to the empty silence of my cell phone. I'm so drained of emotion that I can't even muster up the energy to cry. Useless phone in hand, I just silently look out the window, watching the parking lots, playgrounds, backyard jungle gyms, and houses of successful people pass by. I close my eyes and pretend this isn't happening. That I'm not sitting alone on some dark train back to Philadelphia after the worst conversation I've ever had with Jared in my life, after a terrible interview, back to my friends who will ask how the interview went, back to acquaintances who ask what I'm doing next year and get no sufficient response. Back to my mother's voice asking when Jared is going to propose, when I'm not even sure if we're dating anymore. Majuro has to be better than this. I'd rather move seven thousand miles away to dwell in my own inadequacy as a person than spend the next three months trying (pointlessly) to find out who that person really is.

As schools, American flags, highways and mini-malls rush past my window, I try to stop myself from quietly sobbing. As I wipe my nose on my suit sleeve, I realize I'm ready to go to Majuro. I don't want to be here. I don't want to be myself. I don't want to be anything, or anyone.

My shoulders stop shaking as I take deep breaths, trying to get a hold of myself as I sit hoping that something will happen that will give me hope again, something will make me proud of who I am again, all I know I have to offer, and inspire me to get rid of my gloom-and-doom attitude that repulses Jared—and me too. That something will happen that will inspire me to look for a job I want rather than a job I think I should want. That something will make me realize *what* I want. To stop judging my self-worth based on some interview about haircutters. To stop interpreting job callbacks as in any way indicative of my value as a person.

I look at the fluorescent clock on my neighbor's cell phone. 5:55. I remember that when I was eight I would make wishes any time the clock had one number all the way across. I sigh and mutter to myself, "I wish Jared didn't hate me . . . and I wish I knew how to get a job." If only I had a job, none of this—with Jared, with me, with Majuro—would ever have happened. I'd be happy with who I am. There would be no self-loathing, no jealousy, no selfishness.

Help Wanted, Desperately

Seemingly out of nowhere, a thick Texan voice booms, "First job, huh? Couldn't help but overhear your conversation on the phone."

God is a Texan?

"Hey." The redheaded man sitting next to me pours some gin into his ginger ale.

"Um, yeah." I try to look as uninterested as possible, and I stare blankly out the window in an effort to end this conversation before it begins.

The Texan doesn't pick up on my disinterest. "Well, I'll tell you something. When I graduated college with a technical degree from some know-nothin' university you wouldn't even know nothin' about, I had no *idea* what I wanted to do with my life." Big Red lifts his plastic cup in the air, swirls the drink around and takes a big swig.

"Oh?" I keep staring out the window. *Like I could give a shit, creepy, eavesdropping asshole.*

"So I mowed lawns for three months after college. You know, to get my head together. And then, I made my own company that doesn't have nothin' to do with my technical degree or lawn mowing. I just said to myself, I like money, I want to make lots of it! Ha! So I started my own financial company. I invest. Then I married my high school sweetheart. And I just retired as the CEO of my own multimillion-dollar company today. Just this afternoon, as a matter of fact. What do you think of that?"

"That's great." Nothing helps depression and musings on your own mediocrity like hearing other people's success stories. I continue to look out the window, ignoring him.

"Look, today is your lucky day. Not only am I the CEO of my own company, I'm also a motivational speaker."

Of all the trains in the United States, of all the seats on the train, this motivational speaker had to be sitting next to me. All "logic" would have pointed toward my sitting next to a haircutter. Or a skinny organic yoga instructor. But no. My fairy godmother is a ruddy-faced, rough-and-tumble Texan. How did my life turn into this?

"I'm going to help you get a job, little lady." Big Red wipes his mustache, takes another swig of his drink, and points to his gold watch. "This is a real Rolex, you know. And I didn't get it by fooling around with stupid little jobs I didn't want."

He pulls out a legal pad and begins to draw me a graph. I cannot believe I am sitting next to this drunken version of Howdy Doody, and I'm having an even harder time believing that he is actually attempting to map out my life as we speak. "This here is a ten-year spectrum. See? Where do you want to be in three years? In five years? In ten years? We're gonna make benchmarks on our little spectrum. Let's set five-year goals. Hell, Russia did it! But what do *you* want? A certain salary? A certain job? A certain man?" Big Red winks at me, "A certain lifestyle? Where do *you* want to be in five years from now, huh?" Big Red puts down his Mont Blanc pen and mixes another drink for himself.

"I, uh . . . I don't know. That's sort of my problem."

Big Red swallows and booms, "That's not an answer, now is it? What do *you* want out of life? You've got to have some goals!" He starts pounding his ruddy fists against the armrest. "There's gotta be *something* you want!"

"I, I guess I just want to be happy with my life, in my job . . . to find something that's interesting, helps people, and that pays well."

"That's not an answer either! Stop with the BS, already! What're you, an English major or something?"

"Well, yeah."

"Whoo-boy, you got even more problems, then! Ha! You can take that to a shrink! But what do *you* want out of *life*?" Big Red stares me straight in the eye.

Frustrated more with myself than him, I blurt out (in a voice usually reserved for my parents when I'm on the brink of a breakdown): "I don't know! That's my problem! I don't know! I could be anything—I could be a teacher, a singer, an actress, a consultant, a retailer, a, an an ANYTHING!"

"Huh! Then you've got bigger problems than I can help you with."

"Thanks. Very 'motivational.'"

"What you need is some direction! How can you drive to your destination when you don't even have a road map! You're not going to have the requisite *skills* to get there! You gotta do some soul-searching. You've got to look into yourself, find what you want to do. And then set milestones. And get there." Big Red takes a final gulp of his drink.

"PHILADELPHIA, NEXT STOP!" The conductor takes my ticket.

"This is my stop. Thanks . . . for . . . yeah."

"Remember: milestones! You'll get there!"

My mind still reeling from my conversation with Jared and Big Red's unsolicited "advice," I get home and order Chinese food, and then lock myself in my room, ignoring my housemates' knocks, the phone, my e-mail inbox. I check my voice mail repeatedly to see if Jared's called: he hasn't. By 2 A.M. I give up and assume he'll just never call me, ever again, and that that's the way it's going to be. At 2:01, I call him and get his voice mail. I don't leave a message, and just quickly hang up the phone. Why the hell should he love me anyway? Maybe Majuro is for the best.

As I wallow in the idea that the best two years of my life were because of Jared, and now I'm loveless and futureless with only the soggy, brown-sauced-covered vegetables in my Buddha's Delight Number 9 order to give me solace, a fortune cookie seems to jump out of the brown paper bag. An omen from God. (Or from the Chinese restaurant.)

I shove my leftover vegetables to the side and open the cookie that will give me the key to solving all my life's problems: from Jared to joblessness to jealousy to insecurity, all the way to Majuro and back. As the cookie's yellow shell breaks into stale, inedible pieces, my future will be revealed.

A freak fortune cookie! Not one fortune, but two! Double luck!

The first one: "You will learn something of infinite value today." I'm selfish, I'm insecure, I'm unlovable. There. Oh, and that there are *not* 50 million haircutters in the United States.

The second fortune jeers at me. "You are almost there."

If only I knew where "there" was and how the hell I would find it.

Lessons Learned

1. When selecting a seat on a train, avoid the one next to the guy who looks like a drunken Howdy Doody.

2. If there actually were 50 million haircutters in the United

Help Wanted, Desperately

States, I should at least be able to find one who can give me a decent, well-priced haircut.

3. Never, under any circumstance, mention the words *vibrator, phallus,* or *throbbing* in an interview.

4. Being weird makes me lovable. Being selfish and insecure does not.

11
Baby's Gonna
Be a Star!

3 Months, 14 Days, 10 Hours

The past week has been full of self-realization. I realized three days ago that I've been a selfish, terrible friend/girlfriend/human: jealous, self-obsessed, depressed, insecure, uncaring. Jared hasn't called in three days and I really don't blame him. I'm not sure he'll ever talk to me again, and I'm not sure he's so wrong about that. When my mother calls asking why I haven't been talking about Jared, that's when the tears really come. And make no mistake—it is no drizzle. It is monsoon season.

So for the past 72 hours, I've exclusively eaten egg rolls for breakfast, lunch, and dinner, as if binging on obscene amounts of Chinese food is some sort of normal mourning ritual over lost love (and profound idiocy). Not only that, but I've even sunk to the level of buying an entire bag of fortune cookies. Last night, unable to sleep at 3 A.M., consumed by the kind of spacey delirium associated only with insomnia and broken hearts, I decided I'd write my own fortunes and then neatly tuck them into the cookies using my tweezers. Initially, I started writing fortunes geared toward my own personality, just to pass the time, including: "Grow up already," "A loser is not made; she is only sustained," and "Happiness is the greatest revenge on enemies from high school, college and beyond." Somewhere around 3:45 A.M., just as I had come up with another gem ("Suck it up, admit failure, and go to Majuro already"), I realized that creating my own fortunes for fortune cookies could be the love poem to Jared that I never knew how to write. The apology I desperately owed him, but couldn't phrase.

Frantically, I began writing new fortunes geared toward Jared to fill my cookies:

"I'm an idiot. Period." "I don't care about Lyric, I'm sorry I was cruel, I'm sorry I made you feel like you weren't loved." "I'm sorry I didn't sound more excited for you on the phone." "I'm sorry I didn't show you how much I love you when you needed to be loved and appreciated more than anything." "And worst of all, I'm sorry I made you feel like I didn't care when you are what I care about most in this world." "I'm sorry I didn't say all this then, when you and I both needed to hear it." "I'm sorry. For everything."

At 6 A.M., in a blissful moment of delirious exhaustion, I realized I was happy for the first time in what felt like months. I was doing something important, something worthwhile, something that would increase the happiness in the world (maybe), if only for a second.

Then the cookies were off to New York, and I was off to my bed to sleep off my exhaustion, to dream that Jared would get the cookies and then somehow, maybe, possibly, perhaps at least think of talking to me again.

Help Wanted, Desperately

That was moment number one of self-realization.

The other moment came just before I was working on the fortune cookies, as I sat in my bedroom staring at the ceiling, wondering what the hell went wrong with my job search. Why was Majuro suddenly becoming more appealing by the second?

That was when I realized, in a terrible moment of self-awareness, that I'm looking for jobs that won't necessarily make me happy, but will just be "time-fillers." That these jobs that I seem to "really want" (consultant, retail buyer, earthworm breeder etc.) will in the end just be places where I can spend my time in between weekends that will provide:

1. the comfort of a paycheck;
2. a life outside of Majuro;
3. the luxury of a speedy Internet connection, with which I will presumably check my e-mail four hundred times a day, only to find out that most of my friends are similarly bored at their jobs.

Maybe I could get free fancy pens, but that's about it.

It was time for me to face the "you're on hold" Muzak: the way my job search was going, I wasn't really getting closer to the sneeze-guarded, candy-coated American dream I had assumed would be waiting for me in New York.

It is a terrible, terrible thing to anticipate a future of bland-tasting mediocrity, whether in New York or Majuro. It's almost as bad as agonizing over the idea that your future—whatever it may be—may have been unintentionally ruined because you've made yourself completely and totally unlovable to the people you love most. On top of the idea that you have the potential to be a disappointment to everyone who knows you, it's almost enough to kill you. Almost.

As I sat in my room staring out the window, thinking about whether I should call Jared or not (and also thinking about different strategies to stop my mother from calling me *about* Jared), I realized that in the past, I hadn't resigned myself to searching for passionless gruntwork jobs.

In the past, I had a dream. And I might still have a dream.

In fact, up until this very point in my life (three months, fourteen days and ten hours until Majuro), I've been quite certain I was going to end up in show business. And it's not just because of my stellar performance in a fourth-grade play as Tree #4, my Academy-Award-Winning stint as Chorus Girl #37 in a high-school performance of *Carousel*, or even my tear-jerking performance in my second-grade "December Holidays" play as Latke #8. (To my credit, though, that wintry morning I mustered up all the dynamo my little eight-year-old heart had to give and performed one of the most heart-wrenching interpretations of a latke that Hartshorn Elementary had ever seen.)

Of course, I think most people would be just as shocked as I am that I'm not some famous, fabulously wealthy actress by now.

That being said, perhaps all these people who rejected me for leads in school plays in the past were simply blinded by their overwhelming jealousy, unwilling to let themselves see my incredible potential. Yes—that was it. I would not give up my dream. I was going to act. I just didn't know how. Amidst the unbearable loneliness of Jared's absence in my life, I embarked on a new journey into stardom. I was sure this was when I was going to make it.

Help Wanted, Desperately

* * *

Without Jared to talk to, I suddenly found myself with a lot of spare time. No midnight phone calls, no e-mailing back and forth, no weekend trips to New York, nothing. Until yesterday, I had been keeping myself busy writing new fortunes in my head. As I came up with another winner—one that I think I could give to about thirty or forty people I know ("Get over yourself, you pompous bastard")—I got a call from *More Style* magazine, the New-York-based fashion magazine that I had worked for last summer. They were doing a feature called "Phun in Philly," and had rented out space in some office building downtown to start working on the cover story. They knew I lived in Philadelphia and asked if I would come help them with their "huge" feature, doing important internly stuff for them for a week or so, like stapling things and xeroxing. (It takes a village to collate.) Granted, they didn't want to hire me for a real job in New York. So in a moment of sad loneliness, I said yes, yes, I would come in to do their filing and faxing.

I worked at *More Style* this past summer not because I have some passionate drive for "celebrating the winter in fluffy angora" or "putting the 'Oh!' back in orgasm," or even "finding eight easy ways to more toned abs," but because I had applied to a large magazine company for an internship, and instead of placing me at one of my top three choices, I was instead shoved into working at *More Style* magazine, since "my past experiences showed a real interest in women's magazines." The truth of the matter was that the same thing had happened the year before at another magazine conglomerate, where I had similarly been randomly placed into an internship at *Style* magazine, which then labeled me on my resume as someone "passionate about fashion."

Ariel Horn

It was like there was some sort of conspiracy against me in the magazine world: I was eternally doomed to work at fashion magazines, surrounded by twenty- and thirty-something women named Jasmine, Sky, and Tenanya who ignored my presence to talk to each other about how they would con their relatively overweight and slightly balding boyfriends (believe me, they had about four hundred pictures each per cubicle) into proposing to them. The good thing was that they didn't really care what I did, so long as I seemed like I was doing something "productive" (read: re-alphabetizing their Rolodexes) and didn't make them look bad. And that was exactly what I was expected to do when I came into the Philadelphia office.

So yesterday, I sat in my cubicle at *More Style*'s new Philadelphia office, hoping that someone would perhaps give me something interesting to research. (My research assignment last summer, to "find out which celebrities of the 1940s loved horses," would be difficult to beat.) I had grown accustomed to checking my e-mail about thirty-five times an hour, praying that maybe, just maybe, one of the many writers or editors I had e-mailed requesting—nay, begging for—an assignment would respond with something exciting for me to do (and cleaning the promotional gift closet, an "assignment" I had received several times, didn't count). Without Jared to e-mail, the day felt endless, and more often than not, there was nothing in my inbox, not from him, not from any writers, not from anyone.

Naturally, no one at *More Style* wanted my help. Story of my life: They invite me in to do nothing.

But as I was about to shut the e-mail program, a message popped up: its subject line was marked "Urgent" and it was from my sister Julie. The text was cryptic: "Call me ASAP." Hooray! Something to do! As I reached for the phone to call her, it rang.

"Hello, this is Intern Number Three." (The lowly interns were not allowed to answer the phone by saying our names; we were only to say our number. More like "internment" than "internship.")

Telepathy—it was Julie. "I can't believe they make you answer the phone like that. That's ridiculous."

I agreed, and then started singing my soulful rendition of a song from *Joseph and the Amazing Technicolor Dreamcoat*, soliciting more than a few bizarre looks from the Jasmines and Tenanyas surrounding me. "Just give me a number, instead of my *naaaaaame* . . . forget all about *meeeeeee* and let me *decaaaaay*! I do not matter; I'm—"

Julie interrupted my dramatic interlude, sounding concerned, "Alex, are you okay?"

"Yeah, I guess. I mean, considering that Jared doesn't ever want to talk to me again, considering that I genuinely think I'm going to go to Majuro in about three months, considering I no longer believe I can even get a job in New York that I might like. Oh yeah, all things considered, I'm just fantastic."

I resumed singing and Julie interrupted. "Okay, as much as I'm enjoying this, I have really cool news to tell you—so listen.

"I just read in the *Village Voice* online that there are open-call auditions for *Rent* tomorrow—we've GOT to go! Look, I won't go to work tomorrow morning, and we'll both go audition, okay?" No-nonsense corporate lawyer by day, zesty diva by night. Runs in the family. "Look, I've got to go, but let's meet tomorrow morning at Church and Leonard at six thirtyish. That means you have to take a, I don't know, like a five A.M. train. But the line is going to be *insane* and we need to get there early. Try to look bohemian hip, okay? Oh, speaking of 'bohemian hip,' did you hear that Nina wants us to wear 'eggplant'-colored brides-maid dresses? Shit—I gotta go. Talk to you later. Love you."

She hung up the phone, leaving me only with the vision of my-self standing onstage in an eggplant-colored dress with thou-sands of audience members throwing rose petals at my feet. "Bravo!" "Encore!" "Thank you, thank you, no, really, it's too much." Who needs Majuro when you've got fame?

And with that, Sky jolted me out of my blissful reverie. "Like, could you fax this for me?"

At that moment, as I faxed out sheets detailing what kinds of paper clips the office needed, I really and truly believed I would be a star.

At 5 A.M. I can barely believe I'm awake, let alone going to New York to audition for Broadway when I have no theatrical experi-ence whatsoever. I also can't believe I'm going to New York—only blocks from where Jared lives downtown—and he won't even know that I'm there, since he never picks up his phone and I'm too nervous and sad to leave a coherent message (but not for lack of trying).

The train pulls into Penn Station, and I hop into a cab which speeds south and drops me off on the corner of Church and Leonard, right outside the club where the talent agency is hold-ing their open-call auditions. I chose my outfit carefully this morning to make myself look "bohemian hip," as Julie sug-gested: dirty green cargo pants, a tight white tanktop, a beaded necklace, and a bandana in my hair. At the last minute, I contemplated putting in a fake nose ring, but thought that might be pushing it, even for a "bitchin' punk" like myself (it's my new professional title).

But the second I step out of the cab (oh God, how tragically unhip of me to take a taxi), I realize immediately that my attempt at bohemian chic is a total and utter failure: The hundreds of teenagers and twenty-somethings ahead of me on line ("we camped out all night!") are wearing combat boots, electric blue pleather pants, eyebrow piercings, tight skirts and tighter rhinestone-studded shirts emblazoned with words like "Slut" and "Cowgirl." I look down at my own outfit: pathetic. In contrast, I look like I came out of a Banana Republic ad from 1987. Actually, I think my pants *are* Banana Republic 1987.

I mentally lament the fact that I am unalterably unhip, and that's when Julie shows up. I'm relieved: her attempt to be bohemian is just as miserable as mine: she's dressed in Gap clothes from 1994.

Julie kisses me and then tilts her head as she looks at my face with the same critical scrutiny I'm really only used to receiving from our mother. She squints and focuses on the bags under my eyes. "You look exhausted, Alex. Are you eating? Okay, better question: Are you eating anything other than Chinese food? I mean, Nina's starving herself for the wedding, it's ridiculous, you should see her. I think she wants to have one of her ribs removed or something—Dad was telling me about it last night, how Nina was asking him if he thought rib removal was covered by health insurance. Anyway, is this about Jared?" Julie's face softens and she gently slides her arm around my waist. "Mom was telling me everything—I'm so sorry."

Nothing quite like motherly confidentiality. "Yeah, well," I concentrate very closely on a crack in the sidewalk, avoiding Julie's concerned look.

"Fine, we don't have to talk about it now, but you should talk about it with *someone* at least. Me, or Mom, or even Nina. Okay, not Nina. Anyway, did you bring your resume and your head-shot like I e-mailed you?"

"If 'headshot' means that normal picture of me from vacation, then yes, I brought my 'headshot.' "

Several bohemian hipsters behind us compare their resumes, which hardly resemble mine or Julie's. One of the girls talking has the most perfect stomach I have ever seen (navel pierced, of course), and I can see it well since she's just wearing a black rhinestone-studded leather bra and low hip-huggers which just about expose her pubic hair (Brazilian wax, of course). "So, after I was the understudy for Eponine in *Les Mis*, well, like, it was really hard to just settle for doing something as kitschy as *Lion King,* you know?"

"Jen," replies her flamboyantly gay male friend wearing tighter hip huggers than Jen herself, "You are just SUCH an amazing dancer! Honey, it's a CRIME you didn't do *Lion King!*"

Jen twirls her perfectly straight black hair around her fingers and then says, "Jesse, you KNOW that I changed my name to Gwenyvere! So stop calling me Jen! It's so . . . ugh, SUBUR-BAN!" Jen—nay, Gwen—looks pissed. I squint my eyes and peek at her resume: her address is in Tenafly, New Jersey. "What-EVER. I need to do my warmups."

As Gwen starts warming up (read: adjusting her leather bra to show more cleavage), Julie and I look at each other, stunned. For the first time in our lives, we have no words. For the first time in three days, I've momentarily almost forgotten about what happened with me and Jared. Almost. Then I start to wonder about what Lyric the Thinning Potato looks like now until Julie stops me by filling me in on all the Nina-related wedding chaos I've tried to avoid for the past three days.

After about four hours waiting for the line to inch forward on the sidewalk (and four hours of hearing Gwen and Jesse discuss the benefits of having a cock ring), we make it to the front of the line. Spiky-pink-haired line-mate Colin points out that we're close enough to the door to peek into some girl's audition. The girl, wearing jeans that are ripped right around the crotch, stiletto boots, and a tube top that would barely cover my wrist, rocks out on the song "Heartbreaker," touching her breasts as she dramatically falls to her knees, throwing her head back and forth as she gyrates like a hooker in heat. Julie and I look at each other in awe.

I don't think I've ever seen Julie gyrate.

Would I ever find myself in a situation where I'd need to gyrate in Majuro?

By the time we make it to the front of the line, a relatively normal-looking man (by comparison) from the talent agency separates Julie and me. "You, Blondie, go to the room downstairs. And your friend—upstairs." We part.

I wait outside my audition room and whisper nervously to my fellow auditionee/new best friend Colin, "I'm scared." Colin doesn't care—he's too busy adjusting his nipple pierces so that they're even. (Uneven nipples affect the likelihood of employment in all fields and industries.) Though Colin ignores me, a girl on line with me smacks my shoulder and says, "Girl! You shut up! Shut up! You got to *believe* in yo'self! Remember this moment here, now. This is what it's aBOUT! *Believe*, girl!"

Whoa.

While I'm nursing my bruised arm (she hit kind of hard), Colin has been called into the audition room. I hear him sing "Losing My Religion" by R.E.M. very dully. I wouldn't have expected such lack of gusto from someone with a pink Mohawk. I guess you can't judge a punk by his piercings.

Colin exits the audition room and looks at us. "Sucks. Asshole didn't want me. I'm going home. This fuckin' blows."

If Colin got ousted so quick, who's to say what will happen to me, the quintessential suburbanite? But before I have a chance to ponder my fate, I'm suddenly in the audition room looking at a bald, fat man who holds the key to my potential stardom in his sweaty little hand.

"Headshot."

I give him my "headshot."

"Resume."

I give him my resume. He takes a glance at it, I guess expecting to see his three hundredth resume that listed random roles in crappy unmemorable Off-Off-Off-Broadway plays. "Dean's List" seems out of place here. But good ol' Large and in Charge looks at my resume, looks at me, looks at my resume again, looks at my headshot, and then looks at me again and says, "This your first audition? Sing a song. Don't be offended if I cut you off after fifteen seconds."

Sweatier than ever, I take a deep breath, and rock out on Sheryl Crow's version of Guns N' Roses' "Sweet Child of Mine" as loudly and irreverently as I possibly can. As I'm wailing through the chorus, making hand gestures that make me look spunky and energetic but really have nothing to do with what I'm singing, a lightbulb goes on over my head: I know what I've got to do. But just before I have time to touch my breasts and gyrate à la Hooker in Heat, Large and in Charge barely looks up from my resume and says, "Congratulations. You've made it to round two. Go up to the third floor and wait on line."

My dream will finally be realized! There is a God after all! There is life outside Majuro! I scream a cursory and ecstatic thanks and run out of the room.

"See what happens when you believe in yo'self, girl? You go! Mm-hmm!" Another slap.

I'm so elated I skip every other step as I scamper up the stairs to round two, momentarily forgetting that I am supposed to be "cool" and "hip" and that cool and hip people neither skip nor scamper. I change my scamper to a saunter. But then the second I see Julie, I jump up and down and shout in my most eccentric diva voice, "Baby's gonna be a STAR! Baby's name's gonna be up in *lights*! Baby's gonna be a Broadway STAR!" It's at that moment I'm reminded of my *Meow TV* audition, and how Jared was my loving, supportive stage mom. *I wish Jared were here* . . .

Julie rolls her eyes (as do the other auditionees surrounding us), but is delighted for me. Not having had Large and in Charge as her initial evaluator, Julie hasn't made it to round two. Apparently, "moot court" was not an impressive credential. No hard feelings: this is retribution for all the times she always got the lead in the school play while I was stuck in the back as a yet another underfed, overworked person from Anatevka. Just because I couldn't get callbacks for Tzeitel in *Fiddler on the Roof* in the sixth grade doesn't mean that I can't play a lesbian on Broadway. I smile and think of how proud my parents will be when I tell them that I'm going to drop out of school to be an actress. This tops Nina getting married in a million ways. After all, what more could neurotic parents want for the daughter they hope won't leave for Majuro? (Besides, that is, for her to be engaged.)

The line for round two is much shorter but more complicated. There are cameramen there who are eager to film auditionees for the ten o'clock news. My insatiable hunger for fame flares up. I look at Julie and cry, "I'm going to be on the news tonight! I'm going to have them film my audition!"

Julie looks at me and shakes her head. "You do realize you'll be fired from your part-time gig in Philly, right? Correct me if I'm wrong, but *More Style* thinks you're 'at the doctor' today 'getting a shot'?"

Shit.

The cameraman starts panning the line to get the "full audition" effect. Julie and I hide behind two kissing gay men.

And then, the moment of truth comes. I walk into the audition. A girl about my age from the talent agency says, "Sing. Now."

I wail "Sweet Child of Mine," again, forgetting for the second time that I'm supposed to rub my nipples and fall to my knees if I want to get called back. It's the moment of truth: the girl writes something down on a piece of paper, and I feel like I'm going to vomit, which on the one hand would make me stick out from hundreds of auditionees, but on the other hand would utterly mortify me. She hands it to me and says, "Congratulations. We'll need to see you for callbacks in two days. We'd like to see you for the part of Maureen. You can get the script and the audiotape outside this room. Thanks."

I burst out of the audition room and look at Julie. She sees my face—she knows. "Look out, World!" her face says. "My little sister is going to be on Broadway!" (Alternatively, it might say, "I can't believe I skipped work for this.")

We leave the building and I'm almost crying, I'm so happy. I wish I could call Jared, but after I dial his number, I remember we're not talking. His voice mail picks up, and I quickly hang up. Desperate to share my newfound professional goal with someone, I call my dad, interrupting him while he's with his patients—which he hates—to tell him the great news. (As my dad mentally calculates thousands of wasted tuition dollars, the only response I get is, "Oh, shit.") Julie and I decide that it's time for us to go back to work—it's only one o'clock, and it would be wrong of us not to (as opposed to skipping work to audition for Broadway, which is not "wrong," just stupid).

After a quick lunch with Julie, I take the train back to Philadelphia and get back to *More Style*'s office at around 4 P.M. Fortunately, my coworkers view my Banana Republic 1987 ensemble as "so retro, it's cool." Usually, people at fashion magazines dress in one of two ways. The women in the fashion department come into work wearing feathered boas, fishnet stockings, and denim ballroom skirts, and then compliment each other for looking "so Audrey Hepburn meets Courtney Love." Alternatively, there's the other type of person who works at a fashion magazine: the late-forty-something bitter and unmarried editor who has lost all hope, who shows up wearing the same sweatpants she wore last week because, to hell with it, it doesn't matter—no one will ever love her, and she's "doomed to spend her life writing about other people's sex lives without any sex for herself." (I heard that conversation in the bathroom once when two of the editors thought they were alone.) My outfit is some-

where in between pathetic old spinster and daring young fash-
ionista: For the first time, I fit in.

My intern friend, Kathy (better known to officemates as "Intern Number 2") comes up to me and hands me some faxes, "You
know, since you weren't here this morning, I had to separate all
these stupid faxes myself and distribute them alone. It was a real
pain in the ass. So that's why you get THESE faxes this afternoon. Ha." Kathy, a junior at Haverford, triumphantly drops the
faxes on my desk, looks over each of her shoulders to make sure
no one is around, and whispers, "How'd it go?" I had tried to lie
to Kathy yesterday about skipping work to "get a shot," but in
the end I just couldn't do it. Kathy is just as bored as I am at *More
Style,* and just as upset that her education gets her only faxing
and xeroxing for hours on end, and nothing more. After all, who
will play "see how long you can stare at the clock without blink-
ing" with her after I'm gone? Certainly I owe her an explanation.

I look over each shoulder and excitedly tell her, "You're never
going to believe this. They actually want me for callbacks! I'm
going on Thursday!" Kathy's jaw drops. There's no pain worse
than seeing someone as low as you on the employment food chain
skyrocket up, leaving you stranded in the world of paper-clip
sorting and promotional-gift-closet-cleaning alone. I am supposed to be doomed to sorting people's faxes for the rest of my
life, like her, until we do what our parents really want—that is,
decide that we can't handle journalism anymore and apply to law
school. But in just one morning, I have gone from Intern Number Three to Broadway Star Number One. At first, I feel kind of
bad, leaving Kathy alone like that. Thankfully, that doesn't last
very long.

Kathy makes it her responsibility to tell the news to the other three people in the office who will talk to us: a copy editor who just graduated college and already hates her job, a custodian who barely speaks English, and the intern whose one responsibility is answering reader letters ("Dear *More Style,* I am poor and from Venezuela. I want move to America, and be rich beautiful movie star! *More Style* must help! Please make me beauty model like magazine! Then get to go to America! I love *More Style.*" "Dear Reader, Thank you for writing to *More Style.* We appreciate your readership and dedication. Sincerely, Your Friends at *More Style.*")

For the rest of the day, I am Queen of the Interns. Kathy sorts the faxes for me and even does my xeroxing. The letter-writing intern lets me respond to a letter. And the copy editor just looks at me in awe. I'm movin' up in the world. Movin' on up. Adios, Majuro. Bonjour, fame.

It's Thursday afternoon, a half hour before my train, an hour and a half before my audition. I can't believe I'm heading into New York again unbeknownst to Jared, who by now must have received my fortune cookies. Is he ignoring them? Is he going to ignore me for the rest of my life? Am I truly an unlovable wretch? Shaking the depressing thoughts of Jared out of my head, I go to the bathroom to look at my second attempt at "bohemian hip." A little better, but not much. Still the bandana (what if it was the bandana they liked?), still a tanktop, but hipper, "clubbier" pants. Kathy hugs me and hands me a card: "Forget about me— save yourself!"

After the train pulls into New York, I find my way to the talent agency, which is a dirty-looking warehouse located somewhere in the Garment District. For a split second, I remember this really bad made-for-TV movie that we watched in my fifth-grade class called *Jackie's Last Day*. It's all about this ten-year-old girl, Jackie, who meets some random guy on the street who tells her that she's invited to a special address where there will be lots of presents for her. Jackie enthusiastically discusses the presents with her friends, who advise her with such pearls of wisdom as, "Strangers are bad!" and "Don't go, Jackie!" Jackie, one of the dumber after-school special characters I've ever seen, eagerly goes to the address after school, where she is then molested and killed. Not quite as entertaining as the "Bulimic Becky" video in which Becky stores her vomit in jars in her closet so as to hide her bulimia, but my fifth-grade class got the message anyway: Don't go to unknown addresses given to you by strangers and expect something good to happen. (Another fabulous fortune.)

And yet here I am, ten years later, going to an unknown address given to me by a stranger, expecting to get a part on Broadway. I ride the freight elevator up to the second floor, and when the elevator doors open, I'm greeted by a room with paint chips falling off the walls, loose floorboards sticking up, and about twenty urban hipsters.

I look around and spot my "friend" from the line the other day. Naturally, she's delighted to see me, and smacks me on my shoulder again. "See what happens when you know to believe! Jesus was lookin' out for you, girl!"

Ow. "Um, yeah, he certainly was." I'm scared she'll hit me again if I disagree with her, so I go with the Jesus thing, though I'm pretty sure Jesus doesn't keep an eye out for unemployed Jewish girls who want to be on Broadway.

Help Wanted, Desperately

Finally, they call my name and I go into an even more dingy-looking room. This time, a panel of three people and a piano player stare me down. Large and in Charge is nowhere to be seen. Trouble.

A thin, lanky girl who apparently only speaks in questions outlines what's going to happen in the course of the audition, and then introduces herself as "Stacy?" Stacy? tells me to sing "that part of the song we marked off for you on the music?" and then to "do your dialogue?" The piano player strikes up the music, and I sing the song from the show "Take Me or Leave Me" as loudly, energetically, and enthusiastically as I can.

The panel looks unimpressed. Yikes.

Then I do my dialogue. In this dialogue, the character is supposed to be doing a performance-art piece, which involves impersonating (incowanating?) a cow. Basically, the point of this dialogue was to see how convincingly and entertainingly I could be a cow. I had spent the whole night before begging my house-mate Ethan to critique my moos. "That one's a little too guttural." "Try to make your moo a little less loud and angry and a little more soft and sexy." "Alex, that's good enough, let's get dinner." I wondered if I should call Jared and moo for him, but then decided against it. I'm not sure unsolicited mooing is part of the road towards reconciliation.

So despite Ethan's pleas, I mooed. And mooed some more. And then some. (That's when Ethan left and got dinner without me.) But I was sure that this dialogue was where I was going to shine. This was when the talent agency would tell the other call-backees to go home, they had found their star. I had tried some method acting the night before that I had heard about on a TV show: "BE the cow. Know who the cow is. Imagine yourself doing the cow's daily activities." Milk me. I knew the cow. I was the cow. I was ready to be the cow.

I take a deep breath and begin my dialogue. "Moooo." Good, soft and sexy, nice. Don't give away the milk yet. "Moo!" Build it, Alex, a little more anger, but still seductive. "MOOO!" Bring out the big guns now, Baby! Show them what you're worth! Know the cow! BE the cow! "Mooo, moooooooo, MOO!"

I stop, and curtsy with my invisible skirt for effect. The guy on the panel smoking a cigarette claps slowly. The other two look at each other quickly, and then write something down. Stacy says, "Thanks?"

Mooing aside, I seriously ask, "So, when am I going to hear from you next?"

Stacy's about to open her mouth, but her friend answers for her: "We'll be in touch."

"But when?"

"Could be a week, a month, or even a year. We always keep our applicants on file. Now goodbye."

Ouch. I'll try not to let the door hit me on my way out.

Lesson learned: Go for what you want, try as hard as you can, but if you can't moo the way they want you to, well, you're out of luck. So much for show business.

Back in Philadelphia, I sit on my bed and wonder what comes next. All I want to do is call Jared, to tell him everything—from sorting paper clips at *More Style* to auditioning for Broadway with nipple-pierced, Mohawk'd punks. I want to tell him how much I miss him, how I can't stop thinking about what a shit I was. I want to tell him all about callbacks, how it was Jackie's Last Day-like because I know he'll know what I'm talking about. But more than anything, I want to hear about him. How he's doing. What he's been doing. Is he happy? Does he miss me like I miss him? Can he fall asleep without our before-bed phone call?

I wonder if he got the fortune cookies—not that they said half the things they needed to. As I continue to brood over Jared, I begin absentmindedly to play with the tweezers I used to insert fortunes into cookies just days earlier. Breaking the quiet, the doorbell to our off-campus house rings, and I assume—as I always do—that someone else will answer it. It rings again, and I hear Ethan's angry footsteps thunder down the stairs as he shouts, "Alex, what, are you crippled? Or deaf? I mean, it's not that hard to answer the damn door!"

I mumble "Whatever," as I hear Ethan open the door. From downstairs, he shouts tentatively, "Um, Alex? I think you should come down here . . ."

Grumbling, I get up from the bed. Probably some garbage man yelling at us again for putting our garbage to the left of our front stoop instead of to the right.

I walk down the dark hallway, and then head down the stairs. *Stupid garbage people.* But as I make my way toward the bottom of the stairs and reach our front hallway, I see it. There, standing before me in all its six-foot tall glaringly yellow glory is a man wearing a huge, adult-sized banana costume. Everything about this banana person is yellow: his shoes a bright yellow Converse, his tights a mustardy nylon, his face jaundiced by makeup. The yellow of the banana seems to radiate into our front hall, basking our dreary entryway in a soft, lemony glow. I look at Ethan. Ethan looks at me. We both look at the banana. The banana looks back at us.

"Yo. You," the banana scans a sheet of paper in his hand, "are you Alexa Hoffman?"

I look at Ethan, who responds for me. "Yeah, that's her, all right." Somehow, having had one minute more than me with this gargantuan fruit, Ethan is confident, comfortable, and not at all fazed that what appears to be a giant yellow phallus is standing on our doorstep.

Not knowing of the protocol concerning having a larger-than-life-size piece of fruit in your foyer, I look at Ethan and ask, "Should we invite it in?"

The banana, hearing my "invitation", tries to get in through the doorway, which is apparently too low for his banana head. His felt banana costume slams into the top of the opening, making a muted *pphh* sound, and when Ethan and I wince for him, the banana shakes his head and says, "Nah, I'll just stay out here, it's cool."

Baffled, Ethan looks at me and asks the banana, "Do you want a drink of water or something?"

Ignoring us, the banana looks down at his sheet of paper again, consulting it for fruitly wisdom. "Okay, yeah, that's right, you're the herring chick."

Ethan and I look at each other. "Excuse me?"

The banana rolls his eyes and then reaches into his messenger bag, muttering to himself, "The stupid shit I gotta do to make a living . . ." Fascinated and mesmerized by him, Ethan and I watch as the banana takes a sheet of paper and a sign with a piece of string on it out of his bag. Then, he maneuvers his tremendous banana head through the loop of string, hitting his head again against the door frame. Ethan and I can see that he's now wearing a sign that says, "I am not a banana, I'm a piece of herring."

Help Wanted, Desperately

"Ahem." The banana looks at me and Ethan to make sure we're watching (in addition to the four people on the street who have now fully stopped to stare at our large banana friend). Ethan stares right at the banana's face, clearly amused. I just stare at the banana's sign as the banana offers, "Oh yeah, the guy who called said he wanted, like, some herring or fish-o-gram but we don't have no herring-gram, so I told him I'd wear this sign and dress, like, in our banana-gram suit."

Stuttering, I respond, "Oh, yes, of course." Certainly a huge yellow penis should feel free to dress as he pleases.

Pulling at his banana crotch, the banana apologizes, "Sorry, this costume rides up like hell. Anyway, where was I? Oh, okay, right. Ahem.

"Alex,

> *H is for how I feel when I'm around you, and how I hate*
> *   feeling when you're not there*
> *E is for everything that came before our fight,*
> *   and everything that should come after*
> *R is for how I ran to get my mail when I saw I had*
> *   a package from you*
> *R is for another 'r' word that I can't think of because*
> *   I'm bad at these poems*
> *I is for how I love you always, because of and*
> *   in spite of everything*
> *N is for not sleeping for the past three nights because*
> *   I knew you weren't either*
> *G is for giving you all that I have, and knowing that*
> *   you will give back that much more.*

I love you, Alex. Let's start over? Jared. P.S. I went to the *Meow TV* thing, and you still haven't tried herring. We had a deal."

The banana looks at me, "Aww, that was real sweet, huh? I don't get the whole 'herring' thing, but it was cute."

Smiling so much my face hurts, I feel a lump well up in my throat. "I hate herring."

"Hey, do you want me to do my banana song too, or is that it?" The banana looks at me expectantly and then scratches his crotch again. "Shit, it's hot as hell in here, this costume's like wearing a fuckin' diaper. So?" He wipes some sweat off his face, and his yellow makeup smears onto his yellow-costumed arm.

Still smiling, I say softly to no one in particular, "I wish Jared were here—I have to call him, I have to go . . ."

Ethan then points to the door to a figure behind the banana. "Seriously, could this get *any* weirder? I feel like I O.D.'d on Robitussin or something."

Standing now behind the giant banana is Jared, smiling and wearing a sign that says, "I am not a piece of herring either." Over the banana's shoulder (do bananas have shoulders?) he quietly says, "I missed you. And I loved the fortunes."

Amazed, excited, overwhelmed, I sputter, "You're here? You came? When did you get here?"

"I was on your train, I think, I saw you at the station but then I lost you, why were you in New York? How come you didn't come to me? Why didn't you call?"

"I didn't know you wanted to see me . . . You never pick up your phone. I thought you hated me."

"I couldn't hate you."

Help Wanted, Desperately

I try to find a way around the banana, but it's impossible to negotiate my way around his huge felt body. Looking over the banana's other shoulder I say, "Jared, I was so unhappy—I felt so terrible . . . all I could do was think about you, I'm sorry, I was just, I was stupid about Lyric, I—"

The banana, sensing his work here is done, tries to back up, to get out of the way so that Jared and I can talk face to face. Instead, the banana trips over Jared's feet. Catching himself from his fall, the banana then positions himself next to Jared and coughs, holding his hand out.

Ethan, done with the show, comments, *"Man,* that's one greedy banana," and then heads up the stairs. Jared pays the banana, who looks at me, scratches his banana crotch, and says, "Later." And just like that, the banana disappears from the doorstep and crosses the street, where he tries to fit into his comically small car.

Jared and I stand there looking at each other, and I wrap my arms around his waist and remember all over again what it was like to miss him all this time. His voice. His smell. His hands. "I love you, you know that?"

"I know."

"You're amazing."

Jared smiles. "I know that too."

"I don't get the 'I'm not a piece of herring' sign, though."

Jared pushes my hair out of my eyes, sighing, and explains, "Okay, you know that Magritte painting that's a picture of a pipe but there's a sign in the painting right under the pipe that says in French, 'This is not a pipe'?"

"No . . ."

"Well, now you know. I was trying to do that, but with the banana. You know, 'I am not a banana, I am a piece of herring'? Get it? It's still a banana, no matter what you call it."

"Yeah, I guess I get it now. But it's still not doing anything for me."

"Look, they didn't have a herring-gram costume. In all of Philadelphia, there's no herring-gram. Do I smell a major business opportunity? Oh, I think I do . . ."

". . . Jared, look, I'm sorry I was . . . terrible."

Jared tightens his arms around me and I take a deep breath, inhaling all the Jared my body can handle. It still doesn't feel like enough.

"Oh, but that's not all," Jared squirms out of our hug and reaches into a plastic bag that seems to have materialized out of nowhere. "Look what I've got!" Jared cheerfully thrusts a large half-pound container of herring into my hand.

"Let's go eat it. You owe me."

"Well, I guess this is what starting over's about." I smile and take Jared's hand. "Let's do this thing."

Jared takes my hand and kisses it, and then kisses my lips. "I prefer my kisses before herring."

"And I prefer them without herring at all."

"Too bad. New beginnings."

Lessons Learned

1. Impersonating a heifer is probably better than actually *being a heifer*, although neither occupation yields any personal financial value.

2. The ability to gyrate like a hooker in heat guarantees success. I need to learn how to gyrate.

Help Wanted, Desperately

3. If Banana Republic clothing dating back to 1987 is the closest I can get to "bohemian hip," I am probably doomed to an eternity of tragic un-hipness. That, or it's time to buy some new pants.

4. Being Latke #8 in the second-grade holiday play does not mean I am sufficiently talented to play a lesbian diva on Broadway. It does, however, mean I can refrain from picking my nose for a full half hour.

5. When a six-foot-tall human banana appears at your door, you should assume this is the answer to all of your romantic woes. A man in six feet of yellow felt is just as good as a knight in shining armor.

12
Teeth and
Murses

2 Months, 21 Days,
14 Hours, 3 Minutes

A little bit of herring, and my life—and, for that matter, things with Jared—was better than ever before. (Had I known herring was a magical relationship-repair drug, I probably would've tried it sooner.) In a long conversation with Jared, as I crouched by the toilet (the herring didn't sit well, cure-all or no cure-all), I confessed to being self-obsessed, unnaturally preoccupied by my own desire to avoid Majuro (thereby admitting personal failure), and abnormally fixated on Jared's seemingly effortless job-search success. Jared admitted that he had overreacted, that Lyric was and remains heinous, and in a moment of unfiltered honesty, that if anything, he's afraid I actually will go to Majuro—and that it scares him maybe even more than it scares me. Two hours (no vomit) later, for the first time in a while, things felt okay again, so I'm pretty sure I don't have to go drag myself off to some kind of therapy, and that's (always) reassuring.

Had it not been for my recurring dream, I would've been

happy as a pig in shit. But two nights ago, I had that dream where all my teeth fall out.

It was the fourth time in one month that I had this dream, thus guaranteeing that I will, in fact, never be completely abnormality-free.

I fear I may have to return to Sheila, a.k.a. Galoshes Lady, the therapist.

Anyway, in the dream, I'm sitting at a table in a diner alone, waiting for someone. The diner is cold and dark, and no one is there except for me. All the lights are out, but I can still see the empty booths, the pies on the pie rack behind the plastic guard, and out the window, the empty parking lot lit by streetlights. As I sit waiting, I suddenly develop a very bad cough. The first time I cough, I feel like something is rattling in my head. There's a glass of water on the table, and I greedily drink the whole thing. Then I cough again, and this time, I bring my hand to my mouth. As I cover my mouth, my finger brushes against my front tooth, which I suddenly discover is loose. I wiggle it a little, and it comes out in my hand. Terrified, I try to shove it back into my mouth, but then I start coughing again—and this time, I cough out two or three of my teeth into my hand. The dream continues with me coughing out more and more teeth— more than I think I have in my mouth. Then, I realize I'm meeting someone (whoever that someone is), and I try to cram all my teeth in my mouth at once, securing them into my gums so they don't fall out again.

And that's it. That's the part where I wake up. I never meet the person I'm waiting for—I just sit at the table with my teeth in a napkin, trying to cram them back into my mouth one by one.

I would kill for the "naked in school" dream.

Help Wanted, Desperately

Normally, I don't think dreams mean anything. But this is the fourth time I've had this one in thirty days. Ever since Jared and I ate an entire half pound of herring in ten minutes (that has to be some kind of record), my mind keeps drifting back to the dream.

I blame the herring.

On top of my new obsession with blaming a piece of herring for my psychological hang-ups, last night, when Jared and I ate Chinese food, my fortune read, "Someone new might change your mind." Change my mind about what? Who's this new person? Is it the same person I was waiting for in my dream?

After we finished our dinner and were lounging lazily in each other's arms on the floor, spacing out as we looked at the water damage on my bedroom ceiling, I rolled over and asked Jared, "Are you superstitious?"

Intently picking a crusted piece of brown sauce off his shirt, Jared absentmindedly answered, "What do you mean? Like do I not walk under ladders or something?"

"I mean, do you believe in your fortunes from fortune cookies? Did you ever play Ouija and actually believe that it would tell you something?"

"No. And no."

"Why not?"

"Because my brother was a little bastard and would push the clear game piece toward 'no' and he broke the magnet, so whenever I—"

Interrupting and suddenly very interested in helping him get that crusty brown sauce off his shirt, I began picking. "No, that's not what I mean. I mean, do you believe that every person has a destiny they need to fulfill, and that everything happens for a reason?"

"So after he broke the magnet we got in this huge fight—I don't even remember why—and that was when I broke his arm. But that was an accident. And it wasn't like he didn't deserve it."

Ignoring Jared, I continued, "Maybe I'm destined for Majuro, and this whole me-not-getting-a-job thing is just part of the big plan, you know, so I actually *do* go there. And maybe my fortune is true. Maybe someone new *will* change my mind."

"Gimme a break."

"What do you mean?"

"Look, I'm just saying it's stupid to invest so much meaning into a fortune from a fortune cookie. Or inject so much meaning. And you do it *all* the time. Look at your wall, it's like a joke." My eyes panned across the room to the wall above my laptop, covered with taped-up fortunes. "When I got those fortune cookies you sent me, what was so great about them was that it was like you suddenly realized that those fortunes are all bullshit and that in the end, you can create your *own* fortune. It was like you finally got it." Waving the newest fortune, he continued, "They mass-produce these, Alex. Contrary to what you may believe, this was not 'destined' to fall into your hands. You got it because you paid seven-ninety-five for moo shu." Smoothing my eyebrows, he suddenly looked nervous, like a three-year-old. "Okay, fortune-cookie stuff aside, are you worried about us?"

"What do you mean, us? No! Of course not!" Maybe. *Maybe if I go to Majuro you won't love me anymore.*

"Are you sure?"

"Entirely." Okay, seventy-eight percent.

"It's okay if you feel a little nervous."

"I'm not nervous." Maybe a little.

"I know you don't want to talk about it—"

"There's nothing to talk about."

We were quiet for a little bit, and I knew that, yet again, I messed things up, superimposing my anxiety onto our relationship. I should just carry a sock with me and stuff it in my mouth every time I want to speak. Or have the sock permanently implanted there.

I rolled over to face him and slowly wrapped my arm around his chest, my face sheepishly inching up closer and closer to his face. I worked my way toward his ear and then playfully nibble on the bottom of his earlobe, whispering, "I'm sorry. I love you."

He turned to me and a little smile crept across his face. "I know. Me too."

"It's just that I'm starting to feel like maybe Majuro might be the right thing all of a sudden. I mean, maybe I *need* to go there so I can figure out what the hell I'm going to do with my life. Maybe I *need* a year off in a metaphorical DMV on some random island so I can actually sit and think about my life . . . It's too much. I'm tired." I heaved a sigh that I'd been holding in for what felt like months, then muttered, "I'm exhausted."

Jared sat up and randomly adds, "Well, I don't want you coming to New York for *me*. I mean, I never thought *that* was part of the picture at all, anyway. I want you to come for *you*."

"Yeah . . ." *So you don't want me to be in New York at all? There's no tiny part of you that selfishly is saying, "Alex, stay with me in New York!"?*

"Alex, you should come for *you*. I care about you, I love you, you know that. But if you come to New York for me, you're going to resent it if you're unhappy, and worse, you'll resent me, and then what if it doesn't work out at all? Not that it won't, but what if it doesn't? And who knows, maybe you'd be happier in Majuro or wherever. Or even at home living with your parents."

"Okay, gimme a break. I would not be happy as my parents' unpaid slave for Ninafest. Please."

Jared smiled. "It would be more like indentured servitude, actually."

"For eternity."

"Look, can you do me a favor? Stop thinking about everything so much."

Right. "I don't know that I can do that."

Pulling the covers off the bed, Jared takes his shirt off and gets in. He opens the covers for me. "But you'll try, right?"

"I'll try."

Jared drew me to him as I got into bed, kissing me slowly as he wrapped his arms around me. "I really love you, Alex." Then he turned on his side, and I lay awake, facing the window, wondering what the hell just happened. "You'll resent me, and then what if it doesn't work out at all?" What does *that* mean? Who knew "not working out at all" was an option? Did I not get that memo? When did this become an issue?

As we slowly slipped into sleep together, Jared's fingers found their way into mine like they always have and then he made that weird noise with his mouth that he always makes before he goes to sleep. Then the soft, comforting snoring—like an old, favorite song—began. I turned to look at him, and whispered to him as he snored, "I love you. Even though you don't know what you're saying sometimes, I love you."

After a half hour trying to avoid thinking, I thankfully drifted, finally, into sleep.

* * *

Help Wanted, Desperately

It's the next morning: Jared has to leave for New York on a 7 A.M. train in order to get to a 9 A.M. exam on time. At 5 A.M., he gently wakes me up to say goodbye.

"G'morning, you."

"What time is it?"

"You don't want to know, trust me. Look, I know last night was a little weird, so I just wanted to tell you I love you."

Rubbing my eyes, I smile. "That's a nice way to be woken up."

"So I'll see you Friday, right? Only five days." Jared leans over for a kiss, which I readily offer, with the kind of delicious morning breath that smells something just short of horse manure.

Jared makes a face but kisses me anyway. "We're okay, right? I love you so much."

Suddenly awake and remembering last night, I respond suspiciously, "You do, right?"

"I do."

Stretching, I smile. "Good."

"See you Friday, sweets!"

Pulling Jared toward me one last time, I kiss him so hard he can barely breathe. That'll show him.

"Love you." Jared heads for the door.

"Always," I whisper as I roll over in bed.

And as he shuts the door behind him and the door clicks closed, that's when I remember it: the toothless dream. For the fifth time.

For the rest of the day—at the coffee shop, during *Oprah,* even in the bathroom—I can't stop thinking about the dream: Who was I waiting for? What does it mean to wait for someone who never comes? And why would Jared say it might not work out? And what about that fortune: "Someone new might change your mind"?

Over lunch with Ethan, I begin to obsess out loud. "So then, in the dream, I keep waiting and waiting for this person and they never come. And my teeth keep falling out and I try to put them back in my mouth. That's weird, right? And this is the fifth time I've had it."

After four years of being friends with me, Ethan seems unfazed, and knows better than to join me in my obsessions. Deep in thought, he suddenly answers (to no question *I've* asked), "Would you rather have yellow teeth or yarn for hair?"

Ethan is something just short of obsessed with "would you rather"–type questions, and after four years arguing why I would rather have eight toes instead of twelve fingers (four of which would be thumbs), I've learned to accept his neuroses insofar as he accepts mine.

"Yellow teeth. But seriously, what do you think I should do about this dream—what does it *mean*? Oh, and remember, I got that fortune 'someone new might change your mind' last night too. Don't you think the combination of those two things sends some sort of message?"

"Remember, you can't bleach the teeth. It's yellow teeth—and they're highlighter yellow, not like smoker's yellow . . . or yarn for hair, period. And you can't get hair weaves or anything."

"Fine. Yellow teeth. Wait, what color is the yarn?"

"Orange."

"Okay, yellow teeth for sure. But seriously, what should I do about this dream?"

Ethan rolls his eyes—a reaction that I now frequently solicit wherever I go. "I might go for the orange yarn. It might be kind of cool."

Ethan starts eating his grilled cheese sandwich—one of the three foods he actually eats (french fries, grilled cheese, chicken). "Anyway, there's nothing you can do about a dream. You can forget it, if you're normal." Ethan pauses, and then looks at me. "Okay, you're driven to class every day by a chauffeur who drives a car shaped like a baked potato with sour cream *or* you have a 4.0 average all four years you're at school *but* your diploma and all official records give you a new middle name, 'Tiny Knockers,' and all your professors and friends refer to you that way."

"The baked potato chauffeur—no question. And 'Tiny Knockers'? You're losing your touch . . . Anyway, so you said if I *was* normal, I'd forget the dream. But since I'm not normal, what's the alternative?"

"Okay, fine. Jesus, you're such a pain in the ass. Okay, seeing as how you're not normal, you can actually *use* the dream. I saw a poster about some medical study. They're looking for people with sleeping issues. You go to the hospital and then they watch you sleep or something. This girl I used to date was in medical studies all the time. I think they gave her six hundred dollars for staying there for two nights or something."

"Six hundred dollars!? Just for sleeping?!" Eureka! Money without a career! A ticket off of Majuro and into a self-respecting medical profession! The Holy Grail!

"Yeah, and she did it all the time. I think you can make a lot of money doing those studies too."

"So why don't *you* do it? Let's do it together! Six hundred dollars is about six new shirts at Hugo Boss!" Ethan's weakness: Hugo Boss shirts.

"I don't know—they made her take some pill or something. I think it would make me feel like a lab rat. Anyway—hospital beds are gross. And I'm not like you anyway. I'm normal." Ethan smiles angelically.

"Well, you'll be singin' a different tune when I'm rolling in cash from some medical study. You'll see."

"Or we'll see who has a whole host of new medical problems from some weird pill they give you that makes you grow a third nostril."

"I'd rather have a third nostril and be able to move to New York than have two nostrils, no money, and a life on hold in Majuro."

"Fair enough. A woman who chooses to hypothetically ride in a chauffeured baked-potato car knows how to make a decision."

Right.

It's less than eight hours later, and in my desperation for some kind of employment—*any* kind of employment, at this point—I'm already in the corporate department of the university's hospital, waiting to participate in the sleep study that begins tonight. After about a half hour of questioning, I learn that I've been selected to sleep over at the hospital for one night. All I have to do is sleep—and then they'll give me two hundred dollars. It's like prostitution, except I'm just screwing my own exhaustion.

Not knowing exactly what to expect, I brought some supplies of my own: pajamas, clothing for tomorrow, a toothbrush, a book to read. Everyone around me looks tired or bored—maybe both— and I wonder whether any of these people have had past experiences as medical subjects. Picking up a *Parents* magazine, I notice the guy sitting next to me looks particularly exhausted, as if someone's slammed his body against a wall over and over again.

Help Wanted, Desperately

Having perused the magazine, I now feel I know all I could possibly want to know about curing a baby's diarrhea, and decide that it's time for some human contact: Enough with diaper rash and prenatal yoga. I put the magazine down on the coffee table and try to start a conversation with Exhausted Guy next to me.

Before I begin to speak, I wonder what I should ask. I always feel uncomfortable when friends tell me they went to the doctor or that they just got out of the hospital. Part of me wants to know what happened (more specifically, let's be honest, to know if they're infectious), to find out if they're okay. The other part of me really does not want to know the elaborate details of their gastrointestinal disorders, hernias, or recurring genital infections. I decide to keep my questions simple.

"So, come here often?" Great: I'm either picking up insomniacs for kicks or asking strangers to detail the nature of their chronic illnesses.

The guy slowly turns to me, fighting to open his eyes. I notice that he looks particularly disheveled and dirty and hardly seems interested in talking to me. "I've been here every night for the past week."

"So, um, what do you do here, exactly?" Keep it simple, Alex. Don't want to disturb the profoundly disturbed.

"I don't sleep."

"No, I mean what *do* you do here?"

The guy turns, his eyelids drooping so much I wonder if he's okay. "I mean, that's what I do here. I don't sleep."

Incredulous, I ask, "So you come here . . . to not sleep?"

He opens his eyes as much as he can and says, "Yup. They pay me *not* to sleep. That's what I do. I'm in a medical study."

"So you haven't been sleeping for a week?"

Annoyed, he responds, "That's it. I haven't slept in a week. I'm here so they can put me to bed . . . and keep me awake." He rubs his eyes with his hands and yawns, his mouth opening wide enough to swallow the world. "So what are you here for? Menstrual cycle evaluation?"

Asshole. "Um, *no*. I guess I just *come off* as a bitch, then."

Suddenly awake, Exhausted Guy opens his eyes, "Whoa—that's not what I meant at all. It's not that—it's just that a lot of girls come here for the menstrual-cycle study 'cause it pays the most. Pays way more than the sleep deprivation study I'm in."

A better-paying, menstrual study, eh? More dough for your flow, so to speak.

"Do you, you know, have to actually have your period like right now to be in the study?"

Exhausted Guy turns and finally looks at me head-on. "Well, I don't have *my* period right now and they wouldn't take *me* for the study." Exhausted Guy shakes his head. "How the hell would *I* know?"

"Just asking." Methinks someone is a little cranky-wanky after not having slept a winky-dinky.

Exhausted Guy tilts his head back in his chair, letting his head hit the wall and his eyes roll to the back of his head as he mutters to himself, "Just one more day, then I get paid. Oh, God, and sleep."

Just as I'm reconsidering this whole medical-study thing, a ridiculously handsome thirty-something man in green scrubs opens the door to our waiting room and calls out, "Alexa Hoffman?" A little excited, I pick up my overnight bag and say goodbye to Exhausted Guy, "Have a good night!"

He gives me the finger.

Help Wanted, Desperately

I follow the good-looking guy out of the room as he introduces himself. "Hi, I'm Marc and I'm going to be the registered nurse who observes you tonight."

Ooh. This is starting to sound a little kinky. Are we going to play doctor?

Marc leads me down the hallway into a small hospital room. "So for this study, we're just going to be, well, watching you sleep. I'm going to watch you through the night as you sleep, and take notes on your movements throughout the night, and anything you may say or do. You just pretend I'm not here. I'm going to give you a couple of minutes to get ready for bed, and when I come back, I'll just be observing you through the night. Everything okay?" Marc gets ready to leave.

Suddenly shy, I ask, "So, you're just going to sit here and watch me sleep?"

Marc pushes hair out of his eyes. "Yep, that's it. You don't have to do a thing. Except sleep, that is."

"And you're just going to watch the whole night?"

Marc smiles. Great teeth. Teeth that could fall out of his mouth? "Yeah—the whole night. Look, I know this is a little weird—a lot of people who come in for this study say being watched makes them nervous. But look, you won't even know I'm here." Marc turns around and shuts the door, calling out, "I'll knock before I come in again. Should be about five minutes."

Marc leaves and I look around my room. A sink, a bed, a chair, a small window. A toilet in a small bathroom. Sparse. And a little lonely. I quickly change into my pajamas—an old T-shirt proclaiming I BOOGIED MY BUTT OFF AT ANDY'S BAR-MITZVAH! and boxers that have a fluorescent cow printed on them. Should've brought cuter pajamas tonight—sort of embarrassing that cool

251

and sexy Marc will watch me sleep in a baggy shirt that proves I am not—and never have been—a cool or sexy person. Story of my life, Take #3,756.

I hurry to the bed, draw the covers down, and climb in. The sheets are icy cold, and suddenly I miss Jared more than I have all day.

A knock. "Can I come in? Are you ready?" Marc's voice asks.

Marc opens the door, carrying a clipboard and a cup of coffee. "Comfortable? Everything okay?"

"Yeah," I look around the room and pull the covers up close to my chin. "Um, everything's fine."

"Okay, whenever you're ready." Marc sits down and crosses his leg. "Just go to sleep like you normally would." Marc reaches over to the light switch and flicks it off.

I close my eyes. On your mark, get set, sleep!

The room is quiet and I feel incredibly awkward. I slowly open my left eye and try to sneak a peek at Marc, who watches me slowly open my left eye and try to sneak a peek at him. He softly sips his coffee and watches me. He begins to write something down on his clipboard. Perhaps, "Thinks I'm hot tried to check me out I caught her."

I quickly scrunch my eyes closed again, and flip over to my right side, so I face the wall instead of Marc. I hear his pen lightly scratching away.

I suddenly feel very lonely, and realize that this is the first time in two years that I haven't talked to Jared right before I went to sleep, except for when we broke up that week. I told Jared today that I would be doing a sleep study at the hospital, and he sounded sad— and a little distant?— when I told him I probably wouldn't call.

Help Wanted, Desperately

I want to call.

I need to call.

I turn over to face Marc and open my eyes, "So this study is supposed to be about my normal sleep habits, right?"

Marc nods. "Sure, exactly the way you would sleep at home, except, well, you're at a hospital."

"Can I use my cell phone to call my boyfriend? I always talk to him before I go to sleep." Could I sound any *more* pathetic? Do I need my teddy bear too? Why don't I just put in my retainer and show Marc just how big a loser I am?

Marc smiles warmly and shakes his head no. "'Fraid not, sorry. I don't know why, but we're not allowed to let our subjects do that. Call anyone, that is. I mean, it's not a boyfriend-specific rule or anything."

"Oh." I roll over. For a bed for sick people, this isn't all that comfortable.

"I'm really sorry, Alexa. I wish you could, but you can't. If you'd like, we could simulate that discussion here? Is there anything you'd like to discuss?" Marc recrosses his legs and puts his coffee down on the table next to him.

Okay, this isn't weird or anything. My male nurse wants to have pillow talk with me, without the sex.

"Oh, okay. Maybe we could do that."

Silence. I guess I have to start.

"Is it weird being a male nurse, Marc?"

"No weirder than being a male anything-else, I guess."

"Do people give you a hard time—you know, being a murse?"

Marc looks at me quizzically. "A murse?"

"You know, a male nurse. Like a manny. A male nanny."

Marc: "I think that's an unfair sexual stereotype, the idea that

253

only women are good caretakers and therefore a man who tries to do it—and do it well— is somehow failing his gender irrevocably."

Yikes. "Yeah, you're right."

"I know."

Hmm, maybe we shouldn't talk.

Marc doesn't seem that interested in conversation, but as the time passes and it's suddenly eleven thirty and I still haven't fallen asleep, I decide to talk with Marc the Murse a little more.

"Hey Marc?"

"Yeah?"

"You awake still?"

Marc shifts in his chair. "Yeah, that's my job. *You're* the one who should be sleeping."

"I can't sleep. Can we talk?"

Marc sighs. He's sort of cute when he sighs. "Sure."

"Are you seeing anyone, Marc?"

Marc shifts in his chair, "Alexa, you know we're not allowed to date our patients."

Did someone just spray eau de sexual tension in the air? "Marc, I was just trying to make conversation. I have a boyfriend, remember? The one you wouldn't let me call?"

"Oh."

Awkward silence. I hear a slight drip from the sink. Marc looks up at the ceiling.

"Anyway, I'm engaged."

"Oh wow, Marc, that's great!" All the good-looking guys are always engaged or gay. Minus Jared, of course. "When's the wedding?"

"We're still working that out. She's a surgeon, so it really depends on her schedule."

"Oh."

Awkward silence. A slight drip from the sink. Marc looks up at the ceiling.

Breaking the silence, I offer, "So I have this weird recurring dream. Actually, it's why I came to this study—I sort of thought it would be about dreams or something. Anyway, this dream—I've had it about five times now. I'm in this diner and I'm waiting for someone, and all my teeth fall out. And I keep trying to put them back in my mouth, by, you know, shoving them into the gums, but they don't stay there."

"Hmm."

"My dad's a dentist"—okay, now I'm blabbering on. It's like I'm at a fourth-grade sleepover party. When do we make 'smores?—"and he once had this patient whose teeth fell out, and then when he came in to see my dad, he had made these weird makeshift braces to hold his teeth in, with a luggage-tag thingy."

Finally, Marc the Murse laughs! The moonlight streams in through the hospital room blinds and literally lights up Marc's smile. "You know, I read about something like this on the Internet once. Apparently, dreams about hair loss, teeth falling out, contact lenses falling out—they're all about a fear of getting older. Are you scared of getting older?" Marc poises his pen, ready to write my response.

Why does this suddenly feel like therapy? Most important, am I going to walk away from this with some free Prozac samples? It would be a nice perk . . .

I hear someone talking in the hall outside the room as I think about Marc's question. "Well, I'm scared about what I'm going to do with my life. See, this guy—his name's Jared—and I have been dating for two years, and I really love him"—I turn over so

I don't have to face Marc as I share my life story with him—"but I don't have a job and he does, and he's got his life figured out and I know that I told him that I'm not going to be jealous of him or anything anymore, or worry about Lyric, but—"

"What's 'Lyric'?"

"Oh, she's his ex-girlfriend."

"That's her name?"

"Yeah. I know. Anyway, I can't help being jealous of him . . . and then he says to me last night something like we can't ever be sure anything's going to work out, and I'm like, What the hell is that supposed to mean?"

"What do you think it means?"

Thank you, Freud.

"Whatever, I can't even get into that at this point. I've got major issues, Marc, we can't cover them all, certainly not in the span of just one night. Anyway, all I've ever wanted was to be on my own and get my life started, you know? I think that's why I'm jealous of Jared . . ."

"So you compare yourself and your failures to Jared and his successes?"

"Well, that's one way to put it. I'll just go slit my wrists now, thanks . . ."

"Please, Alexa. Go on."

"Okay, so my sisters, Julie and Nina, are both ridiculously successful too, and Nina's marrying some guy my parents love so it's like there's all that to live up to—"

"Do your parents want you to get married to this guy?"

"Well, you'd think my mom thought I was pregnant carrying Jared's unborn child the way she goes on about my *needing* to get married—"

"You're not pregnant, are you? Because we can't have pregnant people in medical studies . . ."

"Marc! I was saying she's always telling me to—never mind. No, I'm not pregnant. Anyway, I want to be in New York, make it on my own, buy my own crappy IKEA furniture—"

"They make good cinnamon rolls."

"Yeah, they do. Anyway, I just have no clue what kind of job I should have. Not that I can get one anyway." I roll over in bed now and face Marc, who, amazingly, looks totally fascinated with my story. Maybe if I'm good he *will* bring Prozac.

"Anyway, Marc, you wouldn't believe how hard I'm trying, it's like no one in the whole tristate area wants to hear from me, I'm like some kind of disease. Not really. I know you're probably not allowed to have diseased people in studies—"

"Well, not this kind of study at least."

"I mean, there must be some memo or something going around to HR departments warning them about me. Anyway, this girl Lyric just has her dad call up some important guy at Christie's and she gets a job right away. What kind of bullshit is that? Some unqualified yoga-fetishist hand model gets a job because her dad knows someone? What *is* that?"

"Nepotism."

"What?"

"Never mind. Just go on."

"Okay, and then I just totally fuck up these interviews . . . anyway, I do have *something* set up, but it's sort of like a back-up plan, you know? If I can't get a job by the time my lease is up, I'm just going to head off to volunteer to be a teacher in Majuro—"

"Majorca?"

"No, Majuro. It's in the Marshall Islands. I have a brochure in my bag, I think, if you want to see it."

Marc opens my bag and about seven tampons roll out. I can't get my life together, but I seem to be quite prepared for the wall of my uterus to bleed like the Hoover Dam.

"This it?" Marc, politely ignoring the parade of feminine hygiene products rolling all over the floor, takes out the brochure and flips through it. "This sounds amazing! You should definitely go to Majuro—why *wouldn't* you go? I would do this in a second if Lily and I weren't engaged . . . they pay for all your housing—and you'll learn Marshallese!"

"The point is I *could* go to Majuro and teach and have this whole new experience . . . and I agree, it does sound amazing and weird . . . but here's the thing: I feel like Majuro is just a waiting space, you know? If I know I want to go to New York and make a life for myself as an independent person there, what's Majuro got to do with it?"

Marc puts his pen and pad down. "Okay, yeah, I can see where you're coming from, but honestly, that trip still sounds amazing. I think you're nuts not to go. You really only have this one time in your life to mess around, and then it's bills, and marriage, and babies, and mortgages . . ."

"That doesn't change that I'm a failure."

"Don't you think you're being a little dramatic?" Marc absentmindedly asks. Then with more enthusiasm: "Wow, did you see these huts? This looks awesome! You live in these huts for the full year . . . You learn Marshallese cooking too! I can't believe you don't have to pay *them* to do this!"

"Marc! You're supposed to be helping me, not planning your second career here."

Help Wanted, Desperately

"Actually, I'm supposed to be watching you sleep . . ." Marc raises an eyebrow at me, and I realize that if I let him keep looking at the brochure, he'll let me keep talking about my problems.

"So let me get this straight," Marc puts down the brochure on the stand next to him, "You want a job in New York."

"Right."

"You want to make it on your own."

"Right."

"You want to know that Jared cares about you and would care about you no matter where you were in the world, even though you've been jealous, obnoxious, selfish, self-centered—"

"Okay, that's enough. But right."

"So why are you here at this study? Did we get to that part? Did I miss it?"

"Oh, I'm doing this whole medical study just for money, you know, like maybe I could make a career out of being a lab rat and do it in New York. I hear menstrual studies pay well."

As Marc frantically writes down everything I'm saying, it occurs to me that he's really doing me an incredible service. Not only am I not sleeping, I'm also crying my whole life out to him. Just as I feel touched by his humanity, I glance over to where I assume he's writing my story down, and notice instead that he's drawn dancing stick figures in front of the hut on my Majuro brochure.

"So Alexa, what's the problem? If you want my professional opinion, it sounds to me like you're doing the best you can, and that's what's most important here." Marc pushes hair out of his eyes. He's attractive all right, in that Murse kind of way of his. But he's not as attractive as Jared, who I can't stop thinking about. His adorable little grin while he sleeps. His dark, furry eyebrows. The mole on the back of his neck.

"Do you think the whole thing with me and Jared is weird—him being sort of distant and uncaring about me going to Majuro? Sometimes I worry about our future together, though. I mean, not you and me, Marc. Me and Jared. What if it doesn't work out?"

Marc looks at me, and for the first time, we lock eyes. "As for you and me, Alexa, well, I don't think it'll work out. But I'm sure Jared really loves you."

"Do you think it's wrong for me to try to go to New York when I have a back-up plan in Majuro?"

"I think you need to do what your gut tells you. You want to be in New York, you want to make it on your own." Marc has given up doodling headhunters on my Majuro brochure and is now in full form as my free-labor psychiatrist.

"Something like that, yeah."

"I think you know what you need to do then." He smiles.

"I've got to fight like a maniac to get my resume into every office in New York so I can do what I need to do."

"The huts on Majuro sound cool, though. You know, even if the New York thing doesn't work out." To himself, Marc mutters, "This is like Doctors Without Borders . . ." He shifts in his seat and adds, "Well, then, Alexa, it sounds like you've made a decision! I hope our talk has helped you out."

I smile and lie on my back. "Yeah, it really has." I close my eyes and pretend that Jared is lying next to me.

The room is quiet again, and I hear Marc cross his legs again, and shift in his seat.

"Marc?"

"Yeah?"

"You're a really great nurse."

Help Wanted, Desperately

Marc, with just a hint of self-loathing, responds, "You mean a really great *murse*, right?"

"No, Marc. I mean you're a really great nurse. Talking to you has really made me feel better. I want to go to New York. I'm *going* to go to New York. *And* I'm going to get a job there." I smile, and suddenly I feel sleepy. Extremely sleepy. I look at the clock: 12:30.

"Sounds good to me. And Alexa?"

Turning over, I yawn, "Yeah?"

"If you want my opinion, though, um, I don't think you should make a career out of being a medical-study subject. You're a little too . . . talky."

I roll over in bed, and let sleep finally overtake me.

When I wake up, Marc is there, looking exhausted. As I open my eyes he asks, "Any dreams about teeth?"

Thinking about it, I cheerfully respond, "Nope!"

Marc pays me my cash, and I head out of the hospital two hundred dollars richer, and so eager to call Jared on my cell phone I can barely get it out of my bag fast enough. As I take it out, the Majuro brochure falls onto the ground, and I quickly pick it up and shove it back in.

"Hi! How are you? I missed you last night!"

I can hear the smile in his voice, "That's good to hear. How'd it go?"

"Well, remember that fortune I got Sunday night? Well, it was true. Last night, someone new changed my mind."

Ariel Horn

Lessons Learned

1. Never accuse a male nurse of being a murse, unless you're ready to get into a heated discussion on the nature of gender politics and sexual stereotypes.

2. Being a medical subject is just like being in therapy, except your psychiatrist, instead of being a bearded Freud wannabe, is just a really hot guy in scrubs.

3. When you frequently dream about losing your teeth, assume you are losing your mind.

4. No matter how often you think about it, having fluorescent yellow teeth is better than having yarn for hair. Period.

5. It's unlikely that I'll ever need seven tampons at once. It's time to clean out my bag.

6. I can create my own fortune. I just have to figure out how.

13
The League
of Puppets

2 Months, 7 Days, 16 Hours

One haircut (with one of the country's many talented haircutters), four fortune cookies (complete with my own fortunes), two desperate phone calls to my parents, and three loads of laundry have passed since I confessed my life story to Marc the Murse. In countdown time, that means there are now only two months, seven days, and sixteen hours until I head to Majuro.

It's becoming increasingly more difficult to suppress gagging in terror when I think about it.

Whether it's because of boredom, a lack of other job opportunities, or simply because lack of sleep has translated into a chronic case of lack of brain, I can't help but tell everyone I know how I destroy all my chances at employment. And worse, each time I retell the horrors of my attempts at employment, I'm left with the same crippling and debilitating finale: Even though all I really want in life right now is to be in New York as an independent, self-sufficient person, the only place I'm getting closer to by the second is Majuro.

Ariel Horn

Dear Alexa,

As you surely know, you are a mere two months from joining us on the educational journey of a lifetime. In two months, you will begin to mold the minds of your students, shaping their lives with wisdom from your own personal knowledge bank and experiences. While Majuro always proves itself to be a valuable place for our teachers and students to learn and grow together, the Marshall Islands are also—unfortunately—a nurturing environment for various diseases to grow into deadly disasters amongst our volunteers.*

At Majuro Volunteers, your health and safety are of utmost importance to us. For this reason, we recommend that you protect yourself from the indigenous diseases of our beautiful islands. On behalf of your health and the health of your future students, please have these vaccinations or inoculations against the following diseases prior to your arrival on Majuro:

-Hepatitis A or immuno globulin

-Rabies (as you might be in contact with wild or domestic animals in Majuro, depending on where your students live)

-Typhoid

-A booster dose for tetanus-diphtheria

-A booster dose for measles

-A one-time dose for polio

Please don't forget also that antimalarial medication should be taken so as to avoid a preventable infection that, in some cases, can be deadly.** Additionally, you should plan on purchasing a bed net impregnated with the insecticide permethrin or deltamethrin to further protect yourself from the deadly Marshallese mosquitoes.

Help Wanted, Desperately

Please be advised as well that dengue, filariasis, Ross River virus, and Murray Valley encephalitis are also insect-carried diseases that occur on the Marshall Islands. Lastly, though there has recently been no risk in this region for yellow fever, here at Marshall Volunteers we always operate under the "better safe than sorry" mentality. Please protect yourself.

As a new member of Majuro Volunteers, we value your understanding that education is the key to a better tomorrow. We are delighted you'll be joining us as one of the gatekeepers to the future.

*To date, there have only been six volunteer deaths.

**To date, only thirteen of our participants contracted malaria while abroad.

Before I received this letter, Majuro was just a proverbial kick in my ass to get me searching for a job in New York. Suddenly, Majuro has now become a shot in my ass. To be more specific, six shots in my ass.

When I received this letter yesterday, I was positive that this was the nail in the coffin, or the duct tape that would hermetically seal closed any opportunities I might have of actually becoming a New Yorker and living an independent, self-sufficient life. To all intents and purposes, I was pretty sure that my receiving this letter was some sort of unofficial message indicating that it's time for my job search to officially end: My days and nights need no longer be spent proactively searching for a job. Instead, I would be forever trapped in horrible reruns of "Alex's Dumbest Home Videos," replaying in my mind all the stupid things I've done in the past seven months trying to get a job.

This letter from Majuro made me realize what I should've

known all along: that here I was, faced not with a fork in the road, but a spoon—and a spoon that would effectively halt all my personal efforts to get a job. It was time for me to suck it up and get my shots for Majuro. This was just the big Human Resources Department in the Sky's way of saying that the buck would stop here. It was time for me to kill my dream of becoming a New Yorker, of getting diseases only from the gritty, unsanitary subway rather than angry, vengeful Marshallese mosquitoes. Here it was, with all the cards laid out on the table: I would die itchy, sweaty, and impoverished, spelling the ABCs on a cardboard chalkboard in Majuro, surrounded by genuine, eager volunteers who truly wanted to be on the Marshall Islands in their attempts to make the world a better place, one third grader at a time.

But just after I had made an appointment to have eight million needles cushioned into my butt in preparation for the imminent trip to Majuro, just when I had caved in to the most recent piece of fortune cookie prophecy ("Be happy with where you are"— even if that's nowhere), an opportunity pops up on my computer screen this morning. Yet another e-mail from the ever-famed Margaret Kilmore, Queen of the Perfect Sit. Subject: "Interested in Public Relations and Event Planning? Put your money where your mouth is!" I decide to click on it.

To apply to work at Yadda, Yadda!, simply send your resume and cover letter to the address below. Uncreative, inside-the-box thinkers need not apply. As a supplement to your cover letter, please answer the following question:

If you were organizing a dinner party and could invite three people—a person from the past, a person from the pres-

*ent, and a person from the future—whom would you invite
and why?*

Why, I'm creative! If I can show this company that I'm an
outside-the-box thinker, couldn't I—hypothetically speaking, of
course—still achieve the dream of becoming someone other than a
volunteer? Someone who still has the potential to start life in the
Real World rather than waiting on hold in the middle of the Pacific?

I spend a couple of minutes thinking about who I would want
to have dinner with. Could go with traditional answers that
Yadda, Yadda! probably gets all the time: John F. Kennedy,
Gandhi (who probably wouldn't eat much), Madonna, George
Washington? Mussolini or Stalin might be interesting, but I
think it's always a bad idea to say you'd like to have dinner with a
tyrant (taking advice from Hitler didn't get me very far). Barbra
Streisand? The substitute teacher I had a crush on in high school
who looked like a Civil War general? Salma Hayek? Salman
Rushdie? Nelson Mandela? The creator of Barbie? Neil Arm-
strong? Louis Armstrong? The ob/gyn doctor who delivered
me? Theodore Roosevelt? Posh Spice? Fidel Castro? Jesus?
George Bush? The Girl from Ipanema?

After hours of deliberate thought (or ten minutes of careless
thought, which are sometimes just as valuable), I decide to ignore
the politically correct answers and choose the honest (and therefore more embarrassing) route instead. Dinner is on, with Fran
Drescher, Oscar Wilde, and my future child.

And now, I wait.

Amazingly, my resume and answer to Yadda, Yadda!'s question
get a response: my interview is in precisely one week. T-minus

one hundred and sixty-seven hours, thirteen minutes and twelve seconds. That gives me only one week to perfect my poised, non-bullshitty responses. One week for total metamorphosis— for the long and painful journey from unappreciated, untalented unemployable wretch to beautiful, skilled, likely-to-be-gainfully-employed potential candidate. If it's a talented, creative, out-of-the-box thinker they want, make no mistake, it is (the new and improved, cheaper, faster, funnier, vibrator-free) *Alexa Hoffman* they shall get! Move over, Majuro. New York is here to stay.

I show up at the interview wearing the same black suit that won me no friends at my consulting interview. And my retail interview. And, for that matter, every other interview I've had in the past seven months. I wonder briefly if the suit is jinxed, but then realize that for all the stupid things I've done in interviews, I have only myself to blame, not the charming black wool number that screams, "I want to be in an office doing inane administrative tasks from nine to five every day!" My interview is at 1:45, so I sit diligently at the Career Services' office from 1:30 on. I peruse the "informational" pamphlets Yadda, Yadda! has given the interviewees to read. "Free massages every Wednesday!" the pamphlet shouts in bright red letters. "Three weeks paid vacation!" "Medical benefits included!" "Company trips to Hawaii!"

Since it's a Wednesday, I think it's a safe assumption that I'll get a free massage from my interviewer.

As I'm flipping through the propaganda pamphlet, waiting for my interviewer to show up (it's 1:48), a guy from one of my classes—I think his name is Mike Harper? Carper?—shows up and sits down next to me. He's wearing newly polished black shoes and a serious and determined navy suit that professionally and casually says, "I'm on my way to being an executive." My suit pathetically whines, "I will alphabetize your Rolodex and color code your files."

Carper picks up a pamphlet and starts flipping through it carelessly. Five minutes later, as if he has just noticed that I've been sitting here for the past ten minutes wildly tapping my foot against the table to get his attention, Carper looks up. "So what are you doing here, Alex? Don't you have a job already? I feel like I just saw you here for that Sweeney's retail interview. Didn't they want you?"

"Um, no. I'm, um, what you might call 'unemployed.' " Others might call it pathetic, but I prefer the more clinical term.

Carper's eyes light up. "They didn't want me either! I got a rejection letter a week after my interview!"

For the first time in what feels like months, a real smile spreads across my face, I'm so happy that someone else is as unemployable as me. "Lucky! I didn't even *get* a rejection letter."

Carper and I sit in quiet mutual bliss at each other's failures.

"So," Carper casually asks. "What's your major?"

"I'm an English major. You?"

"Humanistic philosophy."

Carper's face darkens. Two points for me! On the scale of Useful Majors, Humanistic Philosophy is WAY below English!

Another awkward pause as Carper and I wait for our interviewers, who are now officially thirteen minutes late for our interviews at 1:45. Carper takes his glasses off and polishes them.

"So, how have your interviews been going?" I ask.

"Okay, I guess." Carper looks intently at his glasses, polishing them with unrelenting vigor. He looks up at me then and says,

"Well, I haven't really, you know, well, I've applied to a lot of stuff, but well, I haven't really had any besides this and the Sweeney's interview." Carper quickly looks down to his freshly polished black shoes through his freshly polished frameless glasses. Perhaps the shoes are not so much "freshly polished" as "never worn before"?

"Me neither, really." *Successful* interviews, that is.

And with my own implied admission of failure, Carper moves to the front of his seat, and gestures for me to lean toward him, which I do. He lowers his voice, "You see, I think I just really screw up interviews badly. I told the Sweeney's interviewer that I hate shopping. Can you imagine saying something that stupid to someone who's interviewing you to be a retail buyer?" Carper laughs at his own stupidity, and then looks around to make sure no one "important" saw him act so unprofessional. So human.

Before I can control myself from picking, yet again, my emotional scab, I blurt out: "I said the word 'vibrator' in a consulting interview!"

Carper looks at me with that what-the-hell-is-wrong-with-you face I've grown so used to. "So I guess we're both pretty much failures, huh?" he says. There's a sadness to his voice I can't really describe—except that I recognize it as the voice in my own head.

"So much for the real world, right?" Carper kicks a leg of his chair, and then looks me in the eye. "But wow, it really makes me feel so much better to know that you still can't get a job either. It means I'm not the only loser around."

"Um, yeah. I guess so." And even though Carper has all but made me into the most pathetic person on the planet, I somehow feel comforted, as if he's an old friend who has just hugged me and started reminiscing about all the things we used to do together. For a minute, I feel even closer to Carper than I have to Jared in weeks.

Just as Carper revels in the repopulating of the Land of Loserdom, a man in a purple shirt and black pants and a relatively uptight looking woman walk into the waiting area sipping Starbucks frappucinos.

"And so I said to him, I said, 'Jason, you can't *possibly* mean that! I mean REALLY!' " The thirty-something man takes a thick slurp. "Oh! They're here! Sorry we're late! But I mean, really, who could pass up a mocha frappucino on a day like *this*?" The man gestures to what should be gorgeous blue sky but in the confines of the dark Career Services' office is instead old, gray, water-damaged ceiling. "Can you BELIEVE the weather we're having? Now which one of you is Alex?" The man takes another thirsty suck from his frappucino.

"That's me."

"Let's get this party started then!"

I look at Carper and he looks back at me, giving me the tiniest little smile. I smile back, but Carper has already turned his head, no longer a human, but a professional.

I follow the man, who I later learn is named, Ricky! ("My name is Ricky! I'm the head of recruiting at Yadda, Yadda!") into the Interview Room. Apparently, everything at Yadda, Yadda! involves unnatural and maniacal excitement. I've never experienced such violation of the exclamation point. And of the 50 million hairdressers in the United States, Ricky! happens to look like mine.

Ricky! gestures towards where I should sit in the interview room, which resembles one of those dank, dark questioning rooms you always see in old movies where they torture the witness to talk. Except instead of one broken light bulb dangling from the ceiling, there's just one uninviting, industrial-looking lamp in the corner of the room. "So." Ricky! takes a long, gurgling sip from his empty frappucino cup, shakes it, holds it up to the light to see if maybe, just maybe he's missed a vagrant frappucinolette, and shakes the cup again. Another loud, obnoxious gurgle. "Let's talk about you." He crosses his legs. "Where do you see yourself in three years?"

Honesty or bullshit? Honesty or bullshit? The scale is weighing the pros and cons in my mind, and I remember briefly where honesty got me at the retail interview, the consulting interview, and even my *Rent* audition: up B.O. Creek without a surgical mask. I opt for bullshit.

"I'd love to be climbing the corporate ladder at Yadda, Yadda!, truthfully." (That is, if by *truthfully* we mean "having no truth whatsoever.") "My real passion is for public relations—I love the excitement of event planning, parties, the creativity, the fast-paced culture," that is, if we ignore the fact that I hate staying out late and am usually in bed by 11:15—well, 10:30 really. " I really can see myself advancing my career at Yadda, Yadda! It really offers the most impressive training I've seen in the public relations companies I've looked at." It's also, coincidentally, the *only* public relations company I've looked at.

Ricky! wrinkles his nose and smiles. "How cute!" He writes something down, and I think things are going decently. "So tell me more about your past job experience. Your resume looks so interesting and fun!"

I wax poetic about my past job experiences, omitting the fact that for the most part, I've spent the past four summers of my life in various fields and industries filing multicolored folders, which no one will ever look at, into metal cabinets.

As Ricky! looks more and more intrigued with my answers, I can't help but feel the same proud feeling I felt the first time I went to the bathroom by myself. Overwhelming, smile-bursting pride. "Look what I've done!" I want to shout. "Here I am, world! And I'm not messing up another interview! I'm gonna get this one! SO THERE!" I feel my face, for the first time in any of my interviews, relax into a perpetual smile. I feel calm. I feel myself forgiving Ricky! for being not ten, but twenty, minutes late to my interview. I'm in it to win it. Majuro, you can just suck it large. I feel the air of employment surrounding me seep into my skin. I have arrived.

"So, Alexa, let's see"—Ricky! scans my resume—"it says here you worked in the research department at the children's television show *Gorky and Pals.* How fun! I love love LOVE Gorky! Oh! Gorky! Such a cute little puppet! So what did you do there?" Ricky! leans in.

"It was a really great opportunity, actually. In the research program, we tested the effectiveness of programming within different economic brackets, so we'd show the same episodes of *Gorky and Pals* to different children who were raised in diverse environments in order to see how they learned best. It was really, really fascinating." Of course they're having a hiring freeze right now, but that's besides the point.

Appropriately, Ricky! is really, really fascinated. "You know what I love love LOVE the most about *Gorky and Pals?* I love how there's so much adult humor. Like, I'll be watching it with my little nephew, Ross-y, and he'll say, 'Oh, Gorky!' and I'll be thinking, wait a sec, that other puppet Mable the Walrus just said

Ariel Horn

something so funny that Ross-y, you know, he's three years old, something that he would just never get! I mean, Ross-y's smart, but he's no genius!"

A moment to shine! Fortunately, I read in the paper what's going on next week on *Gorky and Pals*. "You should definitely watch the show next week, then! They're doing a segment where Gorky interviews Kofi Annan! It should be hysterical." What's that sound I hear? Oh, is it the sweet sound of Victory ringing my doorbell? Why yes, I think it is! Yes, hello, please *do* come in! No, no, you're not in the way at all. Majuro was just leaving . . .

But instead of Ricky! jumping up and down and clapping as I would expect him to do—I get a different, scarier response. "Is Kofi Annan a new puppet on the show or something? I haven't watched it in a couple of weeks."

And that's when I hear Victory galloping away on its golden chariot, and the loud gurgling, sound of a toilet flushing in the back of my mind. Sneakily, happily, Majuro reappears in my mind's eye and all I see is a hut, some inoculation needles, and the apartment and life in New York I'll never have slowly slipping from sight.

Point-blank, the interview has really gone to shit. This thirty-something head of recruiting at Yadda, Yadda! thinks Kofi Annan is a puppet. This is the Real World that I'm so eagerly trying to shove my way into? This is why I'm fighting not to be on Majuro? I'm kicking, screaming, biting, crying just so I can have someone hire me so I can be with people like Ricky!? I'm not saying that I know all about Kofi Annan—I probably know what most people know—that he's an African politician who's head of the United Nations. But at the bare minimum, I know that he's not some purple furry puppet on *Gorky and Pals*.

Help Wanted, Desperately

The room is at a total standstill, and all I hear is Ricky's! watch ticking away. Ricky!—still fascinated by *Gorky and Pals* and what he surely anticipates as the heartwarming story of Mable the Walrus's new best friend—looks at me expectantly for an answer. Ricky! continues to stare at me, waiting for an answer. I stare back. A single drop of sweat rolls down my side. Nothing complements emotional horror quite as well as pit stains, I think.

Delicately, I quietly offer, "Kofi Annan is the head of the U.N."

Ricky! looks stunned. I've just done the second worst thing a person can do in an interview after casually discussing sex toys: I've made the interviewer feel dumb. But what could I do? Should I have lied and said, "Yes, Kofi Annan is the newest puppet on the show"?

Ricky! blinks a couple of times, trying to recover from the fact that Kofi Annan is not a puppet but a fairly important political figure of whom he had absolutely no recollection. "Oh. I thought that he, you know, that he was, and Mable, well she, and they . . . well. You know, just, just never mind what I thought." Ricky! tenses up and no longer looks like he's ready to take me home. He picks up his frappucino and takes a long, hard angry suck through the straw. "Do you have any questions for me?"

This hardly seems like a time to ask for a back massage. Instead, I ask what he likes best about his job. How the environment at Yadda, Yadda! is different from other PR firms.

Ricky! dutifully and unceremoniously answers my questions and looks at his watch. "We're running late, so I'm going to have to wrap up this interview now. Thanks for coming, have a good day." He escorts me out of the room. Just like that, opportunity has melted into defeat yet again.

Ariel Horn

I consider going home to make a sock puppet, whom I plan on naming Kofi Annan. Instead, I realize that Majuro is imminent, and well, I just might want to go there anyway. So without a sock puppet to call my own, or to head the United Nations, I dutifully head to the doctor's office to get six needles stabbed into my ass.

Mable the Walrus—and her press secretary—would not approve.

Lessons Learned

1. Explaining why Fran Drescher is a valuable member of society is a one-way ticket to employment.

2. Never correct your interviewer—even if he unironically declares that diplomatic leaders are, as it were, "puppets."

3. "Kofi Annan," like "Boutros Boutros-Ghali," is a good name for a purple, furry, orange-nosed puppet.

14
To Sniff, Perchance To Dream

1 Month, 9 Days, 14 Hours, 12 Seconds

Drastic times call for drastic measures: There is only one month, nine days, fourteen hours and twelve seconds until I'm shipping off to Majuro, unless another miraculous opportunity comes along, paving the way for me to set up camp in New York and live out the life, which, during more foolish times, I assumed would effortlessly and unconditionally be mine.

The truth of the matter is that, as much as I dread signing off on myself as a personal failure for a year, I've actually grown used to the idea of going to Majuro, and I've begun to truly believe that it a) might be interesting and b) may in fact be the right thing for me. Truth be told, after my interview with the sock puppet's best friend, I don't think I'm ready to spend a year with men like Ricky! talking about which foreign diplomat most closely resembles Elmo. As bizarre as it may sound, I think I might actually prefer spending a year on an island in the middle of nowhere teaching dengue-fever-ridden eight-year-olds how to speak English.

And if Majuro doesn't work out, well, the other option is just a lifetime of destitution in New York. Better than prostitution, I guess. But at this point, can I really rule that out?

Look, I'm not afraid to say it. I am desperate. *Desperate* with a capital, paranoid, neurotic, obsessive-compulsive D.

It's gotten bad enough that today, unbeknownst to Jared, my parents, or my sisters, I am truly doing something bizarre in order to find and secure employment in New York: I am going for an interview to become employed as a professional deodorant sniffer. As in: one who sniffs armpits to see whether deodorant works or not.

What, you ask, has driven me to a newfound love of stinky armpits? See the formula below:

Expectations – Ideals x (Desperate times + Desperate Measures) = Desire to become professional deodorant sniffer

Let me explain why the deodorant-sniffer gig doesn't seem that outlandish to me. Ever since I was a sophomore in high school, I've been an unnatural sweat-er. There I was, minding my own business in eleventh-grade French lit, carelessly writing notes to Miranda when she looked up at me from the note, looked at my armpit, and looked back at me. She shot me a note across our desks. "You've got a problem. You're pitting out."

I responded, " 'Pitting out?' Define."

"Sweating in unnatural proportions. Look at your pits."

Subtly, avoiding the evil glare of Madame Birnbaum (who, I might add, was growing increasingly less pleased with our note passing, which was not "en français"), I lifted my left arm and was greeted by one of the most personally horrific physical absurdities I'd ever seen on my own body: a dark navy blue ring in the armpit of my light blue shirt.

It was every girl's worst nightmare.

A year later, I'm on prescription deodorant that my doctor suggested I put on every night before I go to sleep. It smells like nail polish and burns my skin the way only alcohol-on-armpit can—a feeling I hadn't had the pleasure of knowing only a year before. Four years into my affair with Drysol the miracle drug, I still haven't gone as far as the doctor wants: Without irony, he suggested I Drysol my pits and then wrap Saran Wrap around them each night before I go to bed "to pack it in." Somehow, this Drysol-ing routine doesn't seem like an exactly romantic bed-time ritual, and while asking Jared to Saran Wrap my pits before bed seems like it could be intimate, I think that's something that can wait until we're well into our imaginary marriage, after I've gotten fat and he's gone bald. I'll just wait until the day when I have to help him manage his way into adult diapers and navigate the geriatric world of weak sphincter-hood. Then I'll break out the Saran Wrap. Lucky, lucky boy.

Nothing says "sexy" like a girlfriend who chronically pits out.

But one unfortunate night with Jared, I learned the severity of the situation. Just before Jared left for New York again, as I lay nuzzling his neck while we lazily watched *The Nanny* (despite his protests), Jared tapped my head and said, "Hey there," a telltale sign that something was up, since no one—except characters on daytime TV and aging hipsters—actually says "Hey there."

Sleepy and cuddling, drinking in all the Jared-ness I could be-fore he would leave for New York to yet another Christie's job orientation thing (don't get me started on Lyric the Ever-Thinning Potato again), I looked up at him. "Yeah?"

He stroked my hair, and took my earlobe in his hand, lovingly looking at it as if it were a small, pink seashell . . . well, that, or a nacho. "Look, we're honest with each other, right?"

Uh-oh.

"Yeah, of course! Why?"

"And I can tell you anything, right?"

"Duh." Hmm. There was a phrase I hadn't thought to use since fourth grade.

"And because I love you, anything that I might say to you that might be construed as criticism you know of course is really said in a loving, nice way because we can share anything and everything with each other, right?"

"Jesus, what is this, *Oprah*? What are you talking about?" Is this the preemptive if-you-go-to-Majuro-you-know-it-won't-be-the-same-between-us talk? No! I'm not ready—stop the presses! Should I try to escape? I eyed the door and mentally went over how quickly I could feign a sudden attack of traveler's diarrhea, and then run and lock myself in the bathroom.

A pause. I looked at Jared. He looked at me. He glanced at my (dry) armpits.

Uh-oh.

His eyes quickly shifted away from my armpits, as if he'd looked at me in a lewd way that would somehow offend me. "You know how you have that prescription deodorant stuff?"

"Yeah?"

"And how it gets rid of the sweat?"

All right, no more cuddling for you, bub. I don't like where this is going.

"Yeah?" Now I looked at Jared straight on. The Snuggle Train officially stopped.

Help Wanted, Desperately

Jared focused intently on one of my curls and ran his fingers through it carefully, "Well, it doesn't get rid of the smell."

Dear God.

"Excuse me?"

"I said it doesn't get rid of the smell." Jared dropped his hands to his lap and looked at his fingers intently, as if he'd never seen them before.

"What the hell is that supposed to mean?"

Turning to look at me, he said the unthinkable: "You stink."

"What?!"

"You. Stink. You smell, Alex."

"I smell?"

"You smell."

"*I* smell?"

"I don't know how I can make this any clearer. Look, I love you, you're great, but ya stink. It happens. Get some other weird prescription-deodorant thingy, and you'll be fine. And hey, switch the channel—I think there's a *Three's Company* marathon on, or something."

That was when I knew I really had a problem. Three's company indeed: my pits, my sweat, and now, my stink. I am a triple threat. This has gone way, way beyond the help that Saran Wrap and Drysol can offer.

After reading all I could find in online literature on body odor and excessive sweating (known to the medical world as hyperhidrosis, but let's not get technical—I could go on for hours), I've resigned myself, ironically, to doing it as the French do it: drenching myself in perfume—much to the chagrin of classmates, fellow passengers, and people with allergies. So far, everything seems to be working okay. Unfortunately, as Jared is honest with me, I know he'll tell me if I have a problem again. And as for my mother (the woman who coined the phrase "You look like a sausage" as I tried on a skirt in an overcrowded Banana Republic), the only comment she repeatedly makes is "You smell like Eli Kraus."

Eli Kraus being, of course, my very first date. When my parents and I picked up Eli at his house one cold January day so we could go see some bad teen movie I don't remember, he got in the car and my parents immediately opened all the windows. Eli was wearing enough cologne to clear an elephant's sinuses. As Eli shivered in the backseat and tried frantically to shut his window, I heard the click of my father child-locking all the windows in the car. Then my mother began sneezing. "What *is* that smell? I'm gonna choke, I'm gonna choke! I'm having an allergy attack!"

So began my romantic life.

So, smelling like Eli Kraus aside, I seem to be doing pretty well for myself. No more stink. No more sweat.

But what about other people who still have sweating problems? Isn't there a way for the powers that be in pharmaceutical La-La land to fix all of this?

And that's when I have my vision.

It's time for me to apply to be a professional deodorant sniffer, a job which, I am both horrified and delighted to find out, really and truly exists.

After an hour spent perusing various Web sites on hyperhidrosis and searching phrases such as "deodorant sniffer," "smelly armpits tester" and "deodorant testing," ("pitting out AND job" bring up nothing) I learn that: 1) "the passage of a small electric current through the skin tends to stop the sweat glands from working for quite a while" and 2) there is a dream job waiting in cyberspace for me: a job where I can help myself . . . and help humanity simultaneously. The ad reads

Sensory Consultant Needed.
Evans-Heller Pharmaceutical Company Seeks Freelance Trained Sensory Consultants to Evaluate New Deodorizing Product. Please Have Experience in Field.
Excellent Compensation. Serious Responses Only.

Apparently, the real name for what I like to call a deodorant sniffer is really "sensory consultant." After seconds of (mis)calculated thinking, I come to a decision that sounds a little like this: Alexa *Hoffman,* sensory consultant, at your service.

In terms of experience in "the field," I'm what this pharmaceutical company might call a natural. I sweat! I smell! What more experience could these people want?

Suspecting that Evans-Heller Pharmaceutical might want to see "real" experience on my resume, I decide to spend the rest of the day avoiding my European history class and creating the ultimate sensory-consultant resume. But where to start?

The phone.

"Mom, if you were, say, going to apply to be someone who test-smells products—what sort of experience would you say you had?"

"None. Alex, I've never test-smelled anything in my life. I've never even heard of test-smelling! What kind of job is this? Alex, we didn't send you to college to test-smell or model scout or . . . whatever. I don't know how many times I have to say it . . . Go. To. Law. School."

"Okay, fine, but remember when we were in France one time on vacation—we went to that perfume place—what was it called?"

Heaving a dramatic, exasperated sigh into the phone, my mother responds, "Fragonard."

"Right! Fragonard! Remember, they had people who smelled the perfumes to make sure they were good? Remember, that guide told us they had like a Fragonard Institute, or something, where you had to learn how to smell?"

"Alex, I don't really remember that. Listen, let's talk about something important. Do we really think peach is the right color to go with on Nina's wedding? I mean, pink could be very pretty in May. Or how about *shades* of pink? Rory said the shades of pink would work . . ."

"Mom, Rory also told us a story about how he once saw the mother-of-the-bride giving a blow job to the groom right before some wedding he did." Wow, there's a word I can't believe I just said out loud to my mother. *Blow job.* Does she even know what that word means? Do I even want to know if she knows what that word means?

"Alex, he's a florist—that doesn't mean he doesn't know flowers. And I don't want to talk about that again. He shouldn't have told us that in the first place. And besides, he said that he only watched for three minutes."

"Mom, our florist is allergic to flowers. That's like having a woman with a lazy eye make the wedding dress or a deaf mute play your first song. I think that means it's legitimate for us to second-guess him."

"He's not permanently allergic—he was allergic that one day!"

"Mom, it was more than one day. It wasn't even allergy season."

"Fine, you're right. But we *do* have an obese pastry chef, and that bodes well. Remember this, Alex, you always want a pastry chef who's fat. It means he likes his food. Anyway—what do you think we should go with: pink or peach?"

"Rory calls it 'pêche.' "

"Okay, 'pêche.' "

"I don't know, Mom. I'm sure they'll all look great."

My mother sighs knowingly into the phone, "You know, when it's your wedding to Jared instead of Nina's, well, then you'll care. And then I'll remind you about this conversation when Nina takes no interest."

"Mom, look, I've got to send this resume out to this pharmaceutical company I'm going to apply to for work. I gotta go."

Suddenly, I can hear my mother smiling through the phone. Dare I say she sounds . . . *pleased* with me? "Oh! A pharmaceutical company! I didn't know this whole test-smelling thing was with a *pharmaceutical company!* That's great—pharmaceutical companies are really stable right now. Of course, one day when you and Jared are married . . . well, just find out if they give good maternity leave."

"Right-o. Anyway, Mom, thanks for the Fragonard thing. I'll make you proud."

"You always make me proud. Love you."

I hang up the phone and write on my resume "Sensory Consultant, Fragonard." Desperate times, more desperate measures. This may just be my last chance at a job in New York: only one month, nine days, sixteen hours 'til Majuro. Throw my morals (okay, what's left of them) out the window: I'm a broken woman.

It's time to lie on the resume.

So just how many years should I write that I've worked at

Fragonard? Two. Two seems respectable. We'll say I studied abroad in college, and worked there while I was in France. Almost too perfect.

I look at the resume one more time—seems believable. But is "Sensory Consultant" good enough? They wanted real field experience! The cursor flashes on my screen. In front of "Sensory Consultant" I slowly type "Senior." There. Senior Sensory Consultant. That looks better. Wow, I feel impressive already.

And now, I wait.

Less than two hours after sending my e-mail resume out, I'm called in for an interview with Francine Tucker at Evans-Heller Pharmaceutical. Less than twenty-four hours later, I have arrived in the lobby of Evans-Heller Pharmaceutical in New York.

As I wait, I figure I might as well call Jared and see how he's doing. According to my memorization of his schedule, he should be on his way to his contemporary art history class right now.

"Hi there! How are you?"

"Hey, what a great surprise!" Jared sounds happy. "I didn't expect to hear from you till later . . . Aren't you at the interview?"

"Yup. Just about to go in. Ready to sniff my way to success."

Jared pauses. "Did you really say you were a sensory consultant at Fragonard on your resume?"

Embarrassed for the first time for lying, and even more embarrassed that this is the part of our conversation from last night that Jared remembers, I cough and reply, "Um, yeah."

"Oh, Alex, *why*? You're smart! People would kill to have you work for them!"

"And yet, there are no human resources-related murders surrounding my resume as a motive . . ."

Help Wanted, Desperately

A little out of breath—I can tell he's going to be late—he answers, "Alex, you know what I mean. You're a smart person—you're interesting, you pick up things fast, and you're even a nice person most of the time, well, when you're not lying. Or brooding. Or plotting. Anyway, this is the kind of stuff these people love. The point is, you shouldn't have to lie to get a job. *And* it's just plain wrong. It's *deceitful*."

One of the things I love and hate about Jared: he's a real moralist. And not because he thinks he's better than everyone else, because he doesn't think that—it's because he genuinely believes in doing the right thing. For instance: he won't pay for children's tickets at the movies and then sneak in as an adult (which is a technique that I think has saved me over four thousand dollars). He won't take more than one free sample anywhere—even if it's just a free tiny pencil at the library (those are free, right?). And when he heard that his cousin had tried to steal from a restaurant's tip jar on their ski trip, he almost left the cousin in Killington. For eternity.

I reach into my shirt, blot my pits quickly with a tissue, and reply, "I know it's not right— but I just feel like, I'm not lying per se because I *do* happen to know *a lot* about sweating and deodorant, I'm practically a professional already, and I just need to get my foot in the door! And besides, this is a real job! It's a *pharmaceutical company*! I'll tell them the truth, I swear. I've just got to get this job . . . It's this or dengue fever in Majuro. So the point is, I'll tell them the truth. Eventually. When the time's right."

"When's that? After you get hired for a position that you're not qualified for?"

"What about me being smart, Jared? What about people

killing to have me work for them? Let's go back to that part where you say that I'm smart and nice . . ."

"Just get done with this interview and come visit me, okay? And try not to lie more than you already have. You're much prettier when you're honest."

"And I'll be much prettier, I bet, if I'm in New York rather than Majuro."

Sighing, Jared says, "Alex, we don't have time for this . . . I have to go. Call me when it's over. I love you."

"Always." I hang up the phone, try to shake off the moral ambiguity (or clarity) of what I'm doing, and head into Evans-Heller.

Sitting in the lobby, I peruse the promotional material lying on the impeccably clean coffee table next to me. As I flip through the brochure filled with happy people in lab coats playing with multicolored test tubes, I actually start to respect myself. This is just as respectable and impressive as working in Majuro as a teacher volunteer. Except this is in New York, thus making it even more impressive and respectable, right? This is a *real* job. This is a *pharmaceutical* company: reputable, responsible, impressive. Almost as impressive as my time spent at Fragonard. I am going to be a sensory consultant for Evans-Heller. Or perhaps, based on my past experience, a SENIOR sensory consultant.

As delusions of grandeur dance in my head like newly prescribed Drysol sticks, a short, fifty-something woman in a lab coat approaches me, walking quickly with a determined step. She looks serious, wearing dark-rimmed glasses that look like they were bought in the 1960s and her hair pulled back in a tight, brown, important-looking bun. She looks relatively fit, though her nose seems to be stuck in a perpetual-wrinkle mode. She looks like someone pretending to be a scientist . . . except she probably *is* a scientist. Do I look like someone pretending to be a sensory consultant . . . or someone who *is* a sensory consultant? Do I look like a teacher on Majuro . . . or a person who just plays a teacher on Majuro on TV? The woman's steps slow, and she stops in front of me.

"I'm Francine Tucker, Director of Sensory Consulting here at Evans-Heller. You must be Alexa."

"Yes, I am." As I extend my hand to shake hers, she abruptly steps away.

"I don't shake. It affects my senses and will ruin my work for the rest of the day. Please, accept my nod in lieu of a handshake." Francine nods her head at me, much like unicorns did back in the day when I used to watch *My Little Pony*. Not knowing exactly what to do in response, I suppress the urge to whinny, and simply nod back, with hopes that perhaps she will stroke my face and give me a sugar cube sometime later in this interview.

"Please, follow me. I'd like to take you on an informal tour of the sensory consultation department, and then I'll ask you some questions about your experience at Fragonard."

Francine and I start walking down an empty, clean white hallway that smells overwhelmingly like Lysol. Francine seems unfazed, though I feel like I'm going to choke. I try not to breathe as I respond, "Oh yes, my time at Fragonard. Such . . . fond memories."

Francine and I finally arrive at the end of the hall, and Francine holds her hand up to a hand scan. Staring directly into what appears to be a tiny one-inch camera, she says her name in a clear, loud voice: "Francine Tucker." Who knew deodorant sniffing was so high tech?

The doors open in a silent, swift way and shut immediately behind us—and suddenly, I feel as if we're on a spaceship from *Star Trek*. Francine and I are now in a quiet, clean conference room with no windows. There is definitely something other-worldly about this place. She gestures for me to sit down.

"I know it must seem silly to you—the whole security bit. But, as you can imagine, we have a tremendous security risk here, what with the competition these days among all the companies. Just three years ago we lost one of our best sensory consultants to OBG, and he told them all every little detail of what we were working on. Granted, we can't prevent *that* sort of thing, but now we're doing our very best to make sure that Evans-Heller's ideas stay here at Evans-Heller."

Francine takes off her glasses and begins to rub them intensely. For a second I wonder if she's going to take out her bun, shake her hair, and do the whole sexy-librarian thing. Instead, she simply places her glasses again delicately upon the bridge of her nose.

Would I look wild and sexy wearing island wear outside my hut?

"Excuse me for going on about all that. I hardly have to tell *you* about security issues, what with you having worked at Fragonard for two years." Francine looks down at my resume.

Shifting uncomfortably, my armpits as hot and moist as a sultry summer evening in the Amazon, I nervously look around the room. "Um, yeah. Fragonard was like that in a lot of ways." I would imagine.

Francine smiles at me warmly. "I admit that when I first saw your resume, I was tremendously jealous. In the beginning of my career, I had wanted to go to the Grasse School to become a professional 'nose' for Fragonard. And when I saw that at your young age you were already a senior sensory consultant, well! Amazing, really. But I won't let my jealousy get the best of me— I just know your talents could do wonders here at Evans-Heller."

Magnanimously, I offer, "Well, you know how it is. It's just such a selective process over there at the Gas school. Unreasonable, really."

Francine twitches and looks me in the eye. "You mean the Grasse School."

Does sniffing impair one's brain? Is this woman deaf? "Yes, that's what I said, 'the Grasse School.' "

Francine shakes her head at me. "No, you said the 'Gas' School."

Shifting in my seat, I wipe my brow. "Right. Grasse School. It's been a while."

Francine crosses her legs and tilts her head, looking at me curiously, as if I was one of her little experiments. Then she mutters to herself, "Sort of strange to forget the name of a place as prestigious as the Grasse School." Straightening up, ready to take charge of the interview, Francine then asks, "In any case, would you mind telling me about your experience there—and then at Fragonard?"

"Well, I"—time to pull out the heavy-duty bullshit here— "Grasse was great, I made a lot of really good friends. Some great sniffers over there—really keenly involved in the whole process, you know? It was there I discovered my true passion for becoming a sensory consultant. And as for Fragonard, well, that was great too. I smelled a lot of scents over there. Every day, smelling. You know what it's like. But, well, I knew I wanted to do that sort of thing here in the States when I left France after my time studying abroad, so when I saw your ad, of course I thought it would be perfect . . ."

Francine seems confused. "So you didn't actually create any scents? That's interesting—other people who have come to Evans-Heller from Fragonard have often mentioned that a central part of their daily duties was inventing perfumes. They usually tell us how they worked surrounded by raw materials and used precision scales, coming up with scents through trial and error."

At this point, the sweat is streaming down my sides. I might very well slip off my chair. Francine is staring at me. "I, um, didn't have to make the perfumes because I was just a sensory consultant."

"Yes, that's the other interesting part. Some of our sensory consultants here at Evans-Heller have told me that they're trained as 'noses'—not sensory consultants—to become incredibly creative and original perfumers. You don't seem to have had that experience. In fact, I was completely unaware that they even had something called 'senior sensory consultant' over there."

"Well, honestly, I was so junior there, " *Alex, who's ever heard of a "junior" senior sensory consultant?!*—"being so young and all . . . they sort of made the position up for me." *Sort of like I'm making the position up for* you, *Francine.*

Francine pauses and crosses her legs. "So, did you grow up in France?"

Relieved there is finally a question I can actually answer without lying, I proudly tell Francine, "No, I was raised in New Jersey."

Francine looks assured that I'm telling the truth. "So, you had family members who had worked in Grasse as perfume makers?"

"Nope, it was my own idea. I'm creative like that. See, I like to do new things. Try new stuff out. That's why sensory consulting is such a passion for me. Once you start smelling, you know, nosin' your way around, you can't stop."

Francine looks at me, disbelieving. "Are you sure you didn't have any relatives who lived or worked in Grasse?"

"Nope. My family is from New Jersey and Long Island."

Francine looks positively perplexed. "But that doesn't make sense, does it? When I applied to Fragonard, they told me I couldn't go because I hadn't lived in Grasse, and hadn't had a relative live there either!"

Shit. "Well, you should probably take that up with admissions. They can be real jerks sometimes. So much red tape, you know? And maybe it's different if you're studying abroad there. Who knows, maybe your essay wasn't what they were looking for?"

Slowly, Francine says, "But there wasn't an essay to get into Grasse . . . and there isn't an admissions committee either . . ."

Double shit. "Yeah, well, that was a while ago. Who knows how people get in these days . . . ?"

Francine looks crestfallen. "I can't believe I didn't get into Grasse. I had all the perfect qualities to be a nose!"

Trying to make light of Francine's crushed dreams, I say, "Well, who knows? Get it, knows? Nose?"

Francine glares at me and heaves such a tremendous sigh that even I can feel it echo in my own chest. "Well, I think we've done enough talking. I'd like to see you in action on the floor. Please, follow me."

As we walk through another security check, Francine holds her hand up, and says "Francine Tucker." We've made it through

Ariel Horn

the check, and I feel pretty proud of myself in a disgusting, embarrassing way. I've just lied my way through an interview in unexplainable efforts to become a deodorant sniffer. Could it get more pathetic than this? Maybe, since I've just re-crushed the tattered dreams of some poor, innocent lab-coated woman by lying about my own experience at "Grasse"—wherever the hell that was. Is this an unconscionable act of revolting magnitude? Hmm. Perhaps I can ponder that while in Majuro months from now, as I reflect on the stupidity of all the dumb things I did in my efforts to get a job in New York.

There's no time for me to think about all the lies I've just told. To my total amazement, standing before me in a room that looks like a hermetically sealed airline hanger, I see rows upon rows of lab-coated men and women who look just like Francine Tucker. There are test tubes, and paper dipsticks that remind me of those litmus papers that we used in seventh-grade science class for experiments with ammonia. Maybe they *are* litmus papers. Did pH have to do with deodorant? What was that Secret commercial— "Strong enough for a man, but pH-balanced just for you"? I don't remember . . .

"This is the laboratory where all the sensory consulting occurs. Many of our technicians and consultants can remember and recognize up to three thousand four hundred different smells, and can explain why the products smell the way they do—and how we can get them to smell the way we want them to."

"As you know, you'll be working—should we hire you—on our new deodorant product, which we're tentatively calling Reach. I'll take you over now to meet the Reach team."

Francine's otherwise cloudy disposition suddenly warms up as she walks over to a lab table surrounded by twelve forty- and fifty-something men, all of whom look up at me as if I'm an alien with deodorant oozing out of my mouth. Can they see my sweaty pits through my suit jacket?

Crouching over his experiment, a possessive labbie sneers, "Who's she?"

"This is Alexa, she was a senior consultant at Fragonard."

A tall bald labbie looks me up and down. "I'm John. Fragonard?"

What, does he think I'm not *good enough* for Fragonard? What the hell is *that* supposed to mean? "Yes," I say sweetly, "Fragonard."

"So you went to Grasse."

"Yup, I went to Grasse."

John looks up at me. "But you're not from Grasse itself?"

"Nope."

"Do they actually do that? I've never, ever heard of them taking someone there who didn't come from Grasse or work there."

Francine is starting to look upset again. Changing the subject away from her broken heart, Francine suggests, "So let's test her abilities, boys. Bring out Jane."

Before I have the chance or the insight to wonder who the hell Jane is and why they're going to a closet to get her, Jane is proudly standing before me: a plastic body model—a dummy named Jane. Cute. I guess this is labbie humor.

Tall and Bald John begins speaking. "So, I'm sure they had Janes at Fragonard, but here, well, we use Jane a little bit differently." The men look at each other and grin.

I feel like I'm being hazed.

"We coat Jane in very smelly things—you know, onions, garlic, sweaty shirts, all that good stuff—and then, well, we try

Reach on her." John shrugs and looks around at his fellow labbies, who all nod furiously in agreement. "It's that simple, really.
And then each one of us goes in for the topical smelling at first,
you know, to see if there's a difference. After that, it's back to
plugging away at changes and modifications in the chemical formula for the rest of the day.

"So, today, we've washed Jane up, and reapplied the odors
to her."

I thought I smelled something.

"Now, we're going to see if our calculations the other day
worked—and see if we got the kinks out of the Reach formula we
used yesterday. So. Let the games begin!"

A hush washes over the group. Silence. Then, part artist, part
technician, entirely insane, John gently lowers his head, and lovingly applies Reach to Jane's pits. Then, as his nose ever-so-lightly
grazes the plastic loveliness of Jane's torso, he closes his eyes, his
quivering lips nearly licking Jane's nipple as he eases his body
toward Jane's armpit. The other sensory consultants look on in appreciative awe. Francine smiles, her lips pursed—she is visibly excited (sexually?) and fascinated. With his eyes still closed, John
then takes a tremendous whiff, punctuated by delicate, whimsical
sniffs. Deeply inhaling, the scene is a visual symphony: his nose
the conductor, Jane's body the violin. As I watch in completely
baffled awe, I feel as if I'm witnessing a deeply personal and sexual
moment, and I find myself wondering if this is how John looks before he makes love to a (nonplastic) woman. He opens his eyes
slowly as if waking from a soft, delicious dream, and smiles.
"Don't you worry, Alexa—I saved the best part for you."

"Excuse me?" How is it that, without actually knowing what
the "best part" is, I already feel like vomiting?

Help Wanted, Desperately

"Well, as part of our evaluation of your skill set, we'd like you now to use your Grasse-trained nose to tell us exactly how the Reach formula needs to be improved, based on your sensory analysis."

At the very millisecond that I realize that this means that John wants me to sniff the deodorized pits of a plastic model, all of the sensory consultants look at me in eager anticipation. Francine's smile morphs into a sneer, and that's the moment when I know that Francine knows what I've known for this whole Evans-Heller experience.

I am really full of shit.

Francine looks at me with innocent expectancy. "Please, Alexa, show us how the sensory consultants at Fragonard do it, *vous pouvez le faire, oui?*"

Huh?

John looks at me, his eyebrows raised, as if urging me to go on and take a whiff. And I know what I have to do.

Gently, delicately, I lower my head toward Jane's torso, mimicking John's every move. All eyes watching me, I close my eyes and begin to beg God in a way I haven't since I took the SATs: *If you let me get through this, I will never lie again on my resume, I will become a normal person who will get a normal job in normal circumstances.* I lower my head further and gingerly inch my way toward Jane's Reach-covered armpits, my lips grazing her onion-garnished torso. Then, at that exact pivotal moment of my interview, the stench overpowers me: Something like garlic, sweat socks, locker room, and garbage rolled into one hits me like a wrecking ball. Overpowered, on the verge of some physical reaction, a cross between vomiting and lightheadedness, I squeeze my eyes shut and take a deep, long breath.

The sensory consultants echo, with their own deep, long breaths.

And that's when I feel weak in my knees. I look at Francine and John desperately. Mustering up the last jewel of energy not yet sucked away by the overwhelming odor of Jane, I gasp out: "Reach . . . doesn't . . . work."

And then my body slumps to floor.

"Alexa? Alexa? Are you okay?"

It's like a nightmare: four men in lab coats standing above, and one woman with pristinely overplucked eyebrows. This is what Custer must have felt like . . .

"I'm fine. Just felt a little dizzy from that smell."

Helping me up, John offers, "Such a strange reaction for a sensory consultant to have . . . I've never seen anything quite like it!"

The other lab coats nod in agreement. "Peculiar." "Absurd." "Unusual indeed."

Sort of like this whole experience, no?

John. "Do you feel all right now?"

Please, God, get me out of here. I forgive you for not pulling through on helping me with the smelling test . . . but please, please figure out a way for this to end. I will go to Majuro. I will never think twice about what could've been in New York. I will complete the requisite waiting period in the Marshall Islands. I will admit personal failure, just get me the hell out of here. "Yes, yes, I'm fine. Just embarrassed, that's all." I dust myself off and check quickly to make sure no one can see my own sweaty armpits.

Having given me approximately thirty seconds to recover, the lab coats look at each other excitedly, "So, well, what are your thoughts on Reach?"

Help Wanted, Desperately

Have we forgotten already that I have just *passed out*? Company policy: armpits first, coma later.

"It was okay." When in doubt, lie, lie, *lie!*

John and the labbies look at one another. "'Okay'? What does that mean?"

Giving up completely and totally, I offer, "Well, to be quite honest with ya, John, it smelled pretty damn bad."

Francine and John look at each other, dumbfounded. Figuring it all out for sure for the first time, Francine accusingly and slowly spits out: "You never went to Grasse, did you?"

Smiling for the first time in this sweaty hell known as Evans-Heller, I proudly offer, "Nope."

Gasps all around. The labbies look like I've just told them that Jane isn't a real woman—or that I've figured out a super-effective secret formula for Reach.

"And France?"

"Never lived there."

Disbelieving his ears, John furrows his brow and tilts his head like a curious rabid dog. "I can't believe my ears! Fragonard?"

"Went to the gift shop once."

Francine, no longer amazed so much as pissed, grabs my arm and picks up the walkie-talkie attached to her hip.

"SECURITY! We've got a four-nine-seven-six breach on the lab floor!"

Uh-oh.

Lessons Learned

1. Lying on your resume should be avoided at all costs, unless it can be done convincingly, in which case lying is perfectly ac-

ceptable (unless you're in a court of law . . . in which case it's bad. Very, very bad.).

2. Know thy forged alma mater. Purchase said alma mater sweatshirts, brochures, and admissions materials *before* lying commences.

3. If lying about a past job is absolutely necessary, refrain from giving yourself a skill-specific job title. And from giving yourself undeserved promotions.

4. When a grown man lovingly brushes his lips across the breasts of a plastic woman without even a touch of irony, assume he is simply a touch insane.

5. There is nothing personally shameful in Saran-Wrapping your armpits at night. No matter what they say.

15
Yadda, Yadda! . . .Yadda

15 Days, 3 Hours, 2 Minutes, 0 Hope

Today the shit really hit the fan. Jared's job at Christie's officially started, thus leaving me with even more time on my hands to contemplate why I am so unforgivably unemployable. When he and I said goodbye yesterday at the train station, his face was practically glowing with that deserved self-satisfaction that comes with obtaining respectable employment.

Yesterday, as I stood at the top of the stairs at Track 13 all alone, I watched Jared cheerfully walk down the stairs toward the train, turn around, wave, smile, come back for another kiss, and then rush down the stairs, vanishing off onto an anonymous train that, at the end of his journey, would deliver him to a world filled with all the menial entry-level job tasks I've been lusting after these past seven months. Magically, with an employee ID in hand, Jared would be transported to a place where people needed him, where he did something important (or at least he did *something*), a place in which his sole presence inaudibly proved to friends and snotty relatives alike that he had made something of

301

himself. That he had done it—that all the hard work throughout his life had paid off. Jared had arrived—he was going places.

In contrast, I was going nowhere. As I stood at the top of the stairs, waiting (I'm not sure for what), hoping that Jared would turn around one last time, I felt horribly and unbearably alone. It didn't seem quite real, that now, the one person in my life who always seamlessly understood everything about me (minus my irrational jealousy of Hand-Modeling Yoga Instructors) was shipping out, off to the exotic world of employment—the one place in the world my passport couldn't take me.

Yesterday, the meaning of *pathetic* reached a whole new level. Suddenly, the tears began and it was like I had some sort of ocular infection. All I could think about was the fact that Jared was on a journey where the end destination was Success, and through some sick twist of fate, I was headed for Majuro instead. As I wiped the tears off my face on my already snot-covered sleeve, I felt like one of those sappy girls in the end scene of a romantic comedy. This was the part where the perfect boyfriend left for France (okay, or New York) . . . and then ran back off the plane (or train, in this case) into the deserving girl's arms, hugging and kissing her passionately, telling her he could never leave, not even for a couple of months, not even for a couple weeks, days, or minutes. Except in my unfortunate, unedited version of the story, he actually leaves to pursue his dream. I, on the other hand, find myself suddenly left to my own devices in Philadelphia. In fifteen days, three hours and two minutes, I have to come up with a dream of my own. That or I'm voted onto the Island.

So here I am: crying by myself, unemployed, apparently unemployable, dating a successful guy whom I envy, love, and loathe simultaneously.

Help Wanted, Desperately

But wait, that's not all. When I say shit has hit the fan, we're not playing games.

Miranda was accepted to law school. Worse, she's going. And even worse than that, I am now officially *the* only person I know still un-gainfully unemployed, not attending graduate school next year, with no real understanding of what my future holds.

And worst of all: Today, the tickets to Majuro arrived. I'll be flying to failure on Flight 32, with about thirty connecting flights in between (that's what happens when a volunteer program gives you free flights, apparently). I haven't made a Death Folder. I haven't determined who will pick up my remains should I die in Majuro. I haven't learned any of the important phrases the program coordinators suggested we commit to memory. I have, though, begun to believe that maybe Majuro won't be so bad. Maybe I'll be surrounded by people and mosquitoes alike who are dedicated to what they do. Maybe I'm just not cut out for New York. Maybe I'm not good enough to get a job. Maybe there's some sort of supernatural vendetta against me that's preventing me from achieving the only thing I really want: honest-to-god independence and self-satisfaction. Who knows—maybe that one-year holding pattern in Majuro teaching Marshallese children how to tie their shoes will make me understand that I'm just not "success" material. Maybe. Maybe not.

And let's not forget the fact that despite the thousands of times I have told my parents and Nina that my tickets to Majuro are for two days after her wedding, no one seems to care about anything that is unrelated to: 1) beef negimaki appetizers, 2) how much weight Nina can shed in two weeks drinking only wheat germ juice, and 3) whether or not it will rain on her wedding day.

Which means I'm flying to failure solo, without even the façade of a family pretending to care.

The point is: each of these facts then unofficially crowns me the most pathetic person I know. Under normal circumstances, I'd be happy to have any kind of award. But in this case, I am more than willing to abdicate my throne. Operation Desperation, well under way.

Desperation demands a mother's attention. Time to call.

My mom picks up the phone, and I torture both of us with news of the Majuro tickets.

"Mom, the tickets arrived today—it's really happening. I'm going."

"So really, Alex, Nina has lost six pounds! Can you believe this wheat-germ thing she's doing is really working? She looks fantastic!"

"That's great, Mom. Did you hear what I said?"

"Oh, before I forget: Miranda's mom called me, I heard the fantastic news! I can't believe she's going to law school! I remember when you two were little and she would come over . . . She's been looking good lately too. Maybe she's doing this crazy wheat-germ thing too? Who knew germs could be good for you?"

As my mother ignores my question and talks on and on about how I could benefit from the wheat-germ juice diet, the sweet dinging of my e-mail box wakes me from pathetic self-pity. It's a bold-font message with the subject. "Yadda, Yadda! Recruiting." A rejection? As I click on it, I casually ask my mother, "Do you think I'm the most pathetic person in my graduating class?"

"What about that cocaine addict you went to high school with who just had the baby? Is she still in jail?"

Help Wanted, Desperately

The e-mail opens, and a surge of adrenaline rushes to my brain. I have been reborn.

God has sent me a miracle. My prayers have been answered! Yadda, Yadda! Public Relations wants to see me again, for a final-round interview. I may not have a direct flight to Majuro, a job offer, or even a spot in law school, but praise the Lord: I have been delivered, I've got a final round of *something*!

My mother, hearing the news, offers her typical non sequitur: "This wheat germ thing worked for Nina—you should see her, she's a wreck, but she looks fabulous! And I'm not saying this to be mean, I'm just saying it because I'm your mother, and better you should hear it from me than from Uncle Jerry—you know he never holds anything back. Remember when he said you looked like a poodle? Anyway, Alex, I'm just worried you won't fit into the bridesmaid dress. That's my main concern. I can't have you looking like a sausage."

Ecstatic, I hang up the phone. Not even accusations that I look like a hunk of meat can distract me from the sweet, blissful, decadent truth: *Someone*, maybe, wants to hire me.

After several cryptic, relatively nondescript e-mails from Ricky! that reek of "Jackie's Last Day"ness ("Come to our office on Sunday. At Yadda, Yadda! you'll interview with senior-level management, and learn more about Yadda, Yadda!"), the day of my deliverance has finally arrived. I hop on the train to New York for the interview, eager, nervous, nauseous, and inhumanly sweaty in anticipation of today's interview: Judgment Day.

I arrive at the office building a half hour before my interview to case the scene. Actually, I arrive at the office building a half hour before my interview because I'm ridiculously neurotic, but

I'm trying to get into the swing of being "normal," so we'll just say that I arrive early to "case the scene." Do I go into the building early and risk being the first person there? Or do I show up exactly on time and seem casual, relaxed, and relatively unobsessed with this job, in which I have all but invested my future children's college funds? I choose option A. I am normal. A normal person would not show up at an interview half an hour early. A normal person would not deliberate over whether or not it makes a difference to arrive at an interview half an hour early. A normal person, one might argue, would do something useful with this free half-hour time slot.

To the bathroom I go.

I fight the rain, the New Yorkers, and the pigeons—one of which must have an interview in half an hour, which would explain the splotchy white pigeon shit on my shoe—to get across the street to some sketchy-looking hotel to use their bathroom. I walk into the bathroom, push open a stall, and hang my fifteen-dollar knockoff purse, a "Pravda" original (it was nicer than the "Gukki" one), on the bathroom door.

Mission accomplished, it's time for me to make my way to the interview.

I leave the stall, and exit the building. As the revolving doors throw me out on the street, I spot several gray-suited twentysomethings wandering into the Yadda, Yadda! building. Oh, baby, it's showtime.

Arriving merely minutes before the noon invitation time, I walk into the building and am directed to the fifteenth floor for "the Yadda, Yadda! Sunday Event." I casually ask the guard how many people are expected today.

"Only fifteen of you. And they interviewed over four hundred applicants! Good luck, kid. Knock 'em dead!" The guard winks and then gives me a playful punch on my arm.

I take a deep breath as I walk toward the elevator. It is in fact quite possible that I might get this job. This one might not be the pipe dream that all the others have been. This is a final round. It's just me and fourteen other unbelievably talented bullshitters from across the United States. I need to stay calm. I need to stay calm.

The elevator doors open onto what appears to be a Job Paradise. A handsome man wearing a tuxedo is standing behind a bar serving soda and juice. Next to him is a buffet lavishly sporting bagels, wraps, sushi, fruit, and chicken on sticks. I imagine for a second that my fourteen competitors themselves are skewered on sticks. Think 'normal,' Alex, 'normal.'

Just as I'm about to attack the buffet table, Ricky!, aka "Kofi Annan is a Purple Puppet" rushes to the center of the room. "Welcome, welcome, welcome!" Ricky! claps his hands and jumps up and down. "Let me just say, I am stupendously super excited to see you all here! Let's have a round of applause for all of *you*! You're great! Really, you're great! Yay for Y-O-U *you*!" Ricky! claps for us. And then the fifteen of us obediently applaud ourselves and smile graciously at Ricky! Am I the only one here wondering what kind of uppers Ricky! takes? Or whether his three-year-old cousin Ross-y, with whom he claimed to watch *Gorky and Pals,* was perhaps Ricky! himself?

"Okay! The way this is going to work is that each of you has a schedule, and will be interviewed by six senior partners. You'll each have three half-hour breaks in between your interviews, because, ugh, wouldn't that be super, *super* yucky if you had to have all your six interviews in a row? We would *never* do that to you!

Yay! I'm so excited . . . can you all *feel* how exciting Yadda Yadda!'s Sunday Event is? Why, it's . . . stupendous!"

Obligatory tittering throughout the crowd. I smile at my fellow competitors pleasantly: It is time to befriend the enemy.

"So! Let's get started! Your schedules are in those Yadda, Yadda! folders we gave you, and then you'll see who you're interviewing with. All the interviews take place right down the hall, where there are twelve tables set up. You'll just rotate! Alrighty, let's get started, gang!"

All fifteen of us frantically open our manila folders and look at our schedules. I look at mine. It looks at me. There must be some mistake. I have three half-hour breaks and then six consecutive interviews. I approach Ricky! It would be super, *super* yucky if I had all six interviews in a row. And they would *never* do that to me.

Ricky! looks at my adorably questioning face and flashes his plastered smile. "Oh. I'm sorry about that. One person just *had* to end up with that type of schedule, and I guess it's you. Oopsies! Feel free to relax near the buffet for the next hour and a half."

Mable the Walrus strikes back. It is super, *super* yucky indeed.

Eight pieces of sushi, two glasses of orange juice, one cup of tea, a plate of fruit, and three conversations with the bartender later (he's studying to get his masters at Columbia, bartending on the side, though ultimately he's interested in getting his Ph.D. in architecture), my grueling hour-and-a-half break is almost over. I've talked to several employees who have been at Yadda, Yadda! a year, and as luck would have it, it turns out that I carpooled to nursery school with one of them, who happens to remember that I bit Miranda because she stole my seat, and who happens to be very interested in sharing this horribly embarrassing story with anyone with a pulse. (Talk about the past biting back.) I learned that four of the five people here had no intention of going into public relations and just "sort of needed a job." Sounds familiar.

Between the six of us, we've almost polished off the entire buffet. I'll never be able to say that Yadda, Yadda! didn't give me anything. Currently, it's giving me gas.

As I push the last piece of sushi into my mouth, an unspeakably tall, attractive, wavy-haired man with a British accent pokes his head into the lobby. "Is Alexa *Hoffman* here?" He runs his fingers through his wavy brown hair and flashes those of us stuffing our faces a brilliant white smile. This is clearly a man who uses whitening toothpaste, and perhaps an electric toothbrush.

"Mraths me!" I say. A chewed piece of tuna falls out of my mouth and onto my lap. Graceful.

The British guy looks confused.

I swallow the sushi that managed to stay in my mouth, nearly choking on it, and repeat, "That's me."

"I'd absolutely love to interview you now, if you're free and willing. My name is Daryl."

Free and willing indeed, Daryl. Free and willing indeed.

Daryl and I walk down the long hallway into an even longer room where there are, as promised, twelve tables lined up, each with two seats: one for the interviewer, one for the interviewee. As Daryl escorts me to our table, my eyes catch a glimpse of an older woman interviewer on the other side of the room. Wearing Easy Spirit purple heels. An inauspicious start.

Daryl and I arrive at our table, and he pulls my chair out for me. A gentleman. I decide to befriend Daryl.

"And I thought chivalry was dead! Thanks." I smile coyly and try to pick a kiwi seed out from between my teeth with my tongue. I stop when Daryl looks at me strangely, perhaps assuming that I'm having some sort of tongue spasm.

"Ah. Indeed. No, Alexa, chivalry is only dead in *this* office. But you didn't hear it from me." Daryl sits down and looks over one shoulder, then the other. "The 'company' doesn't like it when people admit that everything isn't as 'stupendous' as Ricky! says it is. But you didn't hear that from me either.

"But enough about my gripes with this place. How about I tell you something about myself? I'm from South Africa originally. I enjoy reading, rock-climbing, and fine wines."

I wonder to myself why this situation feels so strange to me and then realize that it's because I vaguely feel like Daryl has just given me his well-rehearsed three-minute dating spiel. Is Daryl looking for a woman? If a strapping young South African like him can't find a date, then the chances that a relatively average New Jerseyan like myself can get a job are practically microscopic.

I smile at Daryl. So charming. So young. So South African. Why can't he find a woman?

"Enough about me. Let's talk about you, because, after all, that's what this interview is all about, isn't it?" Admittedly, I'm a little too obsessed with his accent to actually listen to what he has to say. Which is perhaps the same problem Daryl runs into on dates.

Daryl and I chat for a bit about my past internship experiences, and before I know it, I'm actually being honest with Daryl—a first in an interview for me. I tell Daryl that I want to be doing creative work. That I'm ready to take on challenges, as long as I'm trusted with them. That I want a job that actually works towards making a positive difference in someone's life. Daryl nods and smiles, and tells me about his first job as a tutor in South Africa. By the twenty-minute mark in our half-hour interview, Daryl and I are all but engaged. Daryl has let down his guard and let me in. I know about his boyhood in Durban. His childhood dreams of being a graphic artist. I know what his mother's homemade mango chutney tastes like.

Daryl does not know, though, that in twelve days my back-up plan will take me to the Marshall Islands.

As the interview winds down, Daryl leans in closer and says, "Be honest, Alexa. Why do you want this job? I personally never want to enter this building again, and I wouldn't wish it on anyone, even my worst enemies. I'd rather be in marketing."

Daryl brushes some hair out of his eyes and flashes his electric-toothbrushed smile. He continues, "I want to challenge myself. To meet smart people. You won't find them here, Alexa. I promise you that. I know, because I've looked for them. So I guess my last question for you is this: How do you, a creative, charming young woman who loves to read and write and sing and perform, expect to deal with the hum-drum, boring, endless monotony of a job that will bring you absolutely no moral or creative happiness?"

That certainly takes the cake for the best interview question anyone has ever asked me.

The words "no moral and creative happiness" echo in my mind over and over again.

As I'm about to tell Daryl that all entry-level jobs must inevitably lead to some sort of emotional and intellectual dissatisfaction, Daryl leans across the table, takes me gently by my arm and whispers, "Don't do this to yourself, Alexa. Promise me. You'll be miserable. That's the one thing I can guarantee you."

As Daryl opens his mouth to offer one last word of wisdom, Ricky! enters the room, claps his hands and shouts gaily, "It's Switch Time, people! Interviews are O-V-E-R over! Move on to your next table!" Ricky! jumps up and down.

I shake hands with Daryl, whose parting words are, "I hope you and I meet again someday. In some sort of happy accident in the crossroads of life."

I smile at Daryl. I feel confident that he will find a woman someday. Daryl adds, "And I hope that those crossroads aren't in this building."

Daryl escorts me to my second interviewer, a redheaded thirty-something named Peter from England. ("Peet-ah.") I'm beginning to think that everyone at Yadda, Yadda! is British-sounding, and wonder if I should start faking my impeccable British accent to win the favor of these Brits and former colonialists. (After all, nothing impresses people more than mocking their culture.)

Peter and I shake hands, and Daryl winks at Peter. I'm not sure what that wink means. Perhaps it's a Commonwealth thing. Peter and I sit down at the table, ready for round two of the interviews. Peter looks at his notes, looks at me, looks down at his notes again, and then says, "I hate these bloody questions. Bloody guidelines. What do I look like, a bloody puppet or something? I mean, really. Do they think I'm not 'stupendous' enough on my own to come up with my own bloody questions? Christ." Peter loosens his tie.

I assume I'm supposed to agree with Peter. I try to look sympathetic. Bloody guidelines.

Help Wanted, Desperately

"Whatever. ("Whut-evah.") Let's come up with our own bloody questions, shall we? What do you think are the most impressive brands?"

I pause. Do I go with the brands Yadda, Yadda! represents, or do I go with what I really think? Bullshit has gotten me nowhere in the past. Honesty, for the second time, wins.

"I think McDonald's is incredible. I think it's amazing that you can go to any third world country, and the children won't be wearing shoes or clothes, but they'll be eating Big Macs." *Does Majuro have a McDonald's?* "Now that's—"

Peter interrupts me, and smacks his fist down on the table hard, soliciting more than a couple strange sideways glances from other interviewers in the room. "By GOD, that's the exact *bloody* answer that *I* gave when I was interviewed ten years ago! McDonald's. It's absolutely un-fucking-real, isn't it!"

Ricky! glances at Peter, giving him a watch-your-language-in-front-of-the-kid look. Peter ignores it. "I feel like I've gone absolutely crackers—you're like a vision of me ten years ago! It's un-fucking-real!"

It *sure* is.

Peter continues, "You know, I remember when I was your age, looking for a job . . . I came in here and some interviewer asked me, 'What's your favorite book?' and you know me, I studied literature at Oxford for Christ's sake!—did I already say that?—and I start rambling on about Joyce and *Portrait of the Artist,* and the interviewer just had no bloody idea what I was talking about! You're an English major, I see. Christ, it's time. It's been *years* since we've had someone who can think—just these mindless, thoughtless idiots who . . . never mind . . . What's your favorite book? Do people your age even read anymore?"

As I'm about to answer (resisting at all costs the overwhelming urge to insert the word "bloody" into my response), he rolls his eyes and interrupts me before I open my mouth. He throws his hands up in the air. "It's a fucking joke, really. It's not like anyone in this room, this company, this bloody *world* could give a pheasant's fuck about literature anymore. And it's not like reading George fucking Eliot is going to make you any bloody better at event planning. I mean, *really*." Peter looks around the room, raises the volume of his voice and gestures to the people surrounding us, "Do any of you even know *how* to read? For piss' sake! Listen, we might as well talk about anything *but* books. Talk about who was wearing what and when. I'm thirty-four years old, and my life has already gone to absolute piss. Do you have any *idea* what that's like?" Peter loosens his tie even more and throws back a sip of "soda."

I know that in a normal interviewing situation my interviewer typically would not be badmouthing the company, trashing the employees' intelligence, or using phrases like "pheasant's fuck." And I know that I should be trying right now to somehow steer Peter back to the situation at hand. But for whatever reason, though I know I should somehow segue into my favorite book, or why I want to work in PR, or even ask Peter about the etymology and history of the phrase "pheasant's fuck" in order to distract him from what is apparently his thirty-four-year-old absolute piss life, I don't.

There's something about Peter that is both relieving to me and terrifying. Worst-case scenario: Here is Peter, thirty-four years old, incredibly unhappy with a job that he figured would make him happy for the rest of his life. I'm relieved because I know I'm not alone now in my fear that I will never maximize my potential, but I'm terrified because Peter's life is tangible testimony to the horrifying reality that my life could become, even if I have an enviable job. Peter's life proves that even with a relatively "successful" job, people are still unhappy. The job doesn't make the man. So the question remains: Can Majuro make the woman?

Instead of bringing Peter back to the interviewing part of the interview, I sit like an obedient dog waiting for its owner to put money in the parking meter. This way, I don't ruin my chances by agreeing that Peter's life is absolute shit ("piss," if you will). Instead, I'm quiet. Loyal. Obedient. And completely and utterly depressed by the entire conversation.

The trick of obedient silence works, and my treat is that Peter moves on. "Well, enough about my pathetic life. Let's talk about something else. Christ." Peter scans the bloody sheet that he didn't bloody need since he's not a bloody puppet. "All right, let's see . . . What do you think of Britney Spears? You know, her publicity."

I wonder if Peter is kidding—if this is one of his little tricks to prove that all young Americans are illiterate, gum-chewing morons who can only appreciate Britney Spears videos, Diet Coke, and Instant Messenger. I think about relating a dream I had only two weeks ago in which Britney got a job I had applied for in the dream: developing photo negatives at MotoFoto of the gargoyles of Notre-Dame cathedral. (One wonders if being an insomniac is better than being a healthy sleeper who has dreams like this.)

Instead, I reply, "I think most people are fascinated by Britney. She can play any role any publicist wants her to play—she's everything: an innocent schoolgirl, a sexpot, a diva. I wish I could be all of those things." Did I really just tell Peter that I wished I could be a sexpot? This is an interview, Alex, not therapy. You're not with Marc the Murse. Stay focused. "I mean, who wouldn't admire that? I mean, I bet even someone as well-read and educated as you, Peter, is fascinated with Britney." Note to self: Flattering the interviewer's intelligence gets bonus points, and will probably protect me from being called a "pheasant fuck" sometime in the future by Peter.

For the first time, a smile spreads across Peter's face and he blushes. I wonder if this is what he looked like before he became so bitter and disenchanted with his job. "I wholly admit that I have an utterly unprofessional obsession with Britney, and if I were to start speaking of her right now I might have to profess my undying love for her. Why, you and I, Alexa, are kindred spirits! Yadda, Yadda! could use someone like you." Peter lowers his voice and leans towards me. "But I don't know that you could use a place like Yadda, Yadda! if you know what I mean . . . hate to see someone take over my piss life, you know?"

As I'm about to respond, Peter stands up and shakes my hand. "Good luck in whatever it is you do. I'm going to recommend you for this job." Peter lowers his voice and casts a sideways glance at Ricky! "But I'll also recommend to you that you don't take it."

Out of nowhere, a buzzer rings and I nearly have a heart attack. "I got a buzzer!" Ricky! shouts. "Isn't it cute?" Ricky! dances with the buzzer. "Now we can buzz when it's switch time!" He buzzes the buzzer again. "You know what that means, people! Switch Time!"

Two grueling hours later, the process is finally over, and all six of my interviewers have thoroughly convinced me that I don't want this job. Interviewer #3, a non-Brit named Belinda, told me how she became legally blind in this job from looking at party lists in eight-point-size type. Interviewer #5 didn't even blink at all.

As I walk down the hallway, finally ready to leave Yadda, Yadda! after an emotionally exhausting day, it strikes me as bizarre that on the one day I acted like a poised, well-qualified, well-behaved job candidate, the world around me seemed to fall to pieces. Ricky! jumped up and down like a caffeine-ated sock puppet, while Peter and Daryl all but convinced me that—in the big scheme of things—Majuro is ultimately a much better choice for me than any of these conventionally "impressive" jobs I've so desperately lusted after these past nine months.

The irony of the Yadda, Yadda! Sunday Event is that as I'm walking toward the elevator to leave the building, I feel both confident for the first time that I'm really going to get this job . . . and just as confident that I'm going to reject it when it comes. For almost the entire past year, I've been searching endlessly for a job—any job, I've always thought. But here I am, walking out on one of the most well-respected event-planning and public relations firms in the country, because I know it's not right for me.

Majuro, it seems, is better than this.

They are going to call me in three weeks and ask me if I want to sign a contract. And I'm going to tell them no, and people will think I'm insane. I will call Jared at Christie's and tell him all about this—and he'll try to convince me that I shouldn't write things off so easily, that this is what I always wanted, that this is the job I've been waiting for, and how can I turn away from it like this when I've spent the past nine months crying over it and determining my self-worth by it? Trying to avoid the waiting period in Majuro that I now seem to welcome. My friends who have been watching me frantically send out resumes for the past year will roll their eyes and tell one another that I'm flighty, ungrounded, and directionless.

For the past year I've been looking for a job that would suddenly transform my life into a significant contribution to the world, a job that would make me proud of who I am. As it's turned out, the jobs that I thought would do this make me hate myself and what I'm trying to become. And the jobs that make me smile are the ones that aren't what I would expect from myself: being the voice of a cat on TV, smelling people's armpits, trying to breed earthworms. Maybe I *don't* want the American Dream. Maybe what I really want is the American Dream, twice removed, as the proud voice of a phone-sex operator, or as a star on Broadway, or even the production assistant for a documentary on butter sculptures. It's taken me a year to realize that it's not some random job that will give me self-assurance and confidence in who I am . . . but myself.

But I'm still going to reject the job offer I have spent the past year fantasizing about. Because if I've taken anything away from this agonizing, hair-tearing, armpit-sweating, bleary-eyed, ego-busting process, it's that what you think you want is rarely what you really need. And what you really want is not something you have to know when you're twenty-one years old. Shove that one in a fortune cookie.

As the elevator takes me down to the lobby of Yadda, Yadda!, I take my suit jacket off and proudly display my armpit stains to the world. There will be no more shameless bullshitting today. No more flattering and begging higher-ups for a job I thought I wanted. As I walk across Yadda, Yadda!'s marble-floored lobby, I can't help but think about the thousands of other people my age who think (like me) that they need to have it all figured out. We're going to be investment bankers. Or consultants. Or lawyers or doctors or advertising executives. We're going to live in tiny little apartments in New York, and make ourselves into the people our parents want us to be. But how can we know what *we* want now? And how can we let our jobs define who we are, our self-worth, our life-defining existential significance as individual people on this planet?

As I push my way out of the building through the revolving door, I don't look back—I don't have to. From here on, I'll only look forward.

I guess it's off to Majuro. At least I'm half smiling.

Lessons Learned

1. "Pheasant's fuck" is a good phrase to add to my vocabulary.

2. British interviewers often hate their jobs . . . but they sound really sexy while hating them.

3. Pit stains may not, in fact, affect job offers. This has yet to be proven.

4. Having a job isn't the same as having a life—a life is composed of the people you love who make your life meaningful. For me: Jared, my family, my friends. A job, apparently, is composed of people you hate.

16
The Hour
of Zero

4 Days

I woke up this morning, my eyes squeezed tightly shut, and prayed that somehow there had been a mistake—that today would not be my last day in college, my last day in Philadelphia, with only two days until Nina's wedding, and only four days until I'm off to Majuro. As I slowly opened my eyes, lying in my uncomfortably warm bed in my chaotically disheveled bedroom for the last time in my college career, I realized with anxiety, nausea—and most of all, horror—that this is it. The Real Deal. Except that instead of the glorious, independent, self-sufficient Real Deal in New York that I had prayed for these past seven months, I was being shipped out to Majuro like some directionless nobody—worse yet, as a product of my own stupid decision. The logic being, of course, that even though I can't fix my own life, I'm somehow qualified to fix the lives of people in third world countries.

For the past year, I've been dangling precariously between the Real World and the comparatively "Fake World" of heading off to Majuro to postpone the life I so desperately crave. Which means that today is the day that could have been so much more: the day when I was supposed to be unceremoniously shoved out of my sugar-coated college universe into the nitty, gritty grunt and grind of Real World obligation, responsibility, independence and self-satisfaction. Today is the day I should've been moving into some cheap, tiny, cramped apartment in some un-trendy, unpopular part of New York City. I'd walk around my two-hundred-square-foot space, enjoying the convenience of a bath-room that also doubles as a kitchen. I'd barely be able to turn around in the tight, dirty space, but I wouldn't care, because it would be home, it would be mine, and it would mean that I was finally on my own. And tonight was supposed to be the night that I discover a twelve-pound rat in my new apartment's bath-tub. (Having had years to envision this, I've just assumed the rat would be part of the picture.) But I wouldn't care (okay, I would care a little), I would handle it, and I would be proud of myself for knowing that I had made it (well, me and the rat had both made it). I would know that I had paid for that shitty little dump on my own, and whatever the apartment was, it was mine and mine alone. It would be the world that *I* created, the world that my own employment made possible. That dirty, cheap apart-ment would be all that I wanted, because it would mean that I was finally making it on my own. It would be my home.

And it would be my rat.

Instead, today is the day my parents will pick me up from Philadelphia and drive me to New Jersey for Nina's wedding, to wait out my last four days before Majuro surrounded by family and friends, all of whom want to know only one thing: Why the hell am I going to Majuro instead of getting a "real job" in New

Help Wanted, Desperately

York like I wanted? Pomp, meet Circumstance. Circumstance, this is Pomp. I think for a moment about how Yadda, Yadda! still hasn't called me back. Half an hour until my parents' yellow Buick pulls up in front of our row house to take me to New Jersey, to take me to Nina's wedding, and to take me, finally, to the airport where I will fly for thirty-six hours on endless connecting flights to Majuro: no time left to find a job. Welcome to the Hour of Zero.

I sit up in bed and look around my room, and listen to the echoing sound of alarm clocks beeping in painful dissonance up and down my street—awakening all the unemployed to face the sobering reality that this time, the party is over for good. As the alarms continue to buzz in aggressive atonality, I look around my room: my cap and gown from yesterday hang on my door, waiting patiently to be hung up in a New Jersey closet, never to be seen again. Oversized brown cardboard boxes line the floor of my room, filled with papers, books, old exams, assignments. Notes I've already forgotten. A pile of photographs I'd pasted on my wall lie in a clump by the closet. A framed picture of me and Jared looking at each other happily. A picture of Nina, Julie and I dancing and laughing at a party. And then the fortunes I'd taped up, born from four years of vegetable lo-mein, lying in a neat three-inch-by-two-centimeter pile on my desk. Sighing, I think to myself, *This is it. It's off to Majuro. No rat for you. Not this year.*

As I get ready and brush my teeth, I hear the obnoxious blare of a loud car horn in the street and know instantly that it's my parents, here to take me from Philadelphia to New Jersey one last time. As I thunder down the stairs to the front hallway, the house feels unbearably silent and I can't help but wish that

Ethan, Laura, David, and Leslie hadn't moved out last night. Or wish that at the very least a large six-foot felt banana was standing at the door. The house is quieter than it's ever been, and suddenly loneliness overwhelms me. If this is the way I feel in an empty house, I can't bear to think about what I'll be like in an empty hut.

Before I have a second to contemplate life in a hut, I open the front door and my mother charges up the front steps and into the house.

Kissing me quickly, she whispers in my ear, "Whatever you do, Alex, don't mention anything related to the wedding. Nina's a wreck! I swear to God, Alex, she's like a wild animal. I'm at the end of my rope here."

My mother hurriedly walks up the stairs to my bedroom and carries down a suitcase. As she walks to the car and hoists the case up to the luggage rack, my father rushes into the house, gives me a quick kiss on the forehead and says, "Between the two of them, I don't think I'm going to live through the drive back home. Nina has gone *completely* insane, and your mother, well, she's got the compassion of a colostomy bag." My father thunders up the stairs, grabs two duffel bags, and then noisily stomps down the stairs. As he walks out to the car, dumps the duffel bags in the back of the wagon, and then rushes back into the house to pick up more of my stuff, I'm left alone, standing in the hallway.

The car door outside slams again, and Julie walks up the front steps. I look at her hopefully, my eyes begging her to tell me why Nina's insane. Julie walks up the steps, rolls her eyes, and heads upstairs to pick up a few boxes. As she walks up the stairs, she just shrugs.

Help Wanted, Desperately

For a moment, the house is quiet again, and all I hear is my father stretching packing tape across the cardboard boxes that line my bedroom. I run upstairs, grab a box, and then head down the stairs again.

From the front door, the box in my arms, I gaze out at the station wagon.

Straining my eyes to see how Nina's insanity has manifested itself, all I can see through the car window is the outline of a figure, its chest rising and falling slowly with its breathing. Nina. Noticing me watching her for the first time, she sharply turns her head toward the window, and that's when I notice that Nina doesn't look quite like Nina: she is a crazed, possessed version of the Nina I once knew. Her fine brown hair, normally blow-dried straight, is wild and unruly. Her cheeks—which had been rosy and dewy at graduation yesterday (thanks to a seven-month "Bridal Beauty Skin Care" plan)—look like they've been scratched, clawed, rubbed raw. I slowly walk to the car, put the box down on the ground, and reach for the door handle. Through the window Nina stares straight at me, her bleary, beady, bloodshot blue eyes piercing my body.

Through the window I say, "Nina, I just want to put the box in the car."

Clenching her teeth, Nina furiously climbs into the front seat and dives for the button that locks all the doors. In the split second that I frantically lift the door handle, a sharp click echoes through the car, and I watch through the window as the car lock shrinks to half its size.

Staring straight at me now, Nina begins to smile. I smile back. Then, breaking her suspicious and evil calm, Nina ferociously screams, "LEAVE ME THE FUCK ALONE!"

Ariel Horn

Time to go upstairs and see if Dad has already packed the tranquilizer gun.

Dropping the boxes, I run away from the car and up the front steps of the house, where Julie and my parents greet me, their faces a uniform display of helplessness.

My mother looks at me. "Nina will get over it. It's just pre-wedding jitters. It's normal to act like that, but I'm not going to welcome it. Was that all your stuff? Lock up the house."

Stunned by my mother's incredibly flexible definition of "normal," I lock the door to the house silently, still amazed by Nina's transformation.

Picking up the last box, my dad nods at me. "Yeah, she's been like that all morning."

Julie corrects him: "She's been *worse* than that all morning."

"Is she rabid?" I ask, half joking, half serious, entirely terrified.

My dad eyes the car. "We don't think so. But none of us has gotten that close." My mother rolls her eyes.

Incredulous, I ask, "What happened? Is the wedding off? Is Brad okay?"

Julie, rolling her eyes again, responds, "Oh, *Brad*'s just fine. He's marrying a psychopath, but for some reason *he*'s fine."

As we walk towards the car cautiously, my dad uses his electronic key chain to unlock the car. Calmly, my dad says to Nina through the window, "Get in the backseat. Now."

Nina gets out of the car, glaring at my father, and then obediently switches seats.

Julie and I look at each other before getting into the car. We look at Nina. Nina glares back at us, her eyes wild and unfamiliar.

Julie glances at Nina and then quietly says, "But Mom, she's going to eat us."

Exasperated, my mother sighs. "Oh, stop it! You're acting like four-year-olds! All of you! Get in the car already!"

Reluctantly, I get in the car and sit next to Nina. Julie heaves a tremendous sigh of relief and flashes me a thankful smile as my father pulls away from the house I've been living in for the past three years without so much as the pomp and circumstance of a "Well, that's the end of Philadelphia!" comment. In a matter of seconds, life as I know it fades away into the distance, and Majuro suddenly feels closer than ever. I eye the bags I packed for Majuro in the back of the station wagon.

The car ride is quiet until we hit the Benjamin Franklin Parkway. No longer able to take the overwhelming silence, I meekly and quietly ask, "Nina, what's wrong?"

Coming out of her animal-like rage for the first time, Nina turns to me and shrieks, "You wanna know what's wrong? I'll tell you what's wrong! I'm getting married in less than forty-eight hours and I don't even have fucking favors for the wedding! Somehow, in spite of four hours spent with the florist last week, eight hours spent with the caterer, six hours spent with the band, and two hours spent with the manager of the catering hall, we don't have fucking favors to give our guests! It's like, why have a wedding at all? Martha Stewart says you can't have a wedding without favors . . . It's like having a Cornish hen without a tomato coulis sauce!"

Anything but that!

"I mean, for the love of God, I'm getting married in two fucking days and there are no fucking favors for my fucking wedding! I might as well not get married at all."

327

My mother rolls her eyes in the front seat, "Nina, get over it. Grow up."

"Get over what? This is my life, Mom! I've fucked up my wedding because we have no fucking favors." Nina screams, and Julie, scared, takes my hand and holds it very tightly.

My mother takes a deep breath and simply responds, "Language."

Quietly, Nina says to herself, "God, I'm so fucking stupid."

My mother chimes in with an obligatory and uninvolved "You're not stupid."

I'm not sure I would agree with that assessment at this point.

Nina continues, "Why would Brad even *want* to marry me?" Nina's small shoulders begin to shake, and she begins to sob quietly to herself, "I tried to make it perfect, and then, Jesus. I'm such a fuck-up. I'm such a fuck-up . . . I'm such—" Nina coughs, temporarily choking on her own sobs. She wipes the tears from her eyes angrily, and more bright red scratch marks appear up and down her cheeks. Her shoulders begin to shake more violently and she slams her hand hard against the car door over and over again. "God, I'm such a fuck-up! I hate myself! How could I fuck up like this?" Nina's sobs grow louder and echo throughout the station wagon.

As my parents try to calm their daughter with words she refuses to listen to, Nina continues to sob, her cries erratically loud and then soft. As we pass through Cherry Hill, her small shoulders continuing to shake slowly, I cautiously put my own arm around her. Nina doesn't resist, so I wrap my other arm around her too. Quietly I whisper in her ear, "I don't know if it means anything, but I don't think you're a fuckup." I give Nina a tight hug, and Nina holds on to me, her small fingers gripping my arms tightly. Julie slowly lies down across the two of us, her seat belt pulling across her chest. Smiling shyly at Nina, Julie whispers, "I don't think you're a fuckup either."

Nina wipes her eyes, looks at me, and then looks at Julie. For the first time since she got engaged, Nina looks like her pre-wedding self: Her pale blue eyes soften, and a genuine smile spreads across her red, tear-streaked face. Almost inaudibly, Nina whispers, "Thank you. But I am." Quietly, Nina begins to cry again.

And that's when I know what I have to do.

With only three days to go until Majuro, and now only one day until Nina's wedding, I find myself feverishly awake at 3 A.M. tirelessly examining the wedding guest list for what feels like the fifteenth time in the past seven hours. The list is covered in barely legible notes. "Wants to learn French" for my cousin Lindsay. "Just ended three-year relationship with girlfriend" for my uncle Jonathan. "Graduated med school, looking to start his own practice" for Nina's friend Steven. Between Jared casually asking my oblivious mother questions about our side of the family ("I'm so glad you want to learn about the family—this will make it easier when it's *your* wedding!") and Brad's senile grandmother in the nursing home (who was willing to talk to anyone about anything), I've been able to collect more personal details than I ever could have imagined about every guest invited to the wedding.

And it's from that point that I start to write the fortunes.

"Thirty years of unwedded bliss will lead to a hundred more" works for Great-Uncle Walt and his girlfriend of thirty years. "A law degree may feel like the end of the world, but it's the beginning of a new one," is okay for Brad's cousin Lisa, but I'm pretty sure I can do better. And despite my better judgment, I follow the advice of Brad's granny, and sneak "Better to be engaged to a woman than engaged to your work" into Brad's brother Nate's cookie. As I tweeze the fortunes into the cookies, I wonder whether Ruthie, Nate's girlfriend, even wants to get engaged. But once Brad's granny wised up to the fact that I was only there so I could pump her for personal information about her family, I promised her that I'd do what I could to guarantee that she would live to see Nate's wedding. (FYI: These are the kind of promises you make to an old lady wielding a walker as a weapon.) Unsure of Granny's physical health, and unwilling to propose to Nate myself, I do what I can to speed up his relationship with Ruthie. As I dip the fortune cookie in chocolate, I try to envision Nate opening his fortune at the same time Ruthie opens hers: "A future with Nate could be so great!" (It's getting late, and the fortunes are slowly becoming second rate.) Would this help their relationship or destroy it?

Either way, it's Granny's fault, and seeing as how she's on her deathbed, well, I am willing to take the blame for it.

Scapegoating a granny in a wheelchair never works anyway.

By 6 A.M. I'm almost done with all the fortunes and all the chocolate-dipped cookies—for all two hundred and seven guests. I paint each guest's name and his or her table number on pieces of blue ribbon, and then I tie each ribbon in a bow around each cookie. By 8 A.M., I'm done. Despite the overpowering exhaustion that has begun to slowly seep through my body, I realize that I feel genuinely happy. My fingers are sore from tweezing out useless, clichéd fortunes and my eyes hurt from squinting to fit the new fortunes in. If I smell chocolate again, I might get sick, and I'm pretty sure that sometime during the night I accidentally *ate* some paint, which would explain the dizziness. But in spite of the aches, the soreness, and the exhaustion, I smile, happy with myself for the first time in what feels like years. Even thousands of miles away in Majuro, I will know that I have made Nina happy. That in spite of my annoyance with her whole Martha Stewart fixation on "the wedding of her dreams" rather than the marriage of a lifetime, I have relieved her of the worry that her wedding will be irrevocably ruined without favors.

Somehow, I reason with myself, this will compensate for my own lack of interest in Nina's wedding and my own obsession with getting a job and starting life in the real world in order to avoid the holding pattern in Majuro. So much for that plan.

But at least Nina will have her favors.

Sleepily, I glance at the bags packed for Majuro in the corner of my room. Unwilling to confront the idea that I'm leaving in forty-eight hours, I pick up the phone and call Jared, who is ostensibly on his way to New Jersey for the wedding . . . but really on his way to New Jersey so he can take me to the airport.

So we can say goodbye.

Jared picks up his cell phone, and despite my overwhelming exhaustion, his voice reminds me that in two days I won't have the luxury of calling him on a whim. Instantly, I become pre-emptively homesick, and my heart literally starts to hurt. (Briefly, I wonder if that's the paint in my digestive tract talking.)

Jared's voice, as always, is cheerful, "Hi! How's the crazy girl!" Jared jokes, but all I think about is how in two days, there won't be any more jokes. Just me in a hut surrounded by illiterate third-grade Marshallese children, all of whom I'm expected to teach.

Ariel Horn

"She's good, she's good," I say, assuming for once that he isn't talking about me. "I haven't seen her in a while—it's been all about the facials since we got back from Philly. The redness has finally gone down in her cheeks . . ."

"Okay, good. More importantly—did you finish the cookies?"

"Thank God, yes, they're done." My eyelids start to droop and I can feel myself fading. "Thank you so much for all your help—you were amazing with my mom."

"Well, she thinks we're going to get married now, so you'd better not go to Majuro . . ."

"Jared—"

"I know. But think about it—you could live at home for a while and still keep looking for a job—you don't have to go yet . . . I hear in the summer a lot more jobs become available . . . I have this uncle who knows a lot of people, maybe he—"

"Jared."

"I know."

Jared's quiet on the other end of the phone, and then he abruptly breaks the silence. "Let's not do this now, Alex—I can't. It's hard enough anyway—"

"I know."

"Look, Alex, the train gets in at ten seventeen. Meet me there?"

"Of course. I can't wait to see you!" For the last time in what will feel like forever.

"Alex?"

"Yeah?"

"I really love you." Behind Jared's words, I hear what he doesn't say: *And I don't want you to go.*

I smile into the phone and whisper, "Always." *I don't want to go either.*

Help Wanted, Desperately

*　　*　　*

The wedding passes in a blur. Nina looks fabulous, of course, as would be expected from the girl who spent the past twenty-six years searching for the perfect dress, the perfect makeup artist, the perfect shoes and the perfect tiara. Brad, in contrast, is a messy wreck, and when I see him I'm amazed Nina let him show up this way without "checking" his outfit the way she checked everyone else's (apparently, despite Jared's disagreement with the contention, I *do* look like a sausage in my bridesmaid's dress). Brad's shoes are old and unpolished, his boutonnière wilted. But despite his appearance, he's the happiest I've ever seen him, and Nina is positively glowing. As Nina and Brad slip rings onto each other's fingers, Nina offers Brad her (meticulously selected) handkerchief as Brad begins to cry. When Brad finishes crying, Nina starts, and the rabbi has to wait three minutes until both of them calm down. By the time Brad breaks the glass and they kiss, all the guests are crying. My parents grip each other's hands, my mother lets her head gently rest on my father's shoulder, and they begin crying with everyone else.

Jared and I cry too, for reasons we can't even think about.

The cocktail hour flies by in a haze—every time I catch a glimpse of Nina, she's laughing, smiling, or kissing Brad, and no one would ever guess that a mere two days ago we thought we'd have to get her a rabies shot. As Jared and I enjoy all the carefully selected different varieties of beef negimaki, baby lamp chops, and beef gyoza appetizers, various relatives come up to us, prying for personal information, unaware that Jared and I now know everything about them from the last time they had their hearts broken to the first time they found out they had precancerous cells. Jared and I look at each one of them differently now, and we

333

hardly even mind when my great-aunt Sylvia asks us when *our* wedding is.

"You two are so cute! Did you try the mushroom caps, they're fabulous!" Sylvia shoves one stuffed mushroom cap into my napkin and one into Jared's mouth, "So when are you two getting married? And such cute kids, oy, from my lips to God's ears I should live to see your children!" Sylvia looks threateningly up at the ceiling, as if she's really begging God to let her live to see our nonexistent children. Then, she lets a little bit of chewed mushroom cap fall from her mouth onto the floor as she looks at us expectantly, still chewing wildly.

"Yeah, well, Alex is expecting, so the wedding may be sooner than you think!" Jared rubs his hand over my un-pregnant stomach.

"Jared!" I laugh and jab Jared in his arm. "You'll kill her!"

Sylvia nearly chokes, and only stops wheezing when Great-Uncle Stu rushes over and explains to her it was a joke. "The kid's stupid, he thinks he's funny. She's not pregnant, Sylvie, it was a joke! A bad joke!" Sylvia stops choking, spits out a mushroom cap and looks at Jared, "That's not funny. God willing you'll be married when it really does happen!" Sylvia then eyes Stu and says, "I gotta go. Now." Stu and Sylvia whisk themselves off to the bathroom.

Jared looks at me, "I should've known better. Your mother told me she has a weak sphincter."

A couple of minutes later, a bunch of cousins come up to me, begging to know about my upcoming trip to "Mexico." I try to explain to them that I'm not spending the summer in Acapulco, but that I'm volunteering in Majuro for a year, but none of them seem to get it. One of Brad's friends joins in the conversation. "You know, Majorca is an amazing place in the summer!"

Nina's friend interjects, "She's not going to Majorca, she's going to Monaco!"

After a couple of drinks, even I'm not sure where I'm going anymore.

After the cocktail hour, the reception pushes on and Brad and Nina are contagiously happy. Everyone dances, everyone drinks, Brad and Nina are raised high on chairs, and even Brad's granny dances with her grandson Nate as he twirls her around the dance floor in her wheelchair. As the cake is wheeled out onto the floor and Nina and Brad playfully paint each other's noses with icing, Brad's granny winks at me.

Exhausted, I slip my heels off under the table, and that's when the waiters bring out the plates of fortune cookies. Jared looks at me, "You ready?"

"I guess I have no choice. I hope to God Nina doesn't kill me."

Jared and I watch each table eagerly as the guests, one by one, open their designated fortune cookies. Uncle Morty reads his out loud to his table. "Thirty years of unwedded bliss will lead to a hundred more. Ha! This is terrific, who did this?" Morty leans over and kisses his girlfriend, who happily kisses back with more tongue than I was willing to see on a sixty-nine-year-old. I read her lips as she whispers "I love you" into Morty's ear.

My cousin Lisa shrugs as she opens hers. "A law degree may feel like the end of the world, but it's the beginning of a new one," but then gets into a detailed discussion with a lawyer at her table who's looking for summer associates.

Nervously, Jared and I look over at Nate and Ruthie's table. Ruthie is crying hysterically, and Nate is glancing around and shushing her, begging her to be quiet. Perhaps "Better to be en-gaged to a woman than engaged to your work" wasn't the best fortune for him after all.

Before I have a chance to think about the moral consequences of forcing Granny's view on Nate's life, Granny wheels over to me and says, "Well, you did it, honey! Nate just told Ruthie that he's seeing another girl at his office—I suppose he was engaged in work in more ways than one! So it looks like we'll get another wedding soon after all, even if it isn't to Ruthie." Jared and I look at each other and cringe, his pained expression a mirror of my own. Granny grabs my arm. "You did a good job, honey. Ruthie had to find out sooner or later, and it's better that she found out sooner rather than later." Granny winks at me, and then adds, "I liked my fortune too— 'You'll live to see more than Nate's wedding—you'll see his children's weddings too.' " Granny winks at Jared and then says, "You stick with this one, kid. She's a keeper!"

Jared looks at me sadly and responds to Granny, "I know."

Scooting away in her wheelchair, Granny adds, "Have fun in Malta!"

Towards the end of the party, the guests begin to leave. Most of them seem happy with their fortunes, and almost all of them have told my parents what a "cute and clever" idea the personal-ized cookies were. I told my parents I did it, and even Nina and Brad— drunk on their own happiness—come up to thank me. Nina whispers to me, "I can't believe you did that for me. All this time I thought you didn't care."

"I didn't."

"What?" Nina's face looks like it's going to burst again, so I quickly add, "I didn't care until now—I was so involved with myself . . . I'm sorry. I'm so glad you like them. I wanted you to be happy."

Nina squeezes my waist and kisses my cheek, "You're wonderful. They were so cute, Martha couldn't have made them any cuter! Well, maybe if there was a different ribbon—"

As Nina contemplates ribbon colors ("Well, the flowers were 'pêche,' so the ribbons really *should* have played off those hues, but you used blue, which was okay but not great, but—"), Brad's uncle, a huge man with red hair, comes over to us and slaps Brad on the shoulder.

In a booming thick Texan accent, Brad's uncle jovially shouts, "Well, well, well, if it isn't little Mr. Just-Got-Married! How's it feel, kid?" Brad's uncle is intensely familiar to me, though I'm not sure from where.

His uncle continues, squeezing Brad's shoulders, "I remember when you were a little know-nothin' nobody knew nothin' about!"

The words *a little know-nothin' nobody knew nothin' about* echo in my brain. Jared, sensing my confusion, looks at me, confused himself.

Before Brad has a chance to respond, his uncle throws back the Scotch and tonic he is holding and slaps Brad on the back again, "Now tell me, son, where did you get these little cookies? They're hysterical! Let me read you mine: 'From a lawn mower to a company owner, you cut the world down to size.' I like that! I *did* cut the world down to size—and then I conquered it! It hasn't recovered yet!" He lets out a booming laugh. "So who made these? Love 'em!"

Nina smiles at me and proudly pushes me forward, "This is my sister, Alex. She saved the day and made these fabulous favors. She is a fabulous, fabulous girl."

Brad's uncle looks me up and down, and for a moment I wonder if he's sizing me up the way one would size up a sausage. "Do I know you, little lady? You look just so darn familiar to me . . ." He scratches his neck, and that's when I see it: the Rolex watch. How do I know that watch?

"Anyway, little lady, I think these fortunes are fantastic! How long have you had your business?"

Embarrassed suddenly about my homegrown art project, I shyly respond, "Oh, I just did it for Nina, you know, it's not a business or anything—"

"Well for Pete's sake, it *should* be! My God, you could make a killing with this little idea here!" He shakes the half-eaten cookie in his hand, "Think about it—personalized cookies for every occasion! Engagements! Divorces! Birth of new babies! Wedding showers! Graduation parties! There are about a billion places this could work! You get the personal info, then you write the cookie! You could do different flavors, different types of cookies—you know, provided they all have a fortune or somethin'—"

Jared raises his eyebrows at me from behind Brad's uncle.

Before I can respond, the Texan slaps Brad on the back again (who has started to become increasingly less enthused about being slapped) and then points his finger at me. "Damn, I know you! I got it! You were on that train from New York a couple months ago! You were that sad little girl without a job!"

Remembering that train ride for the first time in months, it all comes back to me, and I slowly respond, "And you were the drunk, redheaded Texan giving me 'motivational' advice!"

Nina, Brad, and Jared look on in uncomprehending awe. "What's going on here?"

Brad's uncle responds, "This little lady and I have a history,"

Brad's uncle—a.k.a. Big Red—smiles. "And I see you finally found yourself a niche after all."

"Well, actually, I don't have a job exactly, I mean, the cookies aren't a job—I'm actually going to volunteer on Majuro for a year starting tomorrow."

Brad looks at Nina. "I thought she was going to Morocco."

"There's not a chance in hot hell you're going to Majorca or wherever with a great little idea like these cookies—look, what's your name again?"

"Alexa. Well, Alex."

"Okay, Alex, I'm going to give you my number. My name is Morgan Finnegan, but you can call me Red—hell, everyone else does!" Morgan—Red—goes to slap Brad on the back and misses, slapping Jared instead, who seems less than amused.

"Here's my number." Red uses Jared's freshly slapped back as a clipboard—"I want you to call me on Monday. I've got this friend I met back in my lawn-mowing days who now runs this bakery in SoHo in New York, he would love this idea. You two could work together—he did the baking for Madonna's kid's birthday party!"

Nina grabs Brad's arm, her eyes saucers. "Oh my God, I read about that in *More Style!*"

"You call me on Monday, and we'll work this out. This is gonna be huge. This is the next big thing, sweetheart!" Red slaps me on the back, hard, and then pulls me in for a harder hug. "You and me, kid, we were destined to meet. We're gonna become multimillionaires together!"

Astounded, I quietly whisper, "I'd settle for just a job . . ."

Red hears me and smiles, "Oh, this is more than a job. You're in business, kid. You're in business. Call me Monday."

"But I won't be here Monday, I'm going to Majuro the day after tomorrow—" I stammer.

Winking at me, Red smiles. "Call me."

Nina and Brad leave the reception for their honeymoon in Hawaii, and the rest of us, exhausted, go straight home to my parents' house. I let my head rest sleepily on Jared's shoulder on the car ride home as I try to take in all that's happened, and all that will happen the day after tomorrow, when I leave.

Once we're home, my parents and Jared collapse in the living room to gossip about the evening, and I head upstairs to change into my pajamas, unwilling to endure any longer the medieval torture device known as a backless corset (a.k.a. "sausage squoosher").

I sit on my bed and look around my old bedroom, enjoying the fact that my feet are touching soft wall-to-wall carpeting rather than the wall-to-wall dirt floor of a hut. As I unzip my dress, I glance first at the bags, all packed and ready to head for Majuro in less than twenty-four hours. They sit quietly in the corner, dutifully awaiting their trip to the airport, the connecting flights, the eventual semi-permanent seat on the muddy floor of my hut.

Exhausted, I take off my bracelet and necklace and put them back into the jewelry box as my mind wanders aimlessly, reviewing all that's happened in these past nine months and how the events of the past month are more than I could have ever imagined happening in a lifetime. The Meow Mix people might be calling me in the fall to tell me I'm their new spokeswoman, Red suddenly wants me to start some cookie business, Nina's married and seemingly normal again, and after tomorrow I won't see

Help Wanted, Desperately

Jared for God knows how long. Yadda, Yadda! hasn't even called me back yet.

My life is a huge question mark, and I'm leaving without even waiting to find out what the answer will be. There's so much here for me in New York already—why am I running away? As I glance at my desk, my eyes focus on a letter I received months ago from Majuro Volunteers. The phrase, "There are two kinds of people, those who are alive and those who are afraid" glares at me, laughing.

As I take off my pantyhose, releasing my stomach from control-top torture, my eyes wander to the tickets to Majuro sitting on my desk. Sighing, I walk over to the desk to check the time of my first flight.

But on top of the tickets sit two fortune cookies—some loser generics that never made it to the party.

As I glance back and forth from the cookies to the bags, I can't decide what to do. Do I stay here until Monday—and miss my flights to Majuro—to see what happens with this guy Red? Or do I play it safe, go to Majuro, and just assume it won't work out, like everything else I do?

Do I stay on hold or do I hang up?

Exhausted, confused, unsure even of what to think anymore, I slowly crack open the last remaining fortune cookies and read aloud to myself, "Happiness is not something one finds—it's something one makes." I open the second one: "The question isn't why. It's why not."

It's true—and that's when I realize it for the first time.

My fortune has already been written.

Jared pokes his head in the door, "Alex, as much as I hate to say this, we should probably be going to sleep; we've got so much

341

to do tomorrow before you leave." Sighing, Jared loosens his bowtie and unbuttons his shirt. He takes a deep breath, and then heads for the bathroom.

To no one in particular, I whisper, "I don't need to leave—I'm already there."

Alexa Hoffman, tomorrow is *really* going to be the best day of your life.